THE BOOK
OF
HORROR

EDITED BY
ANTHONY GIANGREGORIO

THE BOOK OF HORROR

Table of Contents

SKINS

NICKOLAS COOK

The sun's fiery unblinking eye blazed down on the dusty desert town, as the five-man posse mounted their horses and rode forth to hunt the demon. Without a word between them, the men headed out into the desolation of sand and rock that surrounded the dry spit of buildings. Every rider was a church going man, despite their love for guns and liquor, but they'd all heard enough stories from the Indians with which they plied trade to have a healthy respect and fear for the Redman's ancient pantheon of gods and devils.

Even though they carried between them enough firepower to start a small Mexican revolution, none of the posse put much faith in guns and bullets. This day they hunted something inhuman, and they knew their faith would be much better placed in crosses and prayer.

The leader of the silent posse was Roberto Xavier, a stocky Mexican man, swarthy as the undying sun, and built as tough as the rocky terrain through which he rode. His eyes were like an eagle's, far seeing and vigilant. He scanned the horizon, squinting against the bright glare of the sun on the distant hills. Gypsum and quartz flashed meaningless signals into the air. Cacti stood like shimmering ghosts, dancing in the hellish heat. An inferno wind swept over the men, and despite its heat, they shivered. It was too much like an omen of this day's end.

The oldest man of the posse, Hector Huizar, crossed himself and looked nervously at his silent companions, and in a fit of self-pique, he said, "This is ridiculous, you know. We are men of San Mateo. We have no reason to fear anyone. We have kept our women and children safe in this desert for how many generations? You look like old women huddled together." He spit precious water on the ground in disdain as he eyed the youngest of the men, Juan and Carlito Nunez, brothers and cousins to Roberto. "What are you so afraid of? He's only one man."

Juan swallowed nervously, but tried to look braver than he felt. The solid weight of the gun on his hip should have made him feel as proud and brave as the cock of the yard, instead it felt heavy and useless thumping against his hip—a leaden weight of laughing metal and oil. Carlito saw his younger brother's anxiety and lifted his chin in challenge at the old man. "How do you know it's one man, señor Huizar? What we saw could have been an army of killers for all we know."

"Bah! One man is all. A killer, but he's still only one man." Huizar tugged at his horse's reins to keep him away from a small hole, but stared at the young man across from him. "I never thought I'd see the day that a man from San Mateo would be frightened of one man."

Before Carlito could speak up, the fat horseman behind the brothers chuckled and shook his wild mane. "Shut up, old man. You nip at the heels of these boys because you yourself are scared."

"What the hell do you know, Jesus?" Huizar snapped. His tight, lizard-like face whipped in the fat man's direction, his eyes full of malice. "I'm surprised you can stay on your horse, you drunken fool."

"Drink makes me a better rider, señor," Jesus said with an amiable grin. "At least I can say I don't walk my horse into coyote shit."

Huizar turned his baleful glare from Jesus in time to see his horse stride into a steaming pile of fresh coyote droppings. The men's laughter and Huizar's curses resounded in the blistering air. Roberto barely paid attention; his eyes were for the horizon and the desert floor. He was known far and wide as the best tracker the village had ever produced. The only man who could have given him a run for his money was his father's father, señor Arturo Xavier, a man supposed to have once tracked down a missing girl across four hundred dry miles of Indian territory.

Something caught his eye, a shape that didn't feel right, more instinct than sense, and he drew his horse to a halt. The others fell silent; even Huizar stopped his grumbling long enough to watch the tracker with a tense frown.

"Do you see something, Roberto?" he asked.

Roberto held up his hand for complete silence; even the horse seemed to sense the need for quiet, as they settled their stomping, impatient hooves, and their playful whinnies. The wind whispered across the still landscape of rock and sand; overhead a trio of buzzards flew in high searching circles and a lizard scraped its dry body across a rock a few feet away. All this Roberto felt more than saw, as he let his mind reach out into the empty space between himself and the thing he sought, just as his grandfather had shown him.

You must become the prey to find the prey, boy. Feel what it feels; taste what it tastes, and you will know its mind as well as your own.

"What do you see?" Huizar finally asked when he could no longer stand the unforgiving silence of the desert. "Is it him?"

Roberto stared for a moment more, waiting for his senses to tell him the truth between the sand and wind. But whatever had awakened his senses before was no longer there, and he shook his head and started the horses forward once more.

Carlito and Juan glanced at one another with fearful superstition. They had heard the stories about the Xavier family, how they were unlike other men, how even the Indians feared them for their keen preternatural powers, and how they talked with the gods in their sleep.

Roberto's size and quiet aura of stern power made them feel like little scared boys again, and each of them wondered to himself why he had agreed to ride in this posse. They were old enough to be considered men, had been for years now, but neither felt much like they had imagined they would when given the responsibility of riding a posse for the first time. This didn't feel particularly heroic to either of them, just a lot of sweating and riding and boredom.

After a few minutes of riding, Juan felt he needed something to take his mind off of the tension now settled into his shoulders and back, and he said, "Why do you think he did it?"

Jesus pulled his horse up next to the brothers. "Why do killers kill? Who knows?"

"Oh, the great philosopher speaks," Huizar said with a sneer, but he kept his eyes on the ground this time. He'd been lucky he hadn't steered his horse into a snake hole to twist its ankle. He wasn't about to make himself seem foolish again. Once done in front of the younger men, an old man like him was nothing more than fodder for their laughter and cruel jokes. Once the skin of a man, no matter his strength in youth, became wrinkled as the desert sands after a harsh storm, he no longer was a true man to the young ones—wolf cubs always nagging at his heels.

Jesus ignored him and nodded towards the distant hills. "Better to ask the wind why it blows than to try and figure out why someone kills for the enjoyment of it."

"Don't see how he could have gotten much enjoyment out of what he did," Juan replied. Every time he closed his eyes now he saw the little girl's body, all mangled and abused, like some mountain cat had gotten a hold of her. No man should have been able to do that. No sane man...maybe not a man at all.

"But we don't look for a man, do we?" Jesus asked, as if reading his thoughts.

"Crazy talk," Huizar interjected.

"We hunt for the demon spirit of the hills."

Carlito could see his younger brother watching him for a reaction, so he shrugged as if the man's words were silly. His sneer of derision was forced at best, and sat on his mouth like a lizard's dead skin. "There isn't any such thing," he said. "Right, Roberto?" But their leader wasn't paying them any attention, and he didn't reply, his eyes scanning the ground for signs of their quarry. Above, the buzzards circled ever smaller, ever lower to the earth.

Jesus drew a flask from his clothes and gave himself a quick guzzle of liquor before continuing his gossip. "How do you know there isn't any such thing, Carlito? Are you a medicine man? No...I don't think you are. You've never even known a medicine man, have you? Well, I have. There was once an old man that lived in the village. This was many years before you two were even thoughts in your father's pistola, and he talked with the spirits of the desert."

"He was like you, Jesus," Huizar called back. "He talked more with the spirit of the jug than the desert."

"And do you remember the story he told about the first people, old man?"

Huizar snorted and spat a phlegmatic reply on the desert floor.

"This land is the oldest on the earth," he said. "It is the first gods' home, and they never really left it behind. Death to a god is not like death for us, he told us. They pass into the sand, the brush, the rock. Even into the very creatures of the desert. The coyote, the tarantula, the eagle, the rattler, they become the land."

Huizar turned in his saddle, eyes bulging in irritation. "But what the hell does that have to do with one sick killer who uses little girls as his fuck hole, you fool? Nothing! Damn your silly stories to Hell. And damn this crazy hunt to Hell." The old man swiped at sweat beads dangling from his sharp nose and chin, then turned away.

Juan stared at Jesus. "Do you believe the medicine man?"

Jesus shrugged his lumpy shoulders, wiped at his glossy moustache with two expert fingers, and looked up at the glare of the sun before he answered. "Who knows what the truth is? I only listen. Who's to say Dios is not one of the same ancient gods the Indians speak of?"

Juan and Carlito exchanged a nervous glance at Jesus' blasphemous words. And with that the men became quiet once more, riding behind Roberto's stalwart figure, as he led them deeper into the desert.

The criss-crossing buzzards circled and finally came to earth in a hilly canyon a few miles on. And that's where they found the skinned Indians. The three young braves had been butchered and laid out side by side, as if on display for a potential meat connoisseur. As they rode their horses into the sudden shadow of rising rock and geometry, the buzzards exploded into the air with angry screeches, and the violent beat of wings, that echoed off the narrow, uncompromising stone walls like death laughing.

Juan snapped his horse to a halt and almost fell from the saddle in his haste to vomit. Carlito turned away with a nauseous curse, staggering his horse into Jesus' steed. The horses momentarily tangled, whinnied in panic, adding their high-pitched violence to the gut-wrenching scene. Hesitantly, Huizar followed Roberto as he dismounted and made his way to kneel at the abattoir ground.

"Dios Madres." The old man gulped back vomit and crossed himself.

Roberto paid his rough prayer no mind, stared with calm eyes at the bloody forms before him. They had been carefully skinned, nothing left but the long plaits of grimy, blood-soaked hair to identify them as Indians, the corpses left to rot in the sun.

"He took the skins," the old man said with a quivering voice. "Why in God's name would he take their skins? Christ..."

No one answered.

"Let's move out," Roberto said. He wiped his hands in the dry dirt to purify them of the tacky dark blood on his fingers and ambled back to his horse. The others followed, grateful to be away from the death stench rising up in the hot shadows.

The watchful buzzards waited for the intruders to move on, and then settled in for the remainder of their unquestioned feast.

Day moved inexorably into night.

The sun fell behind the hills like a dying ember, the evening turning cold. A wind from the east carried the scent of far away moisture, reminding the men of their carefully tended well at home, the thirsty fields and cattle, and finally leading their thoughts to the warm beds and soft women waiting for them in San Mateo. They camped in a flat stretch of sand, relatively clear of brush and cacti. Roberto wanted no obstructions in any direction and though it offered no shelter from the tussle of the wind, he didn't need to remind them of the skinned Indians; they would live with the gathering teeth of the wind without complaint. Their dinner was simple—pemmican and water, enough for the trail. After the day's terrible vision, none of them had a particular desire for the dried salty pemmican meat, but it was food to keep them alive in the desolation. They spoke little, each man remembering the stink of the dead, the sight of the flayed bodies. Any doubts of the man they chased being human had been laid to rest. After dinner, Jesus settled down not far from the others, and watched the dancing flames of the small campfire, as he took small, bolstering nips at his dwindling liquor. Carlito and Juan cleaned their guns, making sure to show the older men how careful they were with their weapons. Huizar leaned his head against his saddle and fell into a restless sleep, while Roberto fed and hobbled the horses.

Roberto assigned them two man watches. He told them he would take the last watch alone. Juan and Carlito took the first watch, and a few hours later, they shook Jesus and Huizar awake to take their turns. Then the brothers slept, huddled together as they had as children, each clutching the other's hand, and in the other hand, they held their rosary beads. The susurration of their commingled prayers wafted in the starry night.

Carlito fell asleep feeling as if his very skin was changing because of what he had seen this day. He would never be a child-man again. This he knew with a certainty that scared him. He would have to protect Juan as long as he could from this threshold. Looking at his brother now felt like looking at a backward mirror of himself, at the boy-man he had been before this hunt started. Something grew hard inside at the thought of something so terrible as skinning a man alive.

Jesus and Huizar said little to one another. The coyotes wailed like lost souls in the distance and the moon rolled across the velvet field of a diamond-pricked night. After their watch, Huizar woke Roberto and he fell gratefully into an exhausted sleep again. Jesus rolled his saddle back and was asleep in moments, his snores contesting the coyotes.

Roberto walked the perimeter, checked the horses, and chewed on pemmican. He felt restless, which was good for a solitary watch, but there was a deep uneasiness also. It would dull his edge. The sight of the skinned Indians kept coming back to him when he closed his eyes, disturbing his focus. He pulled a blanket from his saddle, wrapped himself up, and sat before the fire.

The wind swept across the sand, making the flames dance in hypnotic ways. The dance drew his eyes to the patterns as they coalesced into faces. Licking tongues began to form words from the eternal mystery of flame and wood. The wind's voice fell into the cup of his straining ears and even the coyotes seemed to be trying to relay something. The spirits had a message. He leaned forward to catch the almost silent crackles and pops of the wood, picking words from their code.

When the spirits finished, Roberto blinked, let out a heavy exhalation that he didn't realize he'd been holding, and found a stick to stir the dying fire. He gathered his saddle and weapons, prepared his horse, and walked out into the desert night, leaving behind his sleeping comrades. The vision had shown him his duty to his friends.

Just before dawn, Huizar woke. He yawned and looked around for Roberto, but did not see him. Bladder screaming for release, he stumbled away from the camp to find relief. When he came back, shivering in the early morning chill, Roberto was still nowhere to be seen. He glanced toward the horses to see Roberto's black roan was gone. He ran to where the others slept and kicked Jesus awake. "Wake up, you fool!"

The fat man rolled his heavy bulk and gave the old man a bleary frown. "Go away. Roberto hasn't said time to ride yet. Let me sleep, you old bastard."

Huizar found a jagged branch of ruined mesquite and whacked the big man across the back. "Get up, you useless drunk! Get up! He's gone, you fool!"

Dust flew from Jesus' slumped shoulders as he yelped in angry confusion. The ruckus stirred Carlito and Juan from their peaceful slumber.

"Roberto has gone without us," Huizar told them, eyes bulging with unrestrained terror. "He's gone to kill the Diablo on his own."

The brothers scampered up, staring in frightened uncertainty.

"Get your guns," Huizar ordered, giving Jesus one last thump. "Saddle the horses." He ran to gather his equipment, not waiting to see if the others were doing so, too. By the time he had cinched his saddle, and had his first boot through the stirrup, Carlito and Juan were already astride and waiting.

Jesus even managed to move his large frame much faster than usual and sat uneasily on his horse a few moments later.

The last smoking embers of the fire died as the men galloped away.

It wasn't hard for Roberto to follow the Diablo's trail. He just had to look for the buzzards. Like a dire totem for the thing clothed in the guise of human flesh, the carrion feeders followed in its wake as well. Riding to where a covey of the birds circled, circled, and finally landed, he found the first Indian's tattered and stinking flesh hanging from a tall cactus. He could only surmise how the demon had gotten the skin so far up without leaving any sign on the cactus' fragile green exterior. Ancient thorns pierced the stolen skin as the morning wind played with its loose ends. The ragged left hand gave him a false wave—or perhaps it was a warning.

With a kick to the roan's ribs, he rode hard. The stolen skin had still been damp with the dead man's blood, so Roberto couldn't be far behind the Diablo now. The gun riding heavy on his hip felt as useless as a whispered prayer, but he couldn't let the demon escape.

And why was it leaving the skins behind if not to show him the way?

More miles, and more distant buzzards gyrating in the roseate dawn air.

He saw them come to earth and galloped to their bloody feast. The demon had left the skin on the ground this time. The torn flesh had been filled with rocks, giving the dead man's skin the bulges and lumps of counterfeit life. It was propped in a sitting position, its eyeless face pointed east, into the rising sun, the empty gaze aimed at the collection of orange hills in the distance, the only discernible landmark for miles.

Roberto felt a gathering bubble of uncertainty in his stalwart consciousness.

He knew he rode into the Diablo's hands, but he had to trust the spirits. They had told him last night what he had to do to bring this killer to the ground. They said the balance of nature was askew because this inhuman creature walked the earth. Such things had their place, but not here.

But maybe the flesh of the unseen world was changing. Perhaps what was true before was no longer. The world of man shed its skin regularly enough. Perhaps the world of the unseen spirits was no different.

Could the spirits who'd spoken to him his entire life been wrong? What did they want of him? Why had they compelled him to come for the Diablo alone?

The hills drew nearer. The ancient, broken stones climbed and curved up gently to become walls, and the walls became a shadowed canyon trail. Roberto entered the canyon, feeling the cool dimness bath his flesh. He watched the cliffs for a sign of his prey. Nothing moved except the shadows of clouds along the rock's passive face. The trail moved sinuously through narrow cut stone until he came to a cul-de-sac. A massive monolith of gray rock rose into the air. Ancient paintings in faded white and black covered the gray wall. He knew them. The paintings were a story of violence, the story of how man had become an upright creature, how the goddess of darkness had birthed man, and finally how man had betrayed the gods and stolen their land.

Halfway up the stone, one of the paintings peeled away from the primordial diorama and began to move downwards. But it was no painting.

It was the Diablo.

Roberto's hand unconsciously whipped out his pistol before he could think about it. Finger poised above the trigger, he aimed it at the moving thing. The creature was pale and thin, and had given up the ruse of man flesh it had worn to insinuate itself into the village weeks ago. Now it had the narrow face of the snake, the gangly slow limbs of a lizard. It moved head first down the face of the rock, its two blazing black eyes watching Roberto as a sly slither of a smile creased its thin mouth. It had saved the last skin for itself, and had wrapped the ungainly, rotting tissue around its upper and lower torso. Tatters of decaying meat dripped from the makeshift covering.

It dropped to the ground from the last few feet, crouching like a hungry coyote. Those lightless eyes watched him warily.

"You don't belong here, Diablo," Roberto said. "And I aim to make sure you go back where you came from, you hear?"

The thing stayed on all fours, still smiling, still watching.

Then it began to move back and forth like the rattler's warning tail; so fast that he could hardly see its frantic movements. The Indian skin sloughed to the ground and acid bile rose up into Roberto's clutching gorge and he had to close his eyes for a moment until it settled again. Nothing living could make its body move in such a manner. It was a blasphemy against the reality of the flesh.

When he looked at it again, the creature had stopped moving. Now it stared at him with a frank and ravenous hunger. Then it began to creep towards him, a black tongue sliding over the wet weal of its mouth.

Roberto muttered a hurried prayer and kissed the end of his pistol. He fired all six shots in quick succession. Each bullet passed through the demon, ripping chunks of its insipid skin away. He tossed the gun aside. It was useless.

Roberto snatched his Bowie knife from its sheath on his hip and crouched down, ready to take on the beast. His powerful shoulders flexed, the muscles of his thighs standing out in brawny waves.

The Diablo leaped at Roberto, inhuman hands outstretched. Roberto's knife flashed in the canyon shadows. A perfect arc of deadly silver carved a deep trench through the creature's upper torso. The stink of death welled up from the empty wound, but no blood.

The demon's weight carried them both to the ground.

He stabbed upward, while pushing with his other arm to keep the thing's claws from his face. Its cold body lay heavy on him and he knew it wanted his skin. A shriek of hungry rage boiled from the creature's mouth, as it scampered to find purchase in Roberto's flesh with its claws.

The knife found flesh once more, biting deeply. The carrion stink made Roberto gag. This was death personified, the spirit made flesh.

He ripped at the thing's body as fire spewed forth from the open wound. He stabbed again, tearing with all his might, his arm getting weaker with the exertion of holding the demon at bay. Another great rent opened in the belly of the Diablo. A harsh, cold wind blew past Roberto, carrying the dampness of rotting flesh and a rain of copper tasting liquid.

Yet another stab and the creature convulsed above him and sodden clumps of decayed earth spilled from the suppurating gash.

The creature managed to swipe its clawed hand across Roberto's heaving chest. Fire exploded across his flesh and black stars danced in his fading vision, but still he held the thing away from his face. He could smell his own blood now, commingled with the stink of the death thing above him.

Roberto got his knees, and with a grunt of agony, heaved the creature over his head.

The Diablo landed a dozen feet away, on its back, pale face staring up into the noonday sun. Its black, soulless eyes never blinked against the glare.

Roberto struggled to his feet and staggered to the prostrate thing, knife dripping with foul ichor. He felt his skin opening and closing with each spurt of his blood, his life slowly draining away. He stood swaying above the demon as the thing's eyes found him. Instead of fear or remorse or pain, he found a confused and curious gaze staring back at him from the god's face.

"Such weak armor, this flesh," the demon said in a harsh voice. "It can contain multitudes, yet it falls apart at a mere whim. It is hard to understand why the first people lost their world to this pathetic worm-ridden animal. Better to never again walk this world with such cattle."

"Why?" Roberto asked. He wasn't sure if the demon would understand the throng of questions contained within that single word; his head was spinning with death and confusion.

"I thought I could find peace in flesh. But it never came. So I thought by doing some great act I could understand the spirit within. Only no act of goodness brought an answer."

"So you chose something evil."

The demon tried to move a gangly arm, but it fell at its decaying side. "The girl was so innocent that I was sure I'd know then. But nothing came."

Roberto felt his legs bend and he collapsed next to the creature—no demon, no Diablo at all, but a wandering god who only wanted an answer to the puzzle of flesh.

"The skins?" His words came at a price as every word spilled more of his lifeblood onto the gore-spattered ground.

"I tried them on for size," the god said. "But none of them would hold me. Their nature was too small."

The wind whistled down the canyon, blew sand into Roberto's clouding eyes.

"You needed someone who has seen great evil and great good," he whispered.

"Yes, there is a balance I never considered," the god said. "Now I will pass back to the other side without answers. All this death wasted. All this life."

"Not wasted," Roberto said. He fumbled his weakening grip to the god's thin cold hand. He handed him the knife. "The others will teach you..."

The remainder of the posse had ridden hard since the morning, following Roberto's tracks. They had seen the rotting skins, or at least what was left of them, as the buzzards had feasted liberally upon them, but did not stop to examine them.

Roberto's black roan had trotted past them half an hour before, and no matter how much they called to it, the horse would not stop. Then the small figure appeared in the distance, swimming in the scorching desert air. For a moment, it wavered like an illusion of black dust, and then settled into reality again.

The posse stopped.

Juan stood in his saddle. "Is that him?"

"Or the Diablo?" Jesus added.

"I cannot see that far anymore," Huizar grumbled. "Is it...?"

Carlito gazed at the approaching man with eyes that were becoming more eagle-like every year. "No...no, that is Roberto. I think he is hurt."

Huizar kicked his horse to a gallop again, the others following.

ALTHIGUA

ROBERT KUZMESKI

Hal held a straight flush when Timmy burst in, yelling about blood in the well. The boy's momma leaned on Hal's shoulder; she'd been a soiled dove long enough to know who had the hot hand in the room. When the boy raced in, she shot him a look that would normally send him crying. Not this time.

"Easy, Betsy," Hal said to her. "The boy's pretty riled. Let's hear him out."

"Quit your stallin'," Kurt Gaithers snapped. "Some of us want to win back what's lost."

Hal raised his hand to shush him. He hated Kurt's unpleasantness. Ever since the old man lost his shirt when his mine dried up, he'd been nothing but an angry drunk. Kurt ran the mine into the ground, Hal had no doubts about that, but he claimed someone was interfering—sabotaging equipment and bribing his men. When Aldus Merriweather bought the mine, he found a gold vein deep in the tunnels. Everyone knew Merriweather's hard work and smarts made him successful but Kurt insisted he was the culprit.

Hal only put up with Kurt because he was an easy mark at the poker table.

"Flip 'em," Hal said, standing to put on his vest and affix his sheriff's badge.

The players showed their hands—the sheriff had them beat. He scraped up the cash, ignoring Kurt's bellyaching, and told Timmy to show him what he'd found.

The sheriff followed Timmy and Betsy to the town center while the boy told him what happened.

He'd gone to fetch some water for the blacksmith, but when he pulled up the bucket, the water was red. He said it had a funny smell to it, too.

They found a small crowd gathered around the well. The townsfolk knew something was wrong and they were scared. People here were farmers and ranchers; folks who depended on a good source of water. If the well went bad, people would leave town.

Hal pushed through the crowd and pulled up the rope. Before the bucket was in view, he could smell it. Back in Witchita, he'd seen plenty of trouble. Bar fights ending in shootings, drunken remarks that led to duels. He'd come across enough blood in those unruly days to know the smell.

Folks gasped when the pail came up. It was filled with blood—pale red and thinned by the water. Hal hoped it'd just be rust in the water or that he would at least be able to convince folks it was rust. But there was no mistaking what was in that bucket.

The sheriff turned to face the group. "Go on home now," he announced. "There's a dead animal down in there, is all. Can't have you good folks in the way while I fetch it out."

The crowd dispersed, murmuring. He figured they didn't believe the story about a dead animal but he knew they'd do as they were told. People here liked Hal—he was one of them. He didn't grow up in the town and hadn't been there very long, but somehow, he just fit. The fast pace in Witchita had been too much for him. When he tried his hand at running his own ranch, it was too slow. Small towns were his speed. He enjoyed a few drinks at the saloon with friendly folk like he found here. He became a real friend to the town, using a firm hand when necessary but solving most trouble with charisma, not guns.

With the crowd gone, Hal turned his attention to Timmy. "Did you see anything else? Hear anything else around here? If there was someone involved, I need to know."

Timmy shook his head for a moment and then paused. "There was somethin'. But you ain't gonna believe me."

"This ain't a game, honey," Betsy scolded. "Tell Sheriff Hal what you know."

"Well," he said with hesitation and fear in his voice. "When the bucket hit the water, it splashed like normal. I let the rope loose to fill up the pail. Then I felt somethin' tug on it."

"Tug?" Hal asked.

"Yes, sir," the boy continued. "Like a fish that's got your line. It pulled real good at first, then kinda slacked off."

"Then?" Hal asked him.

"Then I ain't sure what I saw," he said. "Somethin' black, all shiny and slimy looking. It sorta slithered up the rope like a big ol' worm and then went back into the water. Made a loud splash, too. Whatever it was, it was real big."

"Thanks, Timmy," Hal said. "I'll look into what made this mess. As for the thing you saw, it was probably just funny lighting, is all. Still, make sure you keep this just between us; especially about what you saw."

Timmy nodded and ran off towards his house.

Hal looked at Betsy. "I reckon I better get down there and see what found its way into the water."

"Why don't you let Jim do that?" Betsy whispered, pressing her body against his. "You've got a jackpot to spend and I have a free night."

Hal knew what she was getting at and it didn't sound half bad. He would get his deputy to look into the well while he went to the saloon for a night with Betsy.

"When are you gonna take me up on my offer?" Hal asked her.

"You're sweet," she said to him, kissing him on the cheek. "But I'm not the marrying kind. Besides, I need the money to take care of my boy."

"Well, at least its money well spent," he grumbled. "Be over just after dark."

He walked to the sheriff's office to find Jim. The deputy was good in a crisis but when there was nothing going on, he was on the lazy side. He would no doubt be sitting back in a chair with his feet up on the desk, hat tipped over his eyes.

On the way over, Hal couldn't shake the feeling that something bad was coming. It wasn't just the blood in the well. The air itself felt heavy, like a storm was brewing. The sky looked menacing; thick gray clouds tinged with a color that wasn't quite brown but not fully orange. It didn't look like it was on fire but it could definitely be smoldering.

The townsfolk could feel something, too. He passed by Hank Greenwood's barbershop and greeted the old man. Hank said nothing in return but just sat on the stoop of his shop, sharpening his straight razor. His eyes bore a maniacal glint that made him look like some kind of predator.

He saw similar stares on others, too. The blacksmith pounded out metal with a particular violence. Preacher Brown yelled to people as they passed by the church, delivering a damnation sermon instead of giving his usual blessings. Anger seethed in every man and woman.

He shivered. He felt like he often did when he'd walked into some kind of ambush.

When Hal reached the jail, he found Jim strapping on his gun holster.

"Evening, Jim," he said to his deputy.

"Hal," the man replied, an edge in his voice. "I was just on my way out to the Yarrow's farm if you want to join me."

"What's the situation?" he asked.

"Martha came in a little bit ago, complaining of someone on her land," Jim said. "Says she saw some redskin slinking around the barn. She reckons he was going to steal her horses or something. Adam stayed behind with his shotgun, yelling that he's going to kill any trespassers he finds."

"The last thing we need is another clash with the Navajo," Hal responded. "Adam shoots one of them and they'll raid us for sure."

"You gonna come?" Jim asked.

"No," he told him. "I used to drink a bit with Adam before he got real bad. Why don't I head out there and talk some sense into him? I need you to check out the well. There's blood in the water and we need to drag it to see what died in there."

"I heard about that," Jim said. "Talk of the town and all. I'll round up a couple of farm boys and we'll haul out whatever we find."

Hal walked out to the Yarrow's farm but he didn't find any sign of trespassers. The gates were intact and there was no sign of anyone trying to break into the barn. Adam wasn't standing sentry on his porch like Hal expected. In fact, he was nowhere to be found.

Hal decided to take one quick look along the tree line before heading inside to talk to Adam. He peered into the woods as he patrolled, not expecting to find anything. He was wrong.

The flash of movement that grabbed his attention might have been dismissed as a trick of the light or a branch swaying in the wind, if not for the way the horses reacted. They neighed and fled in panic, galloping directly away from the tree line.

Gun drawn, Hal cautiously moved into the trees. Though it was probably just an animal, frayed nerves made him jumpy. With the blood in the well and the oppressive feeling of hate in town, he wasn't going to take any chances.

About fifteen paces into the woods, he discovered a mound of blood and fur. At first, it looked like a freshly eaten carcass. He looked around for the predator but nothing moved or made a sound in the underbrush. He took a closer look at the carcass to see what kind of animal it was. If something had gotten at one of Adam's dogs, he'd have to hunt it down so it didn't keep preying on his animals.

Seeing the remains close up made him feel sick as he churned the bloody mass with the butt of his rifle. A human eye peered up from the viscera, staring at him through a bloody glaze. Hal jumped back in horror.

What was going on? Was something hunting humans?

Confused, he went through the remains again. It was mostly skin, a lot of it intact. It looked like someone flayed a man and turned his skin outward, probably to attract scavengers that would feed on the remains and get rid of the corpse. But if that were the case, then the fur didn't make sense. He couldn't tell if the corpse were man or beast, much less figure out what killed it.

Twilight began to creep through the trees, choking Hal's light and bathing the land in shadow. He wasn't going to get to the bottom of this tonight. He decided to check on Adam and let him know he would return tomorrow and take a better look at his findings.

When he went to the house, he found Adam passed out at the dining table, a shotgun across his lap and an empty whiskey bottle in one hand. Hal shook him awake. The man looked up with eyes filled with fear.

"I saw the Injun, Hal," he said. "He walked like a man but he weren't no man. His eyes were yellow. I weren't even drinking when I saw him look at me with those yellow eyes."

Hal slowly moved the shotgun away, putting it out of the drunkard's reach. "What happened, Adam? What did he do?"

"I yelled at him to get off my land but he started coming toward me, smiling. So I fired a warning shot. But it don't scare him one bit. No, sir. He looks at me with those yellow eyes and starts yipping and barking like some kind of dog. Then he runs off, laughing. He weren't no man, Hal. You gotta believe me."

"Whatever happened, I'll take care of it. You just wait here for your wife; she's on her way back. Don't do anything. Stay your gun and just keep your door locked."

Hal left the terrified man behind. He needed to get back to the office, find Jim and tell him what happened. Mostly, he needed a drink himself. His nerves were shot and he found himself jumping at shadows. He kept his hand on his Bluntline all the way back to town.

Hal found Jim still at the well.

"What'd you find?" Hal asked.

"I ain't sure," the deputy replied. "Skin, maybe. Looks like someone killed a man, turned him inside out, then threw him down the well. But there's fur, too, so I ain't sure."

Jim looked like he was going to be sick, so Hal put a hand on his shoulder to steady him.

"We've got one hell of a mystery on our hands, Jim," he said.

Hal told Jim what he'd seen at Adam's place and reassured him that whatever was happening, they'd get to the bottom of it.

"What do we do?" Jim asked when Hal finished.

"Not sure yet," Hal answered. "Tomorrow morning, we take another look at all of this. Go get some sleep, Jim. We're gonna need us some clear heads come mornin'."

The men parted ways, Jim heading home and Hal going to Betsy's bed. He counted on her to take his mind off of things. She didn't disappoint.

When at last Hal slept, evil crept into his dreams. He imagined a massive creature living underground, slithering through the local mines and underground wells. The monster was without shape, morphing and shifting to ooze its way through the tunnels. It entered a large chamber under the town and Hal witnessed its horrifying enormity. It dwarfed the town, its black and warted skin stretching into every tunnel in the mine.

In the center of the mass, an enormous orange eye opened and stared at Hal. It was a cold look, devoid of emotion. He knew at once that this creature was older than the Earth itself–man was of no consequence to it. He felt meaningless; a speck of dust floating through an incomprehensibly large universe. The realization nearly maddened him.

The creature shifted its corpulent body to form long, slimy tentacles, much like what Timmy had described. The tentacles violently shot up through the ground, each one burying itself into the heads of the townsfolk, wrapping around their brains.

Mine, the creature communicated, placing the word into Hal's mind without speaking it.

Hal awoke with a start, covered in cold sweat. He hesitated before looking over at Betsy, terrified he'd find her with one of the creature's oily tentacles piercing her skull. When he got the nerve to cast a glance her way, she was sleeping peacefully by his side. He breathed a sigh of relief; he loved Betsy, even if she saw him as just another 'trick', another 'john' to spend the night with.

"Just a bad dream," he whispered, brushing sweat-matted hair from his forehead.

A woman's pained scream coming from outside told him that he'd spoken too soon. He jumped to his feet, dressed quickly, and peered out the window to see what was happening.

Preacher Brown stood in the street, the widow Jamieson crumpled at his feet. He kept one foot on her chest, pinning her to the ground while he stabbed her in the throat and head with a hunting knife. Her screams ended abruptly, replaced by the preacher's maniacal laughter.

Hal charged out of the room and down the stairs, ignoring Betsy's sleepy voice trailing after him, wanting to know what was wrong. He ran into the street and aimed his gun at the holy man, who knelt over the widow while plucking out his eyes with the knife.

"Stand up and back away real slow," Hal said, gun hand shaking in horror. He looked at the preacher. The killer wore an expression of bliss, despite the blood streaming from his gaping eye sockets.

"Sheriff?" the preacher asked. "Is that you?"

"Yep. And I've got a gun, so you get away from her. Now!"

The preacher stood, knife still in hand. "It's beautiful, Hal. Too beautiful to behold. The Rapture is upon us. Can you feel it? The Bringer of Absence has come!"

The words sent chills down Hal's spine. He could feel something—the presence from his dream perhaps. Its miasma blanketed the town, smothering it with fear and hate.

"Who is this Bringer of Absence?" Hal asked, afraid he might already know the answer.

"The Lord of Nothing," the preacher said. "The Herald of the End."

Before Hal could react, the preacher dragged the knife across his neck, dropped to all fours, and opened his throat to the earth. Blood spread quickly through the dirt, circling the two corpses in a crimson halo.

The sheriff looked around for help...for answers. He found only expressionless faces staring back at him. People watched him from every window in town, yet no one reacted to the grisly scene. After a few moments, they silently turned away from their windows and disappeared back into their homes. His gut told him that the creature from his dream controlled these people, that his dream had been real.

With nowhere left to turn, Hal needed to follow the only lead he had. Somehow, the Indian was the key. He had to go to Chief Rolling Sky and find out what he knew. He wouldn't be greeted warmly and would feel better with a steady gun watching his back, so he made his way to Jim's house.

When he saw the front door open and orange light spilling out from the windows, he knew something was wrong. He shoved the door open, gun drawn to protect himself from whatever waited within. Inside, he found Jim's mutilated corpse in the center of the room. Flames spilled from the fire pit, slithering up the walls and engulfing the back of the house. Amidst the blaze, Hal saw Jim's wife sitting upright in a chair, her two children lifeless at her feet.

"Molly, why?" Hal demanded.

"I did it for *Him*," she answered without a hint of sadness in her voice. "For The Rapture. They are with *Him* now, in *His* place of glory."

"I'm taking you in," he told her.

"No. I must join Him," she said. She tilted her chair back and vaulted into the fire. She never made a sound, even as flames consumed her. She just watched him through soulless eyes, a serene smile on her lips as her skin blackened and her hair erupted into flames.

Hal shot her. He hoped killing her would somehow deny the creature its perverse pleasure.

He staggered away from the house, letting it burn behind him. Jim's death made this more real—more horrible. He fought his rising grief and went to the back of the house, where he knew his deputy kept a few dependable horses. He chose the fastest one he could find and galloped toward the Indian camp.

* * *

The dawn sun began to peek through the mountains by the time Hal reached the Navajo camp. The Indian at Yarrow's farm was the only solid lead so far and he had to be one of Rolling Sky's tribe. Hal wouldn't leave without answers from the Chief.

His presence drew expected results. Several braves readying their horses for a morning hunt encircled him, arrows and spears pointed at his head, throat and chest.

"You die today," one of them told Hal.

"Maybe," Hal replied. Images of Jim's family flashed through his mind, strengthening his will and filling his gut with grit. He was in no mood for delays. "But I expect an audience with your Chief first. Any of you thinks otherwise, I'll take you to Hell with me."

Most of the camp heard the angry exchange of words and came to see what was happening and Chief Rolling Sky made his way to the ring of braves surrounding Hal.

"Lower the weapons," he commanded. "Let us see what brings him here before we decide his fate."

Hal described all that he'd seen. The Chief said nothing, nodding occasionally at some parts; frowning at others. The bizarre nature of the story made the Indians shift uncomfortably from one foot to another and many of them clearly wanted to be somewhere else.

Once Hal finished his tale, Rolling Sky motioned for him to follow. The two men went into the Chief's teepee and Rolling Sky sent for one of his medicine men.

"I know only legends," he explained. "But I've summoned a man who can give you the knowledge you seek."

The medicine man arrived, as ancient as the dirt itself, barely capable of standing without assistance. The milky gray over his eyes told Hal he'd lost his sight, perhaps long ago. Despite his frailty, he carried himself with wisdom and authority. The Chief relayed Hal's story in their native tongue. The old Indian listened intently, giving no indication of his thoughts.

"Your town is doomed," the shaman told Hal in English. "Leave it while you can."

It wasn't the answer Hal expected. "I can't do that. I need to help those people...to stop whatever's happening."

The medicine man eyed him coldly. "Then you will die."

"Fine. Tell me what I need to know so that when I die, I die trying."

"You face a spirit older than the Earth itself," the man explained to him. "It is the nature of destruction itself. It is called Althigua."

"What is it?" the sheriff asked.

"Every force has an opposite force," the Indian explained. "In order to create, you must destroy. Once, this world did not exist. There was nothing. The creation of this world destroyed that nothingness. Althigua is the embodiment of both that nothingness and of the energy that destroyed it. He ushers in a return to nothingness, clearing the way for creation to begin anew."

"Is he the Bringer of Absence?" Hal asked, remembering what he'd heard from the preacher.

"Names are meaningless to Him. Lives are meaningless to Him."

"Well, he's turning people into lunatics," Hal snapped. "They're killing each other as we speak."

"It is Althigua's way," the shaman said. "He uses the forces around him to achieve his goals. In this case, he is preying upon man's weakness, corrupting your people...pushing them to destroy."

"How do I stop it?"

"You cannot," the old man told him. "He intends to put an end to us all. Once his appetite for ruin is sated, he will sleep again, just as he has done for many hundreds of years."

"What if he isn't sated until the world is destroyed?"

"My people will make sure that does not happen. We have rituals that can drive him into early slumber."

"So help me now," Hal demanded.

"Coyote forbids it. He woke Althigua. We will not defy his wishes."

"Coyote? What do you mean?"

"Coyote is the trickster spirit. It was his blood you found—his fur. His were the yellow eyes that watched your farmer. When he visits our world, he creates a host —a soulless body to inhabit—and discards it when he is done. You've seen the remnants of those hosts."

"Why would he do this?" Hal asked. "Why would he help this thing?"

"We have a saying," the chief interjected. "Coyote goes where his feet take him. It means that he has no goal, no destination. His whim is ever changing. Even Coyote does not know why he does what he does."

"If you fail to put Althigua back to sleep, it could destroy the world," Hal said. "Coyote would let that happen?"

"The world will not end...just your people," the medicine man replied. "Greed drove you to take our lands. Lust for power pushes you to expand further still. Violence leads you to massacre our tribes. Your weaknesses make it easy for Althigua to turn you into puppets. Coyote knows that, just as he knows our people are strong. We will survive Althigua."

Hal was furious. "Is there nothing you can do to help your fellow man?"

"There is one thing I can tell you," the shaman said. "One thing that may give you a fighting chance."

"What is it?"

"Coyote would only awaken Althigua if someone asked it of him. A person in your town wanted this to happen. If you can find that man, you might be able to sever his connection to Althigua, returning the spirit to the abyss."

Though Hal thanked the men for the information, he wasn't feeling very grateful. The Indians had left him to the wolves, unconcerned for the safety of his people. He knew he might not be able to stop the creature and he knew he might die trying. But he'd rather go out fighting than wait for the madness to take him.

Hal pushed his horse hard as he made the long ride back to town. The rising sun shone brightly across the valley, highlighting numerous vultures that now spiraled above the town, waiting to pick apart the bones of the dead and dying. He bore down even harder on the mare, speeding into town to make sure the birds had little to scavenge.

The streets were oddly quiet when he arrived. He went to check on Betsy first, where he found the saloonkeeper's corpse draped across the bar; another sacrifice to Althigua. His heart raced as he climbed the stairs and opened Betsy's door. She was nowhere to be found.

Panicked, he ran to Timmy's room, finding Betsy's lifeless body bleeding out from numerous stab wounds. Timmy stood staring out the window, a bloody knife in his hands.

"Howdy, Sheriff," Timmy said without turning.

Hal couldn't take his eyes off Betsy. Tears began to streak down his dust-covered cheeks.

"Who did this?" he demanded.

"I did," Timmy said. "She asked me to; said she needed to be with Him." The boy turned from the window, and Hal saw spattered blood decorating his face and clothes. He took a few steps toward the sheriff, an emotionless face hiding his intent. Still, Hal had seen enough to know what Timmy planned.

"Stop," he said, drawing his gun. "I'm not going to let you kill me, Timmy."

"Yes you will," Timmy said. "The Rapture demands it."

Hal crossed himself, religion something to fall back on, to hold on to. "I'm sorry I couldn't save you, Timmy," he said to the boy before shooting him in the head.

Hal stumbled to the window, leaning on the frame while he sobbed deeply. From his vantage point, he noticed Kurt Gaithers standing near the side of a building across the street, engaged in a heated conversation with an Indian brave. Hal cracked the window just enough to hear without drawing their attention.

"This ain't what we agreed to!" Kurt snarled loudly.

"Oh, but it is," the Indian told him, amusement evident in his yellow eyes. "I have given you exactly what you asked for."

"You said you'd help me kill the men that stole my mine. Not destroy the whole town!"

Coyote laughed. "You asked that I kill those who stole the land. White men took this land from my people...from nature itself. Althigua is killing the thieves, just as you asked."

Kurt lunged at Coyote, who stepped aside and buried a boot into Kurt's side.

"Save your energy," Coyote said. "Soon, you will feel Althigua's compulsion to kill. When that happens, you will need your strength." With that the trickster shed his human disguise...exploding violently from his host and spraying Gaithers with blood. A gore-soaked coyote pulled its way from the grotesque mass, leaving behind the human skin and clumps of fur that it shed in the violent separation. The creature ran to the edge of town to then dart into the woods, howling with glee the entire time.

Hal knew he had to kill Gaithers to sever the connection to Althigua. Maybe that would end the hypnotic madness holding the remaining townsfolk in its deathly embrace.

He ran out of the building and into the street, to be confronted by the townspeople. They stood shoulder to shoulder in a line, blocking Hal's access to Gaithers.

They spoke as one. "We will not let you do this."

They started toward the sheriff, emptiness in their eyes. Hal ran to the jail as they began to charge. He slammed the door behind him, trapping himself in the building. The mob of killers began throwing rocks at the windows, smashing their way in. He grabbed his shotgun and began shooting indiscriminately out the window, alternating between the double-barrel and the two pistols in his holster. He fired until he was out of targets. It seemed like an eternity had passed before it was over. Finally, he stood alone in the center of the room, gunshots ringing in his ears like thunder.

With his head throbbing with pain, he passed out.

* * *

When Hal finally awoke, he could feel someone cinching a noose around his neck. He tried to open his eyes but they wouldn't cooperate. The more he tried, the more his eyes hurt. Hearing voices, he turned his head slightly to hear the two men who were talking nearby better.

"The son-of-a-bitch is waking up," one of them said.

"Good. Now we know he'll feel it when the rope chokes the life out of him."

One of them came over and kicked Hal in the ribs. "That's for the people you murdered in town, you lunatic." He picked Hal up and draped him over the back of a horse.

"Why did he do it?" the other man asked.

"No one knows but him," the hangman said. "The redskin that saw him said he was crazed, spouting nonsense as he gunned people down."

"So why did he put his own eyes out afterwards?"

"Dunno. He was muttering something about The Rapture when we caught him, saying it was too beautiful to behold," the hangman said.

Hal could feel Althigua's tentacles probing him, heard its laughter in his mind. Was it true? Had this all been Hal's doing? He had flashbacks—memories of powerful emotions. Anger at Betsy's continued rejection. Contempt for Kurt's constant whining. But surely he couldn't have done what they suggested—could he?

The horse galloped away and the rope around his neck tightened and went taut, denying Hal an answer.

Moments later, he joined the nothingness of death.

HOWL OF THE WILD BEAST

KELLY M. HUDSON

Whatever was in the bushes circling the hunting party was big and sounded meaner than hell itself. I clutched my rifle tight to my chest and evened my breathing. Over to my left, the dogs, all chained up for the night, were howling something fierce and pulling against their leashes, trying to tear themselves free. I've been around hunting dogs my entire life and for all the money in the world I couldn't tell you if those dogs were trying to attack or run away. I was just as mixed in my feelings as to which I wanted to do, too.

The animal—if that's what it was and not some crazed mountain man—crashed around in the bushes, moaning and grunting like it had been stung by a bunch of bees. It was a nasty wail, a cry the devil himself might have made when Jesus decided to get himself crucified instead of running away. It was the sound of frustration and rage all rolled up into one and it tore at my heart like the claws of a rabid black bear.

I looked around at my buddies, the light of the flickering fire throwing their shadows around like ghosts. There were five of us on the trip this time, down from our usual eight. Couldn't be helped, though. Jerry was up in Canada somewhere doing some business for his company. Tom was laid up sick in bed and Cavanaugh, well, he was always a might unpredictable in his behavior. He was a loose cannon over in 'Nam and he hadn't changed a lick since. So there was just the five of us: me, Ed, Hughie, Ronnie, and Allen. We'd been to Hell and back together in the thick, hot jungles of 'Nam and now here we were, old men right back in the middle of something we didn't understand and scared half to death.

And I couldn't have been with finer men.

"It's stopped," Ed said. We all looked over at the bushes and there was nothing now but silence. Even the dogs stopped their barking and it was almost as if nothing had happened at all. We stood still, clutching our guns and straining our ears to catch a sound, a pop, anything to let us know where the animal was. We got nothing. The situation was just like the ones we'd lived over and over again back in 'Nam and it was funny the way we snapped back into that way of thinking. It was like an old muscle we hadn't exercised, but when we needed it, there it was, ready and willing.

"Maybe it's gone," Ed said. He was tall, skinny as a nail and always had been. Ed was the kind of guy that, when you saw him, you were afraid his Adam's apple was going to tip him over. He had a good heart though, and a keen eye. He was the best shot of the lot of us.

"Or it may be lulling us," Hughie said. He was the chubby one, although it wasn't fair to call him out over his weight. Hughie was one of those fat guys that nobody thought of as fat, but as something my momma used to call 'big-boned'. He had a shock of red hair topping his head and a sprout of gray on his chin. Hughie was our muscle and I can't tell you how many times he carried an extra load for whichever one of us was hurting during the war.

Ronnie spat a big wad of tobacco juice onto the ground at his feet. He kept his rifle pointed where we'd last heard the noise, his face scrunched up in concentration. Ronnie was mean. He was average height and average size, but he more than made up for it by being a bastard. Ronnie would sooner cut your throat than look at you, but if he was your friend, he was your buddy for life. You couldn't buy loyalty like the kind Ronnie offered. Of course, try telling that to the trail of bruised and battered ex-wives he'd left behind and they might flat-out disagree with you.

Allen shouldered his rifle, confident we had plenty of firepower ready when needed. He was a born leader, and even though we had a capable commanding officer when we were in the war, Allen was the one we all turned to when the chips were down. He was a handsome fellow with blond hair and blue eyes; the kind of man the ladies always swooned over. Age hadn't hurt him too bad, adding some wrinkles around those pretty eyes and pushing his hair back a bit, but I'd be damned if he didn't still look like a matinee idol.

"Give it a minute, boys," Allen said. Even out here, after all this time had passed, Allen was our leader.

Me, my name is Steven though I go by Stevie. I wasn't nobody special, just a country boy in over his head in 'Nam and in over his head the rest of his natural born life, as it turned out. I grew up in Kentucky and that's where we were, in my neck of the woods. We were in the mountains of eastern Kentucky, up past Hazard and deep, deep into the forest. It was my turn this year to recommend a place to meet and hunt and I figured it was time my good old buddies finally got a chance to breathe that beautiful Kentucky air. Sometimes, laying there in the arms of one of them Vietnamese women during the war, the wind all hot and likely to choke you with the humidity and cigarette smoke, I used to try and think of Kentucky and the memories came hard and clear and I could almost taste the crisp, clean air.

Those were the days that got me through that nightmare. They got me through that bad time, in My Khe, when me and my troop took part in a terrible, terrible thing. I didn't hardly sleep for weeks after that, and although none of us really got in any trouble for it, we sure deserved it. I can't begin to tell you what it was like back then; if you were there, then you'd understand. You might not agree, and you might hate us, but you'd understand. But if you weren't there, then you'd think of me and my friends as monsters. I've tried to live my life in a good way since then, trying to make up for what we did, but I still get the nightmares, and I still wake up seeing that woman whose kid I gunned down hold her little boy's dead body in her arms.

Who could have imagined, years later, that I'd be knee-deep in a new nightmare right in the blessed home state that I always dreamed of going back to.

"I think it's been tracking us for a while," Ed said. "Maybe since we started out yesterday."

"That's crazy, Ed," Allen said.

"Maybe," Ed shrugged. "But I think we've all seen enough crazy to know it's possible."

Ed was right. We were the kind of unit that always got the dirty assignments, the one that was always sent out to recon so the real soldiers, the pretty ones with the right commendations and the good sense not to piss off the brass, could have a safe passage. We were the grunts that got to wade through the blood and the shit and never got a pat on the back for our efforts. Maybe that's why we got a pass on My Khe. I don't know.

"What in the hell is it?" I asked and all eyes turned to me.

"Thought you might know," Allen said. "This is your turf, after all."

"Now, just 'cause I'm from around here doesn't mean I know every square inch of ground and every critter running around on it," I said. The truth was, I hadn't been hunting up here since my daddy took me when I was ten years old. I remembered it like it was yesterday, though, and it was so beautiful and so full of deer that it was the first thing that came to mind when it was my choice on where to hold our little reunion.

Hughie grunted and nodded. He walked over and stood next to me. He didn't talk much, usually letting his actions speak for him. When a big man like him moved, you noticed.

"I say let's go after it," Ronnie said. He spit another wad on the ground. "Maybe we can bag us a good trophy."

I looked around. The wind whistled through the trees. It was near nightfall. Going out after an animal that big would be a bad idea. Maybe during the day, when we could see, but out in those woods in the dark, that animal would have all the advantages.

"I don't like it," Allen said. And that settled that. "We should stay alert, though, in case it comes back. Keep your guns handy."

Like we weren't already going to do just that. War taught a man a lot of things, but the most important thing it taught you the most was to keep your gun by your side at all times. You never knew when you'd need it.

Ronnie growled a reply, not happy about the decision, but he went along with it. Allen was the unspoken boss and what he said went. We settled in, built a big fire and broke out the coffee and booze. The dogs lazed around, occasionally yawning or moaning. We knew they'd get riled up if the animal came around again, so we relaxed a bit.

As we sat there, I reflected on the day that had been and the more I thought about it, the more I believed Ed was right. The moment we set foot in these woods something hadn't seemed right. I got an eerie feeling right away, like we were being watched by something. I shook it off, though, and chalked it up to my paranoia. A day didn't go by when something didn't happen to remind me of the war, people that I knew in it, or what happened after it. Vietnam was just as much a part of me as the last name my daddy gave me.

"Remember that shit, Stevie?" Ed asked. He was grinning like a cat that had caught a mouse it'd been chasing all day.

"What?" I hadn't been listening.

The entire group laughed.

"There he goes," Ed said. "Trying to pretend it never happened!"

"No, really, what were y'all saying?" I asked.

"We were talking 'bout that whore, the one up near Da Nang, that you got all caught up in," Allen said.

I felt the blood rush to my face. Damn, I wished they'd leave that bit of history alone. "I can't say I rightly recall," I replied. They all busted up laughing anyway. I had to turn the tide. "Besides, I wasn't the only one to fall in love," I said, looking squarely at Ronnie.

"Ah-ha! That's right!" Ed crowed. "You had yourself a regular little Ms. Saigon, didn't you?"

Ronnie turned a bright red. I knew how he felt. He shook his head and smiled.

"You boys don't understand," Ronnie said. "The way she sucked dick, you would have fallen in love, too!"

We all laughed. I stared at Ronnie for a moment, remembering the massacre, remembering when he took out his .45 and pointed it at a baby laying on the ground, all alone, its mother shot dead next to it. I remembered him firing and missing and turning to us and laughing. "I won't miss a second time," he'd said and he was right. He didn't. My stomach turned sour and I took an extra belt of the whiskey being passed around.

We went through bottle after bottle of whiskey, telling old stories, making fun of each other, and updating where we'd been since last time we been together. We didn't speak of My Khe, though. We never did. That was something we all tried to put away and never think on again, even though I knew each of us did.

It was always the same when we met up. We got together once every five years or so, with one of us picking the spot, and we'd go out for the weekend, hunting and carrying on like we did that night.

For all our carousing, we never completely forgot about the large animal we'd heard in the woods and how it had come up on us as we was getting ready to set up our tents. We'd been chatting, Ed having just chained up the dogs, when we heard something growl off behind us to our right. We all stopped, turned and looked. All we could make out was a big, dark shape thrashing around in the bushes, maybe a bear, I figured. It stomped and made a loud racket and I swear it felt like every time it took a step, the ground rumbled beneath our feet. That's when it commenced to howling and crying and working around the perimeter of our camp, staying to the bushes and trees that outlined the clearing we'd camped in. Then, like the snap of a finger, it was gone.

"What do you think it was?" Ed asked, bringing our stories to a halt. All eyes turned to me as I sat, nursing my last swig of whiskey, staring into the fire. There was something I remembered at some point in our conversation; something my daddy had told me about when I was a kid. I'd forgotten about it long ago and couldn't piece it together in my mind, as it was in fragments, but the more I thought about it, the more it seemed to pertain to our situation.

"Well?" Allen asked. "You look like you got something on your mind, Stevie."

I shook my head slowly. "Just an old story my daddy told me. It don't matter, anyway, it was probably just a bear lookin' for food."

"What was it he told you?" Ed asked.

I shook my head again.

"C'mon, tell us," Hughie prodded. I looked up into those big brown eyes of his and had a flash of him opening fire on a group of women huddled against the side of a hut, screaming for mercy. He had the same look in his eyes that day as he did now—haunted.

I cleared my throat and said, "I reckon I was ten years old when my daddy brought me out to these woods for the first time." I stared at the fire the entire time, never looking at any of my friends for fear of what they'd see in my eyes.

"He took me hunting and fishing up here and we had ourselves a ball. Just a kid and his dad, you know? There was so many deer up in these woods that it seemed you couldn't throw a stone five feet and not hit one. And the fish! Oh, I caught a big one on that trip. That's why I wanted you boys to come up here, because of the way it was back then. 'Course, things change. Don't seem there's much deer up here anymore, and I reckon we'll find out about the fish tomorrow when we hit the stream over down yonder."

"Okay, so what's the story?" Allen asked, cocking his head to the right. He had that look about him, like he did often when we were in combat. It was an inquisitive stare, like he was trying to figure something out that didn't make any sense. He had that same look at My Khe, when he was glaring at this old man he'd killed. The old man was pleading for his life when Allen gave him the look and then ran his bayonet right through the man's mouth, splitting it open so he looked like a fish, puckering the air. He ran that blade all the way through and pinned the old man against the hut, the bayonet slicing through the back of his neck like it was meant to. Allen studied the old man while he squirmed against the bayonet, his head cocked to the right, until the old man vomited and died.

I shook my head to clear the memory.

"When we were up here, we built us a big fire, like the one we got tonight. And my daddy, he tells me this story, and at the time, I thought he meant to scare me some so he could get a good laugh. But now, I don't know."

I took a deep breath. I was committed. "He told me a story, about a bunch of Indians that lived up in these hills. He said they were a tribe of fifty or so, pretty small, but they lived well with all the game up here. And when he spoke, I could imagine them, all out here dancing and hunting and I wanted to be one of them. It sounded like a great life to me. But he kept going with the story, and it got fairly twisted. I can't remember all of it, the where's and why's, nor many of the particulars, but it goes something like this.

"One of the Indians, their bravest warrior, got into a beef with another warrior, this one the son of the chief. They got pretty mad at each other, but what the fight was about my daddy didn't know. The chief sided with his son, of course, and so did the rest of the tribe. That brave warrior was banished, and as best as my daddy could tell, he was wronged because he was in the right about the dispute. So this warrior, he left and went into the woods, but the tribe wasn't through with him yet. They took his wife and kids out and skinned them alive, leaving them where the warrior could see them, as a warning against him returning. My daddy said the warrior's heart broke and he went deeper into the woods and made a deal with some evil spirit so he could get revenge for being wronged. That evil spirit entered his body and did some crazy things. I can't rightly remember what my daddy said these things were, and he maybe didn't even tell me, but I recall talk about the brave sneaking into his old camp and killing the son of the chief and his wife and eating her, raw, in his tent. The tribe gathered together and discussed the matter and decided the only thing they could do was to try and kill him. But before they put their plan into action, he came back and killed a couple more people. He ran off in the night and howled at the moon, more beast than man. The warrior scared them pretty bad, my daddy told me, such that they eventually formed a hunting party to find and kill him. That hunting party never came back. The tribe got another party together and they didn't come back, either. So the elders, they decided things were so bad that the whole tribe should up and move, despite the bounty of food surrounding them. They packed up and marched out, declaring that the woods were cursed. On their way out, they ran into the remains of the two parties they'd sent to hunt the wild warrior. They say there wasn't much left of them but bones and a few scattered, rotting fingers and toes. The bones looked gnawed upon, and not by animal teeth, either. They didn't know it, but they'd accidentally stumbled on the camp of the wild warrior, and when they did, he just happened to be coming back from a hunt. Those men, women and children, they all looked up on the ridge that stood over the area and they gazed upon pure evil. The warrior looked down on them with eyes that belonged to the Devil himself. They say he was ten times the size he was when they banished him, and that he wore the skins of those he'd killed. He bore their faces, peeled from their skulls, around his neck like a necklace, so it looked like his head sat upon a half dozen other heads. The warrior jumped from the ridge and landed in the midst of them, and he killed them all, saving the chief for last. He ate their bodies and wore their faces, and people said his spirit still haunts these woods, that he was cursed by the evil spirit to forever roam these lands, seeking justice for people done wrong."

I finished my story and didn't dare look at any of my friends.

"Bigfoot!" Ronnie laughed and spat into the fire. "You're saying we're being watched by a Bigfoot!"

"What?" I said. "I'm not saying nothing of the kind."

"He's saying that what was in those bushes was the ghost of some long dead, crazy Indian," Ed said. His face was screwed up in anger. It made me remember back to that terrible day, when he used the butt of his rifle to crack open the head of this teenage girl who'd been running for her life. She'd fallen to the ground, twitching, and Ed climbed on top of her. He ripped her shirt off as the blood bubbled from her forehead and laughed as her breasts flopped around in the sunlight.

I pushed the rest of it out of my head.

Ed looked at me. "Am I right?"

"I ain't saying nothing. I'm just relating a story I heard, is all."

"Bigfoot," Ronnie shook his head. "I've heard it all now."

"No!" I said. "That's not the point."

"The point is, you're working all of us up, here," Ed said. "That's not good."

"You all asked," I said then decided to keep my mouth shut.

The fire crackled and in the distance, we heard an owl hoot. It was eerie.

"I need more whiskey," Ronnie said.

Ed and Allen laughed. "Not a bad idea," Allen said. He left the fire to get his pack lying next to his tent.

Suddenly, the dogs started howling and Allen screamed. I turned around just in time to see a big black shape emerge from the woods. It picked Allen up by his neck and jerked him back into the bushes to disappear.

Ronnie jumped up first, his rifle blazing, pumping shots in the direction the shape took Allen. He stopped firing and ran after them, his boots digging in and kicking up clumps of dirt.

"Ronnie!" Ed yelled after him, but it was too late. Ronnie disappeared through the same bushes and was gone.

All was silent but the yelping of the dogs. I looked at them and saw three of them were dead. They got caught up in their leashes and broke their necks in their frightened panic. The other three were whining and stumbling around like they'd been struck blind.

"What the fuck just happened?" Ed yelled.

Me and Hughie were standing up, our rifles at the ready, staring off into the woods where the black shape, Allen, and Ronnie had gone. Nothing moved out there. A slight breeze stirred some of the leaves in the trees, causing them to rustle above us. The silence was thick and oppressive. I felt like a big wet, steaming hot blanket had been folded over us.

Just in front of us, the bushes shook.

I aimed my rifle as the dogs fell silent.

Ronnie stumbled from the bushes, his face completely white. He looked just like a ghost, or like someone who'd never been in the sunlight in his life.

"Dammit, Ronnie!" Ed yelled. "I nearly shot your fool head off."

Ronnie looked at us, fell to his knees, and vomited. The sick scent of hot dogs, whiskey, and bile, filled our noses. Ronnie vomited again and again, and one more time until his stomach was empty and he was dry heaving. I'd never seen him like that. The toughest of us, reduced to a shivering mess.

Hughie ran over to him and tucked an arm under him, then carried him over to the fire and sat him down. Ronnie shook and shivered, his body racked by spasms.

"It's okay," Hughie said.

"No it ain't," Ronnie gasped. "I saw it. I saw it, plain as day."

Hughie turned to me. "He needs a blanket."

I took a step towards my tent to fetch one when the wind whistled through the trees again, freezing me in place. The remaining three dogs all yelped and their chains broke as the big dark shape scooped them up and ran into the woods again, dragging the squirming dogs behind it.

I looked at Ed and Hughie and they stared back at me. It had all happened so fast that we didn't even have time to react. I trotted back to the others and we moved as one, without thinking. We formed a circle around Ronnie, putting our backs to each other, so that the entire clearing was covered by our rifles. We crouched down, waited and listened.

"It won't do any good," Ronnie said, his teeth rattling like he'd just been dropped into the middle of Alaska naked. "I saw what it did to Allen."

"Quiet," Ed hissed.

"I saw its face," Ronnie said, shivering. "It missed me but it won't miss a second time."

The wind whistled and we all tensed. Was this the call to arms? The signal that it was about to attack again? Nothing happened. We kept our eyes trained, each covering the area we were assigned, keeping one another safe.

"It would help if you got your gun," Ed said to Ronnie, who laughed in his face.

"You're all stupid. We're dead."

"Shut up, Ronnie!" I yelled.

Ronnie laughed again but didn't say anything after that.

Time passed but we never relaxed. Every five minutes, we shifted our positions as one, like we'd been taught so long ago, to keep our muscles and perspectives fresh. Ronnie kept shaking, he never stopped. He also never got up to help us in any way.

Finally, after a time, Ed spoke. "What did you see, Ronnie?"

Ronnie giggled but didn't reply. I'd never seen him like this before. I'd seen him stand strong, knee-deep in dead 'Charlies', gun blazing, never flinching. I'd seen him take an ass-whuppin' in a staged fight between companies and he never buckled once. He kept going until they had to call the fight for fear he'd not stop until he was dead. But never like this.

"Come on," Hughie said. "Tell us."

"No," Ronnie said, his teeth chattering. "No."

"Leave him be," I said. "He doesn't want to help, that's his decision."

"It ain't like that," Ronnie said, suddenly sobered by my accusation. "It's just, we don't stand a chance. That thing out there, I believe it may be the Devil himself."

One of the dogs howled and then something snapped. Rain pattered the area, dripping down and soaking us. I wiped my forehead, and when I pulled my hand away. It was smeared red.

Blood was pouring from the skies.

We heard the howl of the dogs again. Something else snapped and that dog's cry was choked off. Blood sprayed over the bushes and showered us. The last dog cried out and we heard another snap and its blood squirted over the clearing.

We fired our rifles, blasting away, until the blood stopped spraying. We kept firing, reloading, and firing again, for a full minute afterwards. That may have been the Devil out there, but we were damned well and determined to send it straight back to the Hell it came from, no matter how many bullets it took.

I held my hand up and we stopped shooting. We listened. Silence kissed our ringing ears. There was no cry of a cricket or any hoot of an owl. It was as if time itself had stopped. Nothing moved and nothing made a sound.

"Did we get it?" Hughie whispered.

Nobody said a word, but we all had our unspoken doubts.

"Fellas, I'm nearly out of ammo," Ed said. Each of us checked our guns to find that, we too, were low.

"I've got more bullets, but they're in my tent," Hughie added.

"Mine, too," Ed said.

"What if it's still out there?" Hughie asked. I thought on that for a moment and came up with a plan.

"Ed, you go first. Me and Hughie will cover you," I told them. I turned to Ronnie. He was still shivering. "Grab a gun for Ronnie, too, in case he decides to join us."

"What about us?" Hughie asked.

"When he gets back, then you go next and me and Ed will cover you. And then I go."

It seemed an agreeable plan to them. Ed fell to his belly and crawled, slowly, towards his tent. I kept my gun trained just over Ed's head and toward the darkness beyond him. Hughie crouched over and went back to back with me, keeping his rifle pointed in the opposite direction. Ronnie sat and shivered, staring at the fire.

Ed made half the distance to his tent, maybe five yards, when we heard a noise out in the woods. A twig snapped and a bush shook. Ed screamed and scrambled back to us, his rifle raised. A high whine whistled through the bushes on the other side of Ed's tent and we all tensed, our knuckles white on our weapons.

"Hold your fire," I ordered.

One of the dogs that had been taken crawled from the bushes. Half its body was gone, torn apart at the base of its ribs. The dog whimpered and mewled, dragging itself along, leaving a trail of blood and bits of intestines behind as it inched towards us. I looked into its eyes and I could see the dog had gone mad; there wasn't an inch of normal dog left in its brain. The poor thing moved on pure instinct, edging towards the fire and its masters, seeking comfort from the heat and companionship. It looked up at me, its tongue lolling from its parted, sneering mouth, and its backbone sticking out of its rear, making it look like some kind of obscene popsicle.

And I thought of what I did, long ago, what I'd tried but failed to push from my memories. I thought of that kid, clinging to my leg, screaming and crying as we swept through My Khe. I kicked the boy free and he tumbled across the dry ground and scampered back, clamping onto my leg again. I saw my leg sweep out and shake him free and this time, when he hit with a thump against the side of a hut, I ran over and started kicking him. I kicked that boy in the face until his tongue flew out, joining his teeth on the ground. I kicked him until he didn't move anymore, except for a few twitches. And I remembered my friends, my company, pulling close around me, patting my back, cheering me on.

Right then and there, I knew what the thing in the woods was after us for.

I began to shake like Ronnie was and it was all I could do to get the images of that boy out of my mind. I decide to use one of my last bullets on the poor dog. As my shot echoed between the trees, I looked over at Ed and said, "Get going."

"Not me. Not this time. Hughie should go," Ed said. His eyes were wild with fear.

I turned and nodded to Hughie.

Hughie scratched his chin. "Who wants to live forever?" He got down on his stomach and slithered toward his tent.

Out in the woods, nothing stirred. It was uncanny. I'd been out in the woods most of my life and I'd never heard it be this quiet before. It was so silent it made my stomach sick.

Hughie made it to his tent and scrambled inside. We heard him rooting around, reloading. He stuck his head out and smiled at us.

"I'll get the others, too," he volunteered. It was a good idea.

Hughie crawled over to my tent. He went in and came out a few seconds later, a box of shells in his hand. He tossed them over to me. After that, he crawled over to Ed's tent.

I kept watch with Ed. Nothing moved out there, not even the wind. Hughie stuck his head out of Ed's tent, one hand holding a box of ammo, the other his gun. He grinned wide and hard. "Wasn't a big deal," he said.

From out of the dark, the creature crashed from the bushes, surging forward and landing on top of Hughie in the blink of an eye. It howled and cried and it was big...so big. My mind couldn't take in exactly what it looked like or what it was. All I could see was that the thing was huge, like the side of a house, and its eyes gleamed with black insanity in the light of the campfire. The reflection of the flames shimmered across it, revealing the body of a man three times the normal size, naked except for a cloth around its mid-section and burnt red skin. It had a fat, squat head that sat on powerful shoulders and its lips were curled in disgust and delight all at once. But it was the eyes of the creature that was so horrible to look upon. They were empty and full at the same time, cold and hot.

Ed and I screamed and fired a round off each before it grabbed Hughie by his head and yanked him from the tent, holding him up in the air so that he was between us and the creature. Hughie kicked it right in the face and it dropped him. He crashed to the ground, cracking his ankle and screaming in pain. Neither Ed nor me moved, pinned by our fear and uncertainty.

Hughie turned to us, his face drawn and panicked.

"Run! I'll hold him off!" Hughie cried.

Ed and I stood with rifles in hand. Ronnie joined us, finally snapped out of his spell, and stared at the scene playing out in front of us.

The creature reached out and grabbed Hughie again. It turned him around so Hughie was facing it. Then something happened, something I didn't see or understand. Hughie started screaming like a wild man as the creature wrapped its obscene hands around his torso and squeezed.

"Run!" Hughie wheezed.

We sprinted off to our left, out of the clearing and down the tiny path leading to the river a mile away. I was the last of us and I turned to see what was happening as the creature grabbed Hughie by his head and popped it off like a cork from a bottle of cheap champagne. Blood fizzed and flowed over his shoulders, spraying into the air. The creature dropped Hughie's head to the ground, lifted his body, and tilted it so that the stump of Hughie's neck poured the blood into its mouth.

It stopped and looked at me, its glare a diseased fire of madness. And then it smiled. In its eyes, I saw the massacre at My Khe and I saw the accusations of childless mothers and wifeless fathers. I saw and felt the weight of all the wrong we did on that day, and I knew it had come for us now, borne on the back of a demon from Hell.

I ran as fast as I could, hauling ass after the others, the image of that thing burned into my mind for all eternity. I don't remember how long I ran but I caught up with Ronnie and Ed. We'd run through a set of trees and were out in a clearing, the moon shining down on us, bright and high in the night, nearly full. It was peculiar the way that the pale light fell upon us and the entire area, making the whole thing seem like a weird dream.

To our right, we heard the creature howl and tear through the brush.

We turned and ran for the edge of the trees across from us. Ed reached the forest first, gun in hand and legs pumping. A black shape rose in front of him and I wanted to scream a warning but it was too late. The creature had cut us off and stood before Ed, all hot and full of wrath. Ed froze, stared at it, and screamed. It smashed him to the ground with one swipe of its large hands.

Ronnie dropped to his stomach and opened fire. The bullets peppered what was left of Ed and ricocheted off the creature. It looked up at Ronnie and ran at him, full tilt. As it ran, it came out into the full moonlight, and I could see the abomination that it truly was. Around its throat it wore a necklace made up of the faces of Allen, Hughie, and a few of the dead hounds.

It roared loudly and kicked Ronnie, punting my friend into the air like he was a toy. He landed a good ten feet away, and before he could move, the creature was on him, stomping and smashing him into the ground. His body broke into parts, legs and arms flying through the air, followed by blood, so much blood. I heard his bones crack and the gasses in his stomach hiss as the creature wildly ripped his insides out. Intestines flew and slapped into the surrounding trees, hanging like Christmas ornaments. Ronnie looked over at me, his face white and full of terror, as the creature tore his head off his neck. It held the head up and studied it a moment, then drew a line around Ronnie's face with a claw, tearing it open. The creature peeled the face off and fastened it onto his necklace next to Allen's.

There was nothing I could do for Ronnie. My best bet was to run for my life, to make it to the tree line and keep going. So I ran, my breath rasping in my chest, my heart pounding and fit to burst.

I ran right past Ed, who had in the meantime managed to stand up. He looked like he'd been hit by a train. His right arm was bent backwards, broken, and the left side of his face was one massive bruise, brown like the inside of a rotten apple. Blood sprung from a dozen or so holes where he'd been shot and I didn't know how he was still alive, much less standing. He blinked when he saw me and grunted. I kept running.

I heard the creature howl and run after me, the ground shaking with each step, the air, hot and humid, rushing at me from behind, as if when the creature moved, it pushed the air in front of it. I ducked into the trees and was engulfed in the darkness of the forest. Behind me, I heard the creature crashing about.

And then I heard Ed scream.

I didn't stop; I didn't dare. Ed was dead, there was no way around that; all my friends were dead. All the people I'd sweated blood and tears with, my brothers that I swore I'd never leave behind. But that night I did leave them. I ran like a coward. It was too late for them and it was probably too late for me, but I had to try.

The snapping and cracking of Ed's bones beat a counter rhythm with the snapping and cracking of the twigs under my feet as I ran on. Pretty soon, Ed's screams stopped and so did the echoes of his body being splintered like an ornery walnut. I tried to put all thoughts out of my mind and just concentrate on running, keeping my breath even, and surviving the horrible night.

I ran and ran. I couldn't hear anything but my own ragged breathing and my blood thudding in my veins. I pressed on, ignoring the pain in my legs and the ache in my back. I ran towards where I thought the river was because that's all I could think of to do. Down the river we'd parked our trucks, and if I could make it there...

But something in me knew it was all in vain. Some small voice told me what was happening here didn't have a thing to do with an evil Indian spirit, at least not directly. I thought of those people we'd killed back in the war, so long ago it seemed like a wicked dream brought on by an immoral curse. I thought on what my daddy had said, about the spirit and how it avenged those who've been wronged, and I couldn't think of anyone more wronged in my life than those dead Vietnamese.

Still, I kept going. Maybe I was wrong, maybe I was crazy out of my mind and it was just some big bear attacking us. Maybe being back with my friends brought on all the bad memories, the ones I pushed away so I could live with myself, and the guilt was making things seem different than they were.

Up ahead, over the roar of my blood and the beating of my heart, I heard the river. It sounded as sweet as honey tastes on a peanut butter sandwich. I jumped towards the sound, giggling like a man who'd lost his mind. Maybe I had. Maybe I'd gone nuts, but who could blame me? Who could find fault after what I'd been through?

I hurtled through some bushes and exploded out onto the banks of the river. Standing in front of me, blocking my path, stood the creature. It towered over me, a good eight feet tall, its maroon skin and rippling muscles bathed in sweat and blood. Its eyes glowed in the moonlight that broke through the treetops and shone down on the entire area. Right behind it, the river glittered like a million diamonds. Around its throat, I saw the creature had added Ed's face to the necklace. But that wasn't all I saw. The faces writhed, squirming against the creature's chest as if they were in pain, like they were still alive. The faces turned and stared at me, even though they didn't have eyes, and their mouths opened wide and howled. Their cries burned my ears and stopped my heart in my chest.

They spoke in Vietnamese. I heard the same sounds in the forest that I'd heard that day in My Khe; every scream, every cry, every death rattle of every dead boy, girl, man and woman. Then one face in particular glared at me; it was the face of the boy I'd stomped to death. He stared at me, silent and accusing.

I dropped to my knees and wept.

The creature let out a howl and leapt, landing right in front of me. It looked down at me as the faces around its neck screeched their accusations, the lips popping open and shut with each cry. I looked up at the creature and saw no pity or mercy in its eyes, only betrayal and vengeance.

I nodded and leaned back, ready to die.

In a blur of motion, it ripped my throat out, its claws slicing through my skin like it was made of melted taffy. Its hand dug down, punching through my chest to reach my heart.

It tore my still beating heart out through the hole it had made in my throat, holding the pulsing muscle up high like an offering to the Gods.

The faces of the necklace howled and blood poured from their open mouths, their baying reaching up to appease the stars. I fell face forward, eager to be done with my life of guilt. My body shook but I didn't die. I was still there, my soul trapped and unable to leave. Would this nightmare never end?

The creature tore my head from my shoulders, and I felt the pain of every ripping tendon as my flesh was split and rent. That was when I realized death didn't bring comfort and peace but instead a clear, awful understanding. When the creature slashed my eyes from their sockets, I was still able to see, but now I could truly see the world for what it was, for the first time.

As it peeled my face from my skull, my consciousness went with it, my face joining the necklace. At last I was reunited with my friends, forever this time, damned to an eternity of insanity, of howling at future victims of this wild creature, roaming the forest forever, searching for prey.

I WON'T LET YOU DIE

MATT NORD

My son, Alan, and I were talking a while back about the subject of mortality.

Well, let me clarify. My son is only twelve years old, so our discussion of mortality was mainly about characters in movies and video games getting killed. We've gone through the assurances that they are only actors in the movies and nobody really gets hurt. We've had the talks about video game violence and how killing is wrong.

This conversation, however, was one of those heart to hearts that you so rarely see these days. In the time of television, people don't seem to want to take the time to communicate beyond asking where the TV remote is. This was something different, and, in all honesty, turned into something a little uncomfortable.

That may have been because I didn't have all of the answers for him. Not that that's completely unheard of in our talks. However, those are usually about silly things like discussing what exactly a platypus is or who built Stonehenge. Most of the time, I can simply go to the internet for easy answers.

Unfortunately, when you talk of life and death, especially with a child, the answers don't necessarily come so easily. Was I supposed to take the easy way out and tell him that all of the 'good' people go to Heaven and all of the 'bad' people go to Hell? Then we get into the realm of melding mortality with morality. Is that really the easy way out, or does that just open up an entirely different path of discussion?

I was saved from getting into this by his assertion that 'I won't let you die.' I have to say that I was a bit unnerved at the time. What should have been an endearing thing to hear coming from my child left a lasting impression on me. I didn't know why, but I would come to find out.

* * *

I'm not sure what's going on now. I should be dead. I *was* dead...but now I'm not. Now I'm... something else. Something...not right. I feel well enough most of the time, but I can feel my skin starting to go numb. I thought maybe I'd been placed in the morgue by mistake, but any illusion of that was dispelled when my fingers ran over the autopsy stitches on my chest.

While I felt like I should have gone insane at this point, all I felt was a sense of understanding. My mind wrapped around what was going on, and that's the part that actually scared me. I knew that somehow, by sheer force of will, my son had refused to let me stay dead. Now all I had to figure out was what kind of ramifications that would have on me, on him, and on our family.

Because while my fingers and toes are going numb, there is another feeling rising inside me. A feeling of great hunger.

* * *

I made my way home easily enough. I didn't know where else to go. I'm sure Alan was expecting me and I didn't want to disappoint him but I knew I had to remain hidden from the rest of the family. They wouldn't understand. Hell, I didn't even really understand, but I was in the middle of it. I had to except what was happening to me as reality, even though the rational part of my brain told me I was just in the middle of a very vivid, very long nightmare.

The mile and a half walk home distracted me from the hunger growing in my...stomach, I suppose. It wasn't like any hunger I'd felt in my life. Of course, living in the United States, I'd never felt the hunger that goes beyond starvation, that those who go absolutely without must feel. It was the feeling of your body eating itself from the inside out.

The walk distracted me...but not for long. It was late, dark due to the fact that the moon was behind a cloud. I knew it should have been cold, but I didn't feel this. It may as well have been ninety degrees out, not the February cold that it most likely was. I'd grabbed a long coat from a coat rack at the morgue on the way out the back door, not to keep away the chill, but to cover my naked body. I didn't want to draw attention to myself.

I was deep in thought about the situation that I found myself in when I saw the cat. It was sitting near the bumper of a parked car, visible because of the streetlight above it. At first I just glanced at it, but quickly did a double-take. Something inside of me stirred, something primal and savage. Without thinking, I lunged at the animal. Food was the only thought in my mind, all others were scattered to the fringes of my brain. The reptilian brain had taken over. It was basic survival. Eat to survive.

The cat darted off down the street. I chased it for a short distance before it ran into a line of bushes in the front yard of one of my neighbors. After losing sight of it, I came back to my senses. Apparently, with the absence of seeing prey before me, I was in control. My God, what would happen when I saw my son?

Wait, my neighbors... I hadn't realized that I'd chased the feline into my neighborhood. I was almost home, but was that a good thing. After what had just happened, I wasn't sure. Thoughts swirled in my head. Maybe I should actively search out food. This was crazy, though. I'd seen horror movies, but this was real life. Was I seriously some kind of undead ghoul looking for warm flesh to feed upon?

I heard barking coming from behind a house across the street. Better a dog than a human being, I thought. Thank God I hadn't come across a late night jogger or someone out for a walk.

I went around the side of the house, and the barking increased in volume and pitch. Disgusted with the prospect, but understanding what had to be done, I hurried to the backyard. I needed to be quick, before somebody woke up to see what was disturbing the dog. Unfortunately for the dog, unlike the cat, it was chained up.

*　*　*

I was completely covered in blood. I don't really remember exactly how it happened, I stared down at what was left of the animal. Only a small pile of fur, blood and bones remained. My mind had gone into some form of unconsciousness, because I had no memory of even what kind of dog it had been, how large it was, or if it had fought back. It obviously had, because I had scratches running along my arms. The canine blood mixed with the embalming fluid that slowly oozed from the wounds.

What had I become? How could I go back to my son, the one who had wished or prayed me back to life, like this? Something compelled me, though. Something that I felt I couldn't control, just as I couldn't control the need to feed. Alan's desire for my life was also drawing me towards him, but I didn't want him to see me like this.

I didn't want him to have to see me at all, but I didn't know how long I could resist the urge that was pushing on my very being. I looked down again at the gore dripping down my scarred chest. I probably would have started crying if my tear ducts still functioned. I needed to clean up, at the very least.

Luckily, I finished the dog off quickly enough that no one had woken up. I was able to use the garden hose on the side of the house to rinse off the blood and bits of skin stuck to me. The coat I wore was now a mess and no amount of water was going to rinse the blood stains completely out of the fabric. I needed to find some fresh clothes, but that might prove a little difficult. If I was in a film, I would find a line of clothes that I could pilfer, but who dried their laundry on a line nowadays?

I didn't have many options. I could break into a house to steal something to wear, but what happened if I came across someone and lost control again? I couldn't live with myself...I laughed aloud at the thought. At this point, I couldn't live no matter what I did. Still, I didn't want to be the one to cause the loss of the loved one of somebody else. By no fault of my own, I would be the reason for the sorrow of another family.

It wasn't my fault that I died. I was doing all the right things. I had my seat belt on. I was going the speed limit. I stopped at the stoplight. I went when it was my turn, and then I was T-boned by a kid on a cell phone who wasn't paying attention. The thing about it was that I didn't die from the actual crash. Can you believe I had a heart attack from the whole thing? Talk about a bad turnout. Virtually no injuries, scrapes or bruises, but the old ticker couldn't handle the trauma.

And now here I am, a reanimated corpse, eating dogs, looking for clothes, afraid that I'm going to kill the first person I run in to.

I keep waiting to wake up from a bad dream, but the longer I'm like this, the more I realize that I have no hope. I'm desperate to avoid my son and as much as I want to see him again, to hug him and let him know that his father is there for him, I'm terrified that I would see him as nothing more than food.

* * *

I managed to find some clothes out of a suitcase on a neighbor's rooftop carrier. Apparently they were preparing for a vacation trip and had packed some of the items early. Lucky for me, but unlucky for my neighbor. He'd be short a pair of pants, a shirt and some flip flops.

I couldn't avoid it anymore. The urge to see my son was pulling me towards my house. It was still dark out. Dawn was a couple hours away, and the house was only a little further down the block. I could see my home from where I stood, but Alan's room was on the opposite side, facing the backyard. I walked down the sidewalk with great apprehension. I only hoped that the fact that I was here because of him would also keep me from hurting him.

Once I reached the house, I didn't really know what to do. Should I throw pebbles at his window like some idiotic boyfriend trying to get his girl's attention? Should I just use the key under the planter near the back door and sneak in? What if my wife Erin woke up? What about the rest of her family now staying with her and Alan? I had seen several cars parked out front, her family staying with them to comfort them in their time of need for a few days.

I'm sure Erin's mother was enjoying this. We never got along, and she even told me that I had stolen her daughter away from her. She was very controlling, and Erin had only gotten the courage to stand up to her after several years of marriage and much encouragement from me. Maybe I *should* go into the house and find her... but it was bad enough that Erin had already lost a husband. She didn't need to lose another loved one, and I knew that now she was strong enough for both herself and for Alan.

As I stood in front of my house, wondering what to do next, the answer appeared from around the side of it.

"Hi, Dad," Alan said. "I figured you'd come around back for the spare key."

I stood still, staring at him. I was terrified that if I moved I might suddenly lose control and attack him. After several seconds of silence, I realized that the hunger I felt earlier, and that had slowly been returning since I'd slaughtered the dog, was gone.

"Alan," I said, "I'm really glad to see you."

He ran towards me and I embraced him in a hug for what seemed like several minutes.

"I told you, Dad," he said. "I told you I wouldn't let you die."

"I know you did, Alan," I said. "And I'm so happy I could see you again."

I released the hug, but he wouldn't let go.

"Alan, I need you to..."

He gripped me tighter and I gently pushed him away and looked down into his brown eyes. "I need you to listen to me. Are you listening?"

He nodded and I could see the tears beginning to well up in his eyes.

"I'm not right. I don't know what's happened to me, but when I came back..."

I didn't really know how to tell my son that I was afraid that I'd kill and eat anybody that crossed my path.

"I'm sick, Alan," I said, deciding on that. "I feel very sick, and I'm afraid that if I'm around people for too long I might hurt them. I need you to let me go."

Alan shook his head vigorously. "No!" he yelled. "You're back, and I want you to stay. Mom is really sad, and Grandma needs to go. She's trying to tell us what to do. Please, Dad, just come inside and I'm sure things will be all better."

"Shhh, you need to be quiet, please," I said. I didn't want anybody, most of all Erin, to come out and see us. "I don't think that's a good idea. You don't want me to hurt Mom, do you?"

"Why would you hurt Mom?" He looked at me like I was crazy.

"Well, I wouldn't on purpose," I assured him. "But I don't know if I can control it. Like I said, there's something wrong, and I'm sorry, but..." I trailed off.

I looked at him again. *How do I do this?* I thought.

"Look, Alan... there are certain things that we shouldn't mess with," I said. "The doctors did the best they could to save me, but... it was just my time. I really shouldn't be here, as much as I'm glad I am."

"But it's not fair," he said through tears, though straining to keep his voice down, doing as he was told. *Good boy.* "Why did that guy have to run a red light?"

"I don't know, Alan, but that's something that happened, and it was out of our control."

"But I can control this, Dad!" he pleaded. "You can see that! I mean, here you are."

"I know, Alan, and I'm sorry but I can't stay like this."

He looked down and away, not into my eyes. I waited. When he finally looked up, I could see he'd come to his conclusion.

"I love you, Dad," he said. "I'm really glad I got to see you one more time."

He hugged me and I kissed him on the forehead. He let me go, and started to walk back towards the house and I started to feel weird, lightheaded.

"I love you, too, Al..."

DIG UP HER BONES

KEITH LUETHKE

Summer has lost her luster and the ground is hungry for the dead. Under a late October sky, the corn by Oakrun Cemetery turned into a dried bed. The silent rows are home to more things than snakes and rats. Here, under the rich black soil, lies the body of Sawtooth Jack. He's the lurker in the dark, the shadow creeping up behind your back. He's the monster with red-rimmed eyes and a dozen skulls on his rack. Every Halloween, he rises from the corn, eating unfortunate people from dusk till dawn. He sneaks through the black gates, making the cemetery his home, and that's why in Harvest Town on Halloween night you're never to walk alone.

* * *

The serrated knife plunged into the orange pumpkin and moved in and out until it formed a wicked grin. Chloe Simmons shoved her tiny hand into the raw wound and scooped out yellow innards with her fingernails. She put the remains in a metal pail which sat beside her on the front porch.

"I don't believe in Sawtooth Jack, nobody does," she said.

Dale crossed his arms and shook his head. "I saw him last Halloween."

"Liar, liar, pants on fire," Chloe said.

"I did see him. I wouldn't lie to you."

"Right, like I haven't heard that one before. Just because I'm new in town by almost a year now doesn't mean I'm stupid." She shoved the knife blade above the jagged mouth and cored out two triangle eyes.

Dale leaned in closer, and when he spoke, he used the voice reserved for hidden truths only children knew.

"We never go out after dark on Halloween here anymore, not since he came. I was like you. I didn't believe in Sawtooth Jack either. But last year, Tom and I saw him in Oakrun Cemetery. He was carrying a severed head."

Chloe laughed.

"It's not funny. Sawtooth Jack is real. Look, I know the supernatural isn't something that's supposed to be real, but it does happen."

"I'll keep that in mind tonight," she said.

Dale sat down on the porch next to her. He smelled like dead leaves and football fields.

"Then you're really going through with it?"

She put the knife down. "I miss her, Dale. I can't remember what she looks like anymore. My dad doesn't even talk about her, not since Brittney started coming around. I need to see my mom one last time. I want to make sure she's okay."

"But she's dead, Chloe."

"I know, but that doesn't mean I love her any less. Will you still help me?"

Dale looked at the nearby homes, at the manicured lawns mowed twice a week, the trimmed branches of every tree, the way the trash bins were put out on the driveways, the deceptive smiles, the friendly waves from strangers, and the careful way the neighbors locked themselves in at night. He sucked all this down in a matter of seconds, realizing he never wanted that type of life. A life devoid of risk wasn't a life worth living.

"I'm with you," he said.

"Swear it."

"I swear I'll help you until this is done," he insisted.

"Double spit, pinky, cross your heart hope to die, swear it."

Dale spit into his hand and Chloe did the same. They shook hands, mixing saliva between their palms, then, interlocked their pinky fingers.

He crossed his heart and recited the age old mantra. "Cross my heart, hope to die, and stick a needle in my eye."

They separated hands. The promise sealed forever.

"Good, now all we need is a couple of shovels."

"Mr. Peterson has a bunch of tools in his shed we can take. He paid me to dig a hole for his mailbox last summer."

"Is it locked?" she asked.

"Yeah, but he keeps a spare key hidden above the door. I'll get some equipment tonight."

As Dale finished his sentence, a sleek black Mercedes pulled into the driveway.

"Oh no," Chloe muttered. "Brittney's here."

"Wasn't that your mom's car?"

A slender hand waved at them from the driver's seat, red nails flashing in the sunlight.

"You should go now," Chloe said.

Dale nodded and walked on the lawn to avoid having to speak with Brittney.

"Catch you later," he called over his shoulder.

Brittney strutted from the Mercedes, carrying bags from JC Penney and Wal-Mart.

"Little boy," she called to Dale in her sing song voice. "Would you be a dear and help me with my things?"

"Sorry, I can't. I have to go home and feed the dog." He quickened his pace and vanished around a row of shrubs.

"Chloe, come over here and give me a hand, please."

Chloe shuffled off the porch and went to grab a bag from her.

"Don't take that one, honey. Those are my Prada shoes. I'll carry them." She handed her a bag from Wal-Mart. "This is your Halloween costume. I picked it out for you."

Chloe peered inside the plastic bag. Pink sleeves and white frills looked back at her. "This is a princess outfit. I don't want to be a princess."

"Nonsense, all girls want to be a princess. You look dazzling and everyone wants to hold doors open for you and let you cut in line because you're the most beautiful thing in the world."

"I can open my own doors. And why would I want everyone staring at me? I'd feel like the lobster behind the glass at the grocery store. Why would you want that for me?"

"Oh, Chloe, you'll understand when you're older. Your prince charming will come around and he'll sweep you off your feet. Then you won't have to worry because your true love will buy everything you need and make you a queen."

"You mean how my dad gives you money to buy all these clothes that you only wear once? You're not his queen. You're nothing but a wicked witch and I hate you."

Brittney looked as though she'd been slapped. Her face turned bright red like her fingernails and she dropped all the bags on the driveway except the Prada one.

"You're father is going to hear about this," she huffed, and ran inside the house, clicking her high heels on the walkway.

Chloe sat down on the porch. She picked up the knife and made eyebrows for her Jack-O-Lantern. Inside, Brittney was shouting at her father about how ungrateful Chloe was.

Chloe cut her finger by mistake and sucked on it until it stopped bleeding. She looked up when the front door creaked open.

"Honey, we need to talk," her father said, sitting beside her.

"I don't like her," Chloe said before he could start in on her. "I miss Mom."

"I know you do, sweety, but can't you give Brittney a chance?"

"She bought me a princess costume without asking. I want to be a vampire. Mom made me that outfit last year. I wanted to wear it one more time before it doesn't fit."

He put his arm around her shoulders. "You can be a vampire if you want to, but go a little easier on Brittney, okay? She's trying really hard to fit in here."

Her father left the porch and picked up the discarded bags lying in the driveway.

"Simon," Brittney called from the house. "I'm starting dinner. Can you help?"

"Yes, dear, I'm coming."

"Dad, can I ask you something?"

Her father huffed up to the house, the bags weighing him down. "Yes, honey?"

"Nothing," Chloe replied, hesitating.

"Dinner will be ready soon. Make sure to wash all that junk off your hands," he said.

"Did Mom go to Heaven?" she asked

"Yes, sweety," he replied. "She's with the angels up above."

He went back inside and left the door open for her. Chloe placed her pumpkin near the stairs, then sat on the porch, gazing at the sky until dinner was ready.

* * *

Chloe sat down next to her father and across from Brittney at the dinner table. She stared at the hamburger on her plate.

"I made your favorite," Brittney said. "The hot pepper jack cheese is in the middle of the burger just how you like it."

Chloe lifted the bun and poked her burger with her fork, and sure enough, the meat had cheese in the center. "You didn't have to make them," she said.

"But it's your favorite, and besides, I can't cook much of anything else," Brittney smiled.

Chloe put ketchup and pickles on her burger and used two hands to lift it to her mouth. "This is delicious, thanks Brittney." She continued to devour the hamburger.

Her father smiled. He fixed his burger the same way his daughter did and began to eat.

Brittney poured each of them a glass of milk and addressed Chloe. "What time are you going out tonight?"

"In an hour or two, Dale and I are meeting to go Trick or Treating."

"I want you home before dark," her father said. "The town curfew is in effect."

"Can't I stay out a little after dark?" Chloe whined. "What kind of town doesn't let anyone out past dusk on Halloween?"

"This town," Brittney said. "I know you weren't here last Halloween but I'm sure that you've heard of Sawtooth Jack?"

Her father sighed. "Don't fill her head with that nonsense, Brittney. God, the guys down at the construction site won't stop talking about him."

Chloe leaned forward, "Who is he?"

"He's some crazy maniac who comes out every Halloween to scare people," her father said. "It's just a bunch of small town garbage."

"I grew up here," Brittney said. "And it's not garbage. He's haunted this town for twenty years now. They say he was a pumpkin headed scarecrow in the corn field by Oakrun Cemetery. The farmer who put him there used to give his corn away to people who couldn't afford food, but late at night he discovered a few of the local kids were taking the crop without his permission. He was so angry that he went to a witch in the woods and she taught him a spell to bring the scarecrow to life and protect the corn. As the days went by, a few of the local children went missing. When the police searched for them, the trail always led to the corn field. The farmer discovered his scarecrow was bleeding and when he opened up its flannel shirt, he found the gnawed remains of the children instead of straw. He went to the witch but she couldn't break the powerful spell. She could only give him a curse to bond the scarecrow to walk and feed one day out of the year, and that day was Halloween." Brittney gave a villainous laugh.

"What happened to the farmer after he cursed the scarecrow?" Chloe pressed.

"He wasn't happy about being tricked by the witch so he burned her house down and carried her back to the corn field. Only she escaped and ran into the cemetery. The farmer chased after her and almost caught her but she turned herself into a tree."

"Scylla..." Chloe said.

"That's right," Brittney smiled. "The farmer was so frustrated after the event that he approached the scarecrow with a saw and tried to take off its head. But he wasn't fast enough and forgot that it was still Halloween. And that's how the scarecrow got his saw."

"Did Sawtooth Jack eat him?"

Brittney leapt forward and grabbed Chloe's shoulders. "He gobbled him up!"

Chloe screamed.

Brittney laughed.

"Okay, that's enough," her father said. "Finish your dinner and get ready, Chloe. I want you home before dark."

"I thought you said that story wasn't true, Dad?"

"It's not, but you're still coming home early, and that's final," he said.

Chloe finished her hamburger in silence as Brittney talked about her shopping spree. Once dinner was over, she raced upstairs and got dressed in her vampire outfit.

Kissing the picture of her mother on her dresser for good luck, she said, "I'll see you soon, Mom."

* * *

Late afternoon, two hours before sunset, hundreds of children poured onto the streets of Harvest Town. An endless, candy-starved horde of goblins, zombies, pirates, mummies, ghouls, ghosts, Power Rangers, Ninja Turtles, kings, queens, vampires, and Grim Reapers, made their way down the cracked sidewalks and knocked on every door, asking for treats. They stuffed bags with Milky Ways, Reeses Pieces, Jelly Beans, Hershey bars, and lollipops, and ran back home before nightfall, secure behind locked doors and sensibly shut drapes. All the children were accounted for except two, and as night darkened the skies, the police were summoned to find them.

A lone vampire hid behind a row of pine trees, clacking her plastic fangs together. She wrapped her long satin cape around her body to fend off the bitter October wind.

From the woods came heavy footfalls and snapping branches. Chloe stayed hidden in the darkness. Content to press against the pine trees and run through them if need be. A large bulbous head appeared from the woods; it swayed back and forth, scanning the perimeter.

Chloe gasped and ducked under the pines.

"Hey wait, it's me," Dale said.

She was halfway through the underbrush when he spoke and she turned around in time to see the large round head was an astronaut's helmet.

"Why didn't you say something sooner?" she asked.

Dale removed his helmet. His hair was plastered to his face and beads of sweat rolled off his chin. "I didn't think you were here yet. Great costume by the way. I see you even have vampire teeth, too, awesome."

"Every girl should have a pair of fangs. So, you're an astronaut. Where'd you get the suit?"

"I won it at space camp. I lasted the longest in the gravity chair."

"Do you plan on being an astronaut when you grow up?"

"I hope so. My dad says it's really hard to get into the program, though. Can you imagine blasting off into space and leaving Earth and everyone on it far behind? Now that's an adventure."

Chloe looked up into the night sky and gazed at all the twinkling stars. She shivered. "I could never leave everyone like that." She sniffed and wiped her eyes. "Did you bring the shovels?"

"I tried to get them, but Mr. Peterson was outside."

"Great, now what do we do?"

Dale dug into his flight jacket and produced two crumpled rolls of toilet paper.

"I went back home and got these. We're going to distract him and get those tools."

Chloe wrapped her arms around his neck. "You're a life saver," she beamed.

Dale tried to put his hands on her waist but withdrew them. He settled on giving her a pat on the back. "We should go now, it's a long walk through the woods," he said.

Chloe broke off their embrace. "We're not going into the woods. We'll take the streets." She ducked under the fir trees and disappeared.

"What if the neighbors see us and call the cops?" Dale asked.

"There are plenty of places to hide. We'll be fine."

Dale followed after her, crawling through the sharp needles, and out the other side. "What about Sawtooth Jack?"

"What about him?"

"He's real, Chloe. He'll come after us."

"Let him come. I'm not afraid."

She wandered through a well kept lawn and onto the sidewalk. Dale struggled to catch up. "Why are we doing this tonight? Why can't we dig her up tomorrow or next week?"

"Because, tonight is Halloween, and if she's going to return, it would be tonight."

Dale grabbed her arm and forced her to stop. "She's not coming back, Chloe. I'm sorry. The dead stay dead."

Chloe yanked her arm away. "We'll see about that. Now, which way do we go?"

"Make a left turn on…" Dale tugged her cape and headed for the nearest outcropping of trees.

"What is it?"

"It's the cops," he replied.

They ran behind a withered oak tree near a brown house as red and blue lights stabbed the outlining houses and cut through the darkness.

Chloe hugged the oak tree tighter, melting away into the weathered bark.

"Don't move a muscle," she instructed. "And if they spot us, run in a different direction and meet me at the kissing rock."

Dale gulped.

The police cruiser halted near them. A thin beam of light penetrated the shadows, swooping over the oak tree and scanning the adjacent forest beside the brown house. Chloe held her breath as the light ran past them again.

Then, just when the beam was stabilizing, static hissed, and a steady voice crackled over the radio. The light turned off and the police car sped away. A moment later, the wail from its siren rang across the town in dire warning.

Chloe exhaled. "Come on, let's get out of here before they decide to come back," she said.

"Why do you think they left so quickly? Do you think it was Sawtooth Jack?"

"There's no such thing," Chloe said. "Now lead the way to the old man's house so we can get those shovels."

Dale shuffled in front of her. "But what if you're wrong?"

"Then he'll crack our bones and eat us. You worry too much," she huffed.

*　*　*

"There it is," Dale said, pointing at the house on the hill. It loomed above the tree line like a monolith. The house was an impenetrable fortress of wood and plastic siding and it seemed to stare down at them with a scrutinizing gaze.

"Is he the only person living in there?" Chloe asked.

"Yeah, but it wasn't always so big. Mr. Peterson built it up, barred the windows, and put a fence in the backyard a couple of months ago. He had a son who disappeared last Halloween. The cops only found shreds of his mummy costume and a blood trail leading to the corn fields. Mr. Peterson shut himself in after that. He doesn't talk to anyone anymore. He even grows his own food so he doesn't have to go to the grocery store."

"But you talked to him. You said you helped with his mailbox."

"That was before his son was killed. He's different now, bitter," Dale replied.

A dark shadow peered out of one of the third floor windows, then disappeared.

"Do you think he saw us?" she asked nervously.

"I don't think so. Let's stick to the trees until we reach the fence," Dale said.

They crept under low hanging branches devoid of leaves. Sometimes the wind blew and the tips of the branches would brush Chloe's hair like knobby witch fingers.

When they reached the chain link fence, Dale paused. He fished in his jacket and withdrew the toilet paper rolls.

"He's inside right now so let's get to that shed." He handed her a roll of toilet paper. "Do you want to roll his house first?"

"Dale, we're on a mission. We don't have time for this. He's just an old man," she said.

"Exactly, I bet nobody talks to him anymore. This will let him know he's still a part of the community."

Dale threw the roll of toilet paper into a tree on Mr. Peterson's lawn, where it snagged on a naked branch to then send a stream of white cascading down. He picked up the leftover roll and did it again and again until the tree was completely covered in toilet paper.

"Give it a try," he said. "It's fun."

"Screw this," Chloe said, tossing her roll of toilet paper aside. She hoisted herself over the fence and landed on the other side.

"What are you doing? Are you crazy?"

"He's not here, Dale. Let's get this over with."

Dale sighed and joined her on the other side. "I'll go first."

Chloe took his hand. She was trembling.

Dale was thankful for the darkness as his face turned a bright shade of red. Together, they walked into the backyard, avoiding garden gnomes and rotten fruit leftover from Mr. Peterson's harvest. The shed came into view moments later.

Chloe squeezed his hand.

"It's okay, we're almost there," he soothed.

They continued until they reached the shed. Dale kept eying the house for signs of movement but Mr. Peterson never presented himself. Dale stood on his tip toes and eased his hand along the top of the doorframe.

"Dale…"

"I got it," he said, showing her a small metal key.

"Get it open, please," she pleaded. "I thought I saw someone near the house."

Dale shoved the key into the padlock and twisted. The lock unlatched and they stepped inside. The shed stank of wet hay and was surrounded by endless strings of spider webs.

"I don't think he's been in here for a long time," Dale said, swatting through the webbing until he reached the tools.

"Maybe we should've just taken a shovel from my dad's garage," Chloe mused. She stayed in the doorway, unwilling to venture any further.

"You can't dig up a grave with a normal shovel. We need these tools. You can't back out of this now."

"I'm not backing out. I just don't like spiders," she said.

Dale pulled a long handled shovel with a pointed tip from a pile of tools. He set it aside and searched for something else.

"Why don't you like spiders? They won't bother you. They only eat bugs," he said.

"They don't *eat* bugs," she corrected. "They suck out their blood and leave them in webs like strange hanging fruit. I don't like them, okay?"

"But you're a vampire," Dale said. "You suck blood just like they do."

"That's different. Vampires don't hang around on a web all day long waiting for something tasty to get trapped. They hunt for their prey and because of it they live forever."

Dale pulled a pick axe from the corner of the shed. He slung it over his shoulder and used his free hand to grab one of the shovels he'd set aside.

"I'd never want to live forever. Everything you ever knew would change and what would you do with all that time, anyway?"

"I'd never have to say goodbye to anyone," Chloe answered.

Dale handed her a shovel. "Let's get going," he said.

The moment Dale spoke, a light came on at the house, flooding the backyard in a pale yellow glow.

"Run!" Dale yelled.

Chloe bolted from the shed, Dale chasing after her, dragging the tools behind him.

The backdoor of the house swung open and a lanky figure stormed out. Chloe headed out of the light and to the woods, but before she got there something became caught under her foot and she tumbled to the ground. She landed in a warm puddle and gazed at what she'd tripped over, choking in horror.

An old man lay face up in the soil. His chest was ripped open and his insides were missing.

"Mr. Peterson..." she gasped.

Dale caught up to her and saw the dead man. "Oh, shit." He looked behind them and spotted the tall shape racing towards them in the darkness.

Chloe leapt to her feet. "Come on, Dale. We've got to get out of here, now."

Dale snapped out of his stupor and ran around Mr. Peterson's lifeless corpse.

Blue and red lights suddenly lit up the backyard as a police cruiser pulled into Mr. Peterson's backyard. In the flashing lights they saw Sawtooth Jack. He was a scarecrow with a pumpkin head and he gripped a long handled saw. When he looked at them, they could see his red eyes shone with evil.

Dale helped Chloe over the fence and followed her into the forest.

"Hey! Don't move, stay where you are," ordered a policeman to Sawtooth Jack.

The gaunt form twisted around and headed toward the cop. As the children ran through the woods, they heard a long, agonizing wail.

* * *

The corn field stretched out for a little more than a mile. It was a sea of brown husks, dead and still except when the wind blew and the fields came alive, swaying back and forth like thousands of skeletal arms.

"I don't know if I can go in there," Dale said.

"But we've come so far. We can't pull out now. Where's your sense of adventure? Cowards never go into space."

"I'm not a coward. I'm just being cautious. Sawtooth Jack might be in there. I bet he circled around and now he's daring us to come in."

Chloe adjusted her cape and swung the flat head shovel over one shoulder.

"Then let's not keep him waiting," she said.

"Have you lost your mind? He just killed Mr. Peterson and that policeman, and you still want to go through with this?"

"He can't keep me from my mother."

Dale snatched her by the arms and shook hard. "She's dead, Chloe. D-E-A-D. She's not coming back."

"How do you know that? Has anyone ever tried it before?" She stared at him until he averted his eyes. "Either let me go or take my hand because I'm going in there and nothing's gonna stop me."

Dale straightened his back. "I won't let you go in alone."

With a nod, Chloe took his hand and dragged him into the corn field.

The tall stalks sliced along their arms and legs, restricting movement, and blotting out any available moonlight. It wasn't long before Dale took the lead, thrashing a pathway through the ocean of corn. They were almost there when they found a large hole in the ground where the corn didn't grow. It was as though the ground had vomited out something it didn't want to keep anymore.

Dale paused.

"Keep moving," Chloe said. "I see it. The graveyard is just up ahead."

Corn gave way to pavement as they reached the cemetery. They hesitated at the black gates, the lock on the entrance keeping them at bay.

"Should we look for a place to climb over?" she asked.

"No," Dale said. He dropped the shovel and heaved the pick axe. "Stand back."

The pick axe collided with the lock, sending sparks flying onto the withered grass.

The lock was dented but not broken. Dale lifted the pick axe high above his head again and brought it down with all the strength he could muster. The lock exploded in a clash of metal, sending pieces of the padlock soaring into the corn field.

"Good job, Dale."

Chloe gave him a kiss on the cheek. Dale's eyes widened. She gave him a smile and pushed open the iron gates. They swung onto the grass with an unhurried creak.

Chloe strolled inside as Dale picked up the shovel and followed after her, with the pick axe on his shoulder.

Oakrun Cemetery was home to an infinite collection of swollen hills decorated by thousands of tombstones. In the night, the graves looked like the gray fingernails of giants poking out from the ground.

Chloe and Dale moved among the headstones and avoided stepping on fake flowers left for lost loved ones. They climbed a bloated hill and stopped at the sight of Scylla.

Scylla was the biggest tree in Harvest Town; some even claimed it rivaled the red woods in California. The willow oak clawed at the sky with curled branches, as though it could rip open the heavens and let all the corpses underground climb there way up to paradise. But that was the cruelty of Scylla. The tree had grown so large that its roots snaked above and below ground, holding down coffins, and pushing through the cadaver's within.

"I wish they would cut that tree down," Dale said.

Chloe slapped him on the back. "If we make it through tonight, I promise we'll come back next Halloween with two axes."

"You've got a deal," he laughed.

They marched over the worm turned earth until Chloe halted at a tombstone marked,

JENNY SIMMONS, BELOVED WIFE AND MOTHER.

"Hi, Mom, I came to get you. This is Dale."

"Hello," Dale said shyly.

Chloe took the shovel from Dale and planted the shovel's head into the cold earth, scooping out a pile of dirt.

Dale stood across from her and slammed the pick axe into the ground, chomping off worm ends, and breaking through Scylla's roots. They worked in silence for hours, heaving mounds of earth into a gigantic pile. Dale was forced to remove his astronaut flight jacket and didn't stop digging until his pick axe struck wood.

Chloe wiped sweat from her brow and tossed the shovel aside.

"That's her, we're almost there," she said, and dug out clumps of soil by hand.

Once the coffin was unearthed, Dale climbed out of the hole and sat on his space helmet. Despite everything that had happened thus far, he had still managed to hold onto it, not wanting to lose it.

"We did it," he said, gasping.

Chloe pried the coffin lid open with her fingers.

Inside, Chloe's mother stared up at her with sunken eyes. Her skin was gray and tightly wrapped over poking bones. Her black dress was dusty and tattered.

"Mom, it's me," Chloe sobbed. She intertwined her fingers around a boney hand. "I came back for you. I miss you so much."

The body was still. She was just a hollowed out shell and nothing more.

Chloe let go of the hand, the limb falling back onto the corpse's chest to remain still.

"She's gone isn't she, Dale. She's really gone. Dale..."

Chloe looked up and screamed.

A gnarled hand gripped Dale's hair, pulling it back to expose his neck. Dale thrashed like a baited shark but couldn't break free from his attacker's grasp. The jagged edges of a rusty saw appeared and pressed to his throat.

Chloe crawled out of the grave.

A stick-thin man towered over Dale. His head resembled the pumpkin she'd carved earlier that night and a black tongue protruded from between his triangle teeth. Mr. Peterson and the policeman's severed heads dangled from his belt on a piece of rope.

"Run, Chloe!" Dale yelled. "Get out of here!" His voice was cut short as Sawtooth Jack prepared to use the saw on Dale's neck, ready to slice the boy's throat in two.

Chloe armed herself with the shovel and swung for the ragged head. The shovel connected and Sawtooth Jack loosened his hold on Dale enough for him to wiggle free. He stumbled to Chloe's side and curled his hands into fists.

Sawtooth Jack let out a horrible laugh which resembled fingernails against a chalkboard and ended as though he'd gargled with broken glass. The abomination advanced slowly. He put his back to the open grave and licked the edge of his saw blade. Then, before he cold take another step, a skeletal hand clamped around his ankle and yanked, sending the figure falling forward to land in the upturned dirt.

Sawtooth Jack was dragged into Jenny Simmons' grave. He began screaming but his cries soon became gurgles and then stopped altogether.

Chloe and Dale peered into the hole. There was the body of Sawtooth Jack lying on Jenny's feet. His pumpkin head had been bitten and was missing a large chunk. Her teeth were stained a dark red.

Chloe stared down into her mother's grave and sucked in her lips. Where bright eyes once gleamed there was now empty sockets, but something had glimmered there for just an instant.

"Dale, pass me the shovel," she said.

"Are you sure she won't come back again?" Dale asked, frightened.

"I'm sure."

Dale limped over the pile of dirt and handed her the shovel. "She saved our lives."

"I know. Let's put her to rest for good," she said, pushing the disturbed soil back into the grave.

"Will you miss her?"

"Not like before," Chloe replied.

Dale motioned to Sawtooth Jack. "What about him?"

Chloe leaped into the grave and Dale helped her lift the figure out.

"We'll leave him out here and tell the cops where he is."

Dale picked up the shovel and together they filled in her mother's grave, Chloe using her feet and hands. Once the task was completed, they sat on the ground for a brief rest.

"Thanks for helping me. I couldn't have done it without you," she said.

"Don't mention it. Hey, we're heroes now. Just wait until everyone in town hears how we put an end to Sawtooth Jack." He turned to look where the body was but it was missing. "Hey, he's gone," Dale gasped, looking around but the cemetery was empty.

Chloe's eyes widened. She scooted closer to Dale and quivered. "You're going to walk me back home, right?"

"Maybe we'll just stay here until morning," Dale said, and put his arm around her shoulders.

* * *

So the dead mother was put to rest, content in knowing she'd done her best. Chloe and Dale watched the sun rise and took their parents punishment for staying out all night in stride.

Sawtooth Jack remained forever cursed to walk Harvest Town and come out of the earth. So if you're ever in a sleepy town on Halloween night, watch behind your back for a pumpkin headed fright. Lock your doors and shut the drapes and don't let anyone in for goodness sake, because Sawtooth Jack is on the Halloween prowl, devouring any wanderers with his triangle scowl.

DEMONS LOVE CHOCOLATE

SPENCER WENDLETON

1

"Do you know what dissatisfied demon children do without their candy? They eat each other, Duncan. And do you know what? Next, it'll be you they'll be eating!"

"It's not a problem," I let out, unimpressed with my boss' rant. "Just give me another chance to deliver on my promises. I have an ace up my sleeve." *Way up my sleeve.*

"You and your wife will be leftover slop if I had my way," Mr. Finkle huffed, wishing this time he'd actually get to eat me and my wife. The black gills around his throat puckered and closed with a wet glop, expelling his urgency to fix the situation at hand. "But you're a damn good candy maker, I'll give you that. Those kids are regular hellions without their treats. I want your next idea on my desk by five o'clock sharp. Got it? I'm not messing around. I'll eat you myself if you fail, Duncan. And you know I will." That proboscis tongue crawled across his flagellated lips and drew a slobber gleam over the skin. "I'm always hungry."

I'd much prefer a pink slip.

"Yes, sir," I replied, swallowing an irreverent retort. "I'll have it for you today."

"Five o'clock or you're dead, as well as your wife."

Mr. Finkle slammed the office door, ending the pep-talk.

2

My boss is a demon as well as over three quarters of the population, and this was a serious situation building to critical mass. The executive demon owns and operates 'M' and 'D' Candies, and my job is to create packaging for the customer base—demon children—that's attractive and interactive. And my last five projects were met with dull enthusiasm. I was Mr. Finkle's number one go-to guy until last month. I'd invented numerous hits in the chocolate packaging industry, including a candy heart that spits out chocolate from the chambers, a head that leaks chocolate blood from the neck stump—batteries not included—the expensive and popular human-in-a-casket which has to be dismembered and dissected to retrieve hidden chocolate goodies throughout the anatomy—'Cemetery Death Day' was a holiday created in honor of the product—and then there was my last hit, the fake body made of a chocolate rubber—'The Shred-N-Eat Chocolate Feeder'.

Before this job, I used to be a mortician, a much easier career than being a candy maker for demon children, but that was two years ago before I changed. The new chemical additive in formaldehyde, 'Muelertran', was added to the corpses for burial. It made it so bodies could be above the surface for three to ten weeks without being affected by decomposition. The fumes caused deformation in the living—my left arm, for example, is plated up to the elbow—and full-blown mutations in others, which essentially created the race of demons.

"Come on, Duncan," I whispered, letting go of the past and focusing on staying alive. "Let's get it together. You've done this before many times. You can do it again. Create something for God's sake. *Anything.*"

3

I slapped a blank sheet of sketch paper onto the desk and clutched my fountain pen. I prayed something came out of me that would stick. Each time I prepared to hammer out another idea, I sketched out the male and female body—something simple and easy to build on. The problem: the male sketch, I kept picturing my face on it, and the female would be my wife, Julie. She'd bleed from the neck and plead for her life, begging not to be eaten by the demon children, and I would stand there helpless to her defiling.

"Stop them, Duncan! They're sinking their teeth into me! They're eating *me!*" she'd scream. Then the sketch of her would flop dead onto the paper, bleeding from every wound and broken orifice as the demon children finished her off piece by bloody piece. I had nightmares of the same ilk. They would stalk me, and the ravenous children would pin me down to feast on, but instead of blood firing out of my arteries once my skin was ripped open, it was milk chocolate.

You're lucky. They've given you a job. A chance to live. They killed the ones they had no use for. They all became meat for the plate.

I tucked the pad of paper under my arm and decided to go to Hawkins Park; disturbed, creatively blocked, and soaked through with stinking sweat. Maybe I could think there and wrangle up some effective ideas without succumbing to the pressure of an impossible deadline.

4

In the hallway outside my office, Mr. Finkle was chatting with another demon—the head of demon resources, Jack Garfield. They yucked it up with their flapping faces, staring at me like I was a hot plate of food coming out of the kitchen; I *was* fresh out of the oven, in their opinion.

Mr. Finkle growled, "Where are you going, Duncan?"

"To the park to think. I'll be back long before five."

Jack smirked, knowing I was squirming on the inside. "Make sure you come back, huh? My child's eager for chocolate. I've looked over fifty applications for your job. Creative geniuses, I'm sure." Jack flashed those stalactite teeth, a warning. "I guess you creative types work well under pressure. Delicious pressure."

I rushed to the elevator in retreat from the two vultures. Inside, Helen McTavey was sucking on the ends of her hair. Helen was in charge of payroll. She was mostly human except both her legs were a demon's. Her kneecaps jutted out with a single bone hook, and she couldn't wear shoes, her toenails tipped with five-inch talons and dew-claws. She peeked at me from the corner of her eyes, honestly concerned.

"I'm pullin' for ya, Duncan. You can do it," she said.

"Thanks."

'At least it's not me' is what you're really thinking, I thought.

5

The elevator stopped on the ground floor and I rushed to the front entrance of the skyscraper, in dire need of fresh air. My pace was erratic and quick, and I'd traveled far enough that I was already two blocks from the park. Picketers had surrounded the 'M' and 'D' Candies building by the hundreds. They waved their protest signs: ***Our Children Are Out of Control. Candy for Children! Instead of Chocolate, It Will Be Your Blood. Name Your Price, We'll Pay It.***

A group of jabbering, slobbering, and shrieking children hurled trash cans into the windows of the skyscraper in alarming unison. Another group of the tykes uprooted a fire hydrant, and a jet of water launched ten feet in the air and soaked the streets. A group of security officers arrived and tasered them, and they landed on their backs like bug-sprayed beetles. Another wave of kids repeated the screams in the distance, *"Chocolate now! Chocolate now! Chocolate now, OR DIE!"*

Their mantra was grating to my ears. Brats. They get what they want because they have teeth.

I changed course and took the back way through the alley and crossed through two blocks of slow traffic to arrive at Hawkins Park. The gated-perimeter surrounds an average park: water fountain, open grass field for Frisbee and picnickers, and a pond—though there are no more geese; the children saw to that, you can imagine.

It's the lunch hour, and the park was busy. Most are eating their lunch, fast food human. It's mostly ribs and appendages; the organs they prefer diced up and batter-breaded.

I thought it would be calming in this area, but even here, the demon children are restless. The mother breast-feeding from her flabby breast is nagged by the way the baby is gnawing on the skin and drawing blood.

"Not so hard, Beth, you're hurting Mommy," I heard her say.

The children are bounding up the trees and swiping at the pigeons that swoop overhead. The jungle gyms, swings and slides in the distance are overrun by angry children who uproot the equipment to destroy what was once their haven.

School is out today because of the chocolate crisis. Teachers can't stick to the curriculum without the latest in chocolate technology to abate the kids. I had heard Birmingham Elementary was burned down three days ago; trash cans were set on fire and half the staff was sent to the hospital with eaten limbs.

Why me? Why am I the only one who can help this horrible situation? There are dozens of chocolate makers, but few of our ideas become popular. I've had the best luck out of the staff. The city depends on me, and if I fail, the children will overtake the city, and I'm forced to re-concentrate on my civic and financial duty.

I slap the Steno pad on my lap and draw a male and female body. It's immediate that Julie is gazing up at me with her dying eyes.

"Don't let them eat me alive!" she screams at me, drowning in her own blood, but now, she too is spurting milk chocolate from her wounds. And this time I'm hunched over her, licking up the chocolate, spreading it over my body, and lavishing in the candy.

I can't do it. My hand is locked up. I'm pouring sweat, and I'm nervous as hell. Four hours, and that'll about do it for me. Duncan the dead man. Mr. Finkle will pour Jack Daniels on my corpse and cook it for the flavor. Jack Garfield will be flossing me from his teeth and Julie will be the first on the menu.

A demon child clawed bark from a tree nearby, distracting me from my grand failure, *"Gimme chocolate!"* he yelled.

To the left of me, the breast-feeding mother's chest is spurting blood; the entire sternum has been bared, including her breasts. A local citizen demon rushes to her and pulls her from the baby's voracious sucking mouth. The mother clung to the Good Samaritan as her child is hauled away, manic and biting at nothing, desperate for more flesh.

Then on the horizon, an incoming wave of demon children sweep the area, sneaking through the rails of the fence and others hurtling them altogether. Dozens turn into hundreds. They've escaped their homes and their parents and are now rioting in the streets. The windows of parked cars are shattered. Local businesses are turned inside out, some burning and spitting out smoke. Foaming-mouthed demon children war with each other, reaping flesh and bone in their fervor, killing and maiming each other. The park is busy with adults battling the ankle-biters, and very soon, they'll be upon me, too.

I run to escape the throng, but I'm tackled from behind. The beady olive eyes, the yammering mouth, the click-click-clacking of teeth, the claws digging cherry trenches into my sides and chest, and the mouth drooling burning hot saliva onto me, all paralyze me. The child ogles at my hand, meticulously planning my cannibalization.

"Human? Are you human? Tell me! Tell me!" the child screams.

The child seizes my demon arm and chews it up, munching and snapping bone and squishing on blood and meat. I punch and kick and batter the thing, but the small demon's not budging. Red and green blood mix from my chewed up fingers and his mouth cranks open wider—his entire head expanding like a puppet's—to bite down up to the elbow. One wicked crunch, and my demon appendage is taken.

"*NOW YOU'RE ALL HUMAN!*" he screams.

The sight of my flesh, my bones, and my fat mixing on the little demon's tongue horrifies me as much as it inspires me.

My good arm stretched out and my hand landed on a sizeable rock, and I swung it again and again into the demon's head. The fourth strike gouges out its eyes from the force. Safe, I lean up against the tree and remove my Steno notebook from my backpack. I sketch fervently, but my ink pen is dry.

"Damn it!"

I'm desperate and borderline unconscious, so I dipped the pen into the puddle of my blood and began drawing out the prototype.

6

An ambulance crew located me. The first EMT looks tempted, "Ah, he's a human."

The second EMT shared the same enthusiasm. "Yeah, let's eat him. Gobble him up. He's almost dead anyway. Who cares? Nobody will know."

I dug into my backpack for my identification. They both gawked at me and realized the mistake they almost made. "Oh, you work for 'M' and 'D' Candies, huh? Shit."

The other EMT said, "Yeah, shit is about right. Get this poor sap into an ambulance right now! We can't lose this one."

7

I was delivered to St. Luke's Mercy Hospital, Julie at my bed-side at the ICU ward. She mouthed to me between tears, "My genius is alive."

Mr. Finkle stood on the other side of the bed, and he nodded at me with a fake, seedy smile. "Hey, I really wasn't going to eat you. A bit of at-the-office humor, my boy, that's all. I'm giving you the week off to recuperate. Keep saving up the ideas. You have until Monday to draw up the next innovated new thing." He elbowed me. "By five o'clock, you know the drill." He gave Julie the best honest smile he could, which isn't saying much. "Good day, Julie."

Julie lowered her head in respectful fear. "You too, Mr. Finkle."

I ask her when Mr. Finkle had finally made his exit, "How long have I been out?"

"Two days," Julie replied, kissing me on the cheek. "I love you. Thank God you weren't killed. You lost so much blood. It came close. Those kids murdered two-hundred demons but they were finally calmed by the fact you came up with something new."

"Those brats," I cursed. I looked down at my bandaged arm; the eaten arm had already grown back. "Well, I'll be damned. Seri-ously, I'm damned."

"It's kept us alive," Julie reassured me. "Be thankful, I know I am."

I relaxed in bed. "Hey, what was my idea anyway?"

8

The second day of my sick leave, I was finally home. Enjoying a bottle of Pinot Noir on the balcony of our apartment building, Julie replenished the ice in the bucket. Three stories below, I watched the children play outside. They each had a meat grinder in a plas-tic-wrapped box marked 'M' and 'D' Candies. They open the pack-age and chocolate-flavored pieces shaped as human organs and limbs spilled out. The kids raced to dice them up in the grinder; the straw pieces filter out the spout, and they eat it voraciously.

Like a commercial, the little demons grumble in delight to-gether, "*Mmmmm, chocolate!*"

I shook my head at them, knowing what the days ahead had in store for me.

"My God, what will it take to satisfy you brats next week?"

BLOOD COUNT

JOHN SKERCHOCK

Gordy scurried along the base of the stone wall, hoping he'd gotten away from the massacre. He was sorely out of breath, but he kept running, feelers twitching in a frenzied, chaotic dance, hoping that Boris hadn't followed him. The guilt that stabbed at his brain for leaving so many behind to die hurt him almost as bad as the running.

Oh, it was horrible! Yet it seemed like a good idea at the time. Hunger and despair threatened the Clan. The Count had abandoned them to their fate by failing to provide the subtle crumbs to maintain their meager existence. The Clan could wait no more for it would only bring death. Something had to be done or the Clan would perish, but the wrong choices were made.

Gordy sobbed for the fallen as he ran frantically to save his life.

Upon finally reaching a crack in a damp piece of stone, Gordy scuttled into it and hunkered down tight. He wasn't very big to begin with so he was able to hide in tighter spots than most of the Clan. He tried to catch his breath while being as quiet as possible. The screams of his brothers and sisters still rang in his ears. His lungs ached and his tiny feet were sore. The horror he had witnessed was burned into his brain like so many hot needles piercing flesh. At that thought, Gordy suddenly felt hungry.

Earlier, the Count had returned. He was asleep. The Clan thought this was a good sign even though he hadn't provided for them, and they made their move. Too many nights the Count had been absent, leaving his minions wondering who would provide for them. The Count's return was a signal, or so they thought, that nourishment and sustenance had returned.

That was when Gordy and the rest of the Clan went out in search of food. The Count always dropped something for them in the past before laying to rest. The Count, whether carelessly or with divine intent, had often dropped precious morsels. The Clan had become hopeful and desperate that he had honored them again, so they carelessly set out in search of food.

Fungus and bat droppings were ignored. Their vile taste and lack of nourishment were all the Clan had been able to secure during the waning days. It wasn't much to brag about, Gordy mused as he felt his belly ache with the pangs of hunger. He wished he had some of that fungus now.

The Clan had become lax in their need to survive. The Count, their Master, had returned and caution was tossed to the damp breezes that swept through the dank tunnels and halted against the dripping walls of the rancid dungeon. The Clan had become care-less. They had ventured too far too fast on the mere hope they had been provided for that day.

Gordy and the others had heard the Count's hurried return. The creaking of the ancient wooden door, the footsteps across the gravel-strewn floor, and the labored breathing, signaled the urgent need for the safety of his tomb. When the stone slab that covered his crypt slammed home, they knew it was safe to scurry about, for the Master would not be stepping on any of them. At least they thought it would be safe.

Perhaps they would finally have a feast?

Oh, the sweet taste of blood as it pooled on the floor! The tiny yet tender bits of flesh that found their way into the cracks and crevices were joys to devour. Gordy felt himself salivating beyond control. The feeding frenzy was overtaking him like a water mirage did a thirsty man in the desert. With difficulty, Gordy brought the urge under control; he was panting heavily.

Earlier, the Clan had hurried across the floor hoping to find a gift from the Count. Anything would do: a few breadcrumbs, a drop or two of delicious red blood, or, perhaps, a freshly done in rabbit?

They rushed blindly to His resting place, the feeding urge controlling their movements and making them blind to everything else. As one, they halted in the open as no bit of food could be found. One of the Clan suggested returning to the bat droppings for a warm but unappetizing meal. Afterward, they could rest and dream of when the Count would smile upon them again, but that didn't happen.

They had come too far too fast. Their urges had led them blindly into the open, away from the walls and safety. They forgot there were others in the dungeon as hungry as they were; others that were bigger and stronger.

They forgot about Boris.

Boris, the spider, was a big, black, hairy creature that kept watch near the Count's tomb. It was his job to keep trespassers away and he did it with vehemence and perverted glee that frightened even the bravest members of the Clan.

Boris usually left them alone. He was too busy performing his duties or rebuilding his web after the Count left or returned. He was provided for as flies often followed the Count, but they had stopped coming, too. Boris grew hungry just like everyone else. He had to eat regularly as well.

All of the Clan feared Boris. Some Clan members had been victims to the giant spider's voracious appetite in the past, and their families had never forgotten. The Clan knew to stay away from him. That is until the feeding frenzy overcame their good senses.

Boris' job was to ensure that no one disturbed the Count and in turn, no one sought to disturb Boris. However, no one had counted on Boris not being provided for by the Count. The spider became just as hungry as any member, two members, or more of the Clan. At the time of the Clan's move, he was waiting to end that hunger in a very big way.

Boris wasn't stupid. Due to the lack of abundance in the availability of food, things had changed. He had declared all out war on the Clan, but they didn't realize it at the time. He set an elaborate trap for them. While the Clan rushed as one into the open before the Count's bed of rest, Boris hopped across the walls and became busy laying strand after strand of sticky death, like a minefield, across the damp floor. And when they were all out in the open, that's when he fell upon them like lightning striking again and again and again!

Pouncing down on them from his bungee cord web line, he managed to snap up Gordy's family members and friends one at a time. Each died horribly with a resounding crack of the shell then the sucking and venomous bite. Crack, bite, and wrap, was how he did it. One after another, Boris added to his larder.

Gordy saw his friends Eddie and Rondo snapped up and crushed by Boris' mighty jaws before anyone realized what was happening. Sydney and Alice were trapped in the sticky lines beneath their feet and suddenly became victims, too! Then it was widespread panic as the terror set in!

The Clan scattered, and Gordy crapped on the spot. They were like a herd of wild animals running in every direction with only the thought of escaping death controlling their actions. And Gordy, although he was small, was very fast.

The surviving members ran in fear, hoping to get away but Boris had planted many traps. His fine, near invisible webbing, lined most of the escape routes. Brothers and sisters were entangled. Some died quickly. They were the lucky ones. Others would linger for days as poison set to work within their hard-shelled bodies. Their moans would haunt the survivors forever.

Yet, somehow Gordy had escaped. He ran the only way he could think of and that was in the direction of the Count's tomb, Boris' home turf. It was the one route Boris forgot to cover.

Gordy knew his decision might, eventually, be suicide. It was certainly unheard of, for no one disturbed the Count during his slumber. But it ensured Gordy's survival for at least a little while. Gordy was certain that it would only be a matter of time until he met the same fate as his kin.

He felt himself shake and shiver all over. He was scared, and he showed it. Tears welled up in his beady, black eyes and his feelers rubbed together in nervous self-pity. His stomach ached from the run and the lack of food. It had been a long time since he had dined on anything substantial. And sucking water out of a stagnant puddle wasn't anyone's idea of fine dining.

The entire Clan was in the same fix. The Count had stopped providing, and their future was in jeopardy. They were all His children, and Gordy believed that the Count had abandoned them and today, he had proof of that belief.

It was a struggle of the strong over the weak, evolution at its best. Boris was stronger and more fearsome than ever, and the Clan was weak from hunger and scared. The body count would be high. Few of the Clan would survive to carry on.

Maybe that was the way it was meant to be?

Somehow though, from somewhere deep inside of him, Gordy resolved that he would not fall prey to that big old spider. He'd hole up in a crack too small for Boris to penetrate and just waste away. That would serve the big hairy monster! Maybe the ants would feast on what was left of his dried-out corpse, but Boris would never have it!

Gordy sat and rested. He would wait a long time, days if necessary, then check to see if the coast was clear. Then he would scurry home to the damp crack under the west wall, the one that had once held dozens of his kin, all huddled together to share the latest news and gossip. He began to nod off.

The sound was soft at first, but it grew louder as it came closer. Gordy held his breath for fear that Boris had come looking for him. He leaned forward just enough to be protected by the stone, but still able to see what was making the noise. His feelers worked frantically, trying to pick up a scent, a familiar smell. He swallowed hard in anticipation.

It was Vince. He'd somehow managed to get away!

"Psst," Gordy whispered.

Vince's feelers twisted and turned as he tried to find the source of the sound.

"Vince, over here, it's me, Gordy." He tried not to raise his voice, but he was too scared as it was that he would alert the spider who was no doubt near by.

Vince turned quickly and rushed under the stone, almost crashing into his cousin.

"Man, am I glad to see you," Vince cried. They rubbed feelers and bumped shells. It was as close to a hug and a handshake that they could muster.

"What the hell happened out there?"

"I don't know, man. It's crazy out there," Vince said. He was perspiring and his black eyes were watering. "Boris caught a whole lot of us. It's like he's stocking up for the long haul. I was so scared I almost shed my shell again."

"I'd like to give that ugly bastard one solid kick in the nuts, that is if he had any."

"Shit, man, if it ain't the rats it's that big hairy son-of-a-bitch! The world's coming to an end!"

"How long do you think it'll be until we can sneak back home?"

"That's not happening," Vince trembled. "Boris put up a gigantic web between the Count's tomb and home. It's like he knows some of us came this way. This is home for now, pal."

"I want to kick his ass," Gordy said. But his voice didn't seem to have the strength to convince him, let alone his cousin.

Vince just looked at Gordy with pity. Even for a cockroach, Gordy was tiny. He'd let others in the Clan push him around and take the better scraps of food. Now they were all dead. If they had all fallen to Boris, what chance would Gordy stand against the spider?

"Forget it, man. Before long he'll have us, too. And then he'll probably go after the bats."

"It sucks being this low on the food chain."

"Man, Gordy, we are the food chain," Vince cried. "The bats can come and go. The ants, well, they work like a team and no one gets in their way. It's us versus the spider. He'll have a well stocked larder now. Next he'll want to mate, then breed a whole room full of big ugly spiders just like him. And if he breeds, we're all done for!"

"Something is going on," Gordy mused. "It's like the Count is losing control."

"Watch what you say." Vince's feelers suddenly went wild. "He can still hear our thoughts! He knows all."

"I don't know," Gordy said. "I haven't felt His presence in me in a long time. He was away for so long and now He returns empty handed. It's not like the old days when He would feed and, more often than not, it would be right here in the castle." Gordy's eyes suddenly grew glassy. "Yes, then He would nap and let us have what was left. We'd feed to our delight—us, the bats, even Boris— then sleep a nice peaceful slumber. Oh, those were the days."

Vince nodded. "Yes, I agree, something isn't right."

Suddenly, an earth-shattering crash was heard from above. Gordy and Vince tried to squeeze themselves further into the crack. Then it came again, louder than before. It was the sound of wood splintering.

The door to the dungeon was being smashed open!

And there were voices, human voices, and they sounded angry.

Neither Gordy nor Vince could understand what was being said, but the voices were loud and excited. A lot of humans were yelling. Then came the sound of metal striking against stone.

Gordy hazarded a chance to look out from the crack and saw a number of men rush down the steps with a determined purpose. They were carrying metal poles, mallets, and wooden stakes. They crowded around the Count's resting place and began to slide the stone lid off of its base. There was a resounding crash as it hit the floor and shattered. Gordy and Vince were almost knocked unconscious by the deafening blast.

The voices became louder as men reached into the crypt. Gordy felt the urge to protect the Count, but he knew he could do nothing but run away. And he'd be doing that right now if he wasn't so scared to move.

Then there came the sounds of a mallet hitting a wooden stake, followed by the Count's agonizing screams. Several of the men fell over as the power of His voice knocked them down.

Gordy watched in amazement as blood spurted upwards from inside the tomb like a fountain. The shiny red pulsing sprayed the ceiling of the dungeon and splashed upon the floor. Big, red drops seemed to fall everywhere like rain.

Just as suddenly as it began, it was over. The humans, altogether now, left. They were a lot quieter than when they had entered. Their voices were now low and muffled, but they sounded approving of a job well done.

Gordy stared at the tomb to see smoke rising out of it. He looked at the large pools of blood on the floor. Smoke was rising from them also.

The blood was dissipating into nothingness. Gordy's stomach roared with pain.

"Hey, where are you going?" Vince called as Gordy all but knocked his cousin over.

Gordy ran to the nearest drop of blood, overcome by the feeding frenzy that had doomed the Clan. The starving cockroach made a desperate attempt to fill his belly and end the agony.

The blood was evaporating fast and he only had enough time to get to the closest droplets. He sank his face into the red nectar just as it started to burn away. He drank deeply, willingly. He drank his fill just as the last of the blood disappeared into the ages.

He let out a satisfying burp.

"Hey, man, stop that," Vince yelled. "That's our Master's blood." He paused then cried, "And you didn't save any for me!"

Gordy just smiled, then grimaced as the burning started! His stomach was on fire. His small heart began to pound and his head began to throb. Suddenly, an all-encompassing pain consumed him. It was more terrifying than even Boris' venomous bite was imagined to be.

He screamed.

"Gordy! What's happening?"

He began to run around in circles. His head was on fire. He felt like there was something alive crawling around inside of him, and it hurt.

"Quiet! Boris will hear you, and then we'll both be done for!" Vince hissed.

But Gordy couldn't be quiet. He hurt too much. His pain was eating him up inside. He circled several more times and then fell onto his back. His limbs gave one final shake and were still.

Vince looked to his left and then to his right and satisfied they were alone, he scurried forward and gently tapped his cousin with his feelers. Gordy felt stiff and cold. He wasn't breathing.

"Gordy, are you all right? Hey, this isn't funny." But Gordy didn't respond. "Cousin, if you're dead, man, well, you know—I'm hungry."

Gordy didn't answer so Vince leaned in closer. His feelers ran the length of Gordy's body and satisfied that his cousin was truly dead, he was about to ease his hunger when Gordy's legs moved.

"Whoa..." Vince said as he scurried backwards.

Gordy began to breathe. His limbs shook and he began to rock back and forth. His eyes fell on Vince, and he said, "A little help here, cousin. I feel like I just got stepped on."

"Sure. Sure. No problem," Vince said and came forward to help Gordy upright himself. "Hey, I was only checking. I wasn't going to take a bite or anything."

"Thanks," Gordy said as he shook himself all over.

"Are you okay?" Vince asked.

"Yeah, yeah, sure." He stood silent for a moment as if meditating on something. "Boy, the Count sure tasted good," he said as he looked Vince in his beady eyes. "I feel like I'm reborn, like I'm a new person."

"Gordy, you look different," Vince said. "You look a little pale, too."

He ran his feelers over his body. "I feel okay," Gordy said. "Actually, I feel stronger. I feel like I can take on the whole world."

Gordy started walking proudly, filling his lungs with air. He felt his limbs becoming stronger, larger. His chest grew three times its normal size, and he actually felt like he could beat the shit out of something.

"Gordy," Vince said. "You look so different. You look confident now. You look like a leader. What happened?"

"Maybe our Master did provide." Gordy was beaming with confidence. "I want to kick some ass."

Suddenly, his own eyes flashed red and an evil smile crossed his wide face. The look sent a spark of terror down Vince's spine as he cowered before his suddenly larger relative.

"So what do we do now?" Vince asked softly.

"You don't know?"

"N...no," Vince said, half expecting Gordy to bite off his tiny head.

"We're going to have a party," Gordy grinned, his voice sounding much deeper.

"A party?" Vince asked.

"Yes, you gather up what's left of the Clan while I go take care of that damned spider!" Gordy said in a strong voice, feeling the fangs grow in his mouth as he scurried bravely across the floor.

THE HOTEL ROOM

RICHARD MOORE

It wasn't that the bed was uncomfortable, and after having spent most of the day behind the wheel, Martin was more than ready for sleep. Not long after turning out the light, lying there, drifting off, he heard a noise out in the hall, what sounded to him like footsteps, and the noise brought him fully awake.

Not that there was anything unusual about hearing footsteps. This was a hotel after all. There'd been a few cars in the parking lot, and upon checking in, he and his wife Nancy had seen no other guests, but there had to be other people staying in the hotel, obviously.

His mind, evidently been searching for some reason to deny his body what it needed, had found it. Martin was not in the least surprised. He never slept well in any bed other than his own. Wherever they went it was always the same. By the time they got through with these twice yearly visits to his wife's sister in Arizona, or they went on one of their little sightseeing getaways, he always felt as though he was suffering the effects of sleep deprivation. Something to help him sleep was probably what he needed, something like...

There it was again. Footsteps, treading softly across the carpeting outside the door.

"Nancy," Martin whispered. "Do you hear that? Are you awake?"

His wife answered his question by neither moving nor making a sound. Typical. In forty-two years of marriage, he'd never known Nancy to miss out on a good night's rest. When her head hit the pillow, any pillow, no matter where they were, a minimum of eight hours had to pass before it rose again. Like clockwork she was. Martin remembered one time, there was a party going on in the cabin beside theirs, and even then Nancy...

Voices, whispering. Right outside the door.

Martin lifted his head, cocked one ear as he strained to listen. He stayed like that for a couple of minutes at least, perhaps as many as five.

Nothing, not another sound.

Had he imagined the voices? Was he cracking up in his old age?

He returned his head to the pillow, moved around in the bed, and tried to get comfortable. More minutes passed. He heard nothing else. Sleep pulled at him, taking him down into the darkness. He was just about there, just about free of the tethers that held him to his senses, when he heard what was unmistakably a women's voice, out in the hall, standing close to his room's door.

"Is he asleep?" she asked.

Martin jolted and sat up.

"Shall we see if he wants to come out and play?" asked another voice, belonging to a woman also.

"What're you doing?" said the first voice. "Don't do that."

There came a sudden knocking against the door—four fast raps.

"What's the meaning of this?" Martin yelled.

He threw back the covers and stomped to the door, reached for the handle, fingers grasping it, tensing as he prepared for the confrontation. Out in the hall, he heard footsteps hurrying away. He swallowed, as he tried to rid himself of the lump of fear in his throat.

The stairwell door thudded open and he heard faint laughter. He could only think the two women had been playing some sort of prank—possibly confusing his and Nancy's room with that of another guest.

Still, it wasn't acceptable, first creeping around out there, then knocking on his door, and giving him a fright. The money they'd paid for the room entitled them to a peaceful night's rest. Closing the door and locking it, he went to the phone on the table by the bed. Nancy, he was angry to see, hadn't even moved. She was sleeping soundly, a lump beneath the covers with only the very top of her head visible. He picked up the hand-set and dialed 'o' for the front desk.

It rang and rang but nobody answered.

Probably asleep at his post, Martin thought, remembering the tired-eyed desk clerk. *Doing what I'm supposed to be doing.*

He slid back into bed and turned out the light. If his uninvited visitors came knocking a second time, he wouldn't hesitate in throwing open the door–perhaps even arm himself with some heavy object to let them know he meant business. Yes, that was what he would do. Just let them try it.

He lay there, thinking of what might make an imposing looking weapon, trying to see the objects in the room and thinking of turning the light back on. And that was when he saw a shape near the window; unmistakably the outline of a man.

It can't be real. It can't be real.

The shape made its way across the room, settling into the chair facing the bed.

Martin yelped, his hand fumbling for the light switch on the lamp. A middle-aged man dressed in a tuxedo was seated in the chair next to the dresser, concentrating on opening the clasp of a silver cigarette case, seemingly unaware Martin was there.

"Nancy, wake up!" Martin cried, shaking her shoulder. "There's somebody in our room. Wake up!"

Nancy didn't move. The man, who had a black, pencil-thin moustache and slicked back hair, undid the clasp and removed a cigarette. Setting it between his lips, he returned the case to his inside pocket.

"Who are you?" Martin said. "What are you doing in my room?"

The man looked up suddenly, a look of surprise in his eyes and said, "You're not supposed to be able to see me."

What was this lunatic talking about? What was he doing in his room?

The well-dressed man's eyes moved away from Martin, flicking to the left. "Or them."

Standing in the shadows between the door and the bed were two women. A wordless shout escaped from Martin's mouth. The women moved forwards into the light, not so much walking as gliding. Upon seeing the women, Martin suddenly understood what these people were. His throat constricted, trapping the scream in his lungs, a timid gurgling squeal the only sound he could make.

The woman on the left, middle-aged, whose hair was done up in a beehive and wore a florid tent dress, would have had exquisitely fine features, had a gunshot not destroyed the upper left side of her face, demolishing both the high cheekbone and eye above it.

Her companion was much younger, no more than eighteen, and without signs of ruination to her face or body. She wore cut-off jeans, a crop top that ended just above a snake tattoo coiled around her navel, and muddy combat boots. There were numerous piercings in both ears, a diamond stud in the right side of her nose and a silver barbell in her left eyebrow. She wore her hair short, dyed black and pink and spiked.

Unlike the man in the tuxedo, or the bullet-blasted beehive woman, the girl contained far less of a look of substance. Martin could see right through her.

"What did I tell you?" said the girl to her companion. "I knew he'd be here. He's always here. Good thing we came back, otherwise we'd have missed him."

"Charles," Beehive said. "That was mean, yelling and scaring us away after Jane knocked on the door."

"It wasn't me," Charles nodded towards the bed. "It was him."

Both women looked at Martin.

Beehive frowned. "Him?"

"He sees us?" the girl asked. "How?"

"There's only one way," Charles replied.

Charles stood up and straightened his Dickie bow. "He sees us because somebody's trying to cling to him. Trying to stay where they're no longer entitled to be."

All three of them looked past Martin, their attention turning to the prone figure of Nancy beneath the covers. Martin realized the bedcovers his wife lay beneath did not rise and fall. She made no sound. He should have been able to hear her breathing, should have seen some movement.

Charles took a few steps towards the bed and the two women glided forwards. Now that they were closer to him, he was able to get a better look at all three and saw what had caused their deaths. He saw every detail of ruin on the left side of Beehive's face. He saw a hypodermic needle, before unnoticed, dangling from Jane's arm. And around Charles' neck, above the wing-tips and Dickie bow, was a purple ring left by a tightened loop of rope.

Somehow he knew that all three were suicides.

"You better come out," Jane said to the shape beneath the bed-spread. "You can't stay there forever."

The three visitors at the foot of the bed remained focused on Nancy's unmoving form, waiting.

"If she won't come out," Charles said. "We shall have to retrieve her."

The two women grinned at each other with mischievous delight. First Charles rose up into the air, then the women. They angled their bodies forward, all three floating horizontally across the bed. As they moved, their lower bodies became insubstantial, feet and legs turning to white wisps that trailed behind them.

"Ready..." Charles said when they were directly over Nancy.

"Set..." Beehive said.

"Go!" Jane said.

The ghosts plunged their hands straight down, arms disappearing through the bed covers, deep into Nancy's torso. They tugged at the thing resisting them, their faces straining. There was a plopping sound and first their arms and then their hands again became visible, moving up through the covers, clutching what looked like a mass of dense smoke.

Martin instructively reached out and tried to snatch it back from them. His hand passed straight through.

The ghosts moved away from the bed, remaining horizontal as they hovered in the air, the prize they'd claimed struggling to break free of their hold. The white mass tried to rise up, to ascend towards the ceiling, where a fissure had appeared, shafts of powerful light shooting down into the room.

"She's trying to cross over!" Charles yelled. "We better be quick. Ladies, did you dine tonight?"

"A few paltry scraps," Beehive said. "Nothing substantial."

"Then please, be my guests."

Needing no further encouragement, the two women clamped down with their mouths and tore at the mass of smoke, ripping with their teeth and swallowing the white stuff down. Almost instantaneously, Jane became less transparent. Beehive's face went through a reverse of its ruination, becoming as perfectly flawless as its opposite side. Charles waited until each woman had gobbled a few more mouthfuls, then fell to it, his face pressing against the smoke, his debonair deportment stripped away as he frenziedly feasted.

Martin heard it then—an anguished scream that he knew belonged to his wife. Martin screamed, too. Screamed and screamed. They were eating her. Eating Nancy's life-force—her soul. And there wasn't a thing he could do to stop them.

What remained of the smoke formed into Nancy's facial features—not as he had known her last, but as he'd known her first, when they were young and he was certain the moment he saw her that she was the woman he was born to love. She shrieked in pain as they went on devouring her.

Sobbing, Martin begged them to stop.

The sight of Nancy's young face in such unimaginable agony was too much to take. Martin blacked out—or woke up. For only a moment seemed to pass between him being trapped in the nightmare from which there seemed no escape, to him lying in the bed, sunlight streaming in through the window, the sound of cars passing outside on the freeway.

He turned immediately to his wife and tried to rouse her, still uncertain if what he'd experienced could have possibly been real.

His wife didn't move. He touched her face, feeling coldness where there should have been warmth.

Nancy was dead.

* * *

Charles lay on the bed, his eyes closed, breathing deeply.

"Are you asleep?" Martin asked. "Or only pretending?"

"Our kind never sleep, as you know," Charles said with his eyes still closed. "But I do so enjoy the memory of it—of that peaceful state of being. I miss it enough that I try to fool myself that it's something I can still do."

"Where are your friends?"

Charles opened his eyes and looked at his visitor.

"Friends?" Charles said. "I keep no friends."

"The great Charles Tucker," Martin said. "The notorious reveller and ladies man, without a single friend?"

Charles raised himself onto his elbows and smiled. "You seem to have me at a disadvantage. Who are you?"

Martin returned the smile. "You don't recognize me? I was lying right there the last time you saw me. Right where you are now. Where are they, Charles? Where are the two women? I know they're around here someplace, trying to hide from me."

Martin watched the other man study his face, searching for a clue.

Then his eyes widened slightly.

"The old man..." Charles said, concern creeping into his voice. "That was you?"

"Was," Martin said.

He had stopped being the old man the day he died. The death had been chosen, not natural, and the overdose of sleeping pills meant he would never know that *other* place. Seeing Nancy destroyed filled him with a thirst for vengeance that far exceeded in intensity every emotion he'd ever experienced, except of course, his love for her. Now Nancy was gone. Gone forever. She would not be there, waiting beyond the light, Without her, he wanted no part of it.

Martin removed his lumberjack shirt and placed it on the chair.

Charles looked past him to where the shirt lay draped over the chair back. He ran a hand through his slicked back hair, placed a cigarette in his mouth, fingers trembling.

"Well, that's a first," Charles said, failing to make the observation sound casual, the authority he'd asserted the last time they met gone from his voice. "Never seen one of our kind do that without it disappearing."

"You're afraid of me," Martin realized. "All the time I've spent trying to find the courage to meet you here, and you're afraid of me. I'd built you up as something unstoppable. You're just a parasite. Just like all the rest."

"The rest?"

"Others like you," Martin said. "Eaters of the dead. Some far more powerful than you, Charles. Not that I knew. Not until now."

One of the two women—the living guests—occupying the room this night passed through Martin, unaware he was there. The other, her sister, lay on the bed, looking through Charles at the television, blind to the fact he lay beside her.

"Are you ready to die once and for all?" Martin asked.

Charles licked his lips. "Would you mind terribly if I finished my cigarette?"

"A last request?" Martin asked. "Go 'head."

Charles went to take a drag of the cigarette and found it had turned to ash. His fingers began to fragment, tiny beads of light pulling apart to float through the air. As though magnetically drawn towards Martin, they entered him through his torso.

"Wait, you've already started to consume me!" Charles cried, his hand now gone completely, the un-knitting process moving along his wrist and forearm. "Stop! I'm not ready. Please!"

"Don't worry," Martin said. "You'll have time to come to terms with it. I intend to do this slowly."

RED RAIN

DANE T. HATCHELL

The Daily News headlined a story a few days before it happened. **Earth to Pass Through Cloud of Cosmic Dust**. The article didn't provide much information of what the dust was composed of, nor of why it was now in Earth's orbit. Not even a **Spectacular Meteor Shower!** was predicted. The headline appeared to be just an overblown non-story designed to sell more newspapers.

But no one could have predicted what did happen, and no one could have prevented it either. As the Earth met the mass of dust, areas around the world where rain was falling turned red. The clouds blushed as the rains fell, and then the towns, fields and roads were painted crimson.

Mark Roberts was living alone, a consequence of ten years of a bad marriage and a gambling problem. It was close to noon that day when the rain began, but he wasn't going to let a little rain ruin his lunch plans. The cafe was only six blocks away, so he put on some old sneakers, grabbed his umbrella, and made his way outside.

The sky was unusually dark despite the rain, and cars crept by with their lights on, their wipers slinging water. The sidewalks had a few less people than normal; some respectfully jogged past others for the shelter of an awning.

Mark's first warning was the drops of rain dripping from his umbrella. At first he thought the rain was washing off a newly painted building, but as he continued, the water on the sidewalks and streets turned a pinkish color, and a fear started to swell inside him at the odd occurrence.

A woman screamed from behind him and he instinctually spun around to see what was going on.

Two well dressed women in their sixties were rolling back and forth in the street. They were scratching and clawing at each other in savage abandon. Before Mark could react, more screams and cries erupted from all around him. People up and down the street were turning on each other in physical hand to hand combat. Mark was stunned, mass chaos raged all about as the rain stained everything red.

A voice yelled from behind him, "Oh no you won't, I'll get you first!"

Mark spun around again, just in time to see a greasy teenager running for him full blast. He ducked to his right, missing the outstretched arms, and the boy bounced off Mark's hip. The boy hit the sidewalk on his hands and knees. A far away look held his eyes, and then he started crawling back to Mark. "No, no you won't! I won't let you!"

The frenzied atmosphere of violence surrounding Mark made him shift into survival mode. The boy crawled like a wounded beast straight for him and Mark slammed his right foot square into the boy's temple, the teen rolling on his back, his face frozen to the sky as the rains continued to stain everything a deep scarlet.

Madness, turmoil, and hate charged the air. Mark ran down the block and tried to enter the cafe. The door was locked and there were tens of faces staring out in shock and disbelief. Mark pounded his fist and pulled on the handle, but the door wouldn't budge.

A sharp pain to his back pulled him back into the fray; a man in a business suit had jabbed him with a closed umbrella. Mark pulled the umbrella from his attacker's hand and jerked him off balance, causing the man to fall forward. Mark threw an upper cut to his jaw and sent him to the ground. Without thinking, Mark smashed the heel of his shoe into the man's nose until the left side of his face caved in.

Up ahead, two more men were fighting and Mark recognized the one getting beaten was his neighbor, Mr. Crandle.

"Hey! Hey! Stop it!" Mark cried and grabbed the attacking man from behind and embraced him with a half nelson. Crandle came alive and pulled out a pocket knife and stuck it in the held man's groin, pulling the blade up to the sternum. Blood, intestines, and bile spilled onto the sidewalk, and his screams added to the chorus of the others. Mark threw the dying man aside just as Crandle reached out and grabbed Mark by the throat.

"Damn it, Crandle! Has everyone gone fucking crazy?" Mark yelled, taking a step back and sweeping his right forearm against the wrist of the choking hands. Crandle lost his grip and was surprised with a kick to his midsection. He fell to one knee, gasping for breath, then fell flat on his back as he received a kick to the head.

The rain was still falling, but no one noticed that it wasn't red anymore. Clear rain now fell from the skies, but it didn't wash the red or the madness away. But something did twist in the minds of the infected. The stained street people were turning their attention on those inside the buildings now. They weren't driven to fight each other anymore and were working in unison. Two grabbed a waste barrel and smashed it into a dress shop window and were making their way in. Mark had the urge to help them, but his brain was battling the urge with rationality. His mind was scrambling, adjusting to the unexpected reality around him. He was scared and confused and just wanted to be a million miles away. Mark turned and ran, running as fast as he could. He had to run around cars and jump over the dead. The streets were wet and slick, but he ran without care.

He came upon a motorcycle laid down on its side, the motor still running, the rear tire slowly spinning. There was no sign of the owner, and it didn't matter anyway escape was the primordial force driving him. He lifted the motorcycle, straining his lower back in the process, climbed onto it, gunned the throttle and sped away.

The roads were clogged with vehicles, and he had to take any open path available. He drove down sidewalks, through an alley, and even had to back track a block or two just to keep moving. The violence continued, with the red stained people showing no mercy to those not marked.

Motorist in vehicles were being pulled out of broken windows. Shots rang out and bodies were strewn about as Mark attempted to make them all a blur as the bike sped faster and faster.

He made his way out of town and hit the open highway. The wind stung his face but his mind was too numb to care. The rain was letting up, and the clouds were breaking for the afternoon sun. Few cars passed and he wondered if they had any idea of the madness that had just gone down in town. One thing for certain, he wasn't going to stop and warn them. He looked down at his hands; all his skin was colored red, and little bumps were starting to form. He maneuvered his head to see his face in the mirror; it was the same color as his hands. No rational explanation came to mind. There were no factories or chemical plants near the city for this to be some type of chemical release. He had never heard of a volcano doing something like this in the past. It did remind him of one of the plagues from a story out of the Bible, but this seemed more an act of the Devil, and not of God.

He was leaving civilization behind him, taking every back road that would lead him to undeveloped countryside. He needed to be alone and collect his thoughts; he wanted just to curl up in a ball and sleep forever.

Two hours passed when an old gas station came into view, his fuel gauge pointing on **E**. There were two pumps in front, and a single garage on one side. There was no sign of any life, although his eye did catch the bed of an old pickup truck behind the building as he made the turn into the driveway. He pulled up to a pump and turned off the motorcycle. He sat there a moment and rubbed his face and his eyes. Oil and grime rubbed off, but not the red.

His dismount reminded him of the pulled muscle in his back, and he walked in a small circle to loosen stiff limbs. The gas pump looked ancient, not even a slot for a credit card. He removed the nozzle and lifted the handle, relieved to see the pump come to life. While filling the tank on the motorcycle, he noticed how quiet it was, not even a bird chirping. The world around him no longer felt the same. When the tank reached full, he replaced the cap and cradled the nozzle. He pulled out his wallet and counted eight dollars in cash; it was a little short for his purchase. It was time to settle up with the proprietor, and he hoped the owner took plastic.

Mark walked up to an old wood door and reached for the door-knob. Through the glass he could see a withered old man looking back at him. Without any warning, a loud blast went off and the door exploded with a bang and a flash. Splinters and dust blinded Mark momentarily, and something hot sliced through his left side.

Mark fell back and cursed; he touched his side and felt torn wet flesh. Instead of feeling fear, he was overtaken by rage. He lowered his right shoulder and ran at the door, throwing his body into it. Another loud blast went off as the door broke open and slammed into the old man. The revolver he was holding was knocked from his hand, to go flying down an aisle lined with odds and ends. The old man was lying on his back and Mark was on him with unnatural speed.

His fingers sunk deep into the old man's leathery neck, cutting off any hope for a breath of air. The old man's eyes bulged, and bits of tobacco and spittle flew out of his mouth as he choked. Mark felt hate, intense hate, and an uncontrollable intent to destroy. He removed one hand from his throat while firmly maintaining his death grip with the other. He grabbed the left eyelid of the old man and tugged on it until it ripped off. Blood streamed down his face as the old man attempted to scream. Mark then stuck his index finger into the eye and pushed and dug and wiggled his finger about. Mark wanted to abuse this man, he wanted him suffer, to feel pain. He wanted to dig so deep that he would reach brain, and then pull pieces out bit by bit.

The old man's struggle weakened, and his thrashing slowed to a twitch. As the life passed out of the old man, so too, did the violent madness that gripped Mark.

He looked at the gore on his finger, but it didn't bother him, and neither did the red color of his skin anymore. He wiped his hands on his thighs and straightened out his clothing. The corpse on the floor was no longer of any interest to him.

An annoying high pitch sound caught his attention. A message from the Emergency Alert System was about to play from a radio behind the cash register.

"This is an Emergency Action Notification requested by the White House. All broadcast stations will follow activation procedures in the EAS Operating Handbook for a national level emergency. The President of the United States or his representative will shortly deliver a message over the Emergency Alert System."

The message continued to repeat itself, and Mark scanned through the stations but found that all of them had defaulted to the EAS alert. His mind started to get cloudy again with confusion, and his left shoulder itched in an unusual way. There were noises hiding, lurking behind his consciousness. Shadows, whispers, and voices he could sense but not understand. He broke from his internal conflict and felt again the need to flee.

He went to the cooler and pulled out a can of soda. He opened it and took a deep swig and came up for air. The cool drink felt good to his throat, but by the time it reached his stomach, it felt like a lead weight. He let out an odorous burp, and though he was still thirsty, he tossed the can to the floor. He grabbed a bottle of water and drank it down, and this time there was no discomfort.

Snatching a plastic bag from the counter, he gathered basic supplies of lunch meat, chips, and more water. He noticed the revolver on the floor when he stepped on the barrel; he picked it up and shoved it between his belt and pants. Going back behind the counter, he located a half full box of bullets and shoved them in his pocket. He didn't take the money from the cash register, and he didn't give the dead man on the floor a second thought as he stepped over him to leave.

The road was his only companion for the next few hours, riding further and further away from civilization. He tried not to think to hard on what had happen thus far. With all the unknowns, anything he decided was nothing more than a gamble away. Eventually though, weariness set in, and an old farm house set far off the road seemed like his best chance for rest.

An eight foot wide dirt driveway dented with pot holes led off the road to a small rustic old house. Sections of fencing were missing, suggesting that in its best day livestock were once cared for there. Mark rode slowly to within a few feet of the front porch, his eyes roaming for signs of life. He came to a complete stop and turned off the engine, then lowered the kickstand onto gravel-impregnated clay. There was fresh evidence of oil and antifreeze on the ground; another vehicle had recently parked here also.

Mark walked up four creaking wooden steps and onto the porch, his footsteps echoing hollow in his ears. A lone wooden rocker sat next to an ancient ashtray on a metal pedestal. The ashtray was nearly overflowing with cigarette butts, and the dark gray stains of ashes peppered the boards underneath. Mark banged loudly against the screened door and this time he positioned his body to the side to avoid being shot at again. The unsecured screened door bounced inward off the main door back and forth with each knock. He yelled, "hello!" trying to make himself as obvious as he could, but there was no response.

He made a quick tour around the house, and after peering through a back window, he believed the house was empty. He made his way to a workshop in the back. In it was an old tractor, some gas powered tools, and garden implements. There was an old working well behind the workshop and a small vegetable garden that was at the season's end, the contents rotting in silence. The small, odd-looking building standing alone was the outhouse.

Mark walked back to the house with a two foot axe he'd found in the workshop. He retrieved his supplies from the motorcycle and used the axe to pry open the main door, preserving as much of the door frame as possible.

The door opened to a small living room/kitchen combination. There was one couch and an old wooden table with some opened mail and recent copies of Popular Mechanics and a few other magazines. A weathered bookshelf housed many tattered Old Western paperbacks from the likes of Louis Lamour. The kitchen didn't have a refrigerator, and he realized the house had no electricity either. A Coleman stove provided heat for cooking and a wood stove for heat in the winter. Shelves of canned soup and vegetables looked like the main dietary staples of choice for the home's occupants. The only other room contained a single bed, which lay unmade, revealing dingy white sheets.

Mark began to question if he was as removed from civilization as he thought. The owner must visit a local town to be able to pick up mail and supplies. Still, the house was off the main grid, and he wondered what or who the owner might be hiding from.

Mark's shoulder began the same unusual itch again. It surprised him that he was agitated more by the itch than the flesh wound on his side. He suddenly realized his shoulder was itching in the same location as his medical implant.

Mark had an experimental anti-depressant pellet implanted by a V.A. doctor to help control his gambling urges. It had been in place for a few months and it actually seemed to help him be in more control of his life. But his body was fighting the implant; and the drugs he'd taken for infection were fighting the specter in his head.

He was feeling warm and wondered if he was running a fever, fatigue was now his master. He took his bag of supplies and sat on the dusty old couch, opened a bottle of water and drank it down. He was feeling hungry, but not in the usual way. He opened a pack of pressed ham and pulled out half its contents and took a bite. The flavor was pleasing but the salt in the processed meat made him even thirstier. As he chewed, the meat seemed to expand in his mouth. His throat began to close as if it were preventing him from swallowing. He grimaced a bit and chewed wider and wider until he thought he might gag. He spit out the meat into a magazine, his throat opened again as he drank more water. He opened a bag of chips and tried to eat one, but his body rejected that, too.

Mark finished his water and pulled his shoes off. There was no more fight left in him, he hoped he would wake before the owner came back but he knew he had to rest. He stretched out on the couch and adjusted his body in a fetal position, his eyes closed, and he fell asleep.

*   *   *

When Mark awoke, it took him a few minutes to sort out his situation. The red rain and the events that followed seemed like a surreal dream. He pulled himself up and stretched, his mouth dry as cotton.

His watch informed him that it was around noon. To his surprise, his watch calendar was three days later than when he went to sleep. He rubbed his eyes and looked at the functions on the watch, but everything seemed in order. He supposed that the date could have gotten reset during his escape of the city, but his body told him that he had been asleep for a very long time.

He noticed an old battery radio on a shelf; he flipped it on, adjusted the knob for volume and tuned in a station.

"The following is an Emergency Alert System bulletin, this is not a test. The head of the U.S. Department of Homeland Security's Federal Emergency Management Agency under the authorization of the President of the United States has issued a shelter in place warning for all U.S. citizens. The red rains that fell on May 19th carried an infectious parasite, and the infected victims are visually identified by the red color of their skin. The parasites are short lived without a human host. Birds, fish, and all other animals have not been infected, and water exposed to the rain has no contamination issues and is safe to drink. Avoid any contact with any infected human. Reports of violence from the infected have been issued from all areas of the country. Additionally, a new disease with Swine flu like symptoms has been reported in rain affected and unaffected areas. Cover your nose and mouth when you cough or sneeze and..."

Mark turned the radio off; he'd learned everything he needed to know, and it all made perfect sense after what he'd experienced. The parasites were taking over his body and his mind but the chemicals from the medical implant were somehow interfering and it was allowing him to retain his human will. So now, it wasn't a matter of *if,* but a matter of *when* they would totally take over his mind.

He opened a bottle of water and while drinking, contemplated his next move. The farmhouse seemed to be a safe place to stay. It didn't look like who ever owned the house would be coming back, but he knew he had to move on.

'They' were calling to him. He briefly thought of putting the revolver to his head while he still had some control. But that thought disappeared as the alien consciousness grew a bit larger within him.

A trip to the workshop found enough gas to top off the motorcycle's gas tank. With an uncertain destiny now, Mark left the house with the pull of the 'colony' as his guide.

The wind and the road told strange tales as the twin cylinders hummed between his legs as he drove down the highway. His shoulder continued to itch, and it was visibly swelling now. As he rode on, a hunger inside him grew; the ride was dehydrating and his tongue felt thick in his mouth.

An old, double-wide trailer covered by a framed metal roof was coming up in the distance. Something inside was drawing him there, and the choice wasn't his own. Mark slowed and decided to pull off the road and make his way on foot. He turned off the engine and rolled to a stop, dismounted, and pushed the motorcycle off the road to hide it behind a big elm tree with sagging limbs. He felt it best to approach through the woods, and enter the property from the rear. The brush and trees provided good cover as he snuck towards the trailer, but it also prevented him from seeing if anyone was watching him.

Soon, the woods were cleared and a small barn came into sight. There were two cows tied nearby chewing hay. With the revolver in hand, Mark slowly made his way toward the main door.

Inside the barn, there was a lone man in his late thirties. A Ruger mini-14 rested on its stock against the wall a few feet away and he was busy reloading ammunition with a single stage press.

Mark inched forward with the gun cocked and pointed at the man. "Don't move," he said dryly. The man jerked his head in Mark's direction and his eyes went wide with fear. The man made a lunge for the Ruger, and Mark squeezed off two shots. The first went wide but the second hit the man directly in the head.

Mark didn't expect this; he didn't even have a plan as to what he was going to do after capturing the people here. He needed food and water, but he didn't know what he could eat.

A loud bang came from an aluminum door at the far end of the trailer and a woman came out screaming, carrying a rifle.

"Jessie! Jessie!"

Mark took one step out of the door, raised the revolver, and fired two shots into her chest. She stumbled and fell forward as blood seeped from her death wounds.

Mark loaded the revolver with shells from his pocket and made a dash to the trailer, in full war mode now. The alien influence inside him turned any fear he might have felt to rage; he would leave no one alive. He placed the revolver in the close quarter battle position, turned, and charged into the open trailer door.

He was in the kitchen and Mark quickly moved from room to room. He checked behind doors and underneath the bed, behind a shower curtain and inside closets. He found nothing of any danger, but he also found that he wasn't alone in the trailer.

In a worn baby bed that looked generations old, lay a child a few months in age, dressed in pink pajamas. She was sobbing softly and mouthing her left thumb.

Mark's heart melted and the rage inside turned to tears of guilt and shame. He lifted the tiny infant with the utmost care and placed her chest next to his. Mark's gaze focused on a mirror in the room as he gently rocked the baby from side to side. His hair was a tattered mess and the red face staring back at him looked like Satan himself.

What had he become, what was he becoming?

He rubbed the back of the child's head and felt the silkiness of her hair. The sweet smell of powder reminded him of his own child, of the first time he held his firstborn, the responsibility that had swelled inside him.

It was a boy, his son, and there would be nothing on Earth that could ever come between him and his love and care for his child. No matter how bad things became, he would always make sure his child would have food, clothing, and love. Love like Mark wished his parents had shown him. He vowed he would teach his child, he would challenge his child, he would make and give his tiny baby anything and everything the world had to offer to make him happy.

The child that he now held, this child represented what his son meant to him, and it represented all of what the thousands of years of evolution had accomplished in man. Mark held her tightly and pushed his lips softly against her soft cheek, as large tears streamed down his face.

Mankind was the Universe's greatest creation, and somehow Mark realized that he may be the key to saving it. The implant gave him an edge in humanity's favor. He still had some control of his mind, and he could integrate into the 'colony' and perhaps find a way to destroy it.

Even if not all could be killed, as the last hope of mankind, he would do all he could to sabotage their efforts. He would use his military background and make improvised explosives and slaughter as many as he could. He could take them out one by one, whatever it took. Mankind needed a savior, and God or fate or whatever, had chosen him.

A swell of frenzied euphoria washed down from his head to his feet, a power unknown that charged every fiber of his being. His mind became one with a powerful force, and a sweet release deflated his cosmic journey back to reality.

He became aware of his surroundings again; his shoulder was bleeding at the implant.

He looked down to see his hands were covered in blood, as were his mouth and clothing.

The pink pajamas now bloody, lay torn on the floor, and there wasn't much left to the tiny body, the flesh was juicy and Mark had been very hungry.

The alien consciousness had finally won, and Mark was at peace within himself. He wiped his hands on a blanket and made his way to the kitchen. He opened a few drawers until he located a knife. With a slight jab and a small twist, the hunk of skin housing the implant fell to the floor. The cut bled, but the wound wasn't deep, and the blood coagulated quickly.

The oneness of the colony was calling him; a pod wasn't far away. Mark left the trailer and made his way back to the motorcycle. The woman he shot lay on her back with flies dancing in the gaping holes in her chest. The thought of dead flesh brought feelings of revulsion; it had all the appeal of excrement. His mind turned to the living flesh that so refreshed him moments ago. The fruit of the child was life giving, with its succulent pulp of meat. Mark straddled the motorcycle and started the engine, knowing his life was now predetermined.

*   *   *

Time was no longer a concern, the individual did not exist, the collective was all. Mark resurfaced back into a civilization that now looked like a war zone. Abandoned cars and trucks littered the highway, making it impassable. He maneuvered the motorcycle as well as he could and eventually turned at a green road sign that had **COUNTY PRISON** printed in bold white letters.

The prison was a mile down the road, next to a small, defunct air field, both a product of the 1950's. The prison had long ago reached capacity and several expansions were evident.

Mark's first contact with his brethren was without fanfare. The guards stood idly by as he drove through the main gate. The red faces looking back at him had a sense of knowing, of sharing, of belonging. Mark parked the motorcycle and turned off the engine, a growing sense of exhaustion pulling at his will to stay awake. His brothers and sisters were busy as ants, moving about at the tasks instinctually set for them, and he made sure to stay out of their way.

He entered the north wing and walked onto the main floor; it also served as the dining area. The floors were made of dark spotted terrazzo; it hadn't been cleaned in a while. Above, there were two stories of cells that circled around the main floor. Some of the cells were empty, but many were occupied, a look of fear frozen on their faces as they looked out onto the floor.

An internal clock struck and a number of the red-stained hybrids flooded into the wing and next to Mark, as others made their way up to the cells. Ungodly screams of terror reverberated against the concrete walls, as eight humans were extracted and forced to the dining area below.

The overpowered prisoners were strapped to blood-stained tables and were stripped of their clothing. Mark watched without the least bit of care and concern as his ravenous brethren bit and chewed and gnawed and gnashed at the bodies. The symphony of screams eventually turned to gurgles, and the gurgles gave way to silence. Mark made sure to feed as well, sometimes having to shove another out of his way to get at the bloody meat.

The bones and gore that wasn't consumed were scraped into plastic bags. Those that fed washed up in the kitchen, then marched in silence as they left, Mark with them.

They came to a barracks full of military-style cots. Almost half of them were full, the occupants oblivious to the new arrivals. Mark came to the first available cot and laid his tired body down

After one feeds, one must rest.

*　*　*

His awakening coincided with those who had joined him in his digestion period, and he was unaware that three full days had passed. Each of them pulled themselves up and staggered to the bathroom to relieve themselves. The water pressure was low, but enough to evacuate the toilets and to provide cold water for the sinks. After changing clothing, Mark and the others made their way back to the main floor of the prison wing.

There was no longer a need for words, thoughts and feelings were transferred from one to another in a telepathic bond. The group collective shared the greater goals; the individual sensed his designated duty. Mark and his group were hunter/gatherers, and something was very wrong with the food supply that they had on hand.

The humans in residence, as well as most of the humans newly captured, were in a sickly condition. They would eat no food, and when force feeding was tried, the humans couldn't keep it down. There were a few new captures that were very healthy, with nice plump meat beneath their water-bloated skin. They needed to find more like them, and to bring them back as quickly as possible.

They separated into four groups of four, and left on foot to search the closest town.

The sun was in the noon position as Mark's group made its way into a small, neighborhood. The old wooden frame houses were built sometime in the late 1970's, and were empty, offering nothing for the hungry pod back at the prison. The group moved on in silence, scanning every direction for movement. But no life was evident, only the wind in the trees.

The sun crossed the sky and the group moved down a highway of abandoned vehicles. From up ahead, a metal on metal sound rang out, attracting their attention. The four split into groups of two and maneuvered using the abandoned vehicles to shield their approach to the incoming sound.

Two human men were in front of an auto garage, using a hammer and a screwdriver as they tried to knock a hole in a gas tank on an old truck. The main entry to the office was chained closed, as was the four vehicle service doors behind them.

Mark and his partner made their way towards the humans as the other two men did from the opposite side. The humans didn't appear to have much success with what they were doing, and the banging on the gas tank continued. The two groups stealthily moved to the sides and then doubled back to the unsuspecting prey. They positioned themselves for a two-sided attack, and right before they made their surprise move, a human yelp rang out.

The two humans popped up from the truck and ran through an open single door that led into the main service center. With un-hesitant speed, the two hunting groups joined as one as they entered the door in pursuit.

The four ran head long into darkness and straight into the wait-ing nets that fell upon them from above. Before any had the chance to reach for a side arm, twenty humans came at them from all sides with wooden clubs, and beat them into submission.

"Get their guns! That guy over there has two!" a man yelled. He wore a sweatshirt with the local police logo on the breast pocket, signifying he was in law enforcement.

"Is this all there is, any more coming?" another man asked. By the shirt he wore, he was the local high school coach.

"Just these four, the area is clear," the first man replied. He lit up a cigarette and held the match until it went cold. He hadn't smoked in years, but it helped him cope with events of the past week. "Get'em on the stretchers and let's move on back to the school." He keyed his two-way radio. "We're heading out, fall back and cover our rear."

An elementary school was serving as a makeshift fortress for forty families. Concertina wire was haphazardly stretched to reinforce the chain-link fencing that originally served to keep the school children from wandering off. Armed sentries manned strategic positions, and lookouts used binoculars to scan the area. Boys as old as twelve and women as old as sixty shared in the duties of running the school and keeping everyone safe and fed.

The men arrived with the four infected prisoners—Mark in-cluded—and were given passage into the compound. Wide eyes stared and stomachs churned as the bound, red-skinned devils passed by.

The ex-cop was in the lead as they walked down the main hall, the low ceilings making him feel like a giant. The classrooms had been converted into living quarters, and multiple families now shared the space. He didn't have any idea how long they would, or could, go on living like this. Life was so different than it was before, and there was nothing to distract from the hardships of life other than family and friends.

There were no independent television or radio news reports. The only information they had was from the Government EAS. It had warned them of the rain, and had warned them of the parasite in the rain.

Fortunately, in time, a report was issued that would change the dynamics of the infection; a treatment for the virus was given.

The parasite only directly affected the people on whom the red rains originally touched. But the DNA in an infected victim quickly mutated and jumped to the non parasitic human population and had caused a worldwide pandemic. People suffered flu-like symptoms in the beginning, but just a day or two later their bodies had lost the ability to digest and process food. Had been working round the clock to find a cure, and had found an antibody to treat the virus until a real cure could be found. Since the announcement two days ago, the forty families had benefited from the treatment, and their stomachs were now able to accept food again.

The ex-cop and his crew rounded a corner and pushed a set of double doors open. Mark stirred a little and let out a groan and someone said, "I think this one's awake."

"Doesn't matter, don't hit him again, you might kill him," the ex-cop said. He made his way past a line of people and the crowd assisted in placing a stretcher holding each of the four prisoners on each table.

Mark groaned again.

"Hey, we got any more anesthesia? I don't like it when they holler," a woman said.

"No, we can't waste any on them. We need to keep the medical supplies for ourselves," the ex-cop instructed. "Just put some duct tape over his mouth and let's get on with it. Reverend, you ready?"

Reverend Pike, a man in his late fifties with a bald pate and a pale complexion, nodded and cleared his throat, saying a prayer in sync with the noise of the duct tape being pulled from the roll. "Thank you, Lord, for the many blessings that You bring to us each day. Please instruct us in our time of need that we may learn. And that You will see fit to save us and to accept our praises as worthy of Your goodness. In His name, grant us a new way. Amen."

Mark was fully awake now and those close by could hear the air whistling faster and faster out of his nostrils as he looked around, not understanding what was happening.

"Well, they ain't gonna eat themselves, so dig in!" the ex-cop said as he picked up a knife and sliced off a thin piece of Mark's thigh.

Mark's vocal cords rattled in his throat and snot ran from his nose and onto his cheek as he shrieked in utter agony as he was eaten alive.

The rest eagerly followed, making sure to leave enough so that everyone would get a fair share. Two days ago the thought of eating a person was almost unimaginable, but the mutated virus had altered the chemical needs of its victims, and the red flesh of the hybrids was as delicious as life itself.

"Hey, Dad, what happens if the scientists don't find a cure for the virus?" asked a small child, who was almost ten and had always been an inquisitive boy. "If we can only eat the red guys, what will we eat when they're gone?"

The boy's father shook his head and said, "Don't worry about that now, son. Just eat your meat before it dies."

THE THING ABOUT SKEPTICS

MARK RIVETT

I've always considered myself to be someone grounded firmly in reality. I'm always convinced that whatever 'supernatural' experience occurs, there's always a rational explanation. Now, I certainly do believe that the tales of the macabre and supernatural that I've heard are believed by those that tell them–but the mind is a tricky thing.

The imagination has a tendency to fill in gaps or even create entire scenarios that simply did not occur. A curtain may float with the grace of the restless dead, but it's still a curtain no matter how life-like it seems to behave. A settling house may echo with disembodied footsteps, but it's still just a settling house no matter how rhythmic the footsteps. If I can sit and listen to someone exaggerate a funny story about an event that I was present for a mere few hours prior into something incredibly comical but blatantly untrue, then the truth in any story can be lost to the imagination of years and decades of fading memory.

Throw variables like darkness, wind, and alcohol into the equation...and you'd think there was a ghost hiding behind every corner, a disembodied spirit lingering in every basement, a restless apparition trapped in every closet. I'm sorry to break the news to you, but you didn't see a ghost. You didn't hear the voice of your long-dead relative. Whatever it was you saw or heard, I assure you, there's a perfectly reasonable explanation that doesn't involve the spirit of the love child of Big-Foot and the Loch Ness Monster trapped for eternity in your attic.

Despite my stubborn skepticism about anything supernatural, I have an avid interest. I enjoy ghost-hunting television shows and movies about the living dead. I research and occasionally visit supposedly haunted places around my home in Pittsburgh, PA. I always have time to listen to any ghost story anyone has to tell. But, when personal accounts of ghosts and spirits are exchanged between groups of friends, that's something I never do... I never tell my ghost story.

My tale is different than all the other stories out there for mine is real.

I keep my story to myself, but it's not because I don't think people will believe it. In fact, I think most people—the same people who swear up and down they've captured a ghost on video that turns out to be someone's shadow, the same people who point at 'orbs' and confess to you that the dust, pollen, and insects that reflect the camera flash is a measurement of spiritual activity— these people will certainly believe my story. I keep my story to myself because I'm uncomfortable with ambivalence; my complete disbelief in the supernatural despite having had a very potent supernatural experience. This experience is the one unexplainable event in my life that I'm absolutely certain happened exactly the way I'm about to describe it to you. Seems arrogant, right? My story is true and everyone else's is a figment of their overactive imagination? So, I'm an arrogant and cynical jerk; I don't really care. Despite my ambivalence, this story is fact and telling it in this way protects me from the inevitable question of, *So, if you saw a ghost, how is it that you don't believe in ghosts?*

I was nineteen years old and had moved from Michigan to Pittsburgh to begin my college education. The school in which I was enrolled did not have dorms in the typical sense of the word. Rather, it had off-campus apartments.

The apartment complex I lived in was Allegheny Center, Building 7, apartment 817. Allegheny Center, Building 7 has a history of being haunted. This reputation is largely suspect, however, due to the substances in which my fellow classmates had a habit of indulging—both often and in copious amounts.

What's more, there have been deaths at Allegheny Center. I know there have been deaths because I lived there when at least two students either accidentally or deliberately fell from balconies to the concrete parking lot below. I also remember a story the student housing lady told us about a girl who let a stranger into the building and ended up stabbed to death in her apartment. I don't know for certain if that story is true or just a cautionary fiction woven to keep the students from allowing strangers into the building.

Regardless, there was certainly no shortage of ghost stories pouring out of Allegheny Center, Building 7. Does that mean the place was haunted? No...that means that there were plenty of college kids on drugs with plenty of ammunition to tell, re-tell, and exaggerate the limitless bizarre sounds, sights, and even smells that were so common. But that doesn't mean it wasn't haunted, either, for the truth is that it *was* haunted.

Anyway, I lived in a studio apartment pretty much alone. Lance, my roommate from Ohio, was an enormous jerk. Fortunately, he was never around because he was failing all of his classes and had decided to drop out. As a result, he spent most of his time at home in Ohio, and I had the entire apartment to myself.

It's difficult to describe the layout of the apartment, but—in a nut shell—it was a long rectangle. There was a metal door in the corner of the short edge of the rectangle that served as entry to the apartment. From the door there stretched a long hallway with a connected bathroom and closet on one side. The hallway opened into the studio where my roommate's bed sat against the wall across from the hallway and my bed sat on the other side of the room separated by the television. A small kitchen sat open toward the studio. It wasn't much, but probably way more than most college freshmen ever had.

I had a habit of using a dumb bell to crack the door open when I slept. I was used to getting visitors at all hours of the night, and I was always up for hanging out with friends... particularly female friends. I was, and still am, an incredibly light sleeper so I wasn't concerned with anyone slipping into my room while I was sleeping to steal my things.

On this particular night, Lance was in Ohio as usual, and I propped the door open with a dumb bell...also as usual. I turned the overhead light off, and the lamp by my bed cast the apartment in a warm yellow glow mixed with long dark shadows. I slipped into bed and pulled the cord on my bedside lamp to shroud the studio in darkness... the only illumination was the long shaft of yellow light that stretched from the cracked door into the apartment and onto Lance's bed. The usual sounds of the building danced their way into the silence. A door opening and closing here, some laughter there, the muffled sound of someone's television in the apartment above me, or the thumping of someone listening to music with their bass up; typical sounds of student living that always kept me awake for a while before I grew accustomed to them.

As I lay awake in my bed, I heard the unmistakable sound of my apartment door swinging open and the sliver of light cast across Lance's bed across from me expanded to frame the shadow of a figure moving into my room. I heard the sound of the heavy metal door slamming into the dumb bell and watched as the shadowy figure emerged from the hallway to stand in the apartment for a moment before sitting on my roommate's bed. Coldness uncharacteristic of the outside hall began to fill the apartment. The room was dark but the sliver of light from the cracked door clearly outlined the person now sitting in my apartment facing me.

This was not usual. When someone visited me they usually announced themselves before turning on the overhead light or, if it was a girl, she would have left the light off and sat on my bed. But who would just wander into my apartment and sit silently across from me?

"Lance?" I asked as I sat up.

Of course it was Lance. He must have returned early from Ohio, and after a night of drinking or whatever he had been up to, was merely collecting his bearings before slipping into bed.

There was no answer. The figure cast in shadow simply sat there. I could see no eyes, no face...I couldn't even determine if the figure was male or female. Despite the lack of detail, I could feel the person watching me–the same way you can look across a crowded room to make eye contact with someone who's been watching you.

"Are you okay? Are you drunk?" I asked.

Again no answer was given, but the figure seemed to cock its head. Maybe this wasn't Lance.

"Carolyn?" I asked again.

Carolyn was a very good friend of mine who might visit me, but would not slip into bed with me. She and I had become close friends early on, but it was nothing more than platonic. Of course it was her. Who else could it be?

The figure responded in a hollow voice that was oddly androgynous. "*Maybe I am.*"

Instantly I knew that whoever I was looking at was neither Lance nor Carolyn, and with one quick motion I found my bedside lamp and flicked it on. I had made the mistake of taking my eyes off the figure in that instant, and when I looked back...it was gone.

I sprang from my bed, determined to catch a glimpse of the intruder as he or she escaped down the hall toward my apartment's door... but there was no one there; the door was still propped against the dumb bell. I would have at least heard the sound of the door slamming into the dumb bell if the intruder had bolted from my room...wouldn't I?

He or she was still in the apartment! I dashed down the hall and moved the dumb bell from the door with my foot before closing and locking it.

The bathroom!

I opened the door to the bathroom and turned on the light. I pulled the shower curtain open and glanced about. No one. The bathroom was far too small to serve as a hiding place.

The closet!

I closed the bathroom door and stood before the closet. Quickly, I swung the closet door open and stood confronted by a storage space filled with twice the quantity of items that anyone could have imagined. There wasn't room for a deck of cards let alone an entire person.

"What the hell?" I said, as I pondered what I had experienced.

The kitchen!

I already knew you couldn't really hide in the kitchen but that was the only place left.

As before, a thorough search turned up nothing. I began searching under the beds and then re-checked the bathroom, closet, and then back to the kitchen. I was alone. What the hell had just happened to me? Was I dreaming? Was I sick? Whatever I had experienced, I couldn't sleep for the rest of the night. It actually took some time for me to sleep comfortably in that apartment again. When it came time to consolidate roommates, I was asked if I wanted someone to move in with me or if I wanted to move. Guess which one I picked.

Pretty lame right? Some shadowy figure wanders into my apartment and then vanishes? What kind of anti-climactic ghost story is that?

Well, about a year later I'm still living in Allegheny Center. I've been moved around and now live in a much larger apartment with two roommates instead of one. My life had evolved significantly from the night of a year ago. I had a girlfriend. I was less focused on social activities and more focused on my schooling. I had cut my circle of friends down to a small group of people who I visited a couple times a week.

My friend Mitch's apartment was the typical group hangout. He lived on Lockhart Street, well within walking distance of Allegheny Center. I will mention something now to give the story some context. The Pittsburgh North Side is the oldest section of Pittsburgh. Everywhere you go, there's a historical landmark, like some mansion that was owned by some famous person from a hundred or more years ago now cramped between a rundown red-brick condemned building and a closed down pawn shop or liquor store. But Lockhart Street was something of an exception to the rest of the North Side. If you took the modern cars off the side of the road it would look like you stepped right into the 1800's.

Old red brickwork, black stone buildings, worn cement statues, the entire street was like walking through a museum. It was old, untouched by the rise and fall of the neighborhood around it. Your feet were touching the same stone sidewalk that someone had walked two hundred years ago—what's more, you knew it. You could literally feel the weight of age and history. The overcast Pittsburgh sky or yellow lamp lights always enhanced the antiquity of where you were.

One night I left Mitch's apartment as I had countless times before and would countless times since. The night was quiet— uncharacteristic of Pittsburgh—and the street lights, many of which were burnt out, were not dispelling the darkness as they usually did. A chill wind blew in from the rivers and the wind whistled through the street as litter tumbled along the stone sidewalk.

I felt completely alone.

As I passed the few alleys on my way off of Lockhart, I had a habit of glancing down each one and giving a good look. I didn't think anyone would mug me, but I didn't want to take the chance of someone slipping behind me and catching me by surprise. During one glance down an alley, I turned my eyes back to the sidewalk ahead of me to see a figure cast in shadow standing well ahead of me, the black form outlined by the darkness around it contrasting brightly in comparison to itself.

I slowed as I walked, and kept my eyes glued to the figure. The street was always empty at this hour, and anyone out was going somewhere. No one just stood still.

"Wally?" I asked. Wally was one of my circle of friends who had left Mitch's apartment shortly before me. Of course it was Wally! He and I walked the same direction until we got off of Lockhart. What was he doing just standing there?

There was no answer. I stopped walking and felt—though I couldn't be sure—that the figure was facing me. This wasn't Wally.

"Andy?" Andy was Mitch's roommate. Of course it was Andy! Andy would often run out to buy smokes at the gas station around the corner at any hour of the night. I remember he had gotten up to do just that while I was over. I thought he had gotten back, though.

"*Maybe I am,*" the figure said.

It had been a year, but it was the voice—that oddly androgynous hollow voice that echoed back at me through the darkness. It sounded as familiar as if I had heard it the day before. With a quick sidestep the figure vanished into an alley.

This time I wasn't so quick to investigate. My heart jumped into my throat and I stood stunned for a moment. A few seconds passed, and I remembered where I was—I was completely alone on a windy dark two hundred year old street where the voice of something that had vanished in front of me only a year ago had reappeared to repeat the same three words it had during our first encounter.

Though I had terror screaming inside of me, I calmly walked to the opposite side of the street; I was not about to pass that alley without a wide berth between myself and it. Step by step I moved forward, keeping my eyes focused on the spot where the figure had disappeared.

As I approached, the oddness of the situation grew. What I was focused on, what I thought was an alley was not an alley at all; it was an alcove, no more than, three feet deep. Someone, decades, maybe a century ago had erected a stone wall in the alley for who knows what reason. There was simply nowhere to go.

The rest of my journey home was swift. With every few steps, I glanced behind me. Most times that I looked behind me I saw nothing, but occasionally there was the form of a figure shrouded in shadow disappearing behind the edge of my vision. Was I imagining it? Was my terrified mind exaggerating that I was being followed?

My return to Allegheny Center was a welcome relief. The presence of my roommates gave me comfort that—despite my experience—I was not alone.

As of this writing I've been in Pittsburgh for almost thirteen years, and it has been about twelve since I last saw that shadowy black form on my walk home on Lockhart Street. I can count the people I've told my story to on one hand, and now I'm writing this story for your enjoyment. Whether you enjoyed it or not is irrelevant, however. This story—every word, every detail—is one hundred percent fact. So, if you're a skeptic like me, you're probably thinking of at least a dozen possible explanations for what I experienced. You're probably thinking—as I would be—that this is just a story in a book of fiction without a shred of truth behind it. How can I recall those events in such perfect detail from over a decade ago?

But I'll suggest to you this.

As you're lying alone in bed tonight, accompanied by the sounds of the home you've grown so accustomed to—peering into the darkness of your room—think of this story. Maybe those sounds you hear are nothing more than a pet getting into something. Perhaps it's your house settling, the wind outside, or maybe the water heater or furnace turning on or off. Those are all perfectly reasonable explanations you can arrive at instantly to slow your beating heart before drifting off to sleep.

Or next time you're by yourself outside, maybe on a dark street, in an empty field or vacant parking lot—those fleeting moments where you're truly alone—think of this story. Think of this story and tell yourself calmly, rationally, that there is no such thing as ghosts.

Maybe I *was* hallucinating. Maybe I *was* dreaming. Maybe my eyes and ears were playing tricks on me. Maybe I'm like all the other supernatural nuts out there ready to spin a yarn about ghosts and maybe I'm simply not telling the truth.

But then again...

Maybe I am.

THEY SAY I'M WELL NOW

DAVID H. DONAGHE

They say I'm well now; I guess they think I'm well, because I'm going along with the program. The judge said I was criminally insane, that I'd gone mad; just because I killed my wife and a half dozen other people at the office. I did burn down that homeless shelter in New York City and killed several more across the country, but they were only people in the abstract sense.

My name is Brad Cummings, and I kill monsters.

I used to be a happily married man, but one day my wife and I went for a walk in the park near where we lived. Something fell from a tree, landed on the back of my wife's neck, and she let out a yelp while rubbing the sore spot. I checked out the back of her neck and saw a black slug that reminded me of a glob of Jell-O. It burrowed into her skin, causing her flesh to sizzle for a few seconds. Pleading with her to go to a doctor, I couldn't understand why she refused. Even then, the reptilian larva was taking control, and by the end of the week, my beautiful ray of sunshine was gone.

Only I could see the evil thing lurking beneath the surface.

As a resident of a mental hospital, you have a lot of time on your hands. When I first came here, I spent most of my time either killing, or observing the monsters, trying to grasp their agenda. They go about their daily lives like normal people, but then I thought, *Maybe they're waiting for the mother ship?*

Finally, I gave up and decided to leave them alone. Here in the loony bin, you meet interesting people. I've discovered another variety of monster that makes the reptilian interlopers seem as benign as choirboys. This kind of monster is entirely human and that's what scares me. Here we have serial killers, inbred cannibals, rapists, child molesters, you name it. The ones I hate the most are the ones who hurt children.

One day, they took us to an amusement park and I was standing by a carousel when a little girl came running up to me.

"Mister, are you sick?" she asked me.

"They think I am," I said, shooting her a smile.

"Why?" she asked.

"Because I see monsters."

The little girl gave me a look of utter shock. Her eyes widened and her bottom jaw dropped.

"I see them too," she whispered. "They try hard to look like everyone else, but I can see them hiding underneath. The lizard kind is the worst."

Now it was I who stood in shock with my mouth hanging open. I'd never met another person who saw the monsters.

"Don't let anyone else know that you see them," I whispered.

"Why? Do you think they'll put me in the funny farm like you?" she asked.

I laughed. "No, you're too pretty for that."

The girl's mother called out for her.

"You'd better run. You don't want your mother to get worried," I said. The girl ran off and I heard her mother scolding her about talking to strangers.

Back at the hospital, I sat down in the common room to read a newspaper. I read an article about a serial killer that was killing little girls back east and how the authorities couldn't catch him. They said that his usual MO was to kidnap little girls on their way home from school, take them to some secluded place, and then contact the parents. He tells the mother that if she wants to see her little girl alive, she needed to come alone, and he then asks for money. If the mother comes, he rapes and kills both of them, cannibalizes them while they're still alive, and then he burns what's left. The article said that in a few cases, he broke from his pattern and killed people at random. But in every case, he would cannibalize and burn the bodies. The newspapers called him Billy the Burner.

I thought about the little girl in the amusement park and what a horrible thing it would be if someone did that to her. Billy had to die and that's why I decided to go along with the program. Now, I'm a model patient and my target date for freedom is two years from now. They say I need to stay confined and remain in therapy for at least that long before the authorities would consider releasing me. Then, it would be to a halfway house, but two years is too long to wait, and besides, it's all out the window, now that I have blood on my knife.

* * *

When the woman screamed, the barn owl looked up from the branch of the pine tree where it sat. A flickering light wafted from the interior of the abandoned farmhouse and another blood-curdling scream split the night. The owl spread its wings and took flight. Inside the farmhouse, Billy knelt over the woman laying spread eagle on the hardwood floor. The woman's six-year-old daughter's butchered body lay on the dirty hardwood floor of the farmhouse beside her. Pieces of flesh lay in the coals inside the home's fireplace, sizzling, the fat dripping and hissing. Reaching into the fire with a pair of metal tongs, Billy picked up a piece of half-cooked meat.

"Oooh, that's hot," Billy said. "A man's got to keep up his strength though, so down the hatch it goes." He dropped the small pieces of human flesh into his mouth and wolfed it down. He picked up another piece of meat and quickly ate it, relishing the taste.

"Please. Just kill me. You've already killed my baby girl. I have nothing to live for anyway. Just put me out of my misery," the mother pleaded.

Billy wiped his greasy hands on his pants and picked up his bloody knife.

"You know, you do have sexy legs," he said and then smacked his lips. He cut off several large pieces of flesh from the woman's thighs as she screamed in agony. Blood pooled underneath her body and she let out another scream.

A foul odor permeated the farmhouse and outside a coyote howled, smelling the fresh-cooked meat. Billy tossed the fresh cut strips of human flesh into the fire to cook. After gorging himself, he said, "Ah...I always like to save the sweat meat for last," and then stuck the knife into the woman's belly.

She let out another blood curdling-scream, but after a while, the screaming stopped. Later, his hunger placated, Billy the Burner stuffed several pieces of half-cooked flesh into his soiled backpack, and set the pack outside the farmhouse. Picking up a can of gasoline, he poured gas over the body of the woman and the child, then poured a stream of gasoline across the hardwood floor of the living room to the front door of the house.

On the front porch, Billy slung his pack onto his back, took a book of matches from his pocket, and struck a match. Tossing it through the front door, he stepped back, watching the flames ravage the bodies and the interior of the home. As the flames fully consumed the farmhouse, he strolled down the dirt driveway, made his way to the highway, and headed west.

* * *

Right now, I'm kneeling over the body of John Holiday, and his blood is forming a pool at my feet. Here in the Coo Coos Nest, we call him Little Johnny Boy. Tomorrow was Little Johnny Boy's release date, but I couldn't let that happen. Little Johnny Boy used to suck up to the doctors, expressing remorse about his crimes. They claimed he was cured and no longer a danger to society. This morning I heard Little Johnny Boy bragging about all the young trim he was going to get once he was on the outside. Little Johnny Boy liked young girls between the age of thirteen and sixteen. He would abduct them, take them to some secluded place and then rape them. Finished with that, he would kill them with his knife, taking his time. That's why I killed little Johnny Boy with my blade. Then I heard a noise and looked up.

"Damn, Cummings! You killed Little Johnny Boy! That's about as funny as a fart in church!" Patrick Murphy said, stepping out from the darkness. Patrick Murphy is your typical Irish thug. He likes to rob liquor stores, steal cars, break in to people's houses and shoot them. His last victim had seven bullet holes in his body. The police caught Murphy, but the courts sent him here.

"Help me drag him into the laundry room. Get some towels and help me clean up this mess," I said. Murphy did as instructed. "Now get his feet," I told him. Murphy grabbed the feet and we carried the body into the washroom.

"He's a heavy bugger," Murphy said while we carried the body down the corridor.

"I hear you," I replied. Sweat dripped down my forehead and formed underneath my armpits. We deposited Little Johnny Boy's body into an industrial-sized laundry hamper in the washroom. Reaching up to a top shelf, I brought down a stack of white towels, tossed them into the hamper covering the body and then brought down another stack. Tossing half of them to Murphy, I said, "Let's clean up the mess."

"Why don't I just mop the floor?" Embarrassment shot through me and my cheeks turned red.

"Bring it, but we'll still need the towels," I replied. We spent the next fifteen minutes mopping the floor and cleaning the mess.

"What now?" Murphy asked.

"Now you go back to your room," I said, breathing in the smell of ammonia from the mop bucket.

"What about you?"

"I'm getting out of here."

"Take me with you."

"No way, man."

"Take me with you or I'll scream bloody murder. They'll put you in the padded room again." I grabbed my knife and Murphy took a step back. "You need me," he said. "I know stuff. I can help."

I paused, thinking. Murphy's rap sheet covered everything from petty theft to homicide.

"All right. You can come, but if you ever threaten to snitch on me again, I'll cut your balls off and feed them to you," I said and headed back to the laundry room. Murphy came in behind me and closed the door.

"What's your plan, boss?"

"Weaver will be making his rounds in ten minutes. When he passes by, I'll jump him and take his keys."

"What about me, boss man?"

"You stay here. When I bring Weaver in we'll tie him up."

"Why don't you just cut his big black throat?"

"I don't want to kill Weaver. He's not like the rest."

"If you say so, but even if you don't, they'll still nail you for killing Little Johnny Boy."

"What are they gonna do, throw me in the loony bin?"

Murphy let go with a belly laugh.

"Shut up. Someone might hear us," I whispered.

"Why'd you kill Little Johnny Boy?" Murphy asked.

"Because he needed it. Now shut up."

We hunkered down in the laundry room for another fifteen minutes.

"I wonder what's takin' the black bastard so long? Maybe he had to lay a big black turd," Murphy said and then laughed. This struck my funny bone and I let out a snicker. Soon we were both laughing and snorting.

"Shut up. Shut up. I think I hear him coming," I said, stifling my laughter.

Weaver fiddled with his keys, opened the door to the laundry room, and we dived behind the laundry hamper.

"Who's in here? I could of sworn I heard someone laughing," Weaver said, flipping on the light. He looked around for a few more seconds and then closed the door. I heard his footsteps moving down the hallway. Silently, I stepped into the hallway, crept up behind him, and pulled my knife. Grabbing him by the back of his shoulder with my left hand, I brought the knife over his right shoulder and touched his throat with the blade.

"I always liked you, Weaver. Don't make me do something that we'll both regret," I whispered.

"Good Lord, Brad. I think I just shit myself. Please don't kill me."

I let out a low chuckle.

"I'm not gonna hurt you. Unbuckle your belt and drop it. I need your keys, and empty your pockets."

"You don't want to do this, Brad."

I slid the blade across his throat, just barely nicking the skin. A tiny drop of blood trickled down the front of his neck.

"Don't think about going for that pepper spray on your belt. You'd make an ugly corpse." Weaver unbuckled his belt, let it drop to the floor and I kicked it away. "Now empty your pockets." He did as instructed and I forced him up against the wall. "Get on your knees," I said, tucking the knife in my waistband, I grabbed the keys.

"Good Lord, you are gonna kill me. I got a wife and a family," he said.

"Get up and head to the laundry room. If you want to see that wife and family of yours again, do what I tell you," I said sticking the knife into his back. I forced Weaver into the laundry room and made him sit down next to the oversized laundry hamper. "Get his keys. Get some rope and some duct tape from the storage room," I said to Murphy. A big grin crossed Murphy's face and I saw blood lust in his eyes.

"Why don't you just cut the black bastard, or better yet, let me do it."

"Nobody's going to kill him. If you don't do what I tell you, I just might kill you," I said.

"Fine, you're the boss, as long as you have that knife, anyway," Murphy said and went after the rope and the duct tape.

"If you be nice, Weaver, you just might live through this, but if you get any crazy ideas, just look in that laundry hamper. Go 'head. Take a look," I said flipping on the light. Weaver rose up and peeked inside the laundry hamper. "Move the towels aside so you can get a good look."

"Lord God Almighty. You killed John Holiday. He was supposed to get out of here tomorrow," Weaver said, his face turning ashen.

"I couldn't let that happen. Holiday was a piece of shit, so I killed him. I'll kill you too if I have to."

"I won't cause you no trouble, Brad. Don't let Murphy near me. He'll kill me for sure."

"I'll handle Murphy. I'm the one you've got to worry about."

"You know you're not gonna make it out of here."

"I'll make it. Once I make it to the front gate, I'll ram the gate with your car."

Weaver let out a sigh.

"Damn. I just washed and waxed that car."

"I'm going to have to tie you up and then hit you. I can't have you raising the alarm."

"Just don't hit me too hard," Weaver said.

Murphy came back with the rope and the duct tape.

"Tie him up, put some rags in his mouth, and tape his mouth closed," I said. While Murphy went to work, I picked up Weaver's belt and put it on.

"All trussed up like a Christmas turkey, though he looks a little bit on the burnt side," Murphy said and then laughed.

"Wait for me outside," I said.

"Anything you say, Boss. You've got the plan." When Murphy stepped outside, I opened Weaver's wallet and took out the cash.

"You have over four hundred dollars here. It must be payday. I'll take two hundred and leave you the rest. You do have that family to feed after all," I said and then brought the hilt of the knife crashing down on his temple. He slumped against the wall in a state of unconsciousness and I examined his skull. "Lucky for you, this knife has a rubber grip. Bet you'll have a headache tomorrow, though." Picking up Weaver's things, I stepped out the door. Murphy and I headed down the hallway, breathing in the smell of floor wax, which masked the pungent odor of urine coming from some of the patient's room. Some of our patients had accidents at night. When the bats are in the attic, you don't think about going to the bathroom to make a bowel movement or to pee.

Using Weaver's keys, I unlocked each set of doors as we passed through the wards. A door on our right opened and a mousy girl with long red hair stepped into the hallway. I heaved a sigh of despair. Ashley Courtland stood in her hospital gown watching us, her nipples pressing against the fabric of her thin cotton gown. I glanced at her chest and then looked away. *I ought to cold cock her and save myself some trouble.* Ashley liked to cut herself, she was also anorexic and liked to start fires. Other than that, she was just a little bitch.

"What are you guys doing?" Ashley whispered.

"Mind your own business. Go back to sleep," I said, trying to keep my voice down.

"We're bustin' out of here, darlin'," Murphy said. I felt anger surge through me.

"Take me with you," Ashley whispered. She rushed into the hallway and grabbed Murphy's arm.

"Go back to your room," I said, trying not to let my voice grow above a whisper.

"Why not, boss? Ashley's a kick. I'll share. You can always use some pun-tang."

"If you don't take me, I'll scream," Ashley whispered.

"I'll gut you, if you do," I replied.

Ashley rubbed up against me and put her hand on my back. "Please. I'll do anything you want."

"Shit. All right, but keep your mouth shut and do what I tell you," I said.

We moved down the hallway and then let ourselves outside using Weaver's keys. I crossed the lawn to the employee's parking lot with Murphy swaggering along behind me. I found Weaver's car, an old Chevy sedan and we piled in. Sitting behind the wheel, I fired up the engine, Ashley sat in the back and Murphy rode shotgun.

"Thank you for taking me," Ashley said, putting her hand on my leg.

"Keep your hands to yourself," I said, pushing her hand away. Pulling out of the parking lot, I headed down the road to freedom. Weaver's keys let us out of the interior gate and then I drove down the tree-lined road leading to the perimeter fence.

"What are you going to do about the guard at the main gate?" Murphy asked.

"Watch and see," I replied.

"You could run the son-of-a-bitch down."

"Unlike you, I only kill people when necessary," I said. We came around a curve in the road and approached the main gate. The guard stepped out of the guard shack and turned to face us. When I stopped with the front end of Weaver's car only inches from the gate, the guard shined his flashlight into the vehicle. He raised a handheld radio to his lips and spoke into it. Franticly, the guard shoved his radio back onto his belt and pulled a handgun.

"Do something, Boss!" Murphy yelled. "This old boy smells a rat!"

Jamming the shifter into reverse, I mashed my foot down on the accelerator. The tires squealed and the car shot backward. I slammed on the brakes, breathing in the smell of burnt rubber, and Ashley let out a scream. Three hundred feet of space separated us from freedom. Jamming the shifter into drive, I burned some more rubber, squealing the tires as the car shot forward. The guard ran away, hiding behind the guard shack. The car slammed into the gate, making a loud crunching sound. The gate leaned backward, barely holding onto its track, but Ashley wouldn't stop screaming.

"Shut up, you dumb bitch!" I snapped and put the shifter into reverse. This time when we slammed into the gate, the car knocked it halfway to the ground. When I rammed the gate the third time, the gate fell over and we rolled over it. Murphy let out a wild whoop and we rolled down the road toward freedom. The guard took a few potshots at us with his handgun and a bullet slammed into the back window, causing Ashley to scream again.

"If you can't make that bitch shut up, I'm gonna cut her throat," I said.

"Ashley, darlin', hush now," Murphy said, laying a hand on her leg. Ashley hushed and I turned right onto a two-lane highway heading west at a high rate of speed.

Murphy opened the glove box and said, "Hey, look what I found."

"Give me that," I said and took the gun from his hand before he knew what was happening. Shoving it into the front of my pants, I glared at Murphy. He smiled back and I focused on the road ahead.

* * *

On the road for three days, Billy the Burner was famished. He'd gone through all of the human flesh in his backpack and considered stopping at a store to buy something to tide him over until he found what he considered *real* food. He had passed several restaurants and Quick Marts along the highway, but he loathed eating what most people considered palatable. He would starve himself for days after eating human flesh and only eat something else if he absolutely had to. The early morning chill caused his face to redden, his eyes to tear up, his hands to shake and weakness to suffuse his body.

He heard a rumbling sound and looked up the road. A beat-up, white Ford van backfired, approaching from the east and Billy stuck out his thumb.

The van pulled over and stopped.

"You headed west?" a portly woman with dirty blonde hair asked from the passenger window.

"Yeah," Billy said, peering over the woman to her grossly fat husband behind the wheel. He had a large belly, fleshy jowls and rolls of fat that hung from his arms.

Clinching a big cigar between his teeth, the fat man waved Billy toward the vehicle.

"Hurry up, son. We ain't got all day," the fat man said.

"Ha," Billy chuckled underneath his breath as he climbed inside the van. "Here's lunch."

Five miles down the road, they stopped at a country cross road. Taking his knife from his backpack, Billy reached up and stuck it into the side of the fat man's throat. Blood squirted out as the man grabbed his throat while trying to scream, his portly wife shrieking in terror. Billy took a tire iron he found lying underneath the passenger seat and brought it crashing down on the woman's head, knocking her unconscious. Jumping into the driver's seat, he dragged the body of the fat man into the back and then climbed behind the wheel, breathing heavily when he was finished.

Down the road a few more miles, Billy turned off into a vacant field and parked in a secluded spot behind a clump of trees. Using ropes from his backpack, he tied up both the fat man and his wife, then hung them from a tree. The woman came to a few minutes later, hanging by her feet next to her dead husband. She let out a scream and began to cry.

"You know, I'd consider having some fun with you, but I'm not really into fat chicks," Billy said and then went to work with his knives. A full day later with his stomach full, Billy the Burner climbed behind the wheel of the Ford van, pulled out onto the highway, and headed west.

* * *

The first thing Officer Barrow noticed after receiving the radio call about the bodies was the smell. The smell of cooked human flesh emanated from the smoldering bodies hanging from the trees.

"My God. It's hard to tell they were even human. At first I thought some poacher took a couple of bears out of season," Barrow's partner said and then promptly threw up on his shoes.

"Have you ever seen anything like it?" he asked after he composed himself.

Barrow shook his head, looking up at the two-burnt bodies. Long strips of half-cooked meat hung in the trees next to the bodies, animal tracks lay on the ground, and a small cooking fire was near the base of the tree. The remains of a human hand lay in the ashes, the index finger curled up, the other fingers spread open.

"Hell, no. I've been with the State Police for thirty-two years and I've never seen anything like this. It looks like Old Billy the Burner had himself a feast. We got to catch this motherless son-of-a-bitch before he does this to anyone else," Barrow said and then headed back to the patrol car for the body bags.

* * *

Turning the radio onto a country and western station, I rolled down the window.

"We need to ditch this car," I said, resting my arm on the back of the seat.

"What ever you say, but could we change the music from this country shit?" Murphy asked from the back seat.

"How about some heavy metal?" Ashley said, running her hand down my leg as she sat beside me. Moving my hand to her inner thigh, I ran it up underneath her gown until my pinky finger came to rest against her moist center. Squeezing her thigh, I bore down hard and she let out a playful yelp.

"The station stays where it is and I told you to keep your hands to yourself." Removing my hand, I turned up the radio and saw tears in Ashley's eyes.

"Why do you have to be so mean?" she asked.

"Because that's the way I roll."

"Don't worry, boss, she'll be fine, won't you, darlin'? You play what you want," Murphy said. "As long as you've got that gun, you're the boss."

Ten miles down the road, I saw a mailbox next to a dirt road leading back into the trees. The lights from a farmhouse set back from the road filtered through the trees. Stomping on the brakes, I turned onto the dirt road and Ashley let out another muffled yelp of surprise.

"This farmer probably has a truck in his barn," I said. "We'll leave Weaver's car here. The cops probably have the license plate number and the description by now."

"I told you, you should have shot the bastard," Murphy said.

Glancing out the window, I watched the forest and breathed in the pine scent.

"Maybe I should just shoot you and be done with it?"

"No need to get hostile," Murphy said, raising his hands in surrender. The dirt road opened up into a clearing with a dilapidated old farmhouse in its center. To the east of the house was a rickety old barn. Parking the car next to the barn, I turned off the motor and Murphy started to open his door.

"Wait a minute. They might have a dog. If it starts barking, we're out of here," I said. We stayed in the car, waiting, while crickets sang love songs to the night, but no dogs barked.

"The furry critters must be inside with the old folks," Murphy said.

"Stay here while I check the barn," I whispered. Climbing out of the car, I stretched, letting my eyes grow accustomed to the darkness. After a minute, I crept up to the barn.

The barn door hung on a track with rollers at its top so I leaned against the door and gave it a shove. The rollers squeaked, but the door slid open. A musty smell emanated from the dark interior, the smell bringing back memories from my childhood. Something brushed against my leg and I almost jumped out of my skin. A black and white cat looked up at me and meowed. Inside the barn, was a faded Cobalt Blue 1966 Dodge pickup truck. I went to the front of the truck and raised the hood. Turning to a nearby shelf in the barn, I rummaged around, looking for a piece of wire to hot-wire it. Stopping in mid-search, I heaved a sigh.

"Always check the easy stuff first," I said, grabbed the driver's side door handle and gave it a pull. The door squeaked open and I sat down behind the wheel. The keys dangled from the ignition. Climbing out of the cab, I eased the hood closed and then climbed back behind the wheel and turned the key. The engine cranked slowly at first, but then fired up, and I backed out of the barn.

Expecting to see Murphy and Ashley come running up to me, a fit of rage shot through me when they didn't.

I looked up when muffled gunshots came from the house. I saw bright flashes of light coming from a back bedroom. "Shit! I left Weaver's gun sitting on the front seat of the car!" I screamed, slamming my fist down on the steering wheel. Murphy and Ashley came running from the house and jumped into the truck on the passenger side, breathing hard and sweating. They couldn't stop giggling and laughing. Ashley put her hand on my leg.

"What the hell did you do?" I asked.

"I shot the shit out of them old coots," Murphy said and then laughed.

"You should have seen that old woman's face when we stepped into her bedroom," Ashley said and then let out a nervous giggle.

"Shut up, bitch!" I yelled and backhanded her across the face. "Why did you kill them? We could have got away clean!"

"Take it easy. I've got the gun now. You ain't the boss man no more."

"If you point that gun at me again, I'll gut you like a fish. Besides, the gun's empty. You're out of bullets."

"Bang!" Murphy said, pointing the gun at me. "Shit, you're right. I got no bullets left." Reaching over, my elbow brushed against Ashley's breast as I grabbed the gun.

"Hey! Watch it!" Ashley said. I backhanded her with the back of my fist holding the gun.

"I said to shut up!" I snapped at her. Pulling up next to Weaver's car, I jumped out and grabbed the box of ammunition in the glove box. Back inside the truck, I reloaded the weapon and placed the barrel against Murphy's forehead.

"Never carry an unloaded weapon, you dumb shit. Always reload after you're through shooting." Murphy's eyes widened, but I took it from his hand and tucked the handgun back into the waistband of my pants. I put the truck in gear and stepped down on the accelerator. The truck lurched forward, bouncing over the dirt road. Once we cleared the woods and reached the highway, I headed west.

We'll be lucky if every cop in the state isn't on our tail by day-light, I thought. Keeping my foot on the gas pedal, I hoped to make the next town before the police threw up a roadblock.

* * *

We pulled into Greenwood Illinois at 3:15 a.m. I felt drained, but I needed to ditch the truck. We cruised the main drag, trying to look inconspicuous. So far, I managed to slip by a few road-blocks and we hadn't drawn any attention from the police. We had a close call when we passed a doughnut shop with six police cars parked out front.

"Look at them fat bastards," Murphy said and then laughed. A few blocks down, a green, neon sign announced that Shamrock's Irish Pub was open for business. Pulling into the back parking lot, I pulled up next to a Dodge Charger.

"Time to earn your keep," I said to Murphy and then killed the engine on the truck.

Murphy climbed out. He looked around for a minute and then found a small metal strap lying on the ground. He used it as a Slim Jim and had the driver's side door open in a few seconds. Lying down under the floorboard with his head under the dash, Murphy let out a few curse words. He pulled his head out from under the dash and then looked under the front seat. After pulling out a mesh of wires, he then crawled back under the dash. I heard a spark when Murphy crossed the hotwires and the Charger rumbled to life. He climbed out and I slid behind the wheel. Ashley jumped into the backseat and Murphy climbed in the passenger side.

We rolled out of the parking lot and turned left. Heading down Main Street, I felt nervous and I kept glancing in the rearview mirror, watching for the cops. I studied the businesses lining the street, but most of them looked closed. Slowing down in front of a Sports Mart, I saw a closed sign hanging on the front door. Turn-ing down an alleyway, the Charger's exhaust rumbled off the surrounding buildings. I pulled into the parking lot behind the Sports Mart and parked next to the back door.

"Time to go to work again, Murphy," I said while turning off the motor.

"You got it, boss. I'll get us in there quicker than a rabbit can hump a frog."

"Murphy, try not to set off the alarm if they have one," I added.

He climbed out of the car and swaggered over to an electrical junction box mounted to the brick wall of the building. I got out of the driver's seat and paced the parking lot. Murphy let out a muffled curse and struggled with the junction box. He ripped some wires from it and twisted them together.

"It's a done deal. Pop the trunk, get me a tire iron and I'll get us inside."

"How am I supposed to do that? It's not like I got the keys to this thing," I said. Ashley stepped up next to me. Her right breast brushed up against my arm and I stepped back.

"Try going through the back seat," Murphy said.

"Let her do it," I said, glancing at Ashley. "It's about time she earned her keep." Turning back to the Charger, I climbed in the back and removed the rear portion.

"Here we go, darlin'," I said, trying to imitate Murphy's voice.

"In there? It smells greasy and dirty. I don't think I can fit through that small opening."

"You'll fit," I said. "Just like a hunk of cheese into a fat man's mouth. Now get in there."

She ducked her head into the small opening, wiggling her upper body into the trunk and her gown caught on a piece of metal.

"I think I'm stuck," she said, trying to wiggle her way through. Her gown ripped, exposing her bare ass and giving me the bird's eye view of her shapely bottom. Putting both hands on her ass, I gave her a shove.

"Hey!" she yelled.

"Don't worry about it. Hey, I just saw your best assets," I said and then laughed. Ashley giggled and I said, "See if you can find a way to pop the trunk."

"I think there's a toolbox in here. It's hot in here, I'm going to suffocate. I want out," she pleaded.

"You're not coming out this way, so you better get the trunk open," I said. Ashley rummaged around some more and I heard metal scrape against metal.

"Shit," Ashley spat. I heard a metallic click and then the trunk opened.

"See? You're not entirely useless after all," I said.

After putting the back seat into place once more, I climbed out of the Charger. Murphy walked over and helped Ashley out of the trunk. He carried the tire iron and the toolbox to the rear door of the Sports Mart.

"I'll get you in there quicker than you can swat a skeeter off your peter," Murphy chuckled. He went to work on the door and had it open in less than five minutes.

"Let's get some new clothes. I'm gettin' tired of these hospital rags. Then let's see what they have in the way of guns and ammo," I said.

"You got it, boss. My nuts are hiding underneath my armpit to keep warm. I think I'll find myself a coat," Murphy added.

Searching the store, I found the men's clothing department. Stripping out of my hospital gown, I put on a pair of jeans and a long sleeve flannel shirt. I found a shooting vest and a pair of hiking boots. Ashley stripped down, and then put on a pair of jeans and a white t-shirt, then she went looking for a warm jacket. I smashed open a glass case containing weapons in the sporting goods department and picked up an AR-15 and a Browning .45. Murphy took a Ruger Blackhawk .44 Magnum and a Ruger Mini-14. I found a canvas duffel bag to put everything in and then searched the store for other things that we might need. I found a gas can, a bone saw, a coil of rope, a pair of barbeque mittens, extra clothes, a shit load of ammunition and some barbeque tongs. Taking a ball cap off a mannequin, I put it on my head.

"That should do it," I said, stepping up to Murphy and Ashley. Murphy had on a pair of blue jeans, cowboy boots, a western style shirt, and a cowboy hat. He held a fringed leather coat over his arm and had the Ruger Blackhawk tucked into the waistband of his jeans. A cocky grin crossed his face. Ashley didn't look half-bad in her new clothes and I noticed a hunting knife tucked into the front of her waistband.

"What do you think about my new duds, boss?"

"You look like Cowboy Bob," I said. "At least it's better than those hospital rags. Let's get out of here." I scooped up the duffle bag containing our stolen gear.

"You're not the only one with a gun now, boss. I wouldn't be so bossy," Murphy said, a foul look crossing his face. Whirling around, I pulled my gun and stuck the barrel against his belly.

"You're not smart enough to run things, Murphy. But if you feel froggy, jump, and I'll put a hole in your big fat belly," I said.

Fear shot through Murphy's face and he raised his hands.

"I was just teasin' you, boss. You still run the show."

Throwing the duffle bag over my shoulder, I sauntered toward the door with Murphy and Ashley following behind. Tossing the duffle bag into the back seat, I climbed behind the wheel of the Charger. Ashley climbed into the rear with the gear and Murphy rode shotgun.

"I love my new clothes," Ashley said.

"Where to now, boss?" Murphy asked.

"If we make it out of town without getting stopped by the cops, we'll find somewhere to rest," I said.

Starting the Charger, I drove down the alley, then turned left on Main Street to head toward the edge of town. At the end of the street, I turned left onto the highway and headed west. Ten miles outside of town, I found a dirt road on the north side of the high-way leading into a wooded area. Pulling the Charger behind a stand of trees, I killed the motor and Murphy rolled down the passenger side window. The sound of a stream dancing over rocks filled the night. My breath fogged up in my face. Ashley crossed her arms across her chest and shivered from the cold.

"We'll stay the night here and head west in the morning," I said.

"Okay, boss. I'm about as tired as a one-legged frog trying to hop across the freeway," Murphy grinned. "Ashley, hun, would you mind staying up there with Brad? These legs of mine need some room to stretch out."

"Fine," Ashley said.

Murphy stretched out on the back seat, content and said, "Aww, now, hun, he don't bite."

"Don't believe him. I bite. I bite hard," I whispered. Ashley frowned. "I'm just teasing you girl. As long as you don't start whining again, I got no problem with you." She relaxed, leaning against me and soon began to snore softly with her head against my arm. Noticing the handle of the hunting knife protruding from the waistband of her jeans, I took it and slid it under the front seat. Putting my arm around her shoulders, I closed my eyes and gave in to the night.

* * *

The sun shining through the windshield woke me from a deep slumber. Murphy and Ashley were laughing and splashing in the nearby stream. Climbing out of the Charger, I looked across the hood at their naked bodies. Ashley didn't look half-bad for a skinny girl. Her breasts were small, and if you didn't look at the scars on her arms, she looked kind of cute. Her nipples stood erect, telling me how cold the water must be.

"Come on in, Brad. The water feels wonderful!" Ashley yelled to me while spreading her arms apart.

"It's cold enough to freeze your balls off, but you get used to it," Murphy said.

I stripped out of my clothes, tossing them on the ground, then jumped into the water. Ashley jumped into my arms and kissed me. We played in the water for a while and then got dressed. We were all hungry and needed to get some food.

Back on the road, my thoughts reverted to Billy the Burner. This was something I needed to do alone, both Murphy and Ashley a liability. Noticing a Quick Mart on the side of the road, I looked at the gas gauge.

"We need gas," I said and pulled off the highway.

"And food, too. My stomach thinks my throat's been cut," Murphy said when I pulled up to the gas pumps.

"Stay in the car," I said and then climbed out to fill the gas tank.

When I was finished with the gas, I entered the Quick Mart to pay. Strolling through the store, I picked up a large bag of potato chips, cookies, beef jerky, and a bag of pork rinds. After grabbing a six pack of Pepsi, I headed to the check-out counter to see that Murphy had other ideas.

138

"Give me the money in the drawer before I shoot your fat ass!" Murphy yelled at the clerk.

Murphy stood pointing his .44 Magnum at a terrified sales clerk's face. The chunky young girl looked no more than eighteen years old.

"Please don't shoot me. Just take the money," the girl said, raising her hands. Her hands shook and tears welled up in her eyes.

"Murphy, I thought I told you to stay in the car. We don't need to rob this place. I got money," I told him.

"I know, boss, but we could always use more. Let me shoot this bitch in her big fat ass," Murphy said and then grinned.

"She does have a fat ass but that's not a reason to shoot her. Let me," I said, pulling out my gun. I raised it as if I was going to point it at the sales clerk, but whirled around at the last instant and shot Murphy in the side of his head. The loud boom of the gunshot filled the store and blood, bone and brain matter mixed with strands of reddish-blonde hair, flew through the air to cover every flat surface behind him. With more than half his head gone, blood squirted up like Old Faithful as Murphy's hands twitched and spasmed.

He dropped to the floor as the girl behind the counter screamed and dived for cover. I leaned over the counter and looked at her.

"Miss, I lied. You don't have a fat ass. You have a nice round ass, now stop screaming, you're safe."

"Just take the money and leave me alone!" she yelled, covering her face with her hands.

"I don't want the money. I have my own," I said, tossing two twenties down on the counter for the gas and food. "If you don't want me to shoot you, then stop screaming." The sales clerk quit screaming and tried to control her sobs. "That's for the groceries and the gas. Now I have a question for you."

"What?" the girl stammered.

"How much is your life worth?"

"What? I...don't know."

"Is it worth fifteen minutes? If you give me fifteen minutes to get away before you call the cops, I won't shoot you."

The girl nodded her head.

"So we have a deal?"

She did some more nodding.

"I want to hear you say it."

"Yes."

"Yes what?" I asked.

"Yes, we have a deal."

"Good," I said and tucked my gun in my waistband. The girl stood up from behind the counter and called to me as I reached the exit.

"Do you really think I have a nice ass?" she asked.

"Yeah, but you could stand to lose a few pounds, though. If you lay off the Twinkies it shouldn't be too hard," I said. She shot me a brief smile through her tears.

When I stepped out the front door, Ashley jumped out of the Charger, her eyes wide with fear as she came running at me. I guess she realized that I'd splattered Murphy's brains across the Quick Mart's floor. Blood dripped down Ashley's arms and I saw fresh cuts and I guess she'd found her knife.

It didn't pay to leave Ashley alone with a blade. She flailed her arms about, trying to pummel me with her fists and claw at me with her nails. Putting my hand against her chest, I shoved her back. Pulling her knife, she charged forward. I stuck out my right fist and she ran right into it. The impact caused her to fly backward and land on her butt. Blood dribbled down her face from her broken nose. Stepping forward, I took her knife, grabbed her by her long hair and dragged her to the car. Opening the driver's side door, I heaved her into the passenger seat and slid behind the wheel. Firing up the Charger, I drove out of the parking lot, smoking the tires.

Five miles down the highway, I pulled onto the shoulder and put the transmission into park. Ashley clung to the armrest on the passenger door. Tears streamed down her face and blood dripped from her nose and arms.

"Look at you. You're a mess," I said. Taking off my t-shirt, I ripped it into strips and reached over to bandage her wounds, but she pulled away. Grabbing her arm, I pulled her close to me.

"Be still," I said. I bandaged her arms, cleaned her face, and then leaned back to look at her. Her nose was slightly askew but she'd live.

"Why did you kill Murphy?" she asked.

"Murphy was a piece of shit. He was going to kill the sales clerk."

"So?"

"So, she didn't need killing. Get out of the car," I told her.

Ashley put her hand on my thigh.

"I want to stay with you. I'll be your girlfriend. I'll do whatever you want."

"Look at your arms. I can't leave you alone for five minutes without you cutting yourself. Get out of the car, hike back to the Quick Mart and tell the police that Murphy and I forced you to come with us. Blame everything on Murphy. The police will take you back to the hospital."

"I hate that place."

"You need to be in the hospital, you're sick. Now get out of the damn car!" I yelled, stroking the butt of the .45 in my waistband.

"Can I at least have my knife back?" she asked in a whinny little voice.

"If I let you have the knife back, you'll just sit on the side of the road and cut yourself. Besides, I might need it," I replied.

Ashley climbed out of the car and I pulled away, leaving her in a cloud of dust. Pulling over after dark, I hid the car behind a grove of trees. Studying a map I found inside the glove box, I circled Sioux Falls, Iowa with a pen I found on the dash. After previously studying Billy the Burner's MO, I saw a pattern. He would strike and then move on, usually west.

As I drove, I had heard about a random killing over the car radio where a couple was killed and left hanging from a tree. This didn't fit his pattern, but Billy had a lust for little girls and he would have to fill that need soon. Sioux Falls seemed like the next most likely place he would strike.

On further study, I noticed a small little town on the outside of Sioux Falls known as Cedar Glen. It had a warehouse district on the edge of town and I would bet money that Billy's next stop would be at Cedar Glen. Putting the map away, I stretched out to get some sleep, knowing when I woke up, I was in for a long drive.

* * *

Rolling through Sioux Falls, Iowa the following evening, I rented a cheap motel room in Cedar Glen. The next morning, I drove around looking for the local middle schools. There were three in all and I settled on one near the center of town. I decided to watch this school for a day or two, and if nothing panned out, I'd case the other two schools, but my gut feeling told me that Billy would choose this one. When you hunt a hunter, your tactics have to be different. When a scumbag trolls a school, they park close to where the children scamper down the sidewalk. They try to blend in and make the snatch and grab before anyone is the wiser. When you hunt one of those bastards, you stay back and take in the entire scene.

Parking in the lot of a city park across the street, I watched the school for three days. I thought one man was Billy the Burner, as he seemed suspicious, but then a little girl came running up to his car screaming, "Daddy! Daddy!" and jumped in.

On the third day, I was about to give up and go check out one of the other schools when I noticed an old, white Ford van parked by itself down the street from the school. The bell rang, kids poured out of the school to fill the sidewalk, and the van started up and pulled forward. A pretty, little, dark-haired girl was skipping down the sidewalk when the van stopped. A small, thin man with a scraggly goatee jumped out of the van, ran up the sidewalk, and scooped the little girl into his arms. The girl screamed, the other kids and parents looked around in fear, and the man ran back to the Ford van before anyone realized what was happening. He tossed the girl into the driver's side, climbed behind the wheel, and sped away with his tires smoking, leaving both parents and children alike in shock. A few parents were on cell phones, calling the police no doubt.

Firing up the Charger, I shot out of the parking lot to follow the van. Billy the Burner shot through several red lights and took two quick turns trying to lose me, but I stayed on his ass like Super Glue. He headed west toward the warehouse district, but a big rig pulled in front of me, and by the time I was around the truck, Billy's white van was nowhere in sight.

"Shit!" I yelled, slamming my fist down on the steering wheel. After getting control of my anger, I paused to think things through. "You're not getting away that easy, Billy," I muttered to myself, hoping that he didn't hurt the girl before I found him. Billy usually didn't do too much to his young victims until he got hold of their mothers as well.

*   *   *

A half hour later, I rolled through the gates of a massive industrial complex. Warehouses, some abandoned and some not, filled several acres of land, looking almost like a small city unto itself. I knew Billy was in here somewhere, this was the perfect place for him.

I drove up and down the streets between the buildings for over an hour. I was about to give up, deciding my hunch was wrong, when I spotted the white Ford van sitting in a dirt lot. Pulling up behind it, I turned off the motor on the Charger and walked over to the van. Peering in the driver's side window, I found no sign of Billy or the girl. I gazed about at the warehouses filling the complex, the structures like soldiers standing at attention.

"Where are you, Billy?" I said and then let out a sigh in frustration. Getting back into the Charger, I found a secluded spot near the entrance and parked under a large oak tree. There was only one way in or out and Billy had to leave sometime.

I sat watching the entrance to the industrial complex for a full day. On the morning of the second day, Billy left the complex in his white van and I followed from a discreet distance. He stopped at a liquor store and used a pay phone. After making his call, he bought a six-pack of beer and headed back to the complex. I followed, leaving several car lengths between us, and took up my position near the gate once more. I didn't want to follow him inside; that might spook him. The girl's mother showed up the next evening. My eyes locked with the terrified eyes of a beautiful blonde-headed woman when she pulled up to the gate, my heart almost stopping. I had never seen such a beautiful face or such ocean blue eyes in my life nor had I ever seen anyone with such pain in their eyes.

"I think I'm in love," I said to myself and watched her pull through the gate. Pulling the Charger in behind her, I followed her into the industrial complex. She took several turns, driving between buildings and then stopped in front of a large rust-gray building at the end of the row. Parking three hundred feet behind her, I watched her enter the warehouse carrying her purse and a nylon gym bag. Pulling around the corner, I ate a sandwich and drank a soda while I waited.

Soon, icy fingers of darkness stabbed their way across the land and shadows formed between the warehouses. When darkness covered everything like a warm blanket, I climbed out of the Charger, grabbed a tire iron, and my duffel bag. Entering the warehouse, I became one with the night. In front of me lay a vast open area, but I saw a flickering light in the distance. Someone laughed, a woman screamed as I silently moved toward the light. Stepping up behind Billy the Burner, I peered over his shoulder.

He had the mother naked, tied spread eagle, to a rusty box spring from a mattress set. Unaware of my presence, Billy knelt down and went to work on her with a pair of pliers. The woman screamed, and even with the red welts covering her body, she was still the most beautiful woman I'd ever seen. My eyes danced over her body, taking in every curve.

The little girl lay off to the side in a drug-induced slumber. The mother's dress lay in tatters on the floor along with her purse and the gym bag.

"That one must have hurt a bit," Billy said and laughed. "Fun time's over now. Time to eat." He set the pliers aside and reached for a skinning knife. The woman's eyes widened when she saw me standing behind Billy the Burner. Before she could scream or do anything to alert Billy to my presence, I brought the tire iron crashing down on his head. He dropped to the floor like a sack of wheat, unconscious.

* * *

Pulling my knife—the one taken from Ashley—I cut the woman free, grabbed her coat and took her hand, helping her to her feet. Holding the coat open, I looked into her eyes, trying not to stare at her naked body. Tears streamed down her face, and I reached up and wiped one away.

"Get a grip. You need to take care of your daughter."

"How did you..."

"It doesn't matter. Get your daughter and get out of here," I said.

"How can I ever repay you?" the woman sobbed.

"Take your daughter home and love her. That's payment enough."

"Thank you," she whispered and then hugged me.

"If God forbid something like this ever happens again, and the scumbag tells you not to call the cops, don't listen. The police need to be involved early in a case like this."

"I won't ever let something like this happen again. Are you sure I can't pay you? I have money."

I shook my head. "No. That's not necessary. Take your daughter and go home. I have business with Billy, here."

The woman hugged me one more time, and then picked up her daughter and left. She left the purse and gym bag behind. She must have left the keys in her Mercedes, because I heard the engine fire up and I heard her pull away. Reaching down, I rolled Billy over and got the shock of my life. He was a monster after all with big reptilian features shimmering underneath.

"This is like getting two for the price of one," I said to myself and then grinned. Taking a syringe from Billy's pile of things, I injected him with some of his own medicine. I needed him to sleep while I made things ready. Reaching into my gym bag, I brought out my bone saw.

* * *

Billy woke to the putrid smell of burning flesh. After stripping him naked and tying him to the same box spring the woman had been tied to, I cut off both his hands and feet. Cauterizing the wounds with a torch from a fire I started with scrap wood, I tied him by his stubs where his hands and feet used to be. Billy's severed hands and feet were soon roasting like chestnuts over an open flame. Billy screamed in pain, half delirious from his wounds.

"I hope you're hungry," I said, taking a small piece of sizzling meat from the fire. I leaned over Billy, pried open his mouth, dropped the piece of meat down the hatch, and squeezed his lips closed. Billy gagged and then swallowed the meat.

"What was that? It tastes almost like chicken," Billy said in a raspy sounding voice.

"That was a piece of your left foot," I laughed. "You should have taken better care of your feet. I found them offensive so I cut them off." I paused for a moment while Billy screamed. "Now let's talk about your hands. They were dirty. You should have tried to keep them cleaner. They say cleanliness is next to Godliness, but you don't have to worry about that anymore." Billy let out another terrified scream. Pulling out of the fire the crispy piece of meat that had once been Billy's right hand, I held it up in front of him. "Are you still hungry? Would you care for some more? There's more than enough."

"Who the hell are you?" Billy whispered.

"I'm the Grim Reaper and I'm here to take you home."

"There's money over there. Take it and leave," Billy pleaded.

I shrugged. "I don't need money."

"Then kill me and get it over with."

"I thought I'd give you a taste of the pain and suffering you've caused others before I send you to meet the Devil, you cannibalistic son-of-a-bitch. We're just getting started."

Tossing down the burning piece of meat, I pulled out the stick it had been on and jabbed it into Billy's left eye. Ignoring his screams, I went after the other eye, then tossed both eyeballs into a frying pan Billy had with him, cooking them up like they were a delicacy.

"Down the hatch," I said, forcing Billy's mouth open again. I dropped both of his half-cooked eyeballs down his throat and made him swallow. Picking up the torch from the fire, I ran it up and down what was left of his right leg. The flesh sizzled and Billy's screams filled my ears. Whistling while I worked, I moved the torch to Billy's left leg. I wanted him thoroughly cooked. The flesh on his leg turned black and a putrid smell rose into the air. Moving the flame to his genitals, I fanned the air in front of my face. He let out another blood-curdling scream as his genitals began to cook.

"Talk about stinky," I said. "That hot link looks like it's been on the grill for far too long. I'd make you eat it, but I don't want to touch the nasty thing. Maybe I'll fry up those nuts of yours and you can have huevos rancheros." I tossed another piece of half-cooked human flesh into his mouth. "They say you are what you eat, and you're an asshole." I let out a low chuckle.

Moving the flame to his arms and then to his face, I grew weary. I don't get off on torturing people. When I kill someone, I usually like it to be quick and efficient but Billy was a special case. Disgusted with it all, I sprayed him with lighter fluid—another item Billy had with him—then lit a match. Tossing the match onto his chest, I watched the flames consume him. Billy screamed and his body shook violently as he was burned alive.

Billy the Burner's reign of terror was over.

*   *   *

Picking up my duffel bag, I grabbed the woman's things and headed to the Charger. Rummaging through the woman's purse, I found her ID. I took a local map out of the glove box and found her street. After cruising up and down the street on the lookout for the police, I parked across the street from her house and saw lights on in the living room. Taking her purse along with the gym bag filled with money, I carried them to the front porch and set them down. I rang the doorbell and then hurried back to the Charger.

Looking through the rearview mirror, I saw the woman come to the door as I drove away. Near the highway, I pulled into the parking lot of a 7-Eleven. Walking to a payphone, I called the local police.

"Cedar Glen Police Department," a female voice said. "How may I direct your call?"

"You'll find Billy the Burner in the industrial complex west of town. He's in the rusty-gray building near the back. You'll have to identify him by his dental records though as he's a little over done."

"Sir, can I have your name?"

"If you have trouble finding him, just follow your nose."

"Sir, your name?"

I hung up the phone and ambled over to the 7-Eleven. An older black Mustang with a 5.0 Liter V8 pulled in off the highway and parked in front of the store. A sexy looking blonde wearing a pink tank top and a pair of Daisy Duke shorts climbed out of the passenger side. Her large breasts strained the fabric of the tank top. A friendly looking guy climbed out on the driver's side. Tears welled up in the blonde's eyes, and at the door, she stopped, turned toward the guy and hugged him.

"I'm going to miss her so much, Mike. Why did she have to die?" the woman asked and then burst into full-blown tears. The guy patted her gently on the back, not knowing what to do.

"I don't know, but she's in a better place now. She's in Heaven, Roxy," the man said. He looked over the woman's shoulder, our eyes met, and he seemed to look into my soul. It was as if he knew me in an instant, knew what I was all about and approved. I saw in him a kindred spirit, someone who'd seen things that no one should see—some one like me. I wondered if he saw monsters, too. A trace of a smile spread across his face; I shrugged and walked past them into the store. After buying a soda and a bag of potato chips, I left the store, crossed the parking lot to the highway and stuck out my thumb.

* * *

An elderly couple dropped me off at the road leading to the hospital three days later and it felt good to be home. Walking up to the main gate, I noticed Carl Washington, an older security guard, was on duty at the guard shack. A shocked look crossed his face when I stepped up to him.

"Brad. You decided to come home?"

"Yeah, Carl, I've had enough fun for a while."

"They'll put you back in the padded room for what you did to Weaver and then escaping, you know that, right? And there's a few new murders the police are investigating with your name attached."

"Yeah, I imagine so. I didn't do that old couple at the farmhouse, that was Murphy. I killed him because he was about to kill a clerk that worked at a Quick Mart."

"Murphy was an asshole. The world is better off without him," Carl said.

"Did Ashley show up?" I asked.

"She's here. I'll open the gate and send a car down for you," Carl replied.

"I'd appreciate that." There was a whirring sound as the new electronic gate slid open.

"Was that you that did all that stuff to Billy the Burner?" he asked.

"Yeah, that was me," I said. "That's why I had to escape. I needed to take care of him before he hurt anyone else."

"Really? Hell, Brad, people say you're crazy but I don't think so. Billy deserved what he got. Good riddance, I say."

"I'm not crazy, Carl. I'm just a bad man with dammed good intentions," I replied with a smile.

Stepping away from the guard shack, I walked through the gate and onto the hospital grounds, as the car drove down from the main building to pick me up and lock me away for a long time.

JUST BECAUSE

ANTHONY GIANGREGORIO

The pliers were cold and slippery as they slid into Seth's mouth; he could taste the metal.

The rough metal teeth on the tool scraped against his rear left molar, the operator of the pliers lazy, not worrying about whether or not he was pinching the tongue. The upper and lower ends of the pliers locked down on the tooth and Seth squeezed his eyes shut, knowing what was coming.

There was a slight pause as the owner of the tool braced himself, then there was a blinding white pain and the tooth was ripped from its mooring of twenty-six years.

Blood exploded outward from the gaping hole in his lower gum and Seth let loose a blood-soaked scream that would have shattered glass.

The scream was long and loud, filled with pain and suffering. In time, the screaming abated and Seth grew quiet once more. His lower jaw throbbed with each pulse of his heart and he felt like he was going to throw up. Bile crept to the top of his throat and he knew any second he would vomit.

His vision swam with white light as the agony that was his mouth subsided to a dull roar. When he was finally able to open his eyes, he found himself looking up at his torturer.

The man was tall, well over six feet, with muscles that strained his tight shirt. His simple pair of blue jeans and the tight shirt was now covered in blood splatter. Seth knew that it was his blood splatter he saw.

"Please, no more, don't do this to me," Seth whimpered, but just like before when he'd begged the torturer for mercy, his pleas were ignored. "Why? Why are you doing this to me?" he whispered, wanting to know the answer, but as always the tall man who has caused him so much pain said nothing.

Seth looked up once more at the mask-covered face, wishing he could at least make eye contact, but the mesh over the eyes hid everything, and all he could see was the hint of the orbs hiding within.

The man picked up a four inch long, thin stick, reminding Seth of a shish kabob skewer. Without preamble, the man placed the skewer at the tip of Seth's left index finger, the pointed tip touching just under his fingernail.

As the tip touched the tender flesh under his nail, Seth yelped, knowing what was coming and ill prepared to handle it.

"Please, God, no, don't do it. For the love of all that's holy, don't do it," he begged, tears running down his cheeks in a steady stream.

The man still acted like Seth wasn't there, as if the hand didn't belong to another human being, and with a flexing of his arm, he slid the skewer under the fingernail, causing Seth to shriek in agony. There was no way to truly describe the intense pain he felt and he thought he was going to black out, praying he would, but there was no mercy for him, no relief as he stayed conscious.

His entire hand and his lower arm felt like it was dipped in acid, the skewer sliding in with little difficulty, slicing through the meat of his finger. It felt like the skewer had been shoved in more than a foot, though in reality one small inch was all, and as the white light of pain danced across his vision, Seth prayed for death once more.

But he knew it wouldn't come, for if his torturer wanted him dead, he would have killed him a thousand times over already.

As Seth's mind swam with fog at the pain he felt, he tried once more to remember how he ended up in the chair of a torturer.

He remembered going to the night club, drinking, having a good time. He stayed till closing, and as the few other patrons and himself left to find their cars, he remembered reaching into his coat pocket and retrieving his keys.

It was as he was about to slide the key into the door lock that he caught the hint of a reflection in the side window, then he felt hot pain in his neck as his body began to convulse before he passed out. He now knew it was a taser that was used on him.

When he awoke, he was secured to the chair, his arms tied to each side of the arm rests, and his ankles were tied to the two front legs of the chair.

He was in the same room he was in now; bleak, no windows with peeling paint, dirt on the floor, and one naked bulb hanging from the ceiling on an old extension cord. It reminded him of a small room in a warehouse, a stockroom perhaps, but each time he screamed and no one came to help him, he knew that wherever he was, no one was around to hear him beg for mercy.

He was absolutely and totally at the mercy of his captor, a man who hid his face from view.

He cried out again as the car battery sent waves of voltage into his genitals. The torturer had placed the positive and negative ends to his scrotum, the two inch alligator clips biting into his flesh enough to illicit screams of agony by themselves. But then the man flicked the switch and let the electrical current flow to his groin and the rest of his body, the clips then becoming a mild nuisance in comparison.

His body spasmed and jerked in the chair and his hair stood on end. He wet himself and was glad his pants were now lying in the corner of the room. Even as he twitched from being electrocuted, he found it ironic he would so much as give a passing thought to his pants. After all, at the moment, urine on his pants was the least of his problems.

The torturer flicked the switch and the current stopped. Seth let his head sink onto his chest as he shook his head to clear it, saliva dripping out of the corner of his mouth to spill onto his chest. Electrocution was an agony there was no actual description for either. The closest thing was when a person got zapped messing with an electrical outlet but for some reason couldn't let go. If the current continued feeding into the body, as teeth chattered and limbs locked up, that was as close to a description as was possible. The switch was flicked once more and Seth began to jump in the chair, his arms and legs straining at their bonds. He began to smell an odd odor, sweet, as if someone was cooking meat on a barbeque grill, and when he realized he smelled himself cooking, he threw up, splashing warm vomit between his legs.

The torturer jumped back so as not to be splashed and he back-handed Seth with a blow that had his teeth rattling in his mouth. The switch was flicked and a second later the current ceased.

Finished with this part of the torture, the large man simply yanked at the two electrical cords attached to Seth's scrotum. The metal alligator clips refused to let go of the flesh between their teeth and that skin went with them as they were pulled away. Seth yelled out once more and looked down at a pool of blood in his crotch. His balls were bleeding now and he let out long wail, as any man would do in the same circumstance.

Defiance filled him and he hissed at his torturer, spitting bloody vomit across the distance separating them from one another.

"Bastard, so help me if I get out of this fucking chair, then we'll see how tough you are!"

The torturer's shoulders shook and Seth believed the man was laughing.

"Don't fucking laugh at me! Why are you doing this to me! Tell me, you bastard!"

The large man didn't reply but instead walked over to a small steel table which had on its smooth surface an assortment of knifes and other implements used in torturing a human being. He hovered over the scalpels, knives and needles, and Seth watched with wide eyes, knowing what the large hand landed on would spell more suffering for him.

So when the hand landed on a simple metal spoon, such as one used with tea and biscuits on a sunny afternoon, to say Seth was relieved was an understatement.

"Hah, a fucking spoon? What the hell are you gonna do with that? Make me eat a bowl of soup?"

No answer was forthcoming but Seth still felt a surge of renewed energy. Perhaps his captor had run out of ideas and the torture was finally over.

The man crossed the distance separating them and he hovered over Seth, gazing down on him from behind his mask. Seth watched the man's chest go in and out as he breathed.

The man reached out with his left hand and it locked onto Seth's forehead, pushing it back to the point his neck might very well snap. Seth struggled to break free, but with his limbs firmly secured, he had no leverage. Desperate, he spit a glob of coagulated blood onto the man's shirt, then clacked his teeth to no avail.

He still didn't know what was going to happen and he had to admit that after everything he'd been through, to have his neck snapped now seemed silly, anti-climatic, but he waited for what was to come next.

He didn't wait long.

As the man held Seth's head in place, the right hand holding the spoon slowly came up and hovered in front of Seth's eyes. It waved like a snake in a trance, moving back and forth.

Then, like a striking snake, the spoon dove downwards and the tip slid into the side of Seth's right eye. The metal was cold as it dug in deep, the spoon separating membranes and ganglia as it went in deep enough that the man pulled on the handle and popped out the eye like a melon baller to a piece of cantaloupe.

On the right side of Seth's vision, it was like someone had flicked a light switch, the world going dark as blinding pain filled his skull. He screamed as the spoon scooped out his eye, leaving a bloody, gaping socket behind. As he screamed, the open socket touched the air and Seth could feel the cool air caressing the inside of the raw socket. He blinked with his remaining eye but the right side of his vision remained dark.

No sooner did he slow his screaming, the pain finally subsiding to a dull throb, then the torturer brought back the spoon once more. The tip was now bloody, dripping with a clear fluid, and Seth, even in his madness, wondered where his eye had gone to. Where was it now? Did the man toss it into the trash? Or was it in a jar with chemicals to preserve it?

He never received an answer before the spoon was going in once more and the last image he saw was the mask of his captor, then the spoon went in deep and his other eye popped out to plunge his world into darkness.

Seth sat in the chair, sobbing, his world now nothing but darkness. He could feel the blood and ooze sliding down his cheeks from his gaping eye sockets, his eyes now torn from his skull.

He didn't know how long he was left to wallow in misery but finally he heard footsteps and someone breathing. His head popped up and he muffled his cries, his ears now straining to pick up any telltale noise. With no sight, his nose also picked up the slack and he detected a musky smell that hadn't been there before.

It was his captor, his torturer, returning from whence he came; back to do more evil unto him no doubt.

"Why?" Why are you doing this to me? What did I do to deserve this?" Seth cried as his head fell back to his chest.

Once more there was no answer, but his head was grabbed by the hair and snapped back so his neck was exposed.

Though eyeless, he squeezed his eyelids closed, waiting for the final end, and truth be told, he welcomed it now. He was in so much pain he could barely breathe and death seemed like a welcome release.

Something metallic was being picked up, he could hear the rattle on the nearby table and then he tasted metal again.

"Oh, God no, no more!" he screamed around the end of the pliers but the captor ignored his pleas and went to work once more. Like a dentist from a B horror movie, the man was cruel beyond words. Not settling for one simple molar, this time he began tearing out tooth after tooth, Seth screaming as each one was ripped from his mouth in a bloody spray.

Blood and gruel slid from his mouth to coat his chest in crimson and he howled in utter agony, the unbelievable pain causing him to pass out more than once.

But smelling salt aroused him each time and the torturer went right back to work. Seth wondered if when he passed out the man would go grab a smoke, maybe a cup of coffee. Like a man in an office building, he would pause and run to the smoking area, suck on a cancer stick to then run back to his cubicle and resume working.

When all but two of his front teeth were removed, leaving his gums a wrecked amalgam of raw meat, he left Seth alone again. He couldn't see but nevertheless, white light flashed before his mind's eye as his mouth throbbed with the electricity of exposed nerves. It felt like he was gargling lava, the nerves flaring each time he breathed. He passed out more than once but sooner or later would awake once more.

Time lost all meaning in his prison of darkness and agony. Days, weeks, or perhaps minutes, it all was one large entity to him now.

His captor returned when he was awake one time and the torture began anew.

Seth heard him pause and then the sound of a glass jar being opened. Even in his agony, he was amazed how sharp his hearing had become in such a short time. He had heard when a person loses their sight, their other senses grow stronger, but he had never truly believed it until now.

There was a lull in the torture as the man did something with the jar. Seth continued to move his head to the left and right, trying to pick up a telltale sound.

And then something touched his leg, something cold.

No sooner did the liquid touch him then the cold turned into searing heat that filled him from his toes to his head. He shrieked loudly, spitting blood and phlegm from his mouth. As he shrieked in pain, his nose detected the scent of burning meat and he quickly realized it was *his* meat he smelled.

Acid! It was acid!

Another few drops touched his other leg and he roared in agony as the acid ate into his leg, his flesh and muscle dissolving into a sticky red goo.

He kicked his legs as if he could shrug off the acid but it did nothing to slow its descent into his limbs, and soon he couldn't even do that. The acid had eaten into his legs to the point the nerves to control the legs had been severed.

He passed out again, but was quickly revived, and as he swooned in delirium, he heard something that had his stomach falling out from within him.

He heard his legs drop off and fall to the floor from where they had been severed from his thighs, thanks to the acid eating away at the flesh and bone.

With the wounds cauterized, he wasn't going to bleed out, and though his legs were now long gone, he swore he could still feel them.

As if it was a game, his captor picked up the legs and slapped him with them a few times, his own feet striking him in the cheeks to leave welts and bruises. Just before he passed out, and heard the sound of his legs being tossed into a corner of the room. Then he welcomed the oblivion once more.

Smelling salts revived him and though technically awake, he was so out of it from the pain he could barely think straight.

Suddenly he felt something cold slice across his left bicep and he let out a small yell. A second later, another cold slice went across his lower arm, then another and another all over his body. At first he didn't understand. Though it stung, it was certainly not as painful as the other tortures he'd received at the hands of his captor but then, as the air slowly touched the paper thin cuts, he realized what his captor had planned.

Similar to a Chinese torture, he was being cut, sliced if you will, dozens upon dozens of times. The thin cuts stung with an intensity that a simple slice from a knife could never accomplish, the razor thin slices were similar to paper cuts and each one stung a little more with each passing second until it felt like his entire body was on fire.

He didn't know how many shallow wounds he received, but he knew when his captor was through he was going mad with the stings as each one throbbed and pulsed with a life of its own. It was like an itch he couldn't scratch and he yelled and jumped in his chair, but he was trapped and would never be free.

"Oh God, fucking kill me and get it over with, you son-of-a-bitch!" he growled, the words slurring without all but two of his teeth. And he did want to die. Sightless, no legs, pretty much no teeth, death would be a welcome release from the hell his life now was. And yet he still didn't know why this was happening to him.

He detected the torturer near him and he shifted his head, trying to hear where the man was.

He quickly found out when yet another skewer was placed under the fingernail of his left thumb, the wood jammed deep, causing him to shriek loudly. Red spittle flew from his mouth and phlegm dripped from his nostrils as he cried and shook with agony.

His world was now nothing but blinding pain wrapped in a sea of darkness and he cried and screamed, switching out which one depending on the torture.

And then, through his sobs, he heard the unmistakable sound of a blade being honed on a sharpening stone. By the breadth of the scraping blade, Seth knew it was long, and visions of pangas and machetes flitted through his mind.

He wondered if this was finally it. If this was the time when he would finally be released from the prison that was his mangled body. He felt something being tied around his right wrist—rope by the feel of it—and when it was pulled taut, he yelped but controlled his voice. He knew if he was yelling then he couldn't hear what his captor was doing to him.

No sooner did the rope grow tight then his hand began to hurt as all blood was prevented from flowing into it. The man walked away and the honing of the blade continued.

As Seth's hand began to throb, reminding him of how it felt when as a boy he had wrapped a rubber band around his index finger and watched the tip grow purple from lack of blood, the sharpening stopped. Then he heard footsteps and he muffled his sobs as he listened to the large man step ever closer.

He didn't hear the blade rise into the air nor hear it fall, but he did feel it when the blade chopped off his hand, a bolt of lightning-quick pain filling his mind and causing him to pass out as soon as it suffused his body.

When he awoke, his hand throbbed, but when he tried to move it he could feel nothing. The more he tried to wiggle the hand, the more he could feel nothing, though there seemed to be a phantom ghost of the limb still there.

He could hear heavy breathing near him, and just before another burst of blinding pain filled his insides like liquid fire, he realized his other wrist had been wrapped in rope, then the blade came down and the hand was lopped off to fall to the floor in a splatter of blood.

Once more he slid into unconsciousness, the overwhelming pain too much for his receptors.

He came to again, lost in a world of darkness. He didn't know how long he stayed that way and each time he passed out he hoped it would be his last, but smelling salts would always revive him.

But no matter how much his captor wanted to make him suffer, there was only so long a body could survive the abuse his was receiving and now the only defiance he had was to die, to finally spoil the fun his torturer was having.

But what could he do to kill himself? He was tied to a chair, no legs and no hands, sightless, what felt like a hundred stinging yet shallow wounds covering his body. Even if he lived, if right now he was saved, what kind of a life would he have?

He wracked his pain-befuddled mind to figure out some way to kill himself, but nothing came to mind.

Until one idea, though drastic as it was, finally came to him.

He didn't know if he could do it but he had no choice.

For whatever reason, his captor had left him two teeth, both at the front of his mouth. They weren't properly lined up but he shoved his tongue between them, the slippery muscle slipping out more than once.

He could hear his torturer puttering about, and he heard the sound of metal objects, that noise letting him know more pain was to follow soon.

He clicked his remaining teeth together but each time his tongue slid free. He could hear his captor walking toward him now and he let out a soft whimper and forced his tongue between the two teeth, then clamped down as hard as he could. Pain flared in his head as he began to grind the two teeth together, shredding his tongue into a mangled mess. Even when the two teeth had sliced into the tongue, he opened his mouth, repositioned his tongue, and then slammed the teeth together, more pain filling him until he wondered if he would pass out yet again.

As his teeth shredded his tongue, he tasted blood, a lot of it, as it began to slide down his throat. At first he tried to swallow it out of instinct, but as more and more hot blood gushed out of his mangled tongue and slid down his throat, he found he couldn't keep up.

But that was what he wanted to happen.

He began to drown on blood.

He heard his captor yell, "No!" and the man raced to Seth, trying to pry open his mouth. But with a resolve of a dead man Seth refused to open, though fingers probed around his lips and force their way into his mouth.

Unable to keep his jaw shut, the fingers pried his lips apart but the blood continued to flow, slipping out onto his chest as well as down his throat.

"No, no, you bastard, you can't die, not yet! I'm not done with you!" his captor yelled in frustration.

Seth began to laugh as his lungs filled with blood. He was dying, and best of all, he was cheating his torturer of killing Seth himself.

He began to cough, his breathing becoming difficult, and as the torturer cut his bonds and threw him to the floor to work on him, trying to save him with CPR, Seth knew the man was too late.

His mind was growing fuzzy and he knew this time he would not awake, and he managed one last word to his captor, though he didn't expect an answer.

"*Why?*"

He was sliding into the dark void of death, but this time his torturer replied, knowing his victim was done for.

"No reason, really, just because."

In his last second on Earth, after hearing that statement, Seth knew if he'd had just one more second, he would have laughed at the irony of it all.

But that second was denied him.

REFLECTION OF EVIL

KELLY M. HUDSON

"That was the day we sat here, in this very room, and sold our souls to the Devil," Mrs. Gadsden said. She rocked back and forth, the memory of that moment as fresh on her mind as the day it happened.

Dr. Coleman took a step back and shook his head slowly. It was one thing to investigate hauntings, he believed, but it was quite another to deal with a possession. It was a good thing he'd brought along his reliable friend and psychic, Jacob Sterns, who stood over to the side, looking out at the room, his chubby face white as a picket fence.

Dr. Coleman, a fifty-four year old man with a stooped back, pot belly, balding head with a ring of white hair in the shape of a horseshoe, a long white beard, and tiny spectacles, resembled a younger version of Santa Claus. He never dressed in red for this very reason.

Jacob was nearly the opposite of Dr. Coleman. He was thirty-two, with a thick head of black hair that looked like the last time it saw a comb was the first day his mother sent him out to school as a child, perfect vision and almost hawk-like black eyes, and a dark goatee. He was, as his last name indicated, a very serious man.

"What do you see, Jacob?" Dr. Coleman asked, turning to face his friend. He often wondered how Jacob experienced things and one day had asked him. Jacob had smiled and said it would be like trying to explain the color blue to a blind man. Dr. Coleman left it alone after that, but curiosity remained.

"This place is thick with demons," Jacob said. He stirred the air in front of his face like it was thick brine. Jacob never seemed flustered over any paranormal spirit, and in all the times they'd worked together, Dr. Coleman had never once seen Jacob the least bit worried. But the look on Jacob's face as he stood there, staring off at something only he could see, was one of fear. Dr. Coleman was sure of it. He shivered as Mrs. Gadsden spoke.

"As I was saying," Mrs. Gadsden continued. "We sold our souls and invited a deep evil into our lives. They permeate this place."

Mrs. Gadsden was seventy-five and appeared closer to ninety. She was a small woman, with soft gray skin that hung from her face, and had hands like laundry flapping in the wind. She had blue eyes set inside sockets deep as a fleshless skull, and she wore a black dress that was buttoned tight at her waist, chest, and up her neck to her chin. The loose skin dripped on the edges of the dress and made Dr. Coleman think of angel food cake.

The room they were meeting in was the den of Mrs. Gadsden's large mansion. It was located in the middle of the house and was populated with antique cherry wood furniture; dark, hard and ancient. There were chairs of the sitting and rocking variety, two couches with golden cushions, two tables, and a dresser in the corner on which were situated several family portraits. The walls were dark beige and there were paintings, two to each wall, sagging with age, depicting hunting dogs and feasting peasants. It was a room that seemed once pleasant, but the passing of time had robbed it of its light and replaced it with decay and distress.

"Yes, there is evil here," Jacob said. He turned and stared at Mrs. Gadsden. "What did you do?"

She smiled. "You are the psychic," she stated. "Why don't you tell me?"

Jacob offered an easy smile to counter the cold coming from Mrs. Gadsden.

"You profess knowledge of the dark arts and of Magick in general, and yet you mock me, a person you should feel quite in league with in many respects," Jacob said, a twinkle in his eye. "It makes me wonder if this story you just told us was true in any way at all."

"How dare you question me," Mrs. Gadsden said, fire seeming to jump from her eyes to leap across the room, threatening to burn Jacob's eyebrows off. "If you only knew who I was and what I've done, you would be quivering with fear."

"Oh," Jacob said. "I know who you are and what you've done. Your demon companions all fondly whisper of the debauchery you've done in your life. But you, ma'am, despite your story, appear to be the only one in this room who isn't filled with fear."

Dr. Coleman was certainly scared, and he was a professional. He'd been in dozens of haunted houses and never once had the feeling of dread that was pricking the base of his neck. And for Jacob to admit to being frightened...It made him shudder.

Mrs. Gadsden glared at Jacob but he didn't break his smile. He stood and let her fume. Finally, she ducked her head and sighed, weary. "I am afraid," she said. "My companions that day, not one of us knew what we were getting into. It was a game for us. We were young and had the whole world in front of us, and when we broke out the board and spoke to the spirits, we thought it was all quite fun."

"Until your friends started dying, one by one, every five years," Jacob said.

"But you must understand, when the spirit spoke to us through the board, it promised so much. And its words were like the whispers of a lover in your ear," Mrs. Gadsden sighed, her eyes misting over, lost in her memories. "None of us could turn away."

"The dark spirits always promise much," Dr. Coleman added, finally finding his voice. "They also deliver. But the costs are too much to bear, and never in equality with what's given."

"Very true," Mrs. Gadsden agreed. She fell silent again.

Jacob tilted his head, as if listening to voices only he heard. He stood very quiet and still, observing the room.

Dr. Coleman, feeling better now that he was a participant again, paced the room, tucking his hands behind his back. "The first to die was Thomas Daniels, five years after the pact."

"Yes...Thomas..." Mrs. Gadsden said, her words trailing off.

"He was kicked in the head by a horse in his father's stable," Dr. Coleman said. Mrs. Gadsden nodded. "It was such an ordinary death that none of us took it as being from the Devil."

"Before he died, he made quite a bit of money in horse racing, didn't he?" Dr. Coleman inquired.

"Yes. And again, nothing out of the ordinary. His father owned a stable," Mrs. Gadsden said.

"Next was Abigail Foster. She made a fortune when she discovered, quite by accident it seemed, a large pool of oil on her property," Dr. Coleman said.

"Yes."

"And when she died, five years after Thomas Daniels, drowned in the very oil that had made her rich, you had no suspicions?" Dr. Coleman asked.

"None. It was unfortunate, but…"

"Then your dearest friend, as you described him, Grant Stevenson, he also died five years later, a supposed victim of a curse from the mummy's tomb he'd discovered; a discovery that made him wealthy and famous. He was found dead with one of the gold necklaces from the tomb wrapped so tightly around his neck that it squeezed his head until it had nearly popped from his shoulders."

"Please," Mrs. Gadsden said. "I don't want to talk of my friends anymore. It's too painful."

"Each one died, one every five years, and each death more bizarre than the last, and you would have us believe that none of you once, in all that time, equated your sudden fortunes and deaths with the pact you made that night?" Dr. Coleman asked. He shook his head and stopped his pacing. "I find that hard to believe, ma'am."

"We had our suspicions, yes," Mrs. Gadsden offered. "But it seemed so unbelievable."

"Until you were visited last month," Jacob said, rejoining the conversation. He was no longer smiling.

"Yes," Mrs. Gadsden said. "It's true."

Dr. Coleman opened his mouth to speak, to address this new fact that they were both previously unaware of, but Jacob stuck out his hand and cut him off. It was Jacob's show now.

"You have been very clever, weaving the truth of your situation into a fabric that, at its base, is a complete and total falsehood," Jacob said.

Mrs. Gadsden's eyebrows arched and her hands fidgeted at the handles of her chair. Her left cheek twitched almost imperceptibly.

"You are gifted, sir," she said.

"Yes, and you are full of nastiness," Jacob said. He lifted his head and cried out to no one in particular, at least, no one who could be seen. "Show yourself, vile creature!"

Nothing happened. All went silent for a moment and Dr. Coleman gazed about the room, his eyes wide and full of apprehension. He had no idea where Jacob was going with this, but Dr. Coleman had heard Jacob call out demons before, and he knew that was precisely what was happening here.

The air left the room. For the briefest of instances, a vacuum filled the space between all living and undead things. Dr. Coleman gasped, his throat tight and restricted, his heart pounding, fuelled by pure panic. Then the air returned and he caught his breath. His hand shot out and grabbed the table next to him so that he could steady himself and not fall.

A dark shadow fell on the room. There was nowhere for this shadow to come from, but come it did. It swept through them, large and deep and cold, so very cold. Something in the shadow roared, like a lion, and a cavernous thrumming vibrated the air. Goosebumps erupted across Dr. Coleman's flesh as the demon roared; the humming sound filled his ears and made him dizzy. He lurched to the side and fell face first onto the floor, his stomach churned and he vomited from his mouth and nose. His back arched like he was having a seizure as he lost total control of his bodily functions. His bowels and kidneys let loose, spewing filth inside his pants. Dr. Coleman laid in it, too ashamed, afraid and sickened to move.

The shadow drifted over Jacob but didn't seem to affect him in any way. Then it left Jacob and flew across the room, settling over Mrs. Gadsden. Her body spasmed as Dr. Coleman's had, and she too, vacated her bowels and kidneys. Her head slumped and her chin touched her chest as she suddenly went very still. She raised her head and looked at Jacob.

Dr. Coleman recovered enough to stare up at Mrs. Gadsden, to look deep into her blue eyes and watch them cloud over and turn black. He wished to God that he hadn't.

"You summoned me," she said. But it wasn't her. It was the thing inside of her that spoke. Its voice was ancient and dripped with malevolence. It was as if the words coming from her lips were made of physical properties; heavy, sonorous and abominable.

Jacob smiled a bitter smile and glared at the thing in Mrs. Gadsden.

"What is your name, demon?" he asked.

"What does it matter to you?" it replied. "Do you wish dominion over me? Do you believe it works that way?"

"I am no priest, demon," he said. "I am Jacob Sterns, but you know that already, don't you? You arranged all of this, didn't you? Promising Mrs. Gadsden freedom from her pact if she delivered me to you. Isn't that right?"

"You are clever," it said. "My brothers and sisters have whispered tales of you. Tales of hatred."

"My, how that breaks my heart," Jacob said.

The thing in Mrs. Gadsden studied Jacob for a moment, its foul breath filling the room, soiling the air, permeating deeper than the stench of feces and urine. A slight growl slipped from between its lips and then it laughed, the sound like crushing glass.

"You mock now, but when I deliver you to those that hate you, your mirth will turn to tears," it said.

"What is your name, demon?"

"Do you know what it is like to dwell in Hell? Do you know the pain and the constant torment?" it asked.

"Well deserved, I'd say," Jacob said.

"Do you even know what Hell is? Do you understand why we seek to escape it at any chance we have?"

"I really don't care," Jacob said.

"Hell is a series of mirrors, Jacob Sterns," it said. "You are made to sit and gaze at yourself and you see everything of your past and present, everything that you have done. You see yourself for who you truly are. It is terribly beyond imagining."

"For some, I'm sure," Jacob said.

"It is the absence of God, of any hope of any redemption. It is the hideous truth that you are forced to look upon," it said. "Perhaps now, with my explanation, you can understand why so many that you have sent back to the depths wish a taste of vengeance."

Jacob shrugged his shoulders in a casual way. Dr. Coleman watched, still too afraid to move, astounded that Jacob was so cool, so calm. He'd worked many cases with Jacob but in their time together, they had never encountered anything like this. He wondered about Jacob and his history, about how much he didn't know about the man he called a friend.

Jacob strolled in the general direction of the demon, taking his time, whistling a low tune between his lips. "You know a lot about me, demon," he said. "Why not tell me your name? You seem to be sure of yourself and your abilities. There is nothing to fear from me, is there?"

It howled and lifted up out of the chair, hovering Mrs. Gadsden's body in the air for a moment before setting it back down. Her mouth moved forward, her teeth straining against her lips until they split in half, right down the middle. Blood dribbled down her chin as her tongue lashed the air.

"Cute," Jacob said. "But if you truly know of me, then you know your little parlor tricks mean nothing to me."

"I will send you to Hell where you belong!" it said. Its voice sliced the air like razors.

Jacob continued his walk and stopped briefly by the bureau sitting next to the prone body of Dr. Coleman. On it sat a small hand mirror. He looked down at it, smiled, then looked back up at the demon.

"You do a lot of talking, demon, but you don't do much else," Jacob said.

"You dare to continue to taunt me?" it asked.

Jacob shrugged again. "What have you done to impress me? Fly around the room? Act spooky? Take over the body of an old woman who's already sold her soul? Any demon could do that."

"I warn you," it said.

"Yes, yes," Jacob waved his hand, dismissing the warning. "I'm so very afraid."

It howled and rose out of the seat again and hovered in the air.

"You bore me," Jacob said.

The demon screeched and rolled its eyes into the back of its head.

"So you're the best Hell could send?" Jacob laughed.

Items jumped from tables and counter tops and flew around the room; brushes, glasses, coasters, all spun as if caught up in a whirlwind. Dr. Coleman covered his head with his arms and whimpered. Jacob may not have been impressed, he may have stood there, stoic in the middle of the maelstrom, but Dr. Coleman was more frightened than he'd ever been. He peered out between his arms and watched as Jacob stood calmly and threw his head back and chuckled. His bravery, it seemed to Dr. Coleman, bordered on the foolhardy.

Jacob took a step towards the demon and all of the items flying around the room dropped and clanged on the floor. The demon, still hovering in the air, turned its gaze on Jacob.

"I will crush you and send you to Hell!" it hissed.

Jacob laughed again until something invisible slapped his face and then punched his stomach, bending him over. He was then slapped in the face again with such force that he spun and crashed into the bureau next to him.

The invisible force continued its assault; it grabbed Jacob's hair and yanked him up until his toes scraped the floor and he hung immobile as unseen hands struck him. His cheeks flared red and swelled, visible finger marks in the form of welts appearing and burning against the crisp air of the room. The invisible hand holding him up by his hair yanked again only this time the hair tore free and he crashed to the floor in a heap. The clump of ragged hair that was ripped from his scalp floated in the air for a moment and then fell, softly, like a group of feathers, landing next to him.

"I have only just begun," the demon said. It moved Mrs. Gadsden's body so that it stood and walked awkwardly over to Jacob. "I will make you grovel before me and call me God."

Jacob laughed again. His body shook from the mirth as the demon threw its head back and screamed a cry of rage. The hidden hands returned, grabbing Jacob by his coat and flinging him against the bureau. This time, Dr. Coleman heard bones break and he winced with empathetic pain. He watched as Jacob was punched and slammed into the bureau over and over again. Dr. Coleman knew he must do something, that he must act, but he was too afraid.

The demon lifted Jacob and set him on the top of the bureau. For the briefest of moments, six different entities were visible to Dr. Coleman, each small but very powerful. They danced around Jacob like black vapors, each helping the demon that held Mrs. Gadsden in its thrall, to thrash and assault Jacob. They flickered like waves of heat, shimmering and then gone in the blink of an eye. Dr. Coleman wondered if this was how Jacob saw these things and if so, how horrible it must be to experience them on a daily basis.

The room settled and the demon stood in front of Jacob, twisting Mrs. Gadsden's face into a hideous, rictus grin. It leaned forward, its foul breath filling the room with the smell of spoiled meat and rotten eggs.

"No more smart remarks?" it laughed.

Jacob, his face a puffy bruise, with splotches of purple the color of plums dotting his forehead, chin and cheeks, smiled. Between the bruises were the welts, red as the flame of a candle, flaring and raw.

"I'm through with you, demon," Jacob said, his swollen lips slapping together like a boxer beating a side of beef.

Jacob raised his right hand and in it he held a broken shard of the mirror that had been on the bureau. He shoved the mirror into Mrs. Gadsden's face and the demon shrieked and shrunk back, covering its eyes with it hands. It howled and screamed, memories of Hell screeching in its mind.

Jacob reached into his coat pocket with his left hand and grabbed a plastic bag of iron filings that he always carried with him. He held it up and shoved the bag into Mrs. Gadsden's mouth, tearing the bag open. The iron filings poured down her throat and the demon squalled as it pitched the old woman's body back and forth violently. Her head smacked the chair behind her and her neck snapped like a brittle twig. Mrs. Gadsden's body slumped to the floor, shaking with the death rattles of the demon within her.

Dr. Coleman watched as a dark, thick liquid hissed from her nostrils, steaming out in a thick stream and running down her face until it sunk into her skin like acid, eating away at the flesh and burning deeply.

"Behold, the physical manifestation of the demon," Jacob said.

The liquid flared with a bright yellow light and then dissipated, turning to vapors, sizzling and popping, and then gone.

All was quiet.

Jacob staggered and dipped his left hand back into his pocket. The invisible demons, the ones who had battered him mercilessly, flickered in and out of sight in front of him.

"You saw what I did to your master. Do you want the same?" Jacob warned. Blood dribbled from the corner of his mouth and ran down into his beard, matting the hair. The dark shimmers flickered, hesitated, and then swooped out of the room, shattering a window to the right of him and riding the night air to freedom.

Jacob slumped against the bureau and slid down to the floor, passing out.

Dr. Coleman, freed from the oppression of the demon, jumped to his feet. He couldn't believe what he'd witnessed but, forced by the evidence of his eyes and his ruined pants, he had little choice. He crossed the room and checked on Jacob before going to the bathroom and cleaning up. He went out to the van they'd driven to the house and rummaged through it, finding a change of pants. He put them on and returned to the house, finding it remarkably lighter in spirit, as if a heavy presence had left. Sitting up and leaning against the bureau, Jacob was awake now. He looked up at Dr. Coleman and nodded to acknowledge him.

Dr. Coleman checked Mrs. Gadsden's pulse. She was dead.

He looked over at Jacob and said, "You killed her."

"Don't weep for her," Jacob said. "She was a minion of the Devil, intent on killing us both."

"But it's murder," Dr. Coleman said.

"Destroying evil is never murder," Jacob said. He struggled to his feet, wincing with pain and gasping for breath. "It's justice."

As he fought to stand, he removed his left hand from his pocket, the one he'd used to threaten the remaining demons with.

The pocket and the hand were empty. He had bluffed the demons into surrender and retreat.

The next morning, the fire department put out the blaze consuming Mrs. Gadsden's estate, a conflagration set by Jacob and Dr. Coleman to cover their tracks. No questions were asked and no one sought the two men out.

Jacob stayed with Dr. Coleman for a month while he recovered from his wounds. Dr. Coleman tried to speak to him about the events that occurred that night but Jacob would say nothing. He would just say that God's will had been done, and that was the end of it.

Jacob was a stone. Not once during the healing process did he seem upset or filled with guilt or horror over what had happened.

Dr. Coleman wondered just what kind of man Jacob really was, to face down the evils of Hell itself and come out of it unscathed other than his physical injuries.

He found out on the last night Jacob stayed with him.

Dr. Coleman had awakened in the middle of the night from a nightmare and stumbled to the kitchen to warm a cup of milk to help him get back to sleep. On his way to the kitchen, he passed the closed door of the room where Jacob had been recuperating. He stopped when he heard a ruckus inside.

Jacob was crying, begging and pleading with God

"Take this burden from me!" Jacob cried out. Even through the door, he could feel the tremble in the man's voice. Painful sobs pealed the night air as Jacob begged for release.

No answer came.

Dr. Coleman reached out for the doorknob, thinking to open the door and comfort his friend. But his hand froze just above the handle and he hesitated. Silence, as sudden as a heart attack, filled Jacob's room. Dr. Coleman removed his hand and returned to his bedroom, leaving Jacob to wrestle with his personal demons alone.

The following morning, Jacob was gone with the morning sun.

TORI'S DIARY

KEITH LUETHKE

HANDS OFF!

Reading into my personal life is strictly prohibited. If you've discovered this diary or are just peeking when my back is turned, I strongly urge you to not read it and return it to the address below.
Thanks!

Victoria Maple
7621 Derleth Road
Knoxville, TN 37931

February 1st
It hurts when I pee and the bruises on my arms look like ripe tomatoes rotting in a sea of pale skin. My stomach is sore and I have little suction cup marks on my inner thighs. I don't remember what happened, everything was taken from me, even my memories. It's like before going to sleep at night. I close my eyes, I remember keeping them closed, and then I drift into a deep slumber. When I open my eyes it's morning and all the pain from the night before comes rushing back at me, stabbing and hammering like I was a piece of meat worked over in the butcher shop. I don't recall what happened in the night, but I hope that by writing this down I'll be able to remember and deal with my shame. It's mid-afternoon now and I think I'll go to sleep. Maybe I'll be safer in the daylight hours. I'll close my eyes and *will* the pain to go away.

February 2nd
My name is Victoria Maple but I go by Tori. I'm nineteen years old and love to draw and write. I enjoy drawing more than writing because it's easier not to mess up. When people see drawings they get a tiny peek into your soul, what the world looks like through your eyes, and I don't like that, but I can deal with it because all

they get is a quick glimpse. It's kind of like when I wear my short black skirt to the college and boys look at me but quickly avert their gaze when I glance back. Writing is a different story. Someone in my English Composition 101 class said a writer has to 'bleed onto the page' and that good writing only requires 'cutting open an artery and letting the words flow out'. That's what I don't like about writing. I don't want people to get an inside look. I don't want anyone being that close to me, it's too personal. I'd rather be adored from afar than be scrutinized under a microscope, but I still feel watched all the time, even when I'm all alone in my bedroom with the door locked. My mother says that I'm being silly. She tells me I should enjoy the looks I get from guys because everything eventually fades. Last week she saw a bunch of construction workers outside her job at the law office downtown whistling at young ladies walking on the street. When her lunch break came, she decided to walk by them and they didn't make a sound. I tell her she's pretty every day and she rolls her eyes. Last week, I saw her trying to fit into my pink halter top. Once she got it over her sagging breasts and stomach she looked in the mirror and cried. The halter top is too stretched out for me to wear it now, but I never mentioned it. I crumpled it up and buried it deep in the trashcan so she wouldn't see it. Sometimes it's better to hide things.

February 3rd

I'm drinking lots of tea tonight to stay awake. I like Earl Gray with a splash of milk and a little bit of honey. When I run out of it I plan on starting on Plantation Mint tea. I don't add anything to the mint tea because it would ruin the flavor, and I don't like to alter things that I don't have to.

I'm starting a painting of our house. It's basic, I know, but I have to stay awake tonight, NO MATTER WHAT! Right now it's almost midnight. Drawing should keep me busy until dawn. My mother is shouting at me to turn off my bedroom light because I have school at nine o' clock tomorrow. I'm going to put my blanket under the door jam to keep the light from escaping. I hope she doesn't see it and make me go to sleep. Ever since my father got hurt in that accident at the factory she started treating me like a little girl. I like the attention, but I don't really need it. Luckily, she doesn't ask me to help her wheel him outside or make him dinner. He lost the use of his legs when he fell off a loader and got caught under the wheels. My mother says that it crushed his spine and he was a clumsy moron for getting hurt. I never ask him how he feels. I tend to stay away. Sometimes I see him sitting in his wheelchair by the window and looking into the woods behind our house. He'll just sit there for hours, staring past the creaking oaks and green firs. I wonder what he sees that's so interesting out there. We've been growing apart ever since I turned fourteen. Once I started wearing a training bra and practiced walking in high heels, he stopped speaking to me. I miss the old times when we'd go to my ballerina recitals or just sit on the porch drinking lemonade on a hot summer day. Now, he's just a shell. My mother feeds him, bathes him, and tucks him in at night. He could be her pet.

Outside, the darkness is begging to be let in through my window. I shut the curtains and go back to work on my drawing, basking in my little light, and waiting until dawn.

February 5th

I can't stop crying. Sometime last night I had a black out. I tried to stay awake all night again, but I...something happened and I woke up on my bed. My t-shirt was torn and my blue shorts were missing. I have more suction cup marks on my legs and my body is throbbing. The door was still locked, but the window was open. I don't know what's happening to me. I want to run to my mother, I want to tell her what's been going on but I can't, I just can't. She's had enough problems trying to deal with dad being a vegetable. I need to stay strong, but all I want to do is hide. I'm taking down all the mirrors in my room today. I don't want to look at myself anymore.

And I'm not going to school today, either. I'm going to take a hot bath and stay under the soapy water until my skin feels clean.

February 7th

I took two days off from college to gather my thoughts, and a boy from my English class emailed me the assignment due for the next class. I guess he didn't think I was smart enough to check the syllabus. His name is Brian and I'm not sure who he is. My guess is that he's a creep. He's probably been watching me in class a bit too much and thinks I'm available. Technically, I am, but I don't want to date anyone right now. How can I? It would be cheating them, especially if it got serious. How could I explain the marks on my thighs or the purple bruises on my arms? I don't even know how they got there and he'd think I was sleeping around! No, no boys allowed. No girls either, just kidding, I don't swing that way. I don't feel very attractive anymore, anyway. I stopped wearing makeup and put my cute, black skirt in my closet for safe keeping. I only wear jeans and a pink belt now. No more halter tops either, I'm strictly a long sleeve, no cleavage girl right now.

I found the baseball bat my father used to teach me with when I was a kid. It was in the garage covered up by a dusty box marked for my Barbie dolls. I started laughing when I opened the box. Seeing all those pretty, plastic faces staring at me with big hopeful eyes and thin lipped smiles, all of them eager to wear new clothes and go on a date with Ken. In my make believe land, Barbie and her friends were always hanging out by the pool, shopping, and taking turns driving the red Corvette. I didn't even have a Ken doll for years and all of them were perfectly fine without him. But when my mother purchased the blond-haired, lack-of-a-penis doll, they started having fights over who got to date him. Once they all got together and made Ken choose which Barbie he wanted to be with. He couldn't pick one so they tore him apart limb by limb and stuffed the pieces into the shoe closet. After that, they became friends again. Barbie and her friends were silly girls.

I like the bat I found. It's metal and the grip is a little worn. It feels good to hold onto something so sturdy, even if it's cold. I put it under my bed for safe keeping and wait for what the night will bring.

February 9th

My dad is walking again...the doctors said he would be paralyzed for life and yet there he is; outside with my mother slowly walking around the yard. I guess I should be happy but it's so unnatural. People who can't walk because they have a smashed spine don't get up and start moving around. My mother can't stop smiling and they're actually holding hands. I've never seen the two of them holding hands before or even kiss for that matter. My mother usually pats my father on the back and says goodnight. No kissing, no real hugging, nothing. When I was younger they used to sit next to each other on the couch and laugh together while watching television. Now, they have two separate televisions in different rooms. After my father was injured he didn't watch television anymore. He only stared at the woods in our backyard. And now, he's walking with my mother, hand and hand like they just met for the first time. Maybe life will be different between them now? They might even start watching television together again. I feel a throbbing pain in my lower stomach and have to squeeze my legs shut for it to lessen. I need to talk to someone. I need help.

February 10th

I borrowed a book in the school library today that deals with abuse. It says by writing down a string of ten words at random I can alleviate stress and help myself cope with the traumatic event. I don't really agree with the book but I think it's worth a shot at least. So here's my list:

1. Wailing. 2. Biting. 3. Probe. 4. Loveless. 5. Sin. 6. Musty. 7. Spoil.

I'm going to stop now. This isn't helping at all. I want to go downstairs to where our family photographs are stored and scratch my face out of every picture. I want to break mirrors. I want to pull out all my halter tops, short skirts, and pretty dresses from the closet, drench them in gasoline, and set them on fire. I want to wear sunglasses everyday so I don't have to look at anyone anymore. I want to find Brian and tell him to fuck off. I want to piss on magazines with some skinny bitch wearing almost nothing on the cover and giving a seductive glare. I want...I want...I want all the pain in my body to go away. I want to feel normal again.

February 11th
I feel a little better today. I slept soundlessly last night. I didn't mean to fall asleep but I was so tired I simply hid underneath the covers and closed my eyes. When I awoke, I felt as rested as mice hiding from owls under a pile of dead leaves in the woods. I discovered a sticky translucent slime on my window. I don't think slugs crawl on glass but I could be wrong. My mother said it was going to rain tonight so I'm hoping it'll wash everything away. There's nothing as violent as rain, it splashes and pummels, falling from the sky in a torrent and welds together to form puddles and creeks in the streets. I wish I was more like rain, nothing can stop the rain, and everyone complains about it, but the rain doesn't care. The rain doesn't feel pain, and when it forms into running water it simply crawls over obstacles in the way, and if it can't get around something, it builds itself up and climbs over it. I wish I could be that strong.

When I went to school today, Brian introduced himself before class started. He's a little taller than me and has brown puppy eyes. He asked me all sorts of mundane questions that I didn't feel like answering. How are your other classes? What kind of movies do you like to watch? What kind of books do you enjoy reading? I answered as vaguely and quickly as possible. I wasn't rude with him, just curt. That's what needs to be done. Yeah he's attractive in the, 'I'll carry your books for you' sort of way, but like I said earlier, I'm just not interested right now. I made sure to leave class in a hurry so he couldn't catch up to me. I hope he gets a clue that I'm not interested.

February 13th
Today is one of the greatest days I've had in my entire life. I got my period. I never thought I'd ever beg for that terrible feeling in my stomach or wear a smile when I wanted to throw up.

February 14th

Brian gave me a heart-shaped box of assorted candies and a single red rose today. He was blushing as bright as the pedals. I threw the candies in the trash can when he wasn't looking. I don't really feel like eating anything. I kept the rose and he walked me to my car. He talked about the rain as we walked and how he liked the way it made his shoes squish. I kissed him.

February 15th

I saw my father dragging two black trash bags into the woods last night. He paused right before entering the tree line to catch his breath and I thought I saw him looking at my window. I ducked, and when I dared to look again, he was gone. Maybe he just wanted to take the trash into the woods instead of putting it into the plastic barrels beside the house. It could've been leftover food he wanted to dump out for the raccoons in the woods, although, I don't recall him ever doing that before. He's been acting really strange after being able to walk again. Today he asked how my day was and how school was going. My father hasn't asked me any-thing like that since I was a pre teen. It was like he was trying to take an interest in my life again. I told him a little about Brian, not that I kissed him, but just the kind of person he was. I was trying to make small talk and get to my room as quickly as possible.

Later, I heard him arguing with my mother. I put my head-phones on and listened to Coldplay, and then The Prodigy, not the rapper, the techno band from the UK. I drowned out all the yelling and drew for a while. I still don't understand how my father can be fine after the accident, but I guess I should be thankful. He's going back to work once the doctors confirm he's not handicapped. It freaks my mother out. I think she actually enjoyed feeding him vanilla pudding for breakfast and stirring his pain pills into his oatmeal for dinner. She always wanted another baby but she developed cancer in her uterus and had to have it removed. Maybe she thought she was getting her second chance when her husband became needy. I don't like to hear them fighting but it's better than the silence that's been hiding in the house.

Brian called me on the phone but I didn't pick up. I suppose I should call him back but I don't want him to get the wrong impression. I like him a little but it shouldn't have gone as far as it did. I don't regret the kiss but it feels like I signed away all my freedom rights to a boy I hardly know. Once I kissed him it was like saying I belonged to him and I don't want to be that close to anyone right now.

Tonight, after everyone goes to sleep, I'm going to the forest behind our house to find out what my dad buried there. I'm taking the bat for protection against my father or whatever else I might run into.

February 16th
It's six o'clock in the morning. I've been in the woods all night. I crept downstairs past my parent's bedroom and could hear my father snoring. It was easy to reach the sliding glass door leading to the deck and slip into the night. Once outside, I headed straight toward the woods, armed with my baseball bat and a flashlight. I didn't realize how dark the forest was at night. I couldn't see much of anything past the trees as they groaned in the wind. It almost seemed like they were talking to each other, trying to decide if I was friend or foe. I suddenly realized that I hadn't been out in the forest since I was a teenager. I used to come back here after school to smoke a few cigarettes and call Johnny, my boyfriend at the time. My parents hated him because he was twenty-one and they saw him drinking Budweiser in his Firebird while waiting to pick me up one day. We weren't allowed to see each other but sometimes he would park along the road and meet me in the woods. He was in college and I was in high school. I told my mother that it made no difference. Something like that couldn't affect us. We were in love, and love conquered all. I was a fool then. He left me after I wouldn't spread my legs for him. He wasn't in love with me at all, he was in *lust*.

I stumbled among the tree roots Johnny and I once walked over, and didn't turn on my flashlight until I was a descent trek away from my house. I didn't want my father to stir in the night, see the light, and investigate. I wasn't sure what exactly I was looking for, but I thought I would know it if I saw it. Maybe it would be a slight depression in the ground, or the trash bags would be split open, their vile contents spilling out among the dead leaves. But the further I went in the woods the more I began to think he hadn't been here. Perhaps it was some sort of wicked dream and my mind was slowly rotting away like spoiled cantaloupe festering with maggots. The outside layer would have the familiar texture of grainy sandpaper, but the inside would be squirming and wilting as the bugs sucked out all that was good in the fruit. But that's life. Time slowly eats away at every memory until its one convoluted mess of pudding and oatmeal, and the only thing left to do is wait for the Grim Reaper. Unless a pact was made with the devil and he was granted back everything he once cherished. But what would be the price of such a miracle?

As I continued to search it grew colder. The wind turned into a snapping wolf clawing down my jacket for warmth. I pressed forward and sank down a slope and came upon the darkest patch of midnight I'd ever seen. The earth opened up, erupting in jagged, stone teeth. It was a cave, and it seemed to breathe as it sucked the winter winds down into its bowels to produce a soft enticing whistle.

I went inside and can't remember what happened next. It's as though a scene is missing from my life. The only thing I can even relate it to is when I had my appendix removed and had to go under the knife. One minute everything was fine. The nurses were pumping the IV drip full of knockout juice, and the next I was on my back with an oxygen mask over my mouth. Only, when I awoke from the cave I wasn't in the hospital, I was back in my room, and the window was open.

February 17th
I'm skipping school in order to go through my father's things today. The teachers won't miss me, anyway. I'm just another faceless girl in the crowd. Brian will wonder where I am, though, but he can live without me for a day. My father knows something he's not telling me and I intend to find out what it is.

I'll leave for school today like I always do but instead of going there, I'll buy some coffee at the gas station and hang out in my car for an hour. Then, I'll drive back and make sure his car is gone. The doctor instructed him to stay home but I heard my mother screaming at him the other day for not resting enough and leaving the house when she was at work. I'm betting he'll be gone again today.

I checked to see if my baseball bat was under the bed this morning but it was missing. I guess I left it in the woods. I wish I could just hold it for a little while.

February 18th

I don't know where to start. I can't stop shaking. It's so cold. My mother is banging on my door telling me to sleep. I don't think I can ever go to sleep again. I took a knife from the kitchen. Not a little one either, but a long, serrated blade. My father uses it to carve the turkey on Thanksgiving; its seven-inches of stainless steel with a black, easy grip handle.

I've pushed my dresser in front of the bedroom window and I'm keeping the light on all night.

I found a bottle of Prozac in my mother's medicine cabinet. She takes it to help her stay happy, because everyone knows life isn't happy enough and it needs to be synthesized and altered, changed and demoralized until it's a little blue/green capsule of sunshine in the palm of your hand. It says it might cause insomnia and to take one with a full glass of water. I took four with a cup of mint tea.

February 19th

Brian keeps asking me what's wrong. He says he hasn't seen me smile yet today. I told him I had nothing to smile about. He tried to hold my hand. At first I let him and a warm rush flooded my system, but then I felt a cold draft and remembered the cave, and quickly withdrew. I stuffed my hands into my jacket pockets and he didn't try again. He pouted all the way to my car, so when we got there I gave him a kiss, which cheered him up considerably.

I can't tell him what's going on. He wouldn't understand. But I can tell you. At least here I can be honest. Here I'm bound in paper instead of flesh; the ink, my blood, the drawings, my organs. I've given my diary life, but it's not a very good life I'm afraid, and I can hardly protect myself let alone a bunch of scattered thoughts and random illustrations I've piled together over many sleepless nights.

Yesterday, I did what I said I would. I skipped school and waited at the gas station for an hour. When I drove by my house and my father's car was gone, I went inside and called his name to make sure he'd really left. Once I was certain of his absence, I went to his bedroom. I took off my shoes and socks so I wouldn't track in any mud or leave a trace of my presence. There was a musty smell like aged sharp cheese in the room. His bed was made and his spare shoes were on a small metal rack. The closet was slightly ajar and I could see all of his clothes were in order. There was nothing out of place. I opened up his dresser drawers and sifted through carefully sorted socks, underwear, folded shirts, and the blue silk pajamas I'd bought him for Christmas last year. He said he liked them but I don't remember him ever wearing them. I was about to give up when I reached the bottom drawer. Beneath a pair of folded slacks was a yellowed piece of paper which had been torn out of a book and had strange writing on it. I immediately scribbled it down word for word on the back of my hand and this is what it was.

Ph'nglui mglw'nafh Cthulhu R'lyeh wgah'nagl fhtagn

I've never heard of any of those words before and have no clue what language it was. As I was putting the paper back where I'd found it, I discovered something written in English on the other side.

Feed the Gods

I knew it was my father's handwriting right away. I've practiced forging it enough times to avoid arguments with my parents for getting into trouble during my high school years. I thought back to the other night when I'd watched my dad drag those trash bags into the woods. Was he bringing them into the cave? What was in that cave? I put the paper back and sat on the bed. Closing my eyes, I tried to remember what had happened to me the other night. I was in the woods. It was dark. I found a cave. And there was a low whistle coming from it, drowning out the wind, taking me away. I don't remember anything else.

Something wet and a little sticky clutched my feet as I sat on the bed. I opened my eyes and looked down. A growing pool of blood seeped out from under the bed. I don't scream. I don't make a sound. I just sit and watch as the dark red puddle grew in size, seeping into the cracks of the hardwood floor, to stain my feet red. Slowly, I got off the bed and bent over. Wide eyes stared at me from behind a veil of clear plastic. It was a man, stripped naked, and shoved into one of those plastic coverings used for expensive suits. But there must've been a hole in it because he was leaking. I peered into his agonized face. I've never seen the man before. His cracked lips began to move as he tried to form words.

Then, I was screaming.

He shook in the plastic, like a prized gold fish won at the fair whose bag was leaking. I ran out of the room, leaving a trail of bloody footprints. I shut the door and locked myself in the bathroom. I should've called the police. I should've called my mother. But instead, I threw up in the toilet and spent a good twenty minutes scrubbing my feet clean. Once I was a steady, I went back to my father's bedroom and peered inside. There was still a pool of blood on the floor and my footprints leading away from it. The man under the bed had stopped thrashing.

I heard my father's car pull into the driveway.

I took off my shirt and mopped the bloody prints off the floor and grabbed my shoes. I heard a grunt from under the bed but there was nothing I could do about it. I ran upstairs and locked myself in my bedroom. A moment later, my father was announcing he was home. He knocked on my door and asked why I was back so early. I told him I didn't feel good. He wanted to know if he could get me anything. I told him to go away and huddled in the corner. A few minutes later, I heard a loud, wet *thump* from his bedroom. Life is cheap I guess.

February 20th
Before class, Brian saw the markings on my hand and commented on it. He asked if I was an H.P. Lovecraft fan. I told him I

didn't read romance. Brian laughed and said that Lovecraft wrote horror. I asked him if he could decipher the words. He said that was easy, it was common knowledge among fans. It translated as,

In his house at R'lyeh dead Cthulhu waits dreaming.

I asked him who Cthulhu was and he told me it was a Great Old One who sleeps deep in the ocean waiting to be awakened by his followers. He said Lovecraft had an entire mythos devoted to similar monsters that dwelled in remote places, all dead and dreaming. I asked if they ever helped people or kidnapped girls to impregnate them and he said he wasn't sure. The Great Old Ones were said to be worshiped by a cult of followers but were never granted much of anything good for their trouble. As he understood it, they formed a telepathic bond with the Old Ones and did their bidding. I asked him if he thought it had any real truth beneath the fiction. He said they were just stories.

After class, he walked me to my car and I hugged him for a long time. He tried to break away after a minute but I buried myself deep within his chest and wrapped my arms around his lower back, squeezing. We stayed like that for a good while. We kissed and I asked him over for dinner tomorrow, claiming I could cook him a hot meal. My hope is that he'll see something in my father that I don't, and be able to tell me what might be going on. He wanted to know what was for dinner. I told him we were having spaghetti and meatballs. It's the only thing I know how to make.

February 21st

Dinner was a disaster. My mother wanted to help me cook but I told her that I could do it alone. The spaghetti came out fine and I put a little butter on it while the meatballs simmered in tomato sauce. Every time I went to stir it I kept thinking of that growing red pool under my father's bed and would have to leave the kitchen so I didn't get sick. I burned the bottom of the pot and had to throw away some of the meatballs. Brian arrived on time and brought a bottle of Cabernet Sauvignon. I gave him a quick kiss and introduced him to my parents. He was a little nervous when he shook my father's hand, but soon recovered by commenting on the football trophies on the shelf in the living room. Those were my dad's hunks of tarnished metal and sometimes he would take them down and wipe the dust off and run his fingers over the engraved years, but I hadn't seen him do that in a long time. Now, he was smiling and bringing Brian over to have a look at the cold steel trophies covered in fake gold, talking about how he'd always wanted a son. I set the table and asked what everyone wanted to drink. Brian wanted whatever I was having. My mother wanted the wine. My father wanted a Bloody Mary. And I wanted to lock Brian in my closet and wait together until the sun came up.

Dinner conversation centered on Brian's activities and his plans for the future. He was an Electrical Engineering major and liked to hike in the woods. I never knew his major or that he liked hiking. Every time they asked if he planned to attend a college out of state once he finished his BS he would smile at me and shake his head. I blushed.

After dinner my father pressed his palms to his head, complaining about a headache. My mother ushered him to bed and tucked him in. Alone with Brian, I found myself gravitating closer to him. He thanked me for dinner but couldn't say much more because I started kissing him. He tasted like meat, grated cheese, and fear. He pulled away from me, saying my mother could return at any minute. Let her, I said, and pressed my lips to his. He fought like a baited shark trying to rip a chunk of meat from the hook but not brave enough to take the whole thing. In the end, he gave into my needs and managed to avoid the hook. When my mother returned, he fell out of his chair and onto the floor. I couldn't stop laughing. I hadn't laughed in so long it almost hurt. My mother rolled her eyes and disappeared into the kitchen. Instead of helping Brian up, I fell on top of him. His face turned a brighter shade of red. I wrapped myself around him and pleaded for him to stay. My exact words were "please don't go, I need you now." But despite my pleading, he did have to leave eventually. And once he did I locked myself back in my room, hid from the dark, and told lies to myself about how things would get better tomorrow.

February 22nd

Brian wasn't in class today. I called him six times but he never responded. I hope I didn't do anything wrong yesterday.

When I got home from school my father ignored me. I even offered to make him a mixed drink and he batted the air in front of him like he was shooing away a bothersome fly. I went to the kitchen and drank a glass of milk. He appeared silently, moving to the sink, and started washing his hands. They weren't even dirty.

If I see him sneaking back into the woods tonight I'm going to search his room one more time. I should call the police. I should tell my mother. I should drive over to Brian's house and see where the hell he is, but I never bothered asking him where he lived. Why won't he call me back?

February 23rd

I...I have my answers. There's so much blood on me. It stained the kitchen floor, and oozed onto the indigo carpet my mother insisted on putting in the living room. I never knew people held so many things inside of them.

Last night, I stared out my window and witnessed my father creep out of the house with two more trash bags. Instead of going into his room like I planned, I followed him into the darkness, taking the kitchen knife with me. I stayed far enough back to see his flashlight beam, and whenever he paused, I dropped into the foliage and held my breath. It was easy. When he reached the cave, he fell to his knees and opened one of the trash bags. He dumped the contents onto the jagged rocks and in the light I saw...this is so hard to write. I can't...but I need to put this down. I have to stay strong.

My father dropped the flashlight and I saw Brian's severed head, his mouth gaping open in a silent scream. My heart sunk. My body turned into a wet noodle. I sat among the dead leaves while gripping my kitchen knife. I bit my tongue so hard it bled.

My father began chanting in a strange language I couldn't make out. I crept forward, digging my nails into the hard packed dirt.

He opened the second bag and arms and legs toppled out. One leg was wearing a black high heel distinguished by studded diamonds. It belonged to my mother.

I screamed then and charged him. He never knew what hit him. I stabbed with every ounce of strength I could muster, slicing into his flesh, spreading it wide, and thrusting deep. I pulled it out when he gasped and shoved the knife in again, harder this time, pumping and jabbing. My father screamed in pain, I howled in fury.

I left the knife buried in his side and slumped against an oak tree.

Soft whistling came from the cavern. In the flashlight's dim glow, I saw a handful of elongated spider limbs stretching out from the hole to reach for the leftover pieces of my life. I watched as it cradled the parts in its bristly appendages, as though inspecting the sacrifice. Then, the giant spider legs sunk back into the dark and a long tentacle covered in a translucent slime wrapped around the detached legs, arms, and Brian's head. It slipped back into the cave and I heard crunching and a wet slurp. I squeezed my legs together when the tentacle returned, but it didn't come for me, it wrapped around my father's lifeless corpse and carried him into Hell. I ran, and ran, and ran.

Upon reaching my house, I went to my parent's bedroom to confirm my mother's death. I found a large, dark red puddle of blood in her bed.

I took down my painting of our house and put it in my closet, washed the dirty dishes in the sink, and then called the police. They're on their way now, but don't worry, I still have some more time. I'll be questioned for days, weeks, months, locked away in a padded cell, transferred to one doctor after another, and maybe I'll even forget what happened.

Time is funny like that. But my diary won't forget. You'll never forget. The diary is stained in my ink and drowned in my blood. A little piece of me I might not recognize after the years drift by. I should burn it and stomp on the ashes, but it's my creation and I can't let that happen. I hear wailing sirens outside.

It's time to go.

Tori

CLAWS IN THE TREES

MICHAEL D. GRIFFITHS

"This place is so crazy," Ellie said, her eyes darting from one artifact to another. "Who would've thought that such a cool museum would be way out here, so far from anything else?"

Vance looked over a collection of Kachinas that were over a hundred years old. "Yeah it's pretty strange. I..." his voice trailed off when he spotted what appeared to be an old library hidden in the corner of the first floor of the museum. "Hey, I think I'm going to check that room out."

"Okay, I might want to take some pictures."

"Cool, I'll get back with you in a few minutes."

Crossing the room, he entered the library. It had the smell of dust mixed with a lingering odor of dry leaves. The faded spines of the ancient books contrasted strongly with the dark stained bookcases. His eyes roamed over the titles. There were so many books it was overwhelming.

Then his glance lingered on a tall book entitled, **The Northern Influences of the Mayan Culture.**

Taking it from the shelf and skimming through the book, he stopped when he came upon a section mentioning the Gila wilderness in New Mexico. By coincidence, that was where they were headed. It didn't take long to find a passage that interested him.

Despite the strong influences of the followers of Quetzalcoatl in Chaco Canyon to the north, the cult of Tezcatlipoca continued to grow in strength within the Gila wilderness. The struggles between the two conflicting religions continued until the 1200's when the vast structures and cities of Chaco Canyon became inexplicably deserted. Since the followers of Tezcatlipoca did not keep records of any kind, to this day scholars do not know what may have become of them.

Vance continued his research, trying to focus more on the cult of Tezcatlipoca and the Gila wilderness. The Mayans believed that Tezcatlipoca was the first God, the God who had created the world. He ruled over the natural world, but it was Quetzalcoatl who dethroned him and replaced the power of animals with the power of men, and slowly the humans were able to claim the world for themselves.

The warriors of the Jaguar God were fierce beast-like men who only journeyed out at night. Like their dethroned God, they had claimed the darkness, shunning the light. Brutal sacrifices, kidnapping, and wholesale murder were their tools. According to the author, the members of the cult considered all of humanity their enemy. They sought to return the world to its once primitive and pure state.

"I got some great pictures of that beaded tunic." The sudden voice from behind startled him and his body jerked. Ellie giggled. "That was cute. Did I scare you?"

"No," he said and hurried to put the book away, so he would be able to hide his flushed face. "I think we should hit the road. I don't want to have to find the place at night."

"Okay, as long as I can check out the gift shop on the way out. She moved before him and he watched her chocolate hair bounce in the sunlight. He passed an ancient jaguar skin rug while he was trying to catch up. Its glass eyes glowed red and appeared to follow him as he passed.

He looked at it one more time and shivered.

* * *

They had bounced over a rugged dirt road for over an hour before they saw the cheery light of Dean and Eric's campfire.

"Finally," Ellie said. "Good job finding them."

"Thanks. This place is sure out there." With relief, Vance pulled his SUV beside Dean's pickup truck. He had a beer pressed into his hand before his feet touched the forest floor. Various handshakes and slaps on the back were exchanged and Ellie got two hugs.

Once he returned from setting up the tent, Vance said, "We really are in the boonies, huh?"

"Yeah, I'd say so," Dean replied while he readjusted his Diamondback hat over his messy dark bangs.

"We were a little worried you might not find us," Eric broke in. He scratched his beer belly for a moment and then continued. "It would suck to be lost out here."

Dean went on. "The only reason we found it is because I got a map from my archaeology professor. He said there're supposed to be old ruins out here. He was actually hoping we might scout them out." He smiled. "If I can find them and write it up, it should be worth some extra credit."

"Sounds cool with me. Ellie will probably want to take some pictures, too."

"Where is she?"

"Setting up the sleeping bags. She likes to keep the tent real cozy. We even have a down futon," Vance laughed.

"My professor said that these ruins are..." Dean began but was interrupted when Ellie's scream suddenly tore through the night. Vance was headed her way immediately with Dean close on his heels.

"Ellie, Ellie what is it?" he yelled before reaching her.

She sprang from the tent and ran into his arms. "Something was outside the tent. It tried to push in through the front but I had it zipped. Then it started to claw through the tent. That's when I screamed."

"Oh, wow, check this out Vance. There's claw marks on your tent, man."

Vance peered at the tent opening and saw it was true. Four slices were through the fabric, creating long tears.

Eric came running up with his rifle. "What was it?" he panted.

"Yeah, what was it?" Dean repeated.

"I...ah, I'm not really sure." Vance's mind was already running through a myriad of possibilities or, perhaps even more importantly, wondering if this event was going to be chasing them away. Night had fallen an hour ago and he had no wish to drive back to Tucson in the darkness.

"I suppose it could be a bear or maybe a cougar," Dean suggested.

"What about a jaguar?" Vance asked.

Everyone looked at him and fell silent for a moment. Then Eric laughed. "Jaguar? What're you talking about?"

"There's been some reported in southeastern Arizona. That isn't too far from here."

Ellie wiped her eyes. "No, it seemed to be standing up."

Dean moved away from the tent. "It would have to be a bear then."

The question Vance knew was coming was then asked. "Should we leave?" Ellie said as she pressed her slim frame against his. "That was so scary."

"I'm not leaving," Dean said as he brushed off his pants. "I need the extra credit."

Motioning into the darkness with the barrel of his gun, Eric said, "Don't worry about it. It would be back already if it still wanted to mess with us. If it does come back, my dad's rifle will change its mind real quick. The black bears around here aren't very big, more like black labs."

"It seemed pretty big to me," Ellie said. While she snuggled into Vance's arms, she asked, "What do you think, Vance, should we go?"

"We'll be okay. I'd rather not leave." Vance's voice wandered off, sounding distant. Had something moved in the darkness? "I'll keep an eye on you. As long as we stay near the fire, we'll be fine and I'll be in the tent with you later."

"Okay, but if I so much as smell a bear, I'm sleeping in the car." She managed a smile and he hugged her again. Overhead, the growing clouds obscured the crescent moon.

Looking into the darkening woods, Vance tried to detect movement, but his eyes couldn't pierce the gloom. He double checked that his camping dagger was still on his hip, and with one last glance into the darkness, he followed the others back to the campfire.

* * *

"What do you mean you're not going?" Dean complained.

"Dude, whatever. Vance and Ellie are going. I just feel like chilling," Eric said. "I'm gonna crank up some tunes and read my

English lit book. Don't give me a hard time. If I don't get some of this done, I'll have to leave early."

Groaning, Dean turned away from Eric and finished packing his gear. Soon, the three friends had shouldered their packs and were following Dean into the woods, leaving Eric behind.

The forest was a mixture of thick trees and jagged, rocky cliffs. The latter would often have to be scrambled over. Vance stayed with Ellie and helped her over the harder places.

Before a mile had passed under their feet, they were all drenched in sweat and their packs had become heavy. Dean set a quick pace and the couple continued with determination. The smaller canyon opened into one far larger. Looking ahead of it, Vance saw that this larger canyon disappeared into the bowels of the Gila Mountain range. It was daunting.

"Oh, look, a stream," Ellie squealed as they crested a rise. With happy grins, they jogged to the shore and washed their faces and splashed water on the backs of their necks.

"This will make things easier," Dean said. Tossing his backpack over his shoulders, they soon set out again.

At one point, the canyon narrowed so much they were forced to crawl through the rock faces.

Looking back with a smile, Dean said, "This is pretty cool, huh?"

Vance held Ellie's hand and followed him under the low, rust colored ceiling where the two cliff faces came together, leaving a small opening near the ground.

They hadn't passed much farther when clouds of wet mist formed and soon clung to them, like groping gray fingers.

"Wow, intense," Dean said. The awe was apparent in his voice as he led them across the rough stones that were surrounded by a steaming river. "There must be hot springs all over the place around here." As they continued, the clouds of steam only grew thicker. "This is like the coolest thing I have ever done!"

Ellie gripped Vance's hand harder. "I think it's a little scary. We're so alone out here."

They slowly left the heaviest part of the mist behind, but thin wisps still hovered around them.

"Hey, how much farther is it?" Vance asked.

"We should be pretty close now, but no one said anything about hot springs. It must have been a long time since anyone's been out here."

"Or a volcano is going to erupt," Ellie grumbled.

It turned out, Dean was right. After another half hour of hiking, the mist parted, revealing a large set of crumbling ruins. "Oh, wow!" Dean called out and scrambled up the loose shale without the slightest hint of trepidation.

Vance took a more cautious approach and it paid off when he discovered a trail. "Hey, dumbass, there's a path over here!" he shouted to his friend. Vance led the way since he was in the lead anyway. "Does this path seem well used?" he asked.

"It could be a game trail," Dean panted as he finally caught up.

"I don't think so." Looking up at the ruins that loomed over them, Vance thought he saw something odd. "Is there smoke coming out over there?"

"Naw," Dean countered. "It must be the mist." Then he pushed by Vance and Ellie and once again took the lead.

They came upon a large opening in the rock face, a cave by the look of it, and without asking Vance or Ellie, Dean headed inside.

"Wait, don't go in there," Vance called. "You don't know what might be inside."

"That's the point. We're here to explore so let's explore," Dean said as he continued into the cave. Vance looked at Ellie and she shrugged, the two following Dean.

Crumbling gray walls soon encased them, swallowing the dim light.

"Wow, this place looks really old," Ellie whispered.

"Hey, I smell smoke," Vance said as he ran his fingers over the dry wall. Ancient clay bricks broke into powder and fell to the ground, mixing with the debris below. Large wooden beams held the ceiling up and every eight feet, wooden posts lined the side, creating the feel that they were inside a gold mine. The cave branched off to other tunnels, and entering a new section caused the drifting dust to mix with thin strings of mist, but neither masked the scent of fire from Vance.

"Hold up, Dean. It really smells like somebody's burning something in here!" Vance called to Dean's back.

"Nah, it's fine. Sometimes these old beams hold that smell," his friend called back. Dean had already entered a new section with darkness so complete that he had to take out his flashlight. The couple soon followed suit.

The narrow beams of light did little to illuminate the stygian room.

"Where are you, Dean?" Ellie called out. Her voice betrayed her fear and Vance could tell the dark walls and low ceiling was making her nervous.

"Dean, slow down man," Vance called out.

"You guys have to see this!" Dean called back. "I found an opening in the rock wall."

Dean already had his backpack off when Vance and Ellie caught up to him and was using his flashlight to peer inside the opening. Before him was the outline of a rough doorway no more than four-feet high and half that wide.

"It seems to go back quite a ways," Dean said. "Sometimes they used places like this to store corn and liquor." His dust-covered face looked up at them. "But it might be a ceremony chamber." He smiled. "We might be able to find some really cool stuff in there."

The smell of smoke strengthened. "Maybe we should wait and bring your professor back here before we go in there," Vance suggested.

Laughing, Dean flashed him a puzzled look. "Are you kidding?" Then without another look back, he scrambled into the small opening.

Crouching down, Vance said to Ellie, "I should probably back him up."

Ellie was hugging herself while her eyes danced around the dark room. "Well, there's no way I'm going to be left here all alone. I'm coming, too."

Grabbing her hand, he was just about to lead the way into the small opening when he heard Dean cry out in pain. "Oh damn, damn it! Vance, help me!"

The sharp edges of rock tore into his shoulders as Vance pushed through the opening. Ellie was screaming his name, but he had to help Dean. It sounded like something was attacking him. His thin flashlight beam barely cut through the darkness, but he was able to locate Dean. His friend was holding his arm and Vance could see blood leaking through his fingers as he grimaced in pain. It looked like Dean had caught his arm on a particularly jagged edge of rock as he crawled through the opening.

Just as Vance started to move towards Dean, he heard a loud scraping noise on his right. He aimed his light in that direction but he couldn't locate the sound's origin.

Ellie was behind him now and nearly hysterical. When she saw Dean, she squealed his name shrilly and raced to his side. "Vance help me, he's bleeding real bad!"

Vance moved over to help, but as he did, he heard more scraping sounds on his right. This time he could make out words as well. There was no cougar or bear in the cave with them, it was people.

"We have to get him out of here," Ellie said, knowing Dean undoubtedly needed first aid at once. She helped guide him out, and Dean went through the small opening first. Ellie hurried next. Before Vance's turn came, the voices gathered behind him.

Vance had spent a few summers with the Tribal nations to the north, but this was no type of language he recognized. Whoever the people were, they spoke in a rough, whispered hiss.

The beam of his light dashed back and forth around the cave. The hissing grew louder and the black shapes avoided the light.

"Oh shit!" he shouted and then dove through the narrow tunnel.

Once he was back in the main room, Dean shouted, "What is it? What's back there?"

"I don't know. People, I think."

"What?" Ellie cried. Vance was kneeling before the opening with his flashlight.

"What are you doing?" she asked.

"They don't seem to like the light." As he talked, he pointed the flashlight away from them and back into the opening. Standing up and moving away from it, he turned to see Dean's wide eyes staring at him in the gloom, while Ellie bound his wounded arm. It was plain to see that Dean could now hear the hissing words, too.

"We need to get out of here," Vance said softly.

No one argued. Ellie led the way through the rest of the ruins. Vance had never been so happy to see sunlight as they stepped out of the cave.

Behind him, the whispers continued but he didn't look back.

* * *

The sun had already dipped behind the western range before they arrived at the mist-covered hot springs.

"Hold up," Dean panted while he clutched his arm. "I need to rest for a second before we go any further." They all leaned against the rocks, just trying to breathe.

"What did you see back there, Vance?" Dean asked.

"There were people in there. I wonder…"

"Wonder what?" Ellie asked.

"I was reading something… something about the hidden followers of Tezcatlipoca. The book mentioned the Gila forest."

"But that was like eight-hundred years ago," Dean countered.

"The Gila is one of the least traveled national forests. There aren't any real cities within three hundred miles of here."

"But still man, what you're talking about is crazy."

"You're the one with a messed up arm and what about what Ellie saw last night?" No one said anything, so Vance continued. "Hey, I hope you're right. Either way, we should get going. Even if it was some hungry cougar I heard, I don't want to deal with it. I want to be as close to camp as possible, before it gets dark."

"Didn't you mention a jaguar?" Ellie asked. "Could it just be one of those you heard?"

"Just one of those? Jaguars attack more humans than any other kind of cat."

"Almost the same thing, anyway." Dean said. They both looked at Dean as he forced himself back to his feet. "If you're claiming there's some lost cult of Tezcatlipoca out here, and that they would worship jaguars. They might even…" his voice trailed off while his free hand clutched his wound. Vance was beginning to wonder if Dean hadn't cut his arm on a rock like he'd first thought.

"If they were out there, they would dress like, act like, or even have weapons like a jaguar," Vance said.

"Dean, did you cut yourself on a rock back there?" Ellie asked.

"I don't know. It felt like something was near me and then my arm was bleeding. I assumed I did it to myself but now that you say it, yeah, it's possible. Shit, there was someone in there and they attacked me? And your light must have scared them off like you said."

No more words needed to be said. They began moving again.

The hot mists enveloped them, cloaking the light. Their footfalls moved gravel and stone, slowing their pace. They continued until they were quiet shadows passing through the shade of the overhanging cliffs.

Vance had his hunting knife out and was hopping across the boulders as silently as he could when there came a thundering rattle on the path fifty feet before him and he stopped, freezing in place. Clouds of dust rolled over the trio, displacing the mist and clinging to their damp clothes.

"What the hell was that?" Dean yelled.

Vance didn't answer right away. "Dean, you and Ellie stay here."

The mist dispersed as Vance moved forward. He could see where a crevasse had been cut through the tower of rock before him. The crevasse was gone now, a victim of the resent avalanche. He tried not to think what would have happened to them if they had been inside the crevasse when the avalanche began.

Scanning the cliffs above him, he saw that they would need to scale a steep section of a boulder-strewn mountain, before they could clear the interposing boulders.

He was about to turn back towards the others when he glimpsed movement at the top of the cliff. The silhouettes of two figures were there one moment, and then gone so fast that it left him wondering if what he saw had been real.

The whispering laughter that drifted down convinced him that it was no illusion.

Slowly, they began their ascent as Vance filled Ellie and Dean in on what he'd seen on the top of the cliff.

"Come on," Vance said as he helped Ellie through a difficult section. "We have to beat the sun. We need to get at least over this section before we lose the light. I think there might only be two of them."

Dean looked at him, but said nothing.

Reaching the top was no easy feat and they were each forced to stop and gather their breath more than once. Vance studied the area as dusk began to fall. Lingering mist clutched at the trees around them.

"Let's keep..." Vance was interrupted by a fierce yell. A dark shape was racing towards them. Before they could be sure who it was or what they wanted, the shape was flinging a knife. It spiraled through the air and struck Dean in the chest. He went down with a grunt as Ellie screamed.

Moving quickly, Vance stripped off his backpack. He held it like a shield and stood before Ellie. The attacker had a second knife in his fist. It was a man garbed almost completely in black with only his face exposed. He struck out with an obsidian blade, but Vance was able to block it with his pack. Vance kicked out at the man, but the attacker danced back easily.

The black-garbed man hesitated for a moment and Vance got a better look at him. He looked more like a Ninja from a B movie than any type of Tribal American that Vance had ever seen. The figure hissed a few words at him that made no sense. Then he lunged at Vance again.

Vance kept his pack before him while the man made a series of frantic swings with his blade. Soon, Vance's backpack was being cut into ribbons as the contents slipped out and bounced off the rocks. He tried a counter attack, but only received a deep slash across the back of his forearm for the effort. Vance tried to pull his hunting knife from his hip but it was knocked from his hand a second later. The man flashed Vance a wicked grin as they listened to the knife bouncing down the cliff.

"Death," the man whispered and then sprang. But he never reached his target, as a dying Dean tackled the man. With a mutual shout, they both tumbled over the far side of the cliff, Vance never getting a chance to react to the event before it was over.

Their screaming didn't last long.

"Dean...he saved us," Ellie whimpered.

Breathing heavily, Vance grabbed her hand. "Come on, we need to go," he said through gritted teeth.

They found them both below on the jagged rocks. They shared a bloody embrace in death, Dean's head twisted almost completely around, his eyes wide in death, his limbs broken and bloody. The other man's body was too mangled for Vance to learn anything other than what he already knew. That being that his attacker had an olive complexion and was shorter than average.

Ellie's tears overcame her and she dropped to her knees. Vance gave her a moment, but then brought her to her feet. Darkness had now completely claimed the land. After he found himself a tree branch to use as a reasonable club and walking stick, he used her flashlight, then led the way back to their camp.

Vance knew there was at least one more of them out there. Each snapping twig sent him shining the flashlight in mad jerks. Each shadow could hold the other dark figure.

The going was slow and precise. A missed step could mean death as quickly as any knife.

Somehow, they made it to the bigger trail without receiving a dagger in the back. "I'm not sure why he let us get this far," Vance said as he peered into the surrounding darkness.

"Maybe he wants us to lead him back to our camp," she suggested.

"You could be right. If he does, we'll have a big surprise for him when Eric shoots his damn head off. Come on, let's go."

* * *

How they made it back to camp safely, he couldn't have guessed. The second killer could have surprised them at any time. It would have been a simple matter for the killer to conceal himself behind one of the hundreds of trees, then jump out and drive a dagger into Vance's back. Perhaps Ellie was right and the killer was letting them lead the way back to their camp. He only hoped that Eric was still okay.

Once they were close enough to the camp, he called to Eric. Vance was relieved when his friend jogged into view and also quite happy to see he was already clutching his rifle.

"What the hell's going on?" Eric paused a moment. "Hey, where's Dean?" His jaw dropped when Ellie began to sob, able to tell something was very wrong. "What happened to Dean?" he shouted.

From the rear of the camp, a shadow appeared behind Eric. Before Vance could call out and warn Eric, the shadow darted in and slashed his back. Lurching forward, Eric fell to one knee, his eyes wide in pain and shock. Vance was sprinting to him, but before he could reach him, the killer drew his hand back, poised for another blow. Like a cat, there were some type of long claws attached to the fingers and they were covered in Eric's blood.

The claws descended once more and Ellie screamed when Eric's throat was torn away, releasing a thick stream of blood that bathed the earth red.

Vance was already attacking with his club before Eric's body had fully toppled over. The jaguar-man blocked the blow easily and sent a kick to Vance's jaw who stumbled backwards. The man moved in a blur and Vance didn't stand a chance. He wasn't sure what sort of attack knocked the club from his hands, but a second later, it was lying a few feet away in the dirt.

Another kick to the stomach sent him tumbling across the ground and Ellie helped him to his feet while the man moved slowly towards him, savoring the kill. He had the grace and patience of a feline and the campfire was reflected in the blood coating his claws.

"Two," he said in English with a voice like the hiss of escaping steam.

"What?" Vance asked while trying to regain his wits.

"Their God is one," the man said and spat at the ground violently. "The number of the adversary is two. There has to be two."

"Two what?" he managed to ask as Ellie shivered beside him.

"The followers of Tezcatlipoca form prides of two. You two are mates." It wasn't a question. "You care for each other. If one of you becomes my new apprentice voluntarily, I will spare the other. If you refuse, I will slay you both."

"But neither of us killed your apprentice," Ellie whimpered. "It was Dean that pushed him off the cliff."

"This matters not. There must be two."

"What's to keep the other from getting help and rescuing the one we pick?" Vance asked.

"Erasing part of the departing person's mind is a simple matter for me. They will forget about you completely. It will be like you have never existed."

"You can't be serious," Ellie stammered.

"Deadly serious. You have a decision to make. I will give you a moment. If you attempt to flee or attack me, you will be slain." Having finished, he took a step back and loomed silent in the darkness, his claws at his sides. Blood dripped from the tips to spatter the ground.

"This can't be happening," Ellie said, hiding her face in her hands.

"I have to let him pick me. I'll have a better chance of escaping later," Vance whispered. "Even if he can somehow hypnotize you to forget me, I'll escape and find you."

"I can't just leave you here. He wants to make you like him. He wants to make you into a killer. That's what he is, a killer!"

"It has to be me. Who knows what he would do to you."

"He could do the same thing to you!"

"I'm stronger. Whatever happens, I'll have a better chance. I'll escape and find you, I swear."

Ellie pleaded with him to change his mind, that they could try to run for it, but his argument remained the same.

"Your time is up," the voice was hollow.

"It'll be me." Vance couldn't keep the quivering out of his voice.

"You understand that I am now your master and you must obey me without question. Disobedience will be punished." Vance was only able to nod. "You can start by throwing the rifle into the fire; guns are not needed where we are going."

Sweat broke out on Vance's forehead when he lifted the rifle from the ground, wondering if he had time to use it on the man. The Tezcatlipoca man stared at him with glowing eyes. This had to be a test, Vance thought to himself, but he had to try to shoot him, didn't he? When would he have a better chance than this?

With a jerk, he pointed the rifle at his would be master, but the man was no longer there. There was a blinding pain in the back of his head and then he was claimed by blackness.

* * *

Vance awoke in complete darkness. Slow motions brought him to his hands and knees as he fought against the pain in his head. "Ellie," he groaned.

A voice came out of the darkness. "I allowed her to live, even though you disobeyed me. Now you will be forever in my debt. I shall not be so lenient again."

Exhaustion and pain threatened to claim him completely, but it was a bone deep sorrow that infused him. "Can't you just let me go?"

"Don't be foolish. Your training will begin at once. First you will learn to live in the darkness. Once you have mastered it, your real schooling will begin."

"And what is that...exactly?"

"You will learn the way of the fang and claw. You will be taught to murder your own kind, the invaders to our forest. Ours is the way of the killer."

After a long pause he continued. "Now your first task will be to locate wood for a fire. Then you will make the fire, all in total darkness. Begin now."

DENIZENS

SCOTT M.BAKER

Jack Randall had finally done it. He had landed himself in a world of shit. Figuratively, and literally.

He stood at the entrance ladder leading down into the sewer, breathing in the noxious odors. The stench of urine and feces mixed with ammonia, creating a combination so pungent it stunned his eyes and caused him to gag. It didn't help that the lack of flowing air meant the humidity hung heavy around him. He opened his mouth to breathe, but it did no good. He could actually taste the stench. It worked its way to the back of his throat, mixing with the rising bile and turning his saliva putrid.

Removing a penlight attached to a keychain from his jacket pocket, Jack shone it left and right down the length of the sewer. Not that he could see much, for the beam barely penetrated more than three yards into the dark. The sewer measured ten feet in width and twelve in height, with an arched ceiling comprised of red bricks.

Shining the light down, he noticed a two-foot drop from the landing to the floor of the sewer. A trough eighteen inches wide ran down the center of it, carrying a stream of brackish water with unidentifiable lumps floating on its surface.

Jack jumped down from the landing. When his feet hit the sewer, they slid out from under him. He tumbled backward, the edge of the landing breaking his fall. His back and elbows cracked against the cement, sending bolts of pain along his arms and down his spine. He waited a few seconds for the throbbing to subside and after using the landing for support, he regained his footing. Lowering the penlight beam to the floor, he saw what caused him to slip. Runoff from the trough formed a thin layer of human waste that coated the floor.

"Careful, that stuff's slippery as ice." The belated warning came from Terrell Johnson, who stepped off the ladder onto the landing behind him.

"So I learned," Jack said as he carefully stepped to one side. Terrell jumped down, landing with a sure footing. He stepped over the trough to the opposite side of the sewer, turned his back to the wall, and switched on the high-powered flashlight he had stolen from the convenience store. Its beam sliced through the darkness far more effectively than Jack's pathetic little penlight, penetrating at least fifty feet into the sewer. When Terrell first grabbed the flashlight as they raced out of the store, Jack couldn't figure out why he'd taken it. Now it made sense.

Sadly, it was the only thing tonight that did.

Jack had a gut feeling all night that things were going to go terribly wrong. He learned long ago to trust his instincts. They had kept him safe in Iraq for almost eighteen months. Those same alarms had gone off earlier that night when Terrell suggested they knock off the neighborhood convenience store. Jack and the others had tried to bow out, but Terrell eventually browbeat them into going along. He made it sound so simple. They'd hit the store late at night when the only person working would be the owner, a grouchy old Korean that no one in the neighborhood liked anyway. The four of them would go in, scare the hell out of the old guy with a .357 Magnum, grab the cash, and get out. Nothing to it.

Who could have known that the old Korean would be stupid enough to put up a fight? That he'd pull a baseball bat from under the counter and whack Terrell on the back? That Terrell, who could easily have disarmed the guy, would instead pump six rounds into Korean's face and chest? Jack should have made a break for it right then and turned himself into the police. With luck, he'd do only a few years for armed robbery. Instead, he allowed Terrell to persuade him into escaping down a deserted access road behind the store where the entrance to the sewer was located.

None of this should come as a shock to him, though. Jack had been getting into trouble since junior high. Bullying the weaker kids. Shoplifting from local stores. Occasionally snatching an old lady's purse. His grandma, the only one who tried to raise him right, always warned him living like that would be his death some day. "So ye sow so shall ye reap," she used to quote him. Which was why, when he finally got into trouble with the juvenile courts when he was seventeen, she forced him to join the Army, hopefully instilling a sense of responsibility in him. It had, but only because the military would not tolerate his crap. He might have stayed on a straight path if he hadn't been wounded by an IED attack outside of Al-Ramadi. It earned him a trip to Walter Reed Army Medical Center and an honorable discharge. Within a few days after being released from the hospital, he hooked up with Terrell. And where did that get him? Crawling around the sewers so he wouldn't be brought up on charges of second degree murder.

Right about now, Jack's future looked as bleak as the water flowing by in the trough.

"My, God," Carlos Vazquez said as he climbed down from the landing, hanging onto the ledge until he felt sure of his footing. "Smells like my mom's place on taco night."

"Shut up," Terrell snapped. He switched the flashlight from his right hand to his left, shining the beam down the opposite end of the sewer.

Mike Manson, the last of the group, reached the landing a second later. "Man, this place smells like shit."

"It's a sewer, asshole. What'd you expect?" Terrell replied.

Mike switched on the second of the two high-powered flashlights they had stolen from the convenience store. "Yeah, but why the sewers? Now we're trapped down here."

Terrell shook his head. He swung the beam down the sewer to his right, focusing on the trough. "This is a sanitation line. It runs toward the center of the city and eventually drains into the water treatment plant." He swung the flashlight so it faced in the opposite direction. "Farther down that way the sanitation line becomes a storm drain that carries rain water out to the Anacostia River."

"So?" Carlos asked.

Mike crawled off the landing. "While the cops are looking for us up there, we'll make our way to the river and get away unnoticed."

Terrell smiled at Mike and nodded. "You lead."

Mike went first, followed by Carlos. Jack and Terrell brought up the rear. As they walked, Terrell handed Jack the flashlight, then removed the same Magnum he had used to murder the shopkeeper from the waistband of his pants. Terrell flipped out the cylinder, reached into his pocket for spare bullets, and proceeded to reload.

"How do you know so much about sewers?" Jack asked.

"My old man used to work the night shift down here when I was a kid. After my mom died, he sometimes brought me with him if he couldn't find a sitter rather than lose a day's pay."

"Couldn't he get into trouble for that?"

"Sure, if he got caught. But there's rarely anyone down here at n.... Watch it."

Terrell gently pushed Jack up against the wall as a stream of water drained out of a three-foot-square opening in the ceiling. The opening extended up beyond their line of sight. Some of the water splattered onto Jack's left shoulder. It stank as bad as everything else in the sewer.

"What the hell is that?" Jack asked.

"A lateral dump. All the toilets in the area empty into them, which then empty into the sewer."

Jack grimaced and brushed the water off his shoulder.

"You'll live," Terrell said as he finished reloading his Magnum and placed it back into the waistband of his pants. He took the flashlight from Jack. "Now move."

After a few minutes of walking, the group came to a foot-high retainer wall that stretched across the sewer. The sanitation trough dropped down and disappeared underneath the wall. On the other side, there was no flowing sewage to encrust the floor, so the red bricks paving the floor were clear except for the occasional puddle of water. They stepped over the wall and walking became much easier. The stench of the sanitation trough gave way to a musky odor, similar to the basement of an old house. The trickling of water fell behind them, giving way to an eerie silence.

Terrell tapped Jack on the shoulder. "Not much longer now."

In another five minutes, Mike and Carlos stopped walking.

"What's up?" Terrell asked as he pushed his way to the front.

"We can't go no further." Carlos pointed ahead of him. Water filled the sewer, extending ahead of them for ten yards before the line gradually curved left out of their line of sight.

"You idiot," Terrell said. "That's the Anacostia. Just around that bend the sewer opens into the river."

"But the water," Mike protested.

"It's only three or four feet deep."

Tentatively, Mike waded in. The water rose as high as his waist and leveled off. He waded out twenty feet, but the water never went above his belt. Mike turned to face the others, a broad smile on his face.

"Hey, he's right. This ain't as deep as..."

What occurred next happened so fast it barely registered with Jack. Something lunged out of the water directly behind Mike. Jack could not see it clearly, partly because of the dark, partly because of the speed with which it attacked. He caught a glimpse of three glistening talons at the end of each hand. Of the rows of fangs in its mouth. Of red eyes that glowed crimson. What most unnerved him, though, was the sound it made. A chirping, similar to that of a cricket, only deeper in tone and considerably louder. Whatever the thing was, it plunged its talons into Mike's chest and its fangs into his right shoulder. Mike tried to pull away, but before he could react, the creature dragged him under the water, drowning out his screams. Mike dropped the high-powered flashlight to splash into the water, the beam slowly dimming as it sank beneath the surface. The entire incident played itself out in less than two seconds. When it was over, all that remained of Mike or the creature was the rippling water.

"What the fuck was that?" Carlos yelled, adding a few choice curse words in Spanish. The man was too shocked to move.

Terrell didn't waste time responding. He grabbed Carlos by the collar and dragged him backwards, knocking him off balance. Then he swung him in the direction they just traveled.

Carlos stumbled, but quickly regained his footing and began running. "Where are we going?"

"Back to the manhole," Terrell yelled. "Move it!"

Jack followed a few feet behind them. After a minute of running, they reached the retainer wall separating the storm and sanitation drains. The going became slower now because of the slime and waste. They barely covered a hundred yards when Terrell lost his footing. His first reaction was to save the high-powered flashlight, knowing they would need it to find their way to safety. By doing that, however, he wasn't able to break his fall. His left leg slid into the sewage-filled trough and twisted. Jack heard the crack of a bone, followed by Terrell's cry of pain. Before Jack or Carlos could catch him, Terrell tumbled forward, slamming his left hand and right elbow into the opposite bank of the trough. He lay for a moment in the brackish water, groaning. Jack bent over and helped up his friend. Terrell gasped, gritting his teeth tight, not wanting to cry out again. Jack helped him over to the wall and Terrell leaned his back against it, then lowered the flashlight beam down to his leg to check on it.

The sight made Jack wince.

The shattered tibia of Terrell's left leg protruded through the skin and pant leg. Blood and raw sewage filled the wound.

"Are you okay?" Jack asked, not certain what else to say.

"Do I look okay?" Terrell snapped. He moved the flashlight beam off the wound. "I'm gonna have one hell of an infection by morning. Ah, God it hurts!"

"We'll get you to a hospital once we get out of here."

"And how do we explain what we were doing down here in the middle of the night? If the doctor notifies the cops, we're not gonna be able to talk our way out of it," Terrell said.

"What do you mean 'we'?" Carlos asked.

Terrell glanced at Carlos with an icy stare. "You have something to say to me?"

"Yeah. You got us into this by killing that clerk and then bringing us down here. Now thanks to you, Mike is dead and I don't plan on joining him."

"He might still be alive," Jack said, though he didn't believe it.

"So do you plan on leaving me here?" Terrell asked Carlos, ignoring Jack.

"I owe you nothing, man. Once we get back to the manhole, I'm on my own," Carlos replied.

Terrell pushed himself away from the wall and stood to face Carlos, his stance unsteady but his body rigid in defiance, pain flashing in his eyes. Carlos refused to back down. Their eyes locked. In the dim light, Jack noticed Terrell reaching for the Magnum lodged into the waistband of his pants.

A deep, loud chirping echoed down the sewer. The showdown was quickly forgotten. All three men turned and looked behind them. Terrell drew the Magnum, aiming it and the flashlight down the sewer. Carlos stayed behind Terrell, keeping his back to the wall.

Jack slid up next to Terrell, his eyes on the sewer where the beam of light illuminated it. "How far to the manhole?" he asked.

Terrell shrugged. "Another hundred feet. Maybe a little more. Why?"

"We have a better chance of getting away from that...*thing*— whatever it was— than we do killing it."

"You're probably right." Terrell slid the Magnum back into the waistband of his pants. He turned, groaning in pain from his broken leg. Jack slid an arm around Terrell's back and, supporting his weight, the two limped off down the sewer, Carlos following close behind.

The chirping soon fell away behind them. That didn't stop Jack glancing over his shoulder every few seconds, each time expecting to see death closing in on them.

He tried to rationalize what he saw, but nothing came to mind. What was real was that Mike was dead and other thoughts would have to wait until later.

Thankfully, he saw no signs of the creature. However, Terrell's limp grew increasingly worse with every step until, by the time they reached the landing leading to the manhole, he could barely walk.

Terrell leaned against the landing and winced.

"Will you be able to make it up?" Jack asked.

"I don't have a choice. But there's no way I'm going to move that manhole cover. You go first and open it up. We'll be right behind you."

"No problem." Jack crawled onto the landing.

The chirping began again, then stopped as suddenly as it began. Carlos threw himself against the wall. Jack crouched down on the landing, peering into the darkness. Terrell aimed the flashlight down the sewer to the right, then to the left, then along the ceiling. There was no sign of the creature. The only sound came from sewage flowing through the sanitation trough and dripping from the lateral drain.

The chirping began again, only much closer this time, as if the creature was on top of them. Swinging the flashlight from right to left, Terrell illuminated the sewer once more. Still nothing.

"Where is it?" Jack whispered.

"How the hell do I know?" Terrell hissed.

"Jesus Christ, man." Carlos backed down the sewer, frantically looking around. He stepped through the sanitation trough, momentarily losing his balance. His eyes bulged widely in fear.

"Get back here," Terrell ordered, his voice all but a whisper.

"No way, man. It's coming for us. We gotta get out of here before that thing…" Just as Carlos stumbled under the lateral drain, the creature lunged out of the opening, its lower torso still anchored in the drain. Taloned fingers lodged into Carlos' shoulder, holding him in place as it lowered its open jaw over the upper half of Carlos' head. The creature bit down, taking out a large chunk of Carlos' face. Then, as quickly as it attacked, it withdrew back up the lateral drain, dragging Carlos along with it. His screams echoed from the drain until they were cut off by the sickening crunch of bones and the sounds of chewing and rending meat.

The two men watched as streams of blood and chunks of gore dripped from the opening in the drain.

Jack started to climb the access ladder, but Terrell reached out and grabbed his ankle. "That'll take too long. I can't climb, remember?"

"How far to the next manhole?"

"A hundred meters or so."

Jack jumped off the landing. "You think you can make it?"

A severed hand dropped out of the lateral drain.

"I have to."

Terrell draped his left arm over Jack's shoulder. The two limped away as fast as they could. They slowed down only after the horrible cacophony fell away behind them.

"What are those things?" Jack huffed.

"Damned if I know. My old man used to tell stories about people flushing alligators and lizards down the toilet, and of them mutating down here. They were urban legends told to scare the new guys coming onto the job."

"Yeah? Well, Mike and Carlos weren't killed by no urban legend," Jack said.

"Give me a break." Terrell groaned, the stress on his leg starting to take its toll. "I'm just telling you what my old man told me. He and his buddies never saw one."

"Maybe anyone who ever did see one of those things didn't live to tell about it."

"There's a cheery thought." Terrell stopped. "Hold on a minute."

"What's up?"

Terrell swung the flashlight to the right. The beam disappeared down another sewer line running perpendicular to the one they were in. He pulled the Magnum from his waistband, aimed it in the direction of the beam, and limped along the wall until he could look down the connecting line. He lowered the weapon and flashlight, exhaling loudly.

"What's wrong?"

"Nothing. I just wanted to make sure one of those things wasn't waiting to ambush us." He slid the Magnum back into his waistband. "Come on."

The two barely walked ten feet when the chirping echoed off the sewer walls, this time in front of them. Terrell shone the light down into the darkness and moved it around. It fell on a large, black object nestled against the far wall. At first, Jack thought it was a chunk of debris washed into the sewer and deposited during a heavy rain.

That is until it moved.

The creature slowly rose to its fully extended form, stretching out to eight feet in length. Jack thought it might be an alligator because of the shape of its body, but that was where the similarity ended. Its scales were dark brown, almost black. In place of short, stubby front legs, there were two arm-length appendages that ended in a three-fingered hand with long talons at the end of each finger. The rear legs were four feet long and shaped like a dog's hind legs. It had a stub for a tail. The upper torso tapered into a head half the width of its body, a head conjured out of Hell itself.

Bullet shaped, it had a ridge running from the back, over its scalp and down its face, branching off to form a protective ridge around its eyes. The eyes were set deep into the skull and glowed red, even without the glare from the flashlight. What dominated the creature's visage, was its jaws, a gaping maw the width of its face and lined with triple rows of fangs up to three inches in length.

From behind the men, another chirping echoed down the sewer line. There were more of these monsters and at the moment, the new creature was far enough away not to be an immediate threat, but was approaching rapidly. That left only one avenue of escape open to them.

Terrell pointed to the connecting sewer line. "That way."

With Jack again supporting his friend, the two men limped off down the connecting sewer line while several lateral drains disgorged their contents into the sewer. At various intervals, smaller sewer lines connected with the larger one, the sanitation troughs merging until the one in the connecting line had nearly doubled in size.

At one junction, where the merging sewer line was large enough for a human to pass through, the two men paused, contemplating whether to use it. A sudden, loud burst of chirping emanated from one of the creatures as it scurried up behind them. Again, the decision was made for them. Jack hurried with Terrell down the sewer line. In the dark, Jack could make out the red eyes and white fangs of the creature as it lunged at them. But rather than press its attack, it hunkered down, blocking their retreat.

That was when it dawned on Jack. The last two creatures could have attacked him and Terrell at any time. Instead, they were herding him and Terrell. He had experienced this once before—in Iraq. Insurgents had set up roadblocks on side streets, forcing his convoy down a street where an IED waited—the IED that took out his Humvee and nearly cost him his life. These creatures were doing the same thing, directing the two men deeper in the sewer line. Jack was reasonably certain what awaited them would be far less pleasant than a car bomb.

After several minutes, Jack heard the pleasingly familiar sound of flowing water. The Anacostia lay just ahead of them—and safety.

Jack hurried Terrell along. "Come on. We're almost to the river."

Terrell chuckled derisively.

"What's wrong?" Jack asked.

"That ain't the river."

Before Jack could ask what he meant, Terrell stopped moving. The sound of flowing water was intense, as if they stood along the bank of a raging river. Yet they were still in the sewer. Terrell shone the flashlight directly ahead of them.

Jack's heart sank. What he had mistaken for a river was actually a massive sewer line almost sixteen feet in diameter. The sanitation trough that ran down its center was eight feet wide and filled to the brim with a roaring river of sewage. Terrell flashed the light down the length of the line. Two walkways three feet wide paralleled each other on either side of the trough, each coated in a thick layer of human waste. The light beam eventually petered out, leaving the far end of the sewer in darkness.

"What is this?" Jack asked.

"The main sanitation line. All the other lines pour into this one, which eventually empty into the treatment plant."

"How many other lines dump into this one exactly?"

"Dozens. Maybe more."

"Good." Jack supported his friend. "We'll go to the next line and see if we can circle around those things."

Since the two men couldn't walk side-by-side on the narrow walkway, they sidestepped along it. After ten paces, Jack slipped on the slick surface. He would have tumbled head first into the trough if Terrell hadn't pulled him back, propping him against the wall.

"Thanks," Jack gasped.

"Be careful. If you fall in, the current is too strong for me to save you." Beads of sweat stood out on Terrell's forehead, showing how much pain he was in.

A chorus of chirping echoed off the sewer walls. Terrell focused the beam on the path ahead of them. Jack could detect shadowy movement at the outer edges of the beam of light. As the image drew closer and became illuminated, Jack saw a pair of creatures crawling toward them on all fours, one on each walkway. Terrell swung the flashlight behind them to see a third creature approaching along the opposite walkway, while the one that had been herding them along the connecting line emerged into the main sewer and crouched on the walkway. The four creatures blocked all avenues of escape.

"We're screwed," Jack sighed.

Terrell withdrew his Magnum and cocked the hammer. "If we're gonna be their dinner, we can at least make them work for it." He aimed at the creature approaching them on the walkway. Before he could fire, all four creatures stopped and arched their heads into the air. The chirping momentarily grew more intense, then stopped suddenly. Each of the creatures backed away a few feet before settling into a crouch.

"They're scared of the gun." Jack allowed a glimmer of hope to enter his voice.

"Fat chance of that. They're scared of something else."

"What?"

The sewage off to their right began to bubble and swirl, then swelled upwards. For a moment, Jack feared they would be washed away by a tidal surge of human waste. But only one portion of the sewage was rising. Or more accurately, something was rising from it. The thing broke through the surface and sewage flowed off its sides, revealing the shiny dark brown scales of one of the creatures that had been chasing them. Only this creature was enormous.

Nearly ten feet of its spine emerged before its head was out of the flow. It attempted to stand upright in the trough, but was restricted by the arched ceiling, and so had to hunch over. This creature looked just like the others, only it was nearly fifteen feet tall. As the last streams of sewage flowed off its face, it opened its eyes, instantly focusing on Jack and Terrell. Its mouth gaped, revealing fangs as long as daggers. The creature shifted its head slightly, as if contemplating the two men—or choosing which one to eat first.

'What ye sow, so shall ye reap.' The impact of his grandmother's words now became clear to Jack. He would die as he had spent the better part of his life, being regarded by these creatures as something merely to be preyed upon, just as he had preyed on the clerk.

Grabbing the flashlight from Terrell's hand, Jack pushed his friend away and backed down the sewer, putting a few feet between them. Whether he did it out of a sense of justice for what Terrell had done, or merely for self-preservation, he wasn't sure.

Terrell struggled to stand upright, balancing his weight on his one good leg. He looked confused until he saw Jack slowly retreating. Then the realization hit him. Jack watched the expression in Terrell's eyes go from confusion to anger.

Terrell aimed the Magnum at Jack. "I'm not gonna die by myself, you son of a..."

The enormous creature lunged forward and dived on Terrell, swallowing him down to below his knees. Jack heard Terrell's muffled screams, then the sickening crunch as the creature bit through his friend's legs. The creature dove back beneath the sewage and the backwash slopped over the walkway, carrying away Terrell's severed feet and ankles.

Jack wasn't about to wait around for the creature to return for him. He ran, trying desperately not to lose his footing on the waste-encrusted walkway. The chirping began again. The four smaller creatures sprang from their crouching position and closed in on Jack. The one directly in front closed the distance the most rapidly, and would be on him in seconds. He attempted to stop, but his feet slid out from under him. Bowing to the inevitable, he tumbled sideways, plunging into the river of human waste.

Fortunately, he had enough foresight to take a deep breath before he hit the tainted water. All other senses momentarily were washed away as he plunged beneath the surface. It was just like diving into a river, except this river was toxic. He braced himself, expecting to slam into the cement floor but he never touched it. Instead, he felt himself being rapidly carried along by the current. Kicking, he swam for the surface. Once his head emerged out of the sewage, he shook it violently, trying to shake off as much of the waste as possible. Not that it mattered. After being dunked in liquid feces, if he survived he'd be spending a lot of time in the hospital fighting off a cocktail of diseases.

He opened his eyes, then quickly closed them again to ward off the burning. When he opened them a second time, they still stung, but at least he could see. Turning so he flowed backwards, he lifted the flashlight still clutched in his hand out of the sewage, wiped the lens clean, and aimed it behind him. The four human-sized creatures chased after him, two on each walkway, chirping furiously. Rather than closing the distance, they were falling behind. Because of the rapid flow of the current, they couldn't keep up. He watched for several minutes as the creatures fell further behind, and he dared not to get his hopes up that he was safe. When the creatures could no longer be seen in the flashlight's beam and the chirping faded away, Jack finally allowed himself to consider that he might make it out alive after all.

A change in pitch in the flow of the sewage caught his attention. He turned to face the direction of the flow, shining the light ahead of him. He saw nothing. But the new sound rapidly grew louder, becoming a roar. Then the beam of light reflected off the encrusted metal, and Jack saw his impending doom.

The sewer line ended against a brick wall. Or at least the walkways did. A hole in the wall twelve-feet wide channeled the trough into a slide, creating a waterfall of sewage. Not that Jack would have to worry about the plunge; a metal grate covered the hole. Its rungs were an inch thick, creating openings about three inches square. Empty trash bags, a tire, pieces of wood, and other large debris floated on the surface, all clumped around the grate.

Before he could react, Jack slammed into the grate with enough force to knock the breath from his lungs. The weight of the sewage plunging through the opening threatened to drag him under. He grabbed one of the metal rungs with his left hand and tried to pull himself up, but decades of accumulated waste coated the rungs, preventing him from getting a good grip. He dropped the flashlight to free up his right hand. It sank beneath the surface, the light immediately swallowed up in the foul liquid, plunging the sewer into complete darkness. However, with both hands free, he was able to pull himself up until all but his legs were out of the flow. Sidestepping along the rungs, he moved to his left until his shoulder bumped the brick rim of the opening.

He reached around with his left hand until he felt the edge of the walkway. Normally, he would have been able to grab the ridge and pull himself to safety, but not now. Everything was coated in slime. If he tried to climb onto the walkway, he would fall back into the trough.

Think, Jack cautioned himself. *There has to be a way out of this.*

With a growing sense of terror, he realized there was. Behind him, he heard the faintest echoes of chirping, barely noticeable at first over the roar of the fetid water, but growing louder with each second. As the creatures drew closer, he crawled back to the center of the grate and lowered himself into the current until only his head was above the surface, hoping to conceal himself. The current was strong, shoving him against the grate and making it difficult to hold on. He braced himself for the coming attack.

Only then did he notice that the chirping had stopped. He prayed that the creatures had abandoned the chase having reached the end of the line. He kept his eyes closed and listened for any sound of them. Nothing. It would have been common sense to remain still, but he needed to know. He needed to take a look.

Opening his eyes and turning his head, he wished he had listened to his common sense.

Four sets of red eyes glared at him from the walkways— motionless and silent. Yet the true horror came from farther down the sewer line where a large pair of red eyes rose out of the sewage, floating toward him.

As the eyes grew closer, they slowly rose up toward the ceiling. By the time they had reached the grate, they towered over Jack. He could sense the mouth opening, the fangs being bared as the creature savored its meal.

Then, with a sudden loud chirping, the creature lunged.

ISANDLWANA

JOSE ALFREDO VAZQUEZ

The white man thinks it's over. They came to the Zulu Empire lands from the south, all proud in their red dresses and carrying their long weapons. The king and lord Cetshwayo allowed them to come in. He observed them, and realized that their intent was to conquer Zulu land. Their black clad preachers were the advance party for a long chain of invaders that would set themselves in Zulu land, drinking the life of its soil. That could not be allowed.

The king had observed the might of the weapons of the so called British. He knew that the Assegai, the traditional short stabbing sword, could not compete against the 'death from distance' that the so called Martini Henry rifles inflicted. Having failed to capture any new weapons, and not having men trained in their use, he heeded the advice of his half brother. He needed a new weapon, something to strike fear deep in the heart of the invaders. So he decided on a course of action so dreaded it had only been attempted a few times in Zulu traditions.

All the priests were called and informed of the king's wishes. Many refused to comply, and were killed. Those remaining were loyal enough as to undergo the feat.

Ten thousand young warriors were called. All strong, all single, all volunteers. They had the determination of youth, and were willing to give their lives to repel the invaders.

They were organized into groups, and spent the afternoon getting pumped up with songs and dances about past victories. And to make their last hours alive really something to hate, the unthinkable was done. Five hundred beautiful maidens were brought, and then they were organized in small groups and ordered to beat them to death. For young, pumped-up virgin warriors, that really brought their senses up.

It was then that the old ceremony was started. After the night long ritual, at the first light of dawn, they were put in lines, and every warrior was to strangle to death the one standing on his right. That was to be done after drinking the special concoction prepared for the transformation. Their last minutes in this life were ones of pain, anger and agony. One by one they died, until there was silence in the early morning hour.

By late afternoon, however, something was happening. Some of the now swelling corpses began to move, and soon many stood up to stare vacantly at the other corpses slowly rising as well.

It was at this point that the first red clad scouts from the British found them. What they called a silent impi, or warrior unit, hidden in a rolling ridge, waiting for their advance column to arrive. They opened fire as they retreated, and the multitude of figures rose as one, to slowly follow the path where the horsemen had escaped.

The white explorers went back to report to their superiors their finding of the huge and unarmed impi. The so called Pulleine and Chelmsford sent two thousand of their troops to handle the unarmed warrior unit. They left their carts at the base of the Isandlwana hill, and formed their famous firing line.

The dim afternoon light showed a myriad of shambling figures moving towards the hill. The officers ordered their men to move forward, and they formed for the easy kill. At the sound of the orders, a volley echoed throughout the valley. Hundreds of figures fell to the ground, thrown by the sheer force of the bullets hitting them. The soldiers cheered, and advanced in perfect formation, eager to engage the next lines.

What they had failed to realize was that most of the fallen figures were still moving. Teeth bared, hands clawing, the figures reached out to the upcoming line of soldiers, who kept advancing, oblivious to the danger.

The second column noted that something was terribly wrong when the advancing first line suddenly fell from view; hundreds of men falling to the ground at the same time. The screams of sheer terror filled the otherwise silent evening, as hundreds of corpses swarmed over the men whose legs and ankles had been grasped by the first fallen corpses like hungry ants.

The second column vacillated, torn between helping their fellow soldiers and facing the thousands of figures coming at them. That hesitation was their doom.

The officers in charge of the third column shook off their trance and started to instigate their men to fire.

Only one of them, however, managed to remember that the Zulu attack formation, the impi, resembled a buffalo's head, with a strong center and two flanking arms that attacked once the center was involved. He looked back, and saw some of the Zulu warriors running behind them, coming uphill from the sides. Their arms had been burned, even charred in some cases. But why?

The answer came shambling behind them. On both flanks, thousands of dark figures were following the nauseating smell of burnt flesh. The men were effectively making the corpses follow them, thus surrounding the red clad white men apart from their supply wagons.

The white officer tried to order a retreat to the wagon train, but it was too late. The last white men went down in a fighting mêlée that filled the night with horrible screams.

At the wagon train, the supply men panicked and tried to run, leaving all the munitions boxes locked and scattered on the ground. Only a few managed to escape.

One of them managed to maul an approaching corpse on the head with an ax, and the body dropped, not moving again. The man stared at it for a few seconds, and then decided to repeat the experiment on another corpse. Again, the head blow felled the undead warrior. So that was their weak point. The head could be destroyed, and the walking nightmare would be no more.

He looked around, but realized it would be worthless to warn the few remaining men. Their state of panic was such that no one would listen. He decided to make a run to the small huts called Rorkes's Drift.

He ran as fast as he could, and upon reaching the place, found one hundred and seventy men ready to abandon their post and run, stories of the massacre having reached them from the few survivors. He convinced the captain in charge that they would not outrun the approaching horde, so they hastily placed the munitions and supply boxes to form a small perimeter.

And they got ready to aim for the heads.

It was a dawn that would go down in history, as less than two hundred men mowed down an attacking force of nearly ten thousand undead Zulu warriors. When munitions ran out, sheer force was used. Though exhausted, they fought for their lives. When the morning light came, it was over. The relief column came to find the startled survivors amidst thousand of bodies. The Zulu's fear factor gamble had failed.

Of course, the official story of the first encounter of the war was that the professional British soldiers and their Colonial troops had been annihilated by an unexpectedly strong force that had managed to hide from their scouts. That galvanized the public opinion back in England, and although Prime Minister Disraeli lost his position, the Empire went on to defeat the Zulu African Empire.

In a small padded cell on the Isle of Man, a sick patient was being prepared for the premier treatment of his time for schizophrenia—frontal lobotomy.

The doctors did not care too much for his African war stories, especially the ones about how he found out how living corpses could be brought down by a blow to the head. After all, the shrinks that heard his tales joked amongst themselves that unless they believed the crazy Austrian doctor, a certain Freud, then they would have to listen to the ramblings of crazed men like the young sergeant being readied with chloroform for the surgery.

One of the physicians thought it was funny that the man's last words before the lobotomy erased his personality and memories were, "The white man thinks it's over!"

THE BATTLE OF ANDERSON

MARK RIVETT

May 1, 1865

William lay on his back in the barn, crowded on all sides by the bodies of his wounded brothers in arms. A near constant flow of soldiers were brought from every corner of the battlefield to the makeshift triage unit. The distant pop of gunfire and occasional thunder of cannon fire still echoed in the distance. The bright May morning would be the picture of spring if not for the stench of death, the sight of mangled limbs, and pitiful cries of wounded soldiers.

Before the battle, the Confederate general had given an inspirational speech—even though Lee had surrendered over three weeks earlier, the Confederacy could still be saved, here, now. Even though there were no supplies, no food, and barely enough ammunition to fight, this would be the glorious final stand of the South destined to turn the tide and reignite the struggle for independence. Thousands of starving men would be glorified in history as the saviors of the south.

"What a bunch of shit," William murmured as he looked down at his mangled leg.

"I'll clean the barn, Daddy. I promise." Another soldier, barely fifteen years old, responded. He was delirious, his arm was missing and his uniform was covered in blood. Flies buzzed around his wound almost as if he was already dead. More than likely, he soon would be.

An ear piercing scream drowned out the moans and mutterings of the wounded soldiers. A few raised their heads in alarm, the many that had been here for quite a while sat still, their sanity barely intact. The sound was familiar, but every time it was heard it drove a shaft of terror through every conscious man's heart.

"Hold him down, damn it!" the doctor's voice ordered.

William wanted desperately to look away from the horse stall turned operating room but couldn't. He watched as four assistants struggled to hold a wounded man down. The assistant in the rear gripped the patient's leg by the ankle and wrapped his other arm around the knee to immobilize it. Even still, the shoeless foot that poked out from beneath the assistants arm wiggled and struggled in the vice-like grip.

William swallowed, his mouth dry, as he watched the doctor brace for leverage over the implement he was holding. With a precise but powerful thrust, the doctor's arm moved forward and the patient screamed again. A trickle of blood began to pool in the red hay on the blood-stained floor. The doctor's elbow moved back and the patient screamed. Forward, the patient screamed again. Then back, the patient's scream now continuous. Forward, back, forward, back, the doctor continued, and as he worked, the soldier's screams diminished into moans, then whimpers and then went silent. The man had, as most did, passed out from blood loss and pain.

Wiping his forehead with a gore-stained sleeve, the doctor took a step back and set the bloody saw on a shelf next to other medical implements. The teeth of the bright red blade dripped with dark blood.

The assistant who had been holding the leg also took a step back, but still held the man's leg beneath his arm. As he turned to exit the stall, he held in his gore-covered hand the newly amputated leg of the wounded soldier. Quickly, he moved out of the stall and through the barn, dripping blood from the mangled appendage as he went out the barn door.

With a heave, he flung the limb into a pile of other limbs that had been steadily growing all day. Focused on his work, the assistant was numb to the captivated looks of every soldier within the triage.

Stepping out from the stall, the doctor huffed from exhaustion. The cries of agony and semi-conscious murmurings of the wounded seemed dull in comparison to the piercing screams of torture from the suffering patient within. Two assistants struggled to lift the soldier's body off the operating table and to a stall on the other side of the barn. The man would be placed with the others. He would either die or he wouldn't—regardless, there were many more surgeries to be done. The smell of burnt flesh filled the air, the result of the doctor cauterizing the amputated leg.

With appraising eyes the doctor began to look around the occupants of the room. William's heart thundered in his chest as the eyes of the doctor lingered on him for a moment before moving on to someone else. William had faced combat on many occasions; faced the cannons of the Union, faced cavalry, even stood unflinching against a bayonet charge. It was in the moments between surgeries that he knew real terror. It was that fleeting second that the doctor's eyes rested upon him that his heart stopped.

"Him," the doctor said as he pointed at a group of men lying against the wall opposite William. The faces of the three men laying there froze in horror, none of them sure who the doctor was referring to, each of them hoping beyond hope that it was one of the others.

Two doctor's assistants wheeled a rusty gurney over to the group and paused for a split second before reaching down and hoisting the soldier man up.

"No!" the man screamed. His right arm was restricted in bloody bandages but he flailed wildly with his left before clamping another soldier's arm in a death grip.

"No! No! No!" The man continued to scream as the assistants struggled to break the two men apart. It always took a great deal of effort to pry a terrified man loose from whatever he clung to, but every time the assistants were successful.

As they wheeled their way into the operating stall, William could see tears lining the faces of the two men who had been lying next to the doctor's current patient. They sat shaking and chewed their bottom lip in fear and frustration. Even though it wasn't their turn now, eventually it would be.

William looked down at his bloody bandaged leg and wondered when it would be his turn. He looked to the pile of amputated limbs outside and remembered seeing the very first lonely arm discarded there. The limb had long since vanished beneath a pile of bloody arms and legs and a sloppy puddle of gore pooled in the grass beneath.

As the assistants pinned the man down again, the doctor began cutting once more. The screams began again. And, after the grim work was done, an assistant discarded the lifeless limb, followed by the smell of fresh burnt flesh.

The doctor's emerged from the stall and glanced about the room. This time his eyes fell on William and he lost his breath. The doctor gestured with a bloody hand. "Him."

Two assistants began to wheel the gurney over to William and quickly gripped his arms. Before they could hoist him up, the doctors voice called out, "Wait."

The assistants released him and William sagged back to the floor, his heart beating like a drum in his chest.

The sound of hoof beats could be heard in the distance and they were growing louder. A few moments passed and the squeaking of the wooden hay cart used to carry the wounded from the battlefield was unmistakable.

"We're here, men. The doctor will have you taken care of in no time." It was the voice of an officer as he called out above the moans and wails of the new arrivals.

The officer held a handkerchief to his nose as he stepped inside the barn. The look in his eyes said it all, his thoughts clear to anyone–thank God I'm not in here.

"Six more for you," he said to the doctor as the assistants began bandaging the new arrivals.

The doctor nodded silently.

"Sir, sir. Could you bring us back some moonshine? Please sir. Please?" a wounded soldier spoke up.

The officer shot a glance to the doctor and then back over to the wounded man. "We don't have any alcohol, soldier. We don't even have any food. You're a brave young lad, soldier. You made your momma and poppa proud here today. The Doc'll fix you up good." With that, the officer turned on his heals and exited the barn.

"Fuck you!" screamed the soldier. "Get me a drink! I can't take it any more! You hear me? I can't take this any more! Get me a goddamn drink!"

The only response was the squeaking wheels and the beating of hoofs vanishing in the distance.

The doctor took a look at the new arrivals and motioned to the assistants again. "Him," he said.

The assistants lifted one of the new soldiers onto the gurney. The man had a badly wounded arm but sat smiling at the immediate attention he was receiving. "Thanks, Doc. I didn't expect to jump the line," he said nervously, unaware of what awaited him.

Neither the doctor nor his assistants responded. They simply wheeled him slowly into the operating stall.

"Took a shot in the elbow. I'd still be out there fighting if I could hold a rifle... ...hey, what's that?" the soldier continued his nervous chatter.

The doctor said nothing. The process of restraining the patient and applying a tourniquet was performed well in view of the doctor's tools. Grim, nasty looking instruments seemingly more suited to working with wood than human flesh sat arrayed in a grim testament to the pain they inflicted. Their blades and handles dripped with blood—there was simply no time to clean them between surgeries.

William looked over to the five other men who had just arrived. They looked over to the operating stall in wonder at the treatment their comrade was receiving. William watched their faces turn to a mask of horror as the screams began. Moments passed and the doctor began to saw. William watched the masks of horror transform into the desperate looks of men coming to the realization of their fates. Every man in this barn, including them, was destined for that gurney in that stall with the doctor.

Once again, the doctor finished his work and stepped out from the stall. William kept his eyes on the new arrivals and tried to judge which ones were either more or less severely wounded than him. He struggled to understand the doctor's triage process.

And then, when he felt he had it figured out, he could already tell that he was next. None of the new arrivals were severely wounded enough to jump in front of him nor had anyone else been here longer than he. It was his turn, and as it had so many times before, his heart felt as if it would pound out from within his chest.

"Him," he heard the doctor's words as the assistants grabbed his shoulders and hoisted him atop the gurney. He listened to the squeaking wheels of the table as he gazed up at the barn ceiling, and he listened to the stall door close and lock behind him. He glanced around at the four assistants, one gripping each arm and each leg. On instinct, he attempted to move one of his arms and realized the experienced assistants had him completely immobilized.

The doctor, after applying a tourniquet to his thigh, began to fasten a leather strap around his midsection to the gurney, pulling it tight. William looked over to the shelf occupied by the doctor's bloody tools and could see the teeth-shattered remains of one inch thick wooden bars that had been gripped in the mouths of patients to keep them from screaming and biting off their tongue. Each had long-since broken and there was simply no choice but to let the men scream, and if they bit down hard enough, shatter teeth.

William's adrenaline surged through his system and he struggled to control his panic. The doctor held a bloody scalpel in one hand and William could see the man's eyes focused intently on his leg as he judged the best point at which to begin to cut.

Without warning, a bite of pain shot up his leg. The scalpel had sliced into his flesh and he could feel the doctor carefully, methodically, cutting through the skin of his shin. He let loose a scream of agony and began to struggle violently. The assistants held him tighter and he could do nothing but writhe in his restraints. The cut began on the outside and moved under his leg, inside, then over. William could picture in his mind's eye the bloody ring around his leg just below the knee.

He watched as the doctor turned and placed the scalpel on the shelf, then returned to attend his leg with a small saw. In the next instant, the bite of a new agony began. The small saw moved back and forth as it cut through his calf muscle. William could feel his severed calf roll up beneath his knee and he screamed and struggled. He saw the splatter of his own blood cover the assistant securing his leg and he began to grow faint. He welcomed this new sensation, hoping desperately he would pass out and be spared more suffering.

The doctor returned the small saw to the table and then hefted the large steel saw that William had come to fear. He watched as the doctor placed the saw into position and braced himself for the first cut through his shin bone.

As the doctor took one violent thrust forward, William screamed again. The saw's teeth, grown dull by those that had come before him, bit deep into bone and the pain was exactly as he had imagined—unbearable.

The doctor pulled back and the pain ignited again. The mercy of passing out was approaching and William pleaded for it to arrive. The doctor continued, forward and back, forward and back with the saw until William, losing consciousness, felt the blade bite completely through.

A sense of relief washed over him. It was over. The pain was…

He was pulled from his semi-unconscious state by another explosion of agony. The doctor wasn't done yet. There were two bones in his lower leg and each had to be cut for the amputation to be complete. The last thing William saw before passing out, was the assistant holding his severed leg make his way to the pile of limbs outside the barn and casually toss it to join the countless others lying there.

* * *

William awoke periodically from his slumber to the screams and wails of the remaining soldiers. He was laying on the wood floor of a stall cramped with a half dozen other amputees. At one point, an assistant entered and dragged a lifeless corpse out to make room for an unconscious patient. William's venture in and out of consciousness was perpetually plagued by pain, hunger, thirst, and the phantom feeling of his newly severed leg.

When he finally awoke, he had no idea how many days had passed. It was night and the aroma of something delicious wafted through the barn, overpowering even the vile stench of blood, feces, and death. An officer sat muttering to a man next to him, and when he noticed William was awake, turned to address him.

"How are you doing, soldier?" asked the officer who placed a hand on William's shoulder.

"Been better, sir. How's the battle?" William asked, not really caring but not having anything else to discuss with the officer.

The officer thought for a second before answering and William already knew what his answer would be. "You men gave enough of yourself these past few days and we ain't got nothing left to shoot with. If we had, you can bet your ass we'd bury those yanks."

William said nothing.

"The general's trying to work something out with the locals to get you men fed and moved back home." The officer said as his eyes drifted over to another man making his way through the crowd of wounded soldiers scattered about the barn.

"I'm hungry," William said, knowing the Confederate force had run out of provisions long ago and hoping the officer had connections that pity would drive him to use on William's behalf.

The officer nodded, held his hand up, and snapped his fingers. The man who had been walking through the barn left through the large front doors. Though he was still partially delirious, William could have sworn he was the company cook.

"You're gonna make it, son. Not many of you did," the officer reassured William.

The company cook made his way over to William and handed him a steaming bowel of delicious-smelling stew.

"You get healthy and tell them what you seen here back home," the officer said. "A lot of men died here today and those Yank bastards ain't gonna rewrite history. You understand me?" The officer smiled and William noticed the sound of jovial soldiers outside. For months, as the war had turned against the Confederacy, morale had diminished as quickly as the supplies. William couldn't remember hearing a man laugh let alone make a joke or speak with optimism.

"So we're going home?" William asked as he took a bite of stew. He, along with every other member of the Confederate force, hadn't had a full meal in days and the taste was delicious.

"Yup, first thing tomorrow, you men are heading home. Like I said, the general's working on getting all of you home as soon as possible." The officer looked at William's stew with a mixture of disdain and envy before standing up and looking around the barn. "Eat up. The south is gonna need men like you to rebuild it to its former glory."

William took another bite. The smell was seductive and the company cook had outdone himself. For months, the Confederacy had been running out of supplies and for weeks the company had been rationing more and more. "Where'd the meat for the stew come from, sir? I thought we were out of provisions."

The officer frowned for a minute and then looked over to William as he began to make his way out of the barn. "Don't you worry none about where we got the stew son. Just know that you and the rest of the men gave enough of yourself to earn that stew. It's the last real meal you're gettin' in a long while, so eat up." The officer disappeared into the night.

William took another bite as his eyes lingered on the barn doors through which the officer exited. The night was dark but lanterns lit the barn inside and out. There was something not right–something was missing.

"How 'bout that!" William muttered as he took another bite of his stew, a part of him knowing the truth but unwilling to admit it, and another part feigning stupidity. "It must have taken forever to bury all those limbs."

STRIKE THE HARPY

NICK MEDINA

Wives don't plan on getting pregnant when they cheat on their husbands. And husbands don't plan on killing their wives when they pop the big question. But sometimes, shit happens.

* * *

"What should we sing?" Todd Dunbar asked his wife as he finished strategically tucking the twinkling Christmas lights between the branches of the fresh cut pine.

"You know my favorite Christmas carol," Holly said.

"Deck the Halls? You know that song's not about you, don't you?" he teased.

"Deck the Halls with boughs of *Holly*," she crooned, putting extra emphasis on the word which was her name.

"Fa la la la lah, la la la lah," he sang with a smile.

"What exactly is a bough anyway?" Holly asked.

Todd let go of the strand of glittering garland in his hands and yanked the seldom used dictionary from the bookshelf. He blew dust off the pages and cracked the old leather binding. "Bough," he read, "a main branch of a tree."

"Hmm," she hummed, "that sounds about right."

"Of course it's right, it's in the dictionary."

"Of course it's right, it's in the dictionary," she mocked. She took the old book from his hands and tossed it on the sofa before throwing herself into his arms. They fell backward onto the sofa, their lips locked, and their hands groped for more than just jingle bells and mistletoe.

"How about an early Christmas gift?" she asked.

"Is this part of it?" Todd grinned. He yanked off her blouse and unclasped her bra with the same excitement as a little boy tearing away the wrapping paper concealing a new train set on Christmas morning.

"Part," Holly said, "but not all." She picked up a candy cane, licked the tip and then stuck it in her mouth. She sucked on it suggestively while working to release his belt buckle. When she had him free of all encumbrances, she bit off a piece of the candy cane. "Minty," she whispered upon bending to take him in her mouth as well.

"Oh, God," he gasped. "That's just what I've always wanted."

* * *

Although that was the last merry Christmas Todd and Holly Dunbar spent together, it wouldn't be their last Christmas together. Up until that Christmas Todd and Holly loved one another more than all the other reindeer loved Rudolph when he came to the rescue on that foggy Christmas Eve.

Before that Christmas, Todd and Holly never fought. Before that Christmas, they trusted one another implicitly. Before that Christmas, they had never heard of Marty Powell.

Holly ran into Marty—skied into him is much more accurate— on the slopes of Mount Passavant, a local ski resort not ten miles from the Dunbars' home. The two collided and both fell with their skis intertwined in a bank of snow.

"Sorry," Holly giggled her apology. "I've never been all that good on planks."

Marty dusted the snow from his hair and helped her up. "It's okay," he said, taken aback by Holly's beauty even though her cheeks were red with cold and she had on a pair of goggles that obscured half her face. "Maybe I can give you some pointers?"

Holly didn't have a chance to take him up on the offer before Todd came rushing over. He latched onto her like a grizzly bear claiming a fish from a river and escorted her away to the lodge. Little did he know that while he spent an extra thirty minutes cruising the slopes alone, Holly and Marty ran into one another again inside the lodge where they got to talking over hot chocolate spiked with peppermint schnapps.

That was late January, just one month after that wonderful Christmas, and that was the start of the affair.

Why she did it is a question Holly never got to answer. Whether she would have had a good reason is debatable. During twelve years of marriage, she had never expressed any unhappiness to Todd. Perhaps he could be a bit overbearing at times, downright aggressive when provoked, but he chalked that up to passion. Perhaps it was because Marty Powell was a younger man, just a kid really, looking for a good time and to learn a thing or two from a more experienced woman, especially one as enticing as Holly.

Marty had an apartment on the other side of town where he lived with a ferret named Hank. The place was a typical bachelor pad for a guy just out of college. What it lacked in charm, it made up for with empty beer bottles and overloaded ashtrays. While she could have done without the mold in the shower, Holly didn't mind that they had to act out their fantasies on a futon.

"I love you," Marty said just two months after meeting Holly as he was thrusting into her.

"I love your blue eyes," Holly said in response. She didn't love him—she wondered if he even knew what love was—but even if she did, she knew better than to say it while in the throes of passion.

The affair went on that way, always taking place at Marty's apartment, always when Todd was at work, for eight months without a hitch. Marty made her feel young again and she taught Marty things to do with his fingers and tongue that he never would have learned on his own; things he couldn't even learn from the porn he had saved on his computer.

It was in the tenth month of the affair when things went wrong. It wasn't that Todd finally got a clue, it was that Holly conceived.

"How do you know it's mine?" Marty asked. Visions of his perfect world crashing down in flames flashed before his eyes. Holly could see the fear and disappointment on his face.

"Todd and I have tried many times," she said, "and it's never happened for us before."

"So it could be…" he started, a glimmer of hope shimmering in his baby blues.

She clasped her hands with his. "I'll tell Todd it's his," she said, cutting Marty off before he could finish the thought. In her mind, it was the only option. Todd had always wanted an heir and, unlike Marty, Todd could afford one.

"Hey, hon," Holly said to Todd on the night of December first as her nervous hands rubbed her belly up and down.

"What's up?" he asked. His eyes were on the television instead of on her.

"There's something I've gotta tell you, but I'm a little on edge about it."

This time Todd turned away from the TV. For the first time that evening, he noticed that Holly wasn't sitting next to him on the couch the way she normally did; she was sitting in an armchair across the room.

"What's wrong?" he asked.

"Nothing," she said, suddenly doubting the decision she'd made. The problem was, however, that whether she told him or not, she'd still be lying to him, and eventually her expanding belly would give her away.

Todd tried to chuckle, but it was obvious that Holly had already worried him. "You're scaring me," he said.

"Todd..." she started, pausing for an excruciating ten seconds. "I'm two months pregnant."

Todd's face lit up brighter than the tree at Rockefeller Center. He smiled in a way that she had only seen him smile once before; it was when she said yes to his marriage proposal.

"For real?" he asked.

"For real," she confirmed, finally able to force a smile.

"I thought...you scared the shit out of me...you really had me going there," he spluttered. "I thought something was wrong." He leapt from the couch and yanked on her arms to pull her tight against his chest where he covered her face and hair with kisses.

"No, Todd," she said, "there's nothing wrong." The lie hurt like hell, but there was no other way. Todd could never know the child inside of her wasn't his.

Todd beamed like a snowman with too many pieces of coal in its smile for at least twelve hours straight following her announcement. He couldn't sleep and he couldn't come down from the high created by the fact that he would be a father soon. But then, long after Holly had fallen asleep, he had the sudden urge to know when exactly he'd finally pulled off the feat he'd begun to think he'd never accomplish; he had to know when she had conceived.

"Hol'," he said, nudging her from his side of the bed. "Holly, wake up."

"What is it, Todd?" she groaned sleepily.

"When exactly did it happen? Was it exactly two months?"

"Yeah," she said, too groggy to even open her eyes. "Two months ago."

Todd waited for her to fall asleep again before he slid out of bed and flipped through the calendar. He knew something was wrong. There was a reason he couldn't remember a certain special night with Holly two months ago because two months ago he'd been out of the country on a business trip that lasted for two weeks. He climbed back into bed and nudged her some more.

"Who told you that you're at two months?" he asked.

"The doctor," she murmured. "I saw my doctor yesterday."

Although he assured himself that even doctors could be wrong when it came to determining the exact moment of conception, he had an unshakable feeling of doubt that just wouldn't let him be. It didn't help that she had been so nervous when she gave him the news. Everything, it seemed, was pointing him in one dreadful direction.

In an attempt to spare his wife the humiliation of his nagging suspicion—a suspicion he prayed was baseless with every ounce of his being—Todd did something that made him feel like scum, something he hoped Holly would never have to find out about; he ditched work and followed his wife when she left the house the next day.

She took him straight to Marty Powell.

Todd seethed behind the wheel of his Jeep Wrangler when he saw his wife—his Holly—willingly walk into the open arms of the little shit he remembered from the ski slope nearly eleven months earlier. He immediately wanted to get out of the Jeep and beat the living piss out of the son-of-a-whore who had knocked up his wife, but that would only render temporary satisfaction. What he wanted was permanent satisfaction. He wanted revenge that would last a lifetime. Rather than stroll up the walk and bust down the door to Marty Powell's apartment, he drove away.

Todd let the affair go on for another week. He didn't lay a hand on Holly—out of love or anger—the entire time, and she didn't seem to mind, which only fueled his fury all the more. He followed her twice more just to make sure he wasn't acting on a one time assumption. He wouldn't want to make a mistake —not with what he had planned. But he wasn't wrong. Holly always led him to the same place.

It was three weeks before Christmas when Holly went to meet Marty at his apartment with a wine-shaped bottle of sparkling grape juice. But he didn't answer the door when she knocked and he didn't answer his phone when she called. She returned home to find Todd's Jeep in the driveway although he wasn't supposed to be home from work for another four hours.

"What's up?" she asked as she walked through the door. She had an awkward look on her face brought on by the realization of how dubious she must look entering the house with only a wine-shaped bottle of grape juice in her hands. She tried to play it cool anyway. "You're home early."

"Just decorating the tree," Todd said. He had his back to her. His hands were working quickly, affixing something to the tree that she couldn't see.

"But we always decorate the tree together," she protested, genuine hurt and sadness sounding in her voice.

"Sorry, hon," he said, "I was just too excited. I couldn't wait."

"Excited about what?"

"The new decorations," Todd said.

"You bought new ornaments?"

"Not exactly," he said. He finished what he was doing and turned to face her. His hands were red and the tree was *dripping*. She dropped the bottle of grape juice, which shattered on the floor at her feet, and screamed in horror when she saw what Todd had hung on the branches.

There were fingers and toes, a tongue and ears. She immediately recognized the beautiful blue eyes that once had stared at her as she made love to him. They were Marty's eyes. Impaled at the very top of the tree—the star if you will—was his heart.

Holly heaved in disgust, making some disturbing sound that Todd had never heard her make before, and tried to run.

"Wait," he said, "I have a gift for you, too." He caught her by the hair and dragged her across the carpet to the base of the Christmas tree. Once there, he released her locks, letting her head thud against the floor. She turned her head; from her vantage point on the carpet she could see Marty's mangled and mutilated corpse crammed between the entertainment center and the tree. She screamed again and looked away, but what her eyes landed on this time wasn't much better.

"I bought a new electric saw," Todd smiled. He was standing over her with the gleaming tool raised in his hand. "You shoulda seen how easy it brought down this tree. And it brought down this asshole even faster," he said and kicked Marty for extra emphasis.

Holly retched, and when she tried to get up, he struck her down with a single swing of his closed fist.

"You betrayed me," he said.

"Todd?" she pleaded, clutching her belly, which still showed no sign of the impending birth.

"It's going to be a *red* Christmas," he hissed.

She opened her mouth to cry, "No!" but Todd kicked her in the jaw and went to work burying the spinning blade of the saw deep into the joint of her shoulder; the act instantly turned her protest into a bloodcurdling scream of pain.

"I don't know why you had to do it." He spoke in rhythm with the grating of the saw. "But you did, and you hurt me. So now I must hurt you."

"Todd," she wailed, "the baby!"

"I know it's not mine," he said. He also knew that Holly wasn't Mary and that the bastard in her womb wasn't the result of an immaculate conception.

The saw made easy work of getting deep into the shoulder joint. He stopped before cutting all the way through. He actually snapped—and tore—the arm from her body as blood bathed him from head to toe. He held the severed arm in front of her face so that she could watch the blood drain from her own arteries.

She gazed up at him and the limb she no longer had control over with a look composed of horror and a fascinating expression of confusion, almost as though she didn't think he really would have been able to remove her arm.

"See this?" he asked. He caught the diamond studded watch still sparkling around her lifeless wrist between his fingers. "I gave this to you. And this?" He pointed to the three carat wedding ring on her finger. "I'm taking it back."

He heaved her arm over his shoulder like a baseball bat and disappeared into their bedroom, looking like a ballplayer on his way to the dugout. While he was gone, Holly tried crawling away, but he returned without the arm and stopped her before she could make any real progress.

"We're not finished yet," he said. "It's the most wonderful time of the year, you know. We ought to enjoy it." He picked her up, blood leaking everywhere, and dropped her on the sofa.

"Some people see mommy kissing Santa Claus," he went on, "but not me. I saw you kissing Marty Powell. Some hear the bells on Christmas day, but not me. I hear the screams of sinners. Remember how you used to sing to me beside the fire? You sang, '*All I want for Christmas is you,*' but now I think all you'll want for Christmas is your two front teeth!" he snarled then landed a punch square against her mouth.

His knuckles snagged on her incisors, knocking more than just the front two teeth free.

She sobbed and wailed and hyperventilated all at once, but she didn't beg him to stop. She knew her pleas wouldn't make a damn of a difference.

"What do you think of the tree?" he asked. "I still think it's a little bare," he said without waiting for her to reply. "How about giving me a hand?"

Whether she wanted to give him a hand or not didn't matter. He took the one she had left, leaving her with a bloody stump. He also took her feet, her kneecaps, her hair for tinsel and the flesh from her back in place of a tree skirt. Her breasts, when hung by hooks from the nipples, looked almost like bells.

Holly died sometime before midnight. Her last words were, "I'm sorry."

She fell silent with the glint of the Christmas lights in her eyes. Snow had started to fall outside as Todd pulled back the shades and lit a fire. He hummed *Silent Night*, poured himself a glass of eggnog with a little rum, and sat beside the window to enjoy the sights of the season before putting the finishing touches on the tree.

* * *

"Deck the halls with *bowels* of *Holly*," Todd Dunbar sang as he strategically tucked Holly's intestines between the branches of the fresh cut pine. After all, he and Holly always did decorate the tree together. "Fa la la la lah, la la la lah."

THE HEADMASTER

RICHARD MOORE

Galton knew they'd come for him soon. And when they did: what then? They'd already taken his partner, Phil Murphy, ignoring the man's desperate cries, dragging him out of the darkened room without hesitation. Before long, his screams had fallen silent, making Galton think the worst.

The last time he'd seen his partner's face, they'd been advancing through the woods toward the house. Murphy was cursing under his breath, saying they should wait for back-up. Galton couldn't be sure the call he'd put in on the radio had even gone through, the dispatcher's reply, if there had been one, was lost to an unending hiss of static.

Months earlier, an eyewitness to a kidnapping had seen two women and a man force a struggling woman into the back of a black Ford van. The database had provided an inordinate number of matches that fit the van's description. For Galton and Murphy, part of the team of officers interviewing the vehicles' owners as part of their other assignments and assessing them as potential suspects, it should have been routine duty. But somehow, it had all gone terribly wrong.

Driving the tree-lined road that led to the house, they'd found it blocked, a padlocked gate and nine foot razor wire topped fence, ceasing their advance and setting silent alarm bells ringing inside their heads. An investigation of the perimeter revealed that the fence went into the woods and surrounded the house on all sides. They were about to return to the gate when they heard the screams from inside the house.

Left with no alternative, the officers ran back to their cruiser and attempted to call for backup, then Galton shot the padlock, blasting it to pieces. As the gate swung open and they stepped through, Galton met Murphy's eyes–certain his partner's thoughts matched his own. There was no telling how many suspects were inside the house, no telling if they were armed, no telling what they were up against. Added to that, by discharging his weapon, Galton had just announced their presence.

Knowing they would be sitting targets out in the open, they left the road, using the woods for cover. Through the trees, they could see glimpses of the house, a monstrously large edifice that looked more like an upscale lodge than a simple homestead.

They'd advanced no more than ten feet when something struck Galton on the back of the head, sending him tumbling to the ground, his knees sinking into a carpet of leaves. Dizzy from the blow, his vision blurred, Galton whirled around, trying to locate his assailant.

He only saw Murphy.

"Mike?" Murphy looked down at him, confused. "Are you all right?"

Before Galton could answer, Murphy was also struck, the forceful blow enough to knock him onto his back. Galton looked around but still saw no one. He crawled through the leaves, the sound of them crunching under his weight the only noise he could hear.

Murphy was unconscious, a swelling high on the side of his forehead spurting blood. And then Galton was attacked a second time. It came from nowhere, an invisible force that drove head-on into his consciousness, seeming to hit him smack between the eyes to send him plummeting into blackness.

* * *

When Galton opened his eyes, he was still surrounded by darkness. The only difference was his awareness of it. As his other senses became alert, he recognized the smell of rancid meat. He had just enough time to realize that his hands were bound with rope and behind his back, that a cloth sack had been placed over his head, when a door creaked open and footsteps drew closer. Galton heard a scuffling sound, followed by a muffled yell.

"Get the fuck off me, you son of a bitch!" Phil Murphy yelled. "Get the fuck off me!"

In his mind, creating images to match the sounds, Galton saw them drag his partner out of the room.

"Who put the sack on this cop?" a man's voice asked after Murphy was taken away.

"I did," a second voice said, also a man.

"Why?"

"So he wouldn't sit there and scream."

The first man chuckled. "Don't tell me his screams bother you."

"Not in the least," said the second man. "I just didn't want any to go to waste. I wanted him to keep them."

A chuckle. "Keep his screams?"

"For when the eating begins."

The words sank deep into Galton's mind. The panic churning in his gut spread to his chest, consuming what little air he could breathe in through the cloth.

For when the eating begins.

"Please..." Galton tried to say, but what came out was a quivering, high-pitched sob. "Please..." he repeated. "I have a wife...two daughters. Their names are..."

An open-palmed hand found his cheek through the sack, the sting of the slap silencing him.

"You've caused us no small amount of trouble, Officer Galton," the first man said. "Considerable efforts are going to be called for to divert attention away from this place. My friend here thinks you'll scream more later if you have no reason to do it now. Personally, I'm of the philosophy that where fear is concerned, a man never reaches a point where he runs short of it. Happy screaming, Officer Galton."

When the sack was removed and his head uncovered, Galton didn't scream but gagged instead. The cloth must have worked as a filter, blocking the full force of the smell, because almost immediately after it was removed, his nostrils were assaulted by the stink of rotting flesh. He'd tasted the scent of death before but never on such a massive scale. The stench was so intense that Galton's neural reflexes kicked in. Onto his uniform shirt he vomited the eggs and toast his wife had fixed for breakfast along with a donut and two cups of coffee he'd downed at the station house.

On the way out, one of the men turned on the light. Galton squinted against the glare, his vision returning in time for him to catch a brief look at the man as he closed the door.

There was no time to process what he'd seen, to try to make sense of the impossible. No time to tell himself the man smirking in at him was not the well known movie star Kevin Dunhill—several of whose big budget action flicks Galton owned on DVD—but merely a look-alike with strikingly similar features. No time because a second after the door clicked shut, Galton saw the source of the stench that had caused him to upchuck his breakfast.

A stronger man—maybe of the fictional type Dunhill played in his movies—would have refused to give them the satisfaction of hearing him scream. But Galton, who in his lifetime had not only seen the horror show up close, but had been granted his share of passes behind its curtain, was neither a character in a movie, nor strong enough to stare down the insanity surrounding him and hold himself together.

The room was full of corpses, all without their heads, the bodies in varying stages of decay. There was a vast pile of forty or more right across from him. The walls, which were bare brick and windowless, had more decapitated bodies deposited next to them. Some were stacked on top of each other, seven or more high, and others were left sitting upright, as though the body's owner had sat down for a nap, folding their arms and stretching out their legs, and inadvertently lost their heads.

Galton screamed and screamed, unable to stop now that he'd gotten started. Beyond the room, someplace nearby, Murphy's terrified wails eclipsed his own. He heard him cry, "My head. What are you doing to my head?"

Galton was certain that for whatever insane reason, the movie star Kevin Dunhill and his pals were going to eat his partner's head, and that when they were done, they would eat his next.

An array of unwelcome images flashed behind Galton's eyes. He imagined Dunhill digging in with his perfectly capped teeth, saw the faceless others tearing strips of flesh from Phil's cheeks, saw their teeth clamping down on his nose. Last, he pictured them cracking his partner's balding head open and devouring chunks of his brain. Thinking of his own inescapable fate, Galton screamed all the louder.

Then Phil fell silent. And Galton felt sure his partner was dead.

Sobbing, muttering prayers he'd thought long forgotten, Galton heard the footfalls outside draw slowly closer. The door opened. Two people came through the doorway carrying a body between them. The man backing into the room held it under the arms, the woman carried it by the feet.

Galton didn't know the blond woman's name, but recognized her face instantly. She was a news anchor for one of the TV networks. In her hand-tailored business suit, she was the model example of conservative America. The man was the woman's polar opposite. He wore jeans, a black leather jacket and cowboy boots. Even with his hair dangling in his face, the sidelong glance he gave Galton as he moved past was all he needed to recognize him.

It was Bobby Riggs, lead singer with Wonderbred, a rock band who always topped the charts with their catchy power ballads.

Riggs and the woman carried the body to the pile and dropped it on top. Until now, Galton had been trying to avoid looking at it—as though by not acknowledging in his mind what it was, he could deny the truth. But now, with the rock star and news anchor out of the way, the body was directly in his line of sight. It was his partner, Phil Murphy—minus his head.

"You took his head, you sick fucks!" Galton blubbered, snot running out of his nose. "Why did you… why? You took his fucking head."

Riggs leaned in toward Galton, shook the hair out of his eyes and grabbed Galton's right forearm. "Okay, lawman. Time to get it on."

The news anchor grabbed his other arm. Galton tried to shake free but the pair was unbelievably strong, their fingers digging deep enough to bruise his flesh. Together, they hauled him to his feet. Again Galton struggled to shake them off, thrashing his head and twisting his shoulders.

"Christ," the anchor woman said. "He's getting snot on my new suit."

Riggs shook his head, snorted laughter. "You and your fucking suits."

"This isn't funny, Bobby," she said. "This suit cost two thousand dollars."

Riggs leaned in close to Galton's face. "Hey. You're upsetting the lady. Quit jerking around."

"Please..." Galton sobbed. "Don't..."

Snot flew and landed on the newsreader's lapel.

"That's it," she said. "Now I'm officially pissed."

The punch to the gut came fast and hard; Galton oofed and sagged forward. Coughing blood, he raised his head, and looked up in time to see the news anchor draw a clenched fist and send it rocketing toward his face.

"Oooweee!" he heard her whine as her blow connected. "I broke a nail."

Then he dropped into darkness.

*   *   *

Galton was slow to recover consciousness; the toecaps of his Danner boots scraped across concrete as he was dragged along a narrow descending passageway. He lifted his head. The cop was six one and weighed two hundred pounds, and there was no way the news anchor should have been able to hold him upright, but somehow she was doing it with ease.

Bobby Riggs had a shoulder wedged under his other arm, carrying him the same way as the woman, the expression on his face so relaxed he might have been taking a stroll in the park.

How could they be so strong?

They arrived at a stone archway, the door beneath it made of wood that was old and thick. Riggs knocked and someone on the other side answered. The door swung open, hinges groaning, and Galton was dragged inside.

Flaming torches set in the walls spread their glow across both sides of the room, but left the center in darkness. The area was vast, larger than a banquet hall.

I wanted him to keep his screams for when the eating begins.

With mounting dread, Galton remembered that this place really was a banquet hall. The realization sent a fresh zing of panic buzzing through his head, but he still felt groggy, still too dazed by his last beating to summon the strength to put up any kind of resistance. Not that fighting would do him any good. Even if he did somehow break free, there were just too many of them.

They stood in small groups near the walls, some sipping champagne from fluted glasses, others halting their hushed conversation to appraise him—their eyes lit with an unmistakable glint of excitement. Galton saw more familiar faces. Those he did not know by name he at the very least recognized. Pop starlets were hobnobbing with high profile politicians. Two actors from a smash sitcom were chewing the fat with a TV evangelist, a supermodel, a businessman who appeared in his own commercials and a basketball player better known for what he got up to off the court than on. Realty TV stars abounded.

Light flared up ahead. As he was taken closer, Galton saw Kevin Dunhill, a torch in one hand and Zippo lighter in the other, both aflame. The movie star used the Zippo to light a cigarette dangling from his mouth, then snapped the lighter shut and slipped it into his pocket. In his jeans and muscle-hugging black t-shirt, Dunhill looked like he'd stepped straight out of a scene from one of his movies.

He indicated a wooden chair with the torch, and the rock star and news anchor flanking Galton lowered the cop into it.

Dunhill took a drag on his smoke, then exhaled slowly. He gave Galton his trademark smirk. Then, in a spot on Tony Montana accent, he said, "Say hello to your little friend."

Dunhill extended his arm backward, illuminating the area behind him. Galton's partner, Phil Murphy, narrowed his eyes at the sudden intrusion of light as he lay in the pile.

"Mike?" Phil asked, the word wetly gargled. "Is that you, Mike?"

Galton jolted at the sight of Murphy, the shocked flinch so violent he would have toppled to the floor if not for Bobby Riggs and the news anchor bearing down on him with their weight, their hands pinning his shoulders to the back of the chair.

Galton twisted and jerked. "What the fuck?"

"Now," Dunhill took a backward step, raised the flaming torch over his head, throwing more light onto the darkness at his back. "Say hello to ours."

What waited behind the actor was a nightmare made flesh. The thing was comprised almost entirely of human heads. Those at the center, forming a torso of sorts, were squashed and misshapen, some so compressed they'd split open, their brains exposed, fluid leaking out of the openings. There were hundreds of heads, perhaps even as much as a thousand, all melded together into a central mass. The eyes of each were rolled up, glistening white in the torchlight. As the light from Dunhill's torch touched their bleached white faces, a thousand toothless mouths softly moaned.

Extending from the torso were hundreds of veined stalks; pinkly translucent stems that wavered, tentacle-like, in the air. Attached to the end of each was a human head. Unlike those in the center, these looked far more alive, the skin tone almost normal and most of the hair was still intact. These had to be those most recently sacrificed—had to—because Phil was one of them. Some of the stalk-heads stared glassy-eyed into space, all emotion gone. Others continually sobbed, lips drawn back in agonized grimaces. More than a few were laughing, their eyes roving and tongues thrusting, clearly driven insane.

"Oh, God," Galton moaned. "What the fuck is it?"

Still smirking Dunhill cocked his head and looked back at Galton. "Its real name is unpronounceable. We've always just called it The Headmaster. Kind of a cute name for it, don't you think?"

The news anchor used one of her long red fingernails to tickle Galton behind his ear. She leaned in close, said in a breathy voice, "At one time or another we all sat where you sit now, Officer Galton. Who knows? Maybe The Headmaster will see in you what it saw in us. Believe me, to live in its service is to know life as most people can only dream." She paused, and when she continued, she didn't speak with her mouth, her words instead forming directly inside Galton's mind.

You want to talk benefits? We're talking a package offered by no other employer on this Earth. We have the power to influence what people think. To make them believe they need whatever we choose to sell them. Hell, I was a sixteen year old crack whore when The Headmaster chose me to work for it. Look at me now. All you gotta do is want it bad enough, Mike. All you gotta do is pledge your soul right here and now, and maybe, just maybe, you can be one of us, too.

Galton whipped his head around, the curved side of his forehead striking the news anchor's nose, resulting in a satisfying crunch. "Never, bitch. You hear me? Never!"

"You bastard," the news anchor sobbed, backing away, her hands trying to stem the blood flow. "This nose job cost six fucking grand."

Galton watched her flee into the darkness. The other celebrities, he saw, were closing in, forming a semi-circle behind him.

"Mike?" Phil gurgled. "Mike?"

Galton faced forward. "I'm right here, buddy. I'm right here."

"You are?" Phil asked. "Why can't I see you? Mike? What's happened to me? Every time I start a thought I can't... I... can't finish it. And my memories... It's like they're... like they're slipping away from me... Like..." Phil's eyes rolled back in his head. His features twisted in anguish. "My mind..." he cried. "It's eating my mind!"

Galton had to look away. The excruciating death he anticipated was coming for him was nothing compared to this. Tears streamed down his face. It wasn't his flesh that was going to be consumed, The Headmaster was going to feast on his identity—take him apart piece by piece until nothing remained.

Back in the room where he'd worn the sack over his head, he had tried to keep it together by telling himself the agony he would soon endure would only last a few minutes. But now, as a chill spread through his bones like none he'd ever experienced, it dawned on him that his suffering might never end. Even after this thing had sucked him dry, when there was nothing left to take, he would be absorbed into the mass at its center, would become one with the many.

Dunhill moved the flaming torch away from the creature, his attention returning to Galton. A stalk reached out from the darkness, fell onto the movie star's shoulder, and seemed to caress it with tenderness. It slid forward, then thrashed excitedly in the air over Galton's head.

Galton looked up. The stalk moved closer, a sphincter like hole at the end stretching, widening. He stared into the opening to see tiny rows of needle sharp teeth, and beyond them a squirming mass of connective tissue—a closed arterial vein that dangled within the maw at the tip, sputtering blood.

"Are you ready for your close up, Officer Galton?" Dunhill laughed. "Roll sound. Roll speed. And...action!"

Mike Galton sat up in bed. The woman he loved was propped up on one elbow beside him. She smiled, and the look she gave him was one he often thought about when he went too long without seeing her.

"I've been waiting for you to wake up and give me a kiss."

It seemed to him she'd said this before, maybe just yesterday, but he wasn't going to complain about it.

"Happy to oblige," he said.

She leaned in, and a moment before their lips touched, her face changed, her features reforming, taking on the appearance of another woman. It was Mrs. Hunter, his eighth grade English teacher. Galton jerked away.

"What are you doing here? Where's my wife?"

"I didn't know you had a wife," Mrs. Hunter said. She took off her heavy framed reading glasses and used the top sheet to polish them. "What's her name?"

Galton thought about it. He couldn't remember.

On the portable TV on the dresser, last night's episode of NCIS—the last thing Galton had watched—played in reverse.

"I graded your poem," Mrs. Hunter said, producing an exercise book from beneath the sheets. "I especially like the part that goes 'I wanted him to keep his screams for when the eating begins'."

"You're not my wife," Galton grabbed her by the shoulders. "Where's my wife?"

"I don't know," Mrs. Hunter said. "Maybe you should ask him." The closet door opened and out stepped Galton's father, an ax slung over his shoulder. Inside the bedroom it was snowing.

"Dad?"

Whistling, his father got to work chopping firewood on the block at the foot of the bed.

"Dad, have you seen..."

His father set the ax in the block, then turned and looked at him. "Seen who, Mikey? Your mother's in the kitchen fixing lunch, if that's who you mean."

Galton realized they were standing outside. He was now nine years old, the woods surrounding them the landscape of his childhood. His father had called him Mickey, a name he hadn't heard for more than twenty years.

"No, I don't mean Mom..." he said, his voice now high with his youth.

"Who then, Mikey?" his father asked.

He frowned. He could no longer remember the question he'd asked.

Somewhere nearby, but in no place little Mikey Galton could pinpoint, a man was screaming.

ABOUT THE WRITERS

Scott M. Baker lives in Virginia with his wife and 6 house rabbits. He has authored several short stories, many with LDP. The Vampire Hunters, his first full-length novel, was published as an e-book by Shadowfire Press in March 2010. Scott is currently putting the final touches on the last two volumes of The Vampire Hunters trilogy, both of which have been accepted for publication by Shadowfire Press, and is working on a fourth novel detailing the struggle between humans/vampires and zombies. For "Denizens," Scott would like to thank the guys of the D.C. Water Authority for giving him a tour of Washington's sewer system, which inspired this short story. Please visit the author's blog at http://scottmbakerauthor.blogspot.com.

Nickolas Cook lives in the beautiful Southwestern desert with his wife and three pugs. He is an editor (The Black Glove Magazine), a horror critic and reviewer, with close to a hundred articles in print, the author of a couple of dozen published short stories and three novels, THE BLACK BEAST OF ALGERNON WOOD (Dailey Swan Press), BALEFUL EYE (Stonegarden.net Publishing) and ALICE IN ZOMBIELAND (Coscom Entertainment). To contact the author: Nickolasecook@aol.com.

David H. Donaghe lives and works in the high desert of southern California. In 1995, he took the First Place prize in the California Writer's Club short story contest with his Western short story, Blind Justice. His short story, Some Call it Madness appeared in Nocturnal Ooze, an online journal in 2009 and he has three other stories published with Living Dead Press. He invites you to come join his readers network at http://www.authornation.com/MCRIDER
He is currently enjoying life and working on his next novel.

Michael D. Griffiths lives in Arizona with his wife, Cathi. He has won the Withersins 666 award, and several contests at Golden Visions. Mike has published two underground zines and has had his Skinjumper Series published in M-Brane magazine. He is currently a part of Abandoned Towers and Innsmouth Free Press magazines. Mike's first book, The Chronicles Of Jack Primus, was recently published by Living Dead Press.

Anthony Giangregorio is the author and editor of more than 40 novels, almost all of them about zombies. His work has appeared in Dead Science by Coscomentertainment, Dead Worlds: Undead Stories Volumes 1-6, and Wolves of War by Library of the Living Dead Press. He also has stories in End of Days: An Apocalyptic Anthology Vol. 1 - 3, the Book of the Dead series Vol. 1-4 by LDP, and two anthologies with Pill Hill Press. He is also the creator of the popular action/zombie series titled Deadwater.
Check out his website at www.undeadpress.com.

Dane T. Hatchell grew up in Baton Rouge Louisiana and has lived there all his life. In his youth he was a fan of old school horror movies, and a collector of magazines such as Creepy and Eerie. Now in his early fifty's, he is devoting his free time to writing to satisfy a lifelong passion.

Kelly M. Hudson grew up in the wilds of Kentucky and currently resides in California . He has a deep and abiding love for all things horror and rock n' roll. He's had many stories published in such esteemed collections as Dead Worlds, Book of the Dead, End of Days, The Death Panel, and The Bitter End and also has a novel (Men of Perdition) on Amazon Kindle. If you wish to contact Kelly or find links to other stories he's had published, please visit www.kellymhudson.com for further details.

Robert M Kuzmeski lives with his family and a menagerie of pets in his home state of Massachusetts. He writes in a variety of genres with a focus on science fiction, horror and modern dark fantasy. He's published several short stories and has multiple novels in the works. When not writing, he can usually be found playing role-playing games, doing photography or dabbling with music.

Keith Luethke enjoys writing horror fiction and lives in Knoxville, Tennessee. His novel zombie, "Dead House: A Zombie Ghost Story" is available through Living Dead Press as well as having multiple short stories published with LDP as well.

Nick Medina is a young author from Chicago, Illinois. Since 2009 he has appeared in several magazines in the U.S. and the U. K. Dressed in Black is a tribute to his family's funerary ties - although his family had never gone to such extremes as Thomas Tuttle. To read more of Nick's work, visit http://sites.google.com/site/nickjmedina/.s

Rick Moore, originally from Leicestershire, England, moved to the U. S. ten years ago and now lives in Phoenix, AZ. Rick's fiction has appeared in numerous zines and anthologies, including The Undead: Flesh Feast, History Is Dead, The Beast Within, Cthulhu Unbound, Harvest Hill, Dark Animus, the 2009 Stoker nominated Horror Library 3 and Bound For Evil (his inclusion in which still regularly sends Moore into a geekified frenzy of frothing at the mouth fanboy excitement as the collection also contains fiction by two of his childhood heroes, H.P. Lovecraft and Ramsey Campbell). Visit him online at http://www.myspace.com/zombieinfection

Matt Nord is a janitor by trade, a business owner by association, a network technician by education, and a fledgling writer of horror fiction by choice. He is currently working on several short stories for future anthologies. He lives in Central New York with his wife, Karen, and their two sons (and one in the oven).

Mark Rivett possesses multiple degrees from The Art Institute of Pittsburgh and lives in Pittsburgh Pennsylvania where the city's long zombie history inspires his writing. In addition to writing, Mark paints, builds models, and works as a web developer. Check out his other stories in Dead History and Book of the Dead 3

John Skerchock professional work came first in the form of an article for Fantaco then with a horror story for Twilight Zone's sister magazine Night Cry. Work then followed with Druktenis Publishing, Horror Biz, Chiller Theatre and several websites. John also produced the classic Zacherley Scrapbook.

Jose Alfredo Vazquez is an eye surgeon in private practice. Has written the best selling Living Dead Epic "The War Against Them", and his work also appears in "Dead Worlds 5 and Dead History." He can be reached at Thewaragainstthem@ hotmail.com

Spencer Wendleton has published two novels under his penname "Alan Spencer." One is entitled, "The Body Cartel," the other, "Inside the Perimeter: The Scavenging Dead." His work has also appeared in numerous Living Dead Press anthologies. The author welcomes e-mails at alanspencer26@hotmail.com.

DEAD RAGE

by Anthony Giangregorio
Book 2 in the Rage virus series!

An unknown virus spreads across the globe, turning ordinary people into bloodthirsty, ravenous killers.

Only a small percentage of the population is immune and soon become prey to the infected.

Amongst the infected comes a man, stricken by the virus, yet still retaining his grasp on reality. His need to destroy the *normals* becomes an obsession and he raises an army of killers to seek out and kill all who aren't *changed* like himself. A few survivors gather together on the outskirts of Chicago and find themselves running for their lives as the specter of death looms over all.

The Dead Rage virus will find you, no matter where you hide.

CHRISTMAS IS DEAD: A ZOMBIE ANTHOLOGY

Edited by Anthony Giangregorio

Twas the night before Christmas and all through the house, not a creature was stirring, not even a. . . zombie?

That's right; this anthology explores what would happen at Christmas time if there was a full blown zombie outbreak. Reanimated turkeys, zombie Santas, and demon reindeers that turn people into flesh-eating ghouls are just some of the tales you will find in this merry undead book. So curl up under the Christmas tree with a cup of hot chocolate, and as the fireplace crackles with warmth, get ready to have your heart filled with holiday cheer. But of course, then it will be ripped from your heaving chest and fed upon by blood-thirsty elves with a craving for human flesh! For you see, Christmas is Dead!

And you will never look at the holiday season the same way again.

BLOOD RAGE

(The Prequel to DEAD RAGE)

by Anthony Giangregorio

The madness descended before anyone knew what was happening. Perfectly normal people suddenly became rage-fueled killers, tearing and slicing their way across the city. Within hours, Chicago was a battlefield, the dead strewn in the streets like trash.

Stacy, Chad and a few others are just a few of the immune, unaffected by the virus but not to the violence surrounding them. The *changed* are ravenous, sweeping across Chicago and perhaps the world, destroying any *normals* they come across. Fire, slaughter, and blood rule the land, and the few survivors are now an endangered species.

This is the story of the first days of the Dead Rage virus and the brave souls who struggle to live just one more day.

When the smoke clears, and the *changed* have maimed and killed all who stand in their way, only the strong will remain.

The rest will be left to rot in the sun.

THE BOOK OF CANNIBALS
Edited by Anthony Giangregorio

Human meat . . . the ultimate taboo.

Deep down, in the dark recesses of your mind, can you honestly say you never wondered how it might taste?

Honestly, never wondered if a chunk of thigh tasted like chicken or pork?

Or if a hunk of an arm was similar to steak? And what kind of wine would be served with it, red or white?

Would a human liver be no different than one from a cow, or a pig?

For all we know, human flesh is as tender as veal, better than the finest tenderloin. And that is what the stories in this book are about, eating each other. But be warned, after reading these tales of mastication, you may just become a vegetarian, or at the very least, think twice before taking your first bite of that juicy steak at your local restaurant.

DEADFREEZE
by Anthony Giangregorio
THIS IS WHAT HELL WOULD BE LIKE IF IT FROZE OVER!

When an experimental serum for hypothermia goes horribly wrong, a small research station in the middle of Antarctica becomes overrun with an army of the frozen dead.

Now a small group of survivors must battle the arctic weather and a horde of frozen zombies as they make their way across the frozen plains of Antarctica to a neighboring research station.

What they don't realize is that they are being hunted by an entity whose sole reason for existing is vengeance; and it will find them wherever they run.

VISIONS OF THE DEAD
A ZOMBIE STORY
by Anthony & Joseph Giangregorio

Jake Roberts felt like he was the luckiest man alive.

He had a great family, a beautiful girlfriend, who was soon to be his wife, and a job, that might not have been the best, but it paid the bills.

At least until the dead began to walk.

Now Jake is fighting to survive in a dead world while searching for his lost love, Melissa, knowing she's out there somewhere.

But the past isn't dead, and as he struggles for an uncertain future, the past threatens to consume him. With the present a constant battle between the living and the dead, Jake finds himself slipping in and out of the past, the visions of how it all happened haunting him. But Jake knows Melissa is out there somewhere and he'll find her or die trying.

In a world of the living dead, you can never escape your past.

DEAD MOURNING: A ZOMBIE HORROR STORY
by Anthony Giangregorio

Carl Jenkins was having a run of bad luck. Fresh out of jail, his probation tenuous, he'd lost every job he'd taken since being released. So now was his last chance, only one more job to prevent him from going back to prison. Assigned to work in a funeral home, he accidentally loses a shipment of embalming fluid. With nothing to lose, he substitutes it with a batch of chemicals from a nearby factory.

The results don't go as planned, though. While his screw-up goes unnoticed, his machinations revive the cadavers in the funeral home, unleashing an evil on the world that it has not seen before. Not wanting to become a snack for the rampaging dead, he flees the city, joining up with other survivors. An old, dilapidated zoo becomes their haven, while the dead wait outside the walls, hungry and patient.

But Carl is optimistic, after all, he's still alive, right? Perhaps his luck has changed and help will arrive to save them all?

Unfortunately, unknown to him and the other survivors, a serial killer has fallen into their group, trapped inside the zoo with them.

With the undead army clamoring outside the walls and a murderer within, it'll be a miracle if any of them live to see the next sunrise.

On second thought, maybe Carl would've been better off if he'd just gone back to jail.

ROAD KILL: A ZOMBIE TALE
by Anthony Giangregorio
ORDER UP!

In the summer of 2008, a rogue comet entered earth's orbit for 72 hours. During this time, a strange amber glow suffused the sky.

But something else happened; something in the comet's tail had an adverse affect on dead tissue and the result was the reanimation of every dead animal carcass on the planet.

A handful of survivors hole up in a diner in the backwoods of New Hampshire while the undead creatures of the night hunt for human prey.

There's a new blue plate special at DJ's Diner and Truck Stop, and it's you!

DEAD THINGS
by Anthony Giangregorio

Beneath the veil of reality we all know as truth, there is another world, one where creatures only seen in nightmares exist.

But what if these creatures do actually exist, and it is us that are only fleeting images, mere visions conjured up by some unknown being.

Werewolves, zombies, vampires, and other lost things that go bump in the night, inhabit the world of imagination and myth, but all will be found in this collection of tales.   But in this world, fiction becomes fact, and what lurks in the shadows is real. Beware the next time you sense you are being watched or catch movement in the corner of your eye, for though it may be nothing, it might just be your doom.

INCLUDES THE EXCLUSIVE DEADWATER STORY: DEAD GRAVE

THE DARK
by Anthony Giangregorio
DARKNESS FALLS

The darkness came without warning.

First New York, then the rest of United States, and then the world became enveloped in a perpetual night without end.

With no sunlight, eventually the planet will wither and die, bringing on a new Ice Age. But that isn't problem for the human race, for humanity will be dead long before that happens.

There is something in the dark, creatures only seen in nightmares, and they are on the prowl. Evolution has changed and man is no longer the dominant species. When we are children, we're told not to fear the dark, that what we believe to exist in the shadows is false.

Unfortunately, that is no longer true.

SOULEATER
by Anthony Giangregorio

Twenty years ago, Jason Lawson witnessed the brutal death of his father by something only seen in nightmares, something so horrible he'd blocked it from his mind.

Now twenty years later the creature is back, this time for his son.

Jason won't let that happen.

He'll travel to the demon's world, struggling every second to rescue his son from its clutches.

But what he doesn't know is that the portal will only be open for a finite time and if he doesn't return with his son before it closes, then he'll be trapped in the demon's dimension forever.

SEE HOW IT ALL BEGAN IN THE NEW DOUBLE-SIZED 460 PAGE SPECIAL EDITION!

DEADWATER: EXPANDED EDITION
by Anthony Giangregorio

Through a series of tragic mishaps, a small town's water supply is contaminated with a deadly bacterium that transforms the town's population into flesh eating ghouls.

Without warning, Henry Watson finds himself thrown into a living hell where the living dead walk and want nothing more than to feed on the living.

Now Henry's trying to escape the undead town before he becomes the next victim.

With the military on one side, shooting civilians on sight, and a horde of bloodthirsty zombies on the other, Henry must try to battle his way to freedom.

With a small group of survivors, including a beautiful secretary and a wise-cracking janitor to aid him, the ragtag group will do their best to stay alive and escape the city codenamed: **Deadwater.**

DEAD END: A ZOMBIE NOVEL

by Anthony Giangregorio

THE DEAD WALK!

Newspapers everywhere proclaim the dead have returned to feast on the living!

A small group of survivors hole up in a cellar, afraid to brave the masses of animated corpses, but when food runs out, they have no choice but to venture out into a world gone mad.

What they will discover, however, is that the fall of civilization has brought out the worst in their fellow man.

Cannibals, psychotic preachers and rapists are just some of the atrocities they must face.

In a world turned upside down, it is life that has hit a Dead End.

BOOK OF THE DEAD 2: NOT DEAD YET

A ZOMBIE ANTHOLOGY

Edited by Anthony Giangregorio

Out of the ashes of death and decay, comes the second volume filled with the walking dead.

In this tomb, there are only slow, shambling monstrosities that were once human.

No one knows why the dead walk; only that they do, and that they are hungry for human flesh.

But these aren't your neighbors, your co-workers, or your family.
Now they are the living dead, and they will tear your throat out at a moment's notice.

So be warned as you delve into the pages of this book; the dead will find you, no matter where you hide.

ANOTHER EXCITING ADVENTURE IN THE DEADWATER SERIES!

DEAD SALVATION

BOOK 9

by Anthony Giangregorio

HANGMAN'S NOOSE!

After one of the group is hurt, the need for transportation is solved by a roving cannie convoy. Attacking the camp, the companions save a man who invites them back to his home.

Cement City it's called and at first the group is welcomed with thanks for saving one of their own. But when a bar fight goes wrong, the companions find themselves awaiting the hangman's noose.

Their only salvation is a suicide mission into a raider camp to save captured townspeople.

Though the odds are long, it's a chance, and Henry knows in the land of the walking dead, sometimes a chance is all you can hope for.

In the world of the dead, life is a struggle, where the only victor is death.

INSIDE THE PERIMETER: SCAVENGERS OF THE DEAD
by Alan Spencer

In the middle of nowhere, the vestiges of an abandoned town are surrounded by inescapably high concrete barriers, permitting no trespass or escape. The town is dormant of human life, but rampant with the living dead, who choose not to eat flesh, but to instead continue their survival by cruder means.

Boyd Broman, a detective arrested and falsely imprisoned, has been transferred into the secret town. He is given an ultimatum: recapture Hayden Grubaugh, the cannibal serial killer, who has been banished to the town, in exchange for his freedom.

During Boyd's search, he discovers why the psychotic cannibal must really be captured and the sinister secrets the dead town holds.

With no chance of escape, Broman finds himself trapped among the ravenous, violent dead.

With the cannibal feeding on the animated cadavers and the undead searching for Boyd, he must fulfill his end of the deal before the rotting corpses turn him into an unwilling organ donor.

But Boyd wasn't told that no one gets out alive, that the town is a death sentence.

For there is no escape from *Inside the Perimeter*.

DEADFALL
by Anthony Giangregorio

It's Halloween in the small suburban town of Wakefield, Mass.

While parents take their children trick or treating and others throw costume parties, a swarm of meteorites enter the earth's atmosphere and crash to earth.

Inside are small parasitic worms, no larger than maggots.

The worms quickly infect the corpses at a local cemetery and so begins the rise of the undead.

The walking dead soon get the upper hand, with no one believing the truth. That the dead now walk.

Will a small group of survivors live through the zombie apocalypse?

Or will they, too, succumb to the Deadfall.

LOVE IS DEAD: A ZOMBIE ANTHOLOGY
Edited by Anthony Giangregorio
THE DEATH OF LOVE

Valentine's Day is a day when young love is fulfilled.

Where hopeful young men bring candy and flowers to their sweethearts, in hopes of a kiss...or perhaps more. But not in this anthology.

For you see, LOVE IS DEAD, and in this tome, the dead walk, wanting to feed on those same hearts that once pumped in chests, bursting with love.

So toss aside that heart-shaped box of candy and throw away those red roses, you won't need them any longer. Instead, strap on a handgun, or pick up a shotgun and defend yourself from the ravenous undead.

Because in a world where the dead walk, even love isn't safe.

ETERNAL NIGHT: A VAMPIRE ANTHOLOGY

Edited by Anthony Giangregorio

Blood, fangs, darkness and terror...these are the calling cards of the vampire mythos.

Inside this tome are stories that embrace vampire history but seek to introduce a new literary spin on this longstanding fictional monster. Follow a dark journey through cigarette-smoking creatures hunted by rogue angels, vampires that feed off of thoughts instead of blood, immortals presenting the fantastic in a local rock band, to a legendary monster on the far reaches of town.

Forget what you know about vampires; this anthology will destroy historical mythos and embrace incredible new twists on this celebrated, fictional character.

Welcome to a world of the undead, welcome to the world of Eternal Night.

BOOK OF THE DEAD
A ZOMBIE ANTHOLOGY VOL 1
ISBN 978-1-935458-25-8

Edited by Anthony Giangregorio

This is the most faithful, truest zombie anthology ever written, and we invite you along for the ride. Every single story in this book is filled with slack-jawed, eyes glazed, slow moving, shambling zombies set in a world where the dead have risen and only want to eat the flesh of the living. In these pages, the rules are sacrosanct. There is no deviation from what a zombie should be or how they came about. The Dead Walk.

There is no reason, though rumors and suppositions fill the radio and television stations. But the only thing that is fact is that the walking dead are here and they will not go away. So prepare yourself for the ultimate homage to the master of zombie legend. And remember... Aim for the head!

REVOLUTION OF THE DEAD

by Anthony Giangregorio

THE DEAD SHALL RISE AGAIN!

Five years ago, a deadly plague wiped out 97% of the world's population, America suffering tragically. Bodies were everywhere, far too many to bury or burn. But then, through a miracle of medical science, a way is found to reanimate the dead.

With the manpower of the United States depleted, and the remaining survivors not wanting to give up their internet and fast food restaurants, the undead are conscripted as slave labor.

Now they cut the grass, pick up the trash, and walk the dogs of the surviving humans.

But whether alive or dead, no race wants to be controlled, and sooner or later the dead will fight back, wanting the freedom they enjoyed in life.

The revolution has begun!

And when it's over, the dead will rule the land, and the remaining humans will become the slaves...or worse.

KINGDOM OF THE DEAD
by Anthony Giangregorio
THE DEAD HAVE RISEN!

In the dead city of Pittsburgh, two small enclaves struggle to survive, eking out an existence of hand to mouth.

But instead of working together, both groups battle for the last remaining fuel and supplies of a city filled with the living dead.

Six months after the initial outbreak, a lone helicopter arrives bearing two more survivors and a newborn baby. One enclave welcomes them, while the other schemes to steal their helicopter and escape the decaying city.

With no police, fire, or social services existing, the two will battle for dominance in the steel city of the walking dead. But when the dust settles, the question is: will the remaining humans be the winners, or the losers?

When the dead walk, the line between Heaven and Hell is so twisted and bent there is no line at all.

RISE OF THE DEAD
by Anthony Giangregorio
DEATH IS ONLY THE BEGINNING!

In less than forty-eight hours, more than half the globe was infected.
In another forty-eight, the rest would be enveloped.
The reason?
A science experiment gone horribly wrong which enabled the dead to walk, their flesh rotting on their bones even as they seek human prey.

Jeremy was an ordinary nineteen year old slacker. He partied too much and had done poorly in high school. After a night of drinking and drugs, he awoke to find the world a very different place from the one he'd left the night before.

The dead were walking and feeding on the living, and as Jeremy stepped out into a world gone mad, the dead spotting him alone and unarmed in the middle of the street, he had to wonder if he would live long enough to see his twentieth birthday.

THE CHRONICLES OF JACK PRIMUS
BOOK ONE
by Michael D. Griffiths

Beneath the world of normalcy we all live in lies another world, one where supernatural beings exist.

These creatures of the night hunt us; want to feed on our very souls, though only a few know of their existence.

One such man is Jack Primus, who accidentally pierces the veil between this world and the next. With no other choice if he wants to live, he finds himself on the run, hunted by beings called the Xemmoni, an ancient race that sees humans as nothing but cattle.   They want his soul, to feed on his very essence, and they will kill all who stand in their way.   But if they thought Jack would just lie down and accept his fate, they were sorely mistaken.

He didn't ask for this battle, but he knew he would fight them with everything at his disposal, for to lose is a fate worse than death.

He would win this war, and he would take down anyone who got in his way.

THE WAR AGAINST THEM: A ZOMBIE NOVEL
by Jose Alfredo Vazquez

Mankind wasn't prepared for the onslaught.

An ancient organism is reanimating the dead bodies of its victims, creating worldwide chaos and panic as the disease spreads to every corner of the globe. As governments struggle to contain the disease, courageous individuals across the planet learn what it truly means to make choices as they struggle to survive.

Geopolitics meet technology in a race to save mankind from the worst threat it has ever faced. Doctors, military and soldiers from all walks of life battle to find a cure. For the dead walk, and if not stopped, they will wipe out all life on Earth. Humanity is fighting a war they cannot win, for who can overcome Death itself? Man versus the walking dead with the winner ruling the planet. Welcome to *The War Against Them*.

DEADTOWN: A DEADWATER STORY
B OOK 8
by Anthony Giangregorio

The world is a very different place now. The dead walk the land and humans hide in small towns with walls of stone and debris for protection, constantly keeping the living dead at bay.

Social law is gone and right and wrong is defined by the size of your gun.

UNWELCOME VISITORS

Henry Watson and his band of warrior survivalists become guests in a fortified town in Michigan. But when the kidnapping of one of the companions goes bad and men die, the group finds themselves on the wrong side of the law, and a town out for blood.

Trapped in a hotel, surrounded on all sides, it will be up to Henry to save the day with a gamble that may not only take his life, but that of his friends as well.

In a dead world, when justice is not enough, there is always vengeance.

END OF DAYS: AN APOCALYPTIC ANTHOLOGY
VOLUMES 1 & 2
Edited by Anthony Giangregorio

Our world is a fragile place.

Meteors, famine, floods, nuclear war, solar flares, and hundreds of other calamities can plunge our small blue planet into turmoil in an instant.

What would you do if tomorrow the sun went super nova or the world was swallowed by water, submerging the world into the cold darkness of the ocean? This anthology explores some of those scenarios and plunges you into total annihilation.

But remember, it's only a book, and tomorrow will come as it always does. Or will it?

www.ingramcontent.com/pod-product-compliance
Lightning Source LLC
Chambersburg PA
CBHW070619170726
48291CB00003B/802